GRIEFTIME

GRIEFTIME

Heather Bulpett

Book Guild Publishing
Sussex, England

First published in Great Britain in 2014 by
The Book Guild Ltd
The Werks
45 Church Road
Hove, BN3 2BE

Typesetting in Sabon by
Ellipsis Digital Ltd, Glasgow

Printed and bound in Great Britain by
CPI Group (UK) Ltd, Croydon, CR0 4YY

A catalogue record for this book is available from
The British Library.

ISBN 978 1 909984 51 6

1

When the noise began, she was immersed in solving the emerald drop problem and it was a while before she realised that somebody was pounding at the door. The room had grown dim around her as she focused on her design and she got slowly to her feet, taking time to save her work to date, before walking along the passage to the front of the house.

Outside, Judith was shifting impatiently from foot to foot, her breath white in the freezing air. She was bending to call through the letterbox, and looked annoyed.

'What the hell kept you? I'm freezing to death out here.'

'Was I expecting you?'

'You would have been if you bothered to check your emails, or opened your post or even looked on the Bulletin.'

In response, Lyn turned and walked back down the passage leaving Judith to close the door and follow her. 'You haven't even decorated . . . this place is like a tomb.' Her voice tailed off as she took in the piles of paper, the drifts of cobwebs and the littered state of the kitchen. 'Scrub that – tombs are cleaner, tidier and smell better.'

'Coffee?'

'I'm not sure yet. How about you give me an hour to clean up in here and then I'll consider it.'

Lyn sighed, waved her hand generally in the direction of the leather sofa by the French doors and sent a burst of steaming water into the sink. 'You sit. I'll wash up while the coffee sorts itself out and you can tell me what's happening in the real world.' As the sink filled, she swiped the coffee breaker and keyed in her code number times two.

'Why don't you use the dishwasher?'

'To make coffee?'

'Alternatively, try a career change to comedy hour?'

'Because it's only me now – it's not worth it.'

'But it's hardly hygienic to leave it all in the sink for weeks on end. Anyway, that isn't what I'm here for.'

'OK, niceties done with. Don't think I'm ready to start socialising again, though.'

'Lyn, you haven't read any post or anything, have you?'

'Not for a while ... it'll keep. I'm still on grieftime, remember.'

'You're not, not any more – the rules have changed. Actually you're now in breach of Section 10.'

There was a sudden, heavy silence as Lyn stopped sloshing water around in the sink and Judith drew a breath. The coffee breaker announced 'mug needed, mug needed' in its gentle but firm Mary Poppins accent. Judith jumped up and pushed two mugs onto the collection tray. The comforting smell of rich coffee was completely at odds with the startling tension in the room. Then Lyn turned. 'You'd better tell me slowly and clearly, because if I'm about to be sent to Citizen Rehab I'd like to know why.'

Judith sat back holding her coffee. 'No, God, no – it isn't that bad. I've been able to prove you haven't logged on for six weeks apart from working on your Step Ups thing and I can take your unopened real mail back. The neighbours will declare that you haven't been out. You just have to go along with the selection and everything will be fine.'

'Selection?'

'Oh, I'm doing this all backwards. You've been selected and you have to be at the centre tomorrow for the formalities.'

'But I can't have been selected – for one thing it's my turn and for another it's too early.'

'Sit down. Drink your coffee. Listen to me. When you started grieftime you thought you had thirteen weeks.'

'I did have thirteen weeks.'

'Well, a new sliding scale was implemented two months ago based on the age gap between the parties and the length of the relationship. Greg was thirty-one years older than you and you were only married for four years. You get one week for each year up to a maximum of thirteen weeks and you are deducted one week for every ten years of the age difference.'

'I'm struggling with this.'

'OK, technically you were only entitled to one week but the centre approved additional weeks to cover the time people had used prior to the new system coming in, so you got an extra two weeks. Then you should have registered available at the centre. If you'd kept in touch you would have known all this!' She finished on a note of irritation. 'Anyway, you've managed an extra three weeks, so it's not all bad.'

Lyn nursed her coffee. 'OK. My fault. I stupidly thought that we were still allowed time to grieve in our own way but I realise that the centre knows best. But even so it's my turn to select, isn't it?'

'The selection rules for the bereaved have changed. It was found that following the loss of their first partner, people had poor judgement in selecting another, so now you don't get a choice – regardless of whether you had a choice the first time. In fact, females don't get a choice at all.'

'What do you mean – at all?'

'I mean never. But the good news is that you only have to marry three times.'

'Three?'

'Yes. The theory is that . . .'

'Oh, shut up!' Lyn spat, 'it's all theory this and research that and we're just supposed to go along with it. Doesn't it bother you at all?'

3

'Hardly. I'm in a reserved occupation. And, actually, the latest research does show that the longer the spell of grieftime, the more likely you are to sink into depression . . . and look at the state of this place.'

'I'm not depressed, I'm naturally messy. I'm naturally grieving for the loss of my husband. I'm also still working and sure, I haven't redecorated yet but there's no new rule that says I have to – or have I missed that as well?'

'Sure, the loss of Professor Langdale must have hit you hard.'

Their eyes met. 'OK, tell me the rest.'

'The age restrictions have shifted a bit. Something to do with the female availability demographic and an increase in young males.'

'That sentence doesn't even mean anything,' Lyn mumbled.

'But you're lucky,' Judith ploughed on, 'as soon as you went on the available screen you attracted a lot of interest and the centre has chosen a younger man who is self-sufficient with no current dependants and a good career. Since you have the larger property, he is happy to move in here and his apartment will be returned to the centre.'

'What do you mean, younger? Eighteen or something?'

'No, of course not. He's 24.'

'Next you'll tell me he's someone I used to teach.'

'Well, yes, he is – but you liked him. Your report said he always had an opinion in class and contributed regularly.'

'I said that about all of them.'

'The thing is, it's a done deal. You have no choice. Look, have you got anything stronger than coffee?'

'Yes, but I'm up to my allowance for this week.'

'Fine. I'm not, so we'll just cheat a bit.' She crossed to the alco store, keyed in her access code and the door swung open. Inside, a glorious selection of single unit alcoholic drinks hung in sections. 'Good grief – you've got enough here for a siege.'

'Oh, that was Greg. He couldn't get used to the idea that you weren't allowed to drink over the allowance so he was always buying too much and it sort of stockpiled. I haven't bought anything for ages – I'm slowly drinking my way through it. Of course, if I was allowed I'd be getting down it much faster.'

Judith retrieved four units of red wine and found two glasses. 'Well, you wouldn't, you'd be unconscious. As I recall, four was about your limit.'

'Still is really but it locked down on me last week and hasn't let me back in yet. I can't quite understand it because I didn't think I was going over my weekly allowance, but I must have been.'

She waited until Lyn had taken a slug then drew breath. 'Listen – you need to wear this.' Without warning she clipped a chunky plastic bracelet to Lyn's wrist and pressed the alert button. 'We've had some accidents with people unhappy about the new regime and this will just warn centre if there's anything wrong.'

'What, like running away?'

'Yes, or a suicide attempt – I know you wouldn't but it's the rules. You can have it removed after one month.'

'A month?'

'Yes. Now let's go through the details for tomorrow. By the way . . . just a hint but you'll probably want to wash your hair and sort out something decent to wear. Although you are looking a lot better than the last time I saw you.'

After Judith had gone, Lyn wandered through the desolate house. She had no idea who the young man was that she had to accept into her home at a moment's notice – well, actually what the centre described as a 'very fair' twenty-four hours. She didn't recognise the name, she couldn't bring any picture to her mind – if he was now twenty-four it must have been eight years ago, so her sixth teaching year. She could summon up several of the classes from that period but none had had any young men who sounded the type to want to marry her.

Judith had only drunk one unit of wine, so she had another

two available. She filled her glass and went and sat in the living room – she supposed she ought to make a list but she couldn't be bothered. She wanted Greg, with his ironic smile and his firm hand on the reins.

She had been so enormously flattered to be selected by him – a well-known academic with a string of erudite publications who was happy to let her run her own design business from home. So what if he was a bit set in his ways and had ferocious flashes of temper? Some of her acquaintances thought the age gap was creepy but at twenty-seven she was hardly a child and neither of them were particularly bothered by the centre's propaganda at the time. So what if he turned out to be very exacting and thought nothing of beating her if she made a mistake? She'd taken enough punishments in the dump to be able to cope with it, on the whole. Most of the time she had felt protected and she thought she made him happy enough. He'd never really hurt her apart from the last time and certainly they had enough in common for her to enjoy living with him for weeks at a time. Whatever Judith said, their sex life had been perfectly adequate ... well, she supposed it had. Who needed kindness when she had someone who loved literature as she did and had a regular TV slot?

She missed him all right. There seemed to be nothing that she had done for the past four years that didn't involve him. He was in every room in the house – and not there at all. Telling her what to do, directing her work, ruffling her hair when he was pleased. She felt – literally – aimless without him; she had spent all of her time trying to make him happy. Now she had to start again with somebody new. It hardly seemed worth the effort. She leant back in the sofa and tears squeezed their way out of her closed eyes. She knew she was never going to get over this. What if her new husband beat her every day? If he was younger he was probably stronger ...

2

It wasn't that she was extra good-looking or anything. That first day she was just wearing jeans and a black T-shirt with a black jacket over the top. But she had this long scarf that she'd just looped round everything and it swung when she walked – not a fluttery, wispy thing, more like a heavy, shiny bird's wing, so when she turned suddenly it flew out a bit as though she was going to take off.

The group was a bit rough, a bit noisy, and certainly not looking forward to an hour of Writing Studies. She started like they all did by going through the programme week by week. It was the usual rubbish: how to structure your CV, how to write a letter of application, how to make a formal complaint. It was enough to bore anyone to tears. Of course nobody was listening, or only with half an ear, so when she stepped back and looked up at the presentation board and muttered, 'Oh, what are they thinking of? This is completely impossible,' before flicking to the next screen, only Ryan at the front heard her.

'Miss! What was that, Miss?' There was a frozen pause that rippled back through the class as people registered that Ryan had asked a teacher a question. Before she could answer he was off again. 'Who are you calling a rhinoceros?' The class began to snigger but it was the teacher who fell about laughing. She laughed so hard she couldn't speak and her eyes ran and the weird thing was that nobody minded, not even Ryan. He just waited until she'd finished then asked again. This time she managed a smile instead of a guffaw and said, 'I said "impossible" not "rhinoceros". But it's so noisy in here I'm not surprised you couldn't hear me – that's a homonym by the way.'

Luke looked up from the middle of the room. 'Are you really posh, Miss? Because we don't know all those long words.'

'Ahh . . .' She swung back to the presentation and flicked it on. The screen lit up with dictionary practice. 'Look it up,' she quoted, then pulled up the dictionary page and keyed in 'homonym', pressed enter and the screen filled with a glaze of words and symbols. 'Just look at the highlighted phrase for now: "Word with same spelling or sound".'

'That doesn't mean anything.'

'Well, I agree it's not very clear but it's a start point.'

'But impossible isn't the same as rhinoceros.'

'If I was a rhinoceros I bet I'd be the chief one.'

'Oh yeah? Says who?'

'You mean like beer and bear.'

'They don't sound the same.'

'Bear and bare then.' More sniggers from the class.

Luke called out again. 'We're supposed to be doing the course introduction.'

And she looked him straight in the eye and said, 'Yes, we are. But this is just another way of looking at it. You wouldn't plaster a wall without learning how to use a trowel and you wouldn't write a letter without learning how to use words.'

There was a very brief silence then just as Luke said, 'Hey, I wouldn't do either.'

She burst out laughing again and spluttered, 'That was what we call sententious.'

And I fell completely in love.

3

She was early at the centre. There didn't seem any point in not being. All the decisions had been made for her and the tag on her wrist was a constant reminder that if she didn't toe the line she faced detention at the very least and a protracted series of rehab programmes. She wandered round the atrium looking at the notices, amazed at how quickly things changed. The health board now held suggestions for ensuring that 'treats' were phased across the week and not consumed in one mad binge on a Friday night. A smaller notice advised that this would become mandatory in the near future and citizens were expected to invest in treat 'calorie lockers' to monitor their individual consumption.

Finally she drifted into the restroom area. She regarded herself in the mirror, and took the opportunity to smooth her very uninteresting hair and check that she was basically tidy. She'd put on a bit of make-up but it looked odd against her pale face. She felt very sick. The tag on her wrist was registering amber, which she took to be a warning of some kind of emotional state, probably measured by temperature and pulse rate. She sat down for a while but it stayed amber, so she wandered back into the atrium. Then she decided that she needed some fresh air and headed outside. Immediately the tag clicked to red and to her amazement a guard appeared at her elbow.

'Sorry, madam, but you can't go outside for the next thirty minutes.'

'Why ever not?' Despite herself her voice wobbled. 'I only wanted some air – it's so hot in here.'

'You can see for yourself – you're checked in until noon.' He waved at the screen on the left wall. 'Now just take a seat and we'll call someone to wait with you.'

Lyn sank helplessly into a nasty, fake leather chair while the guard radioed for back-up. When Judith appeared she put her head in her hands.

'Hey there, what's going on?'

'Nothing. I was really early and then I started to feel sick so I went to go outside and they won't let me.'

'No, sorry. It's a new system – once you're in the centre you have to stay until your check-out time. It means we don't lose track of people.'

'It's awful. I look like a criminal.'

'No you don't. Do you want to get some water or something?'

'No, I just want it to be over.'

'Well, it will be any minute. Here's Mitch now.'

'Who?'

'Mitch – Michael. Your new husband.'

The blonde sitting next to her pointed me out and her head shot up. I was too far away to read her expression but her stare skittered across me and away, then back. It was quite obvious she had no idea who I was. Nine months in her class and I'd made no impression at all. Despite trying to look confident I could feel my pace slowing and my mouth curving down. Then she stood up and her gaze lightened. 'What's all this Mitch rubbish?' she said. 'It's Mikey, isn't it? I'm so sorry – I just didn't recognise the name and it took me a moment to place you.'

I'd like to say that made it all right – it certainly improved things – but I knew her too well to be fooled. Yes, she'd managed to remember me but that wasn't the point – she had seen I was bothered and she was making me feel better. I'd seen it a hundred times in class; awkward or embarrassing moments easily charmed away with some diversionary tactic: a joke, a sudden change of subject, a smile. She was smiling now and holding out her hand.

I took it in both of mine. I looked into her eyes. 'You're not happy.' The blonde flinched visibly and automatically glanced at the nearest camera.

'What's happy got to do with it?' she squawked. 'You're both here on time, that's the main thing.'

'Judith . . .' It was a sigh. 'Can Mikey and I just have a moment? We won't make a break for it, I promise.' She smiled into my eyes and my heart did a very slow flip. Her head came to my shoulder and she sighed again. 'You've grown.'

'A couple of inches.'

'Have you brought anyone with you?'

'My mum – over there. No one else could get time off. But she's really excited. You won't remember but she met you at an open day – she thought you were lovely – apparently you said nice things about me.'

'I expect I did.'

'So – a big adventure, then.'

'Have you done it before?'

'No. I know you have though, and you've lived to tell the tale.'

The blonde hurried towards us. 'Come on you two, you're on next.' She began to bustle towards one of the interview rooms that lined the atrium.

'Wait a moment. We mustn't forget Mikey's mum.' She looked round and caught Mum's eye with a smile and a wave and as Mum caught up with us her smile widened. 'Hello – how lovely to see you again.'

Mum positively sparkled. 'Michael said you wouldn't remember me after all this time.'

'Of course I do. I never forget a face, although sometimes I struggle with the names.'

'It's Claire.'

'Yes, Claire.' We were almost at the door by now and she clasped Mum's hand.

'Thank you so much for coming today, it means a lot.'

Oh yes – she was smooth all right.

4

A brief fluttering activity at the centre barrier caught Dylan's eye as he looked down into the atrium from the third floor balcony. 'Good heavens,' he murmured, 'surely that's Professor Langdale's wife. Whatever is she doing here? She's very pale.' He frowned as the slight figure was joined by a blonde security guard. 'And she's been tagged ... that's appalling.' He clicked into his hand-held infopad. 'How very odd.' He glanced round for his assistant, who practically sprang to his side looking eager and alert.

'That young lady there ... according to her file she's been called in to confirm her selection but her husband, Professor Langdale, only died about five weeks ago. Can you just check her grieftime allocation and see why she's been tagged? I've got a liaison meeting or I'd do it.'

'Special interest, sir?'

'No, Larissa, not at this stage, anyway. Oh – check who's selected her as well, won't you?'

Larissa nodded, then peered more closely at the action going on below. 'No need, sir. It's Mitch Jones, I remember him from college – he's a chef.' She sighed heavily. 'She's done well for herself.'

'Has she indeed?'

'Yes. She must be thirty at least, hardly young, and he's only my age.'

'Ah, I see what you mean. She doesn't look as though her good fortune is making her happy though.' His alarm flashed discreetly. 'Quick as you can, Larissa.'

13

'Do you want to be interrupted when I've got the information, sir?'

'No, just priority message it to my infopad. I'll decide what steps to take then.'

He took one more glance as he turned away but the little group had already disappeared into one of the cubicles that lined the atrium.

5

The registration took minutes ... in fact, printing the documents took longer than completing the forms. Outside, Claire was disappointed. 'In my day we still did all that "You may now kiss the bride" stuff, as though it was a real ceremony.'

Lyn smiled at her. 'I know. It sounds so romantic. Even the last time they acted as if we were doing something special and that was only four years ago.'

They all stood about in the atrium, not sure what to do next. There was an audible click and Lyn noticed that her tag had turned back to green. Judith nodded but didn't say anything. Again it was Claire who broke the silence. 'I've got to get back to work, they only gave me an hour, but perhaps you could come round for lunch on Sunday and we can have a bit of a party then?'

'That would be lovely if that's OK with ... ?' She looked at Mikey, who nodded.

'See you then. Umm, Michael knows the time.' She walked away without glancing back. Judith nodded again. 'Back to the grindstone then,' and disappeared through a door into the bowels of the centre.

'Shall we go for a drink?' His voice made her jump but she managed another smile.

'Yes, OK, if you don't have to get back to work.'

'Nope. I've taken the rest of the week off to move in and stuff.'

'Stuff?'

'Yeah, you know ... new routines and things.'

It was cold outside and her eyes began to run almost immediately. He took her arm and hurried her along to the nearest bar. 'Cold, huh? What do you want to drink?' She looked round anxiously. The screen was advertising a non-alcoholic hot toddy with ginger and spices. 'One of those.'

'Oh, right. Stay there, I'll get them.'

She leant back on the slithery plastic banquette. Her heart was pounding and she noticed that she was actually wringing her hands like some distressed maiden. Her tag had gone amber again and she tried to slow her breathing. What the hell would happen if it went red in public? Why didn't it come with a user guide? She fumbled for her mobile.

'Jude . . . emergency. I've gone amber again. What do I do?'

Judith's voice was calm as ever. 'Nothing. Where are you?'

'In a bar. He's getting a drink.'

'OK, take deep breaths. Just pull your sleeve over it so he doesn't notice.'

'But what if it goes red? Will I be arrested?'

'No, you're not in a controlled situation, although the centre will log it as a distressed episode. Just stop thinking about it. Got to go.'

'Here we are.' She jumped again. 'Just had a call.'

'So I see. Anything interesting?'

'No.' She looked down at the table. In front of her were one non-alcoholic hot toddy, two double brandies and a can of beer. She looked up.

'I know you're up to your units for this week but you get extra for a celebration and anyway I've got loads left. I would've got champagne but I didn't know if you liked it and brandy's good in cold weather.'

She reached for the brandy and to her fascination her hand was shaking. They both stared at it, then Mikey suddenly put his hand out as though trapping an escaped hamster and held it still on the table.

'I'm sorry.'

'That's OK.'

Flushing, she slid her hand away.

'This has obviously come as a bit of a surprise to you, Lyn.'

'You could say that. I only found out yesterday.'

'I selected you last week.'

'Oh. Gosh, that long ago. I've been out of the loop a bit. Your mum's nice,' she added.

'Yes.' He reached for the beer and took a gulp. 'Come on, your non-alcoholic toddy is getting cold.' She forced a smile and when she picked up her drink her hand was almost steady. It was disgusting and she was quite unable to repress a shudder of distaste.

'What's wrong with it?'

'Nothing. It's probably just me.' To her fascination he picked up the glass, held it to the light for a second then took a cautious taste. 'Umm . . . ginger, lemon, cinnamon . . . far too much sugar . . . watery base. You're right, it's pretty disgusting. I'll get you a beer instead.'

She watched him head back to the bar. Obviously a man who knows his ingredients, she thought.

6

Not that we gave her an easy ride that year. Sure, we liked her and she made the classes as interesting as she could but we still gave her some stick. It wasn't like with the others, though. If anyone got completely out of line there was always someone else who'd shut them up before things turned really nasty because we felt she was on our side. Other teachers got locked in the supply cupboard or had their mobiles nicked but nobody tried that with her. Occasionally someone – usually one of the girls – had a go at her but although she gave as good as she got at the time she never brought it back to the next session.

Luke used to say she was an eternal optimist – she'd come in with these centre-sponsored lesson plans designed for six-year-olds, slap them up on the screen and then start asking what we'd done at the weekend or how our volunteer tasks were going. Before you knew what was happening we'd covered the class targets for the session and were doing something useful, like writing a realistic plan of how to get the job we wanted or practising how to be a journalist because she reckoned you could earn easy extra money that way by doing stuff for community sheets. Luke watched her a lot, openly, as if he had something to say. She ignored him.

I watched her a lot, too, but carefully. I didn't want her to catch me staring.

Writing Studies was a new way of saying 'remedial English' and it was the class they usually gave to the worst teachers, so none of us could see why she'd got it, although we weren't complaining. Then one day we heard old Matthews talking to her in the corridor outside. He was moaning that we were making a noise and she replied that class hadn't started yet. He ignored that and told her that she'd 'better watch her step or she was never going to get out of the stink pit'. We couldn't hear what she said in response, but when she bounced through the door her eyes were round with fury.

The class gave her a hard time that day – give a dog a bad name and all that – but she just kept going. It was a real performance, but I looked back as we were leaving and she was sitting at the teacher's station with her head in her hands. We'd been doing one-word descriptions: desolate seemed about right.

7

The house looked even gloomier than usual. She opened the door and ushered Mikey inside with a travesty of welcome. 'Here we are. Umm, just through here . . . the kitchen!' Mikey was staring and it made her uncomfortable. 'I should have cleaned up a bit. Still, nothing I can't sort out.' She glanced back. His expression was unreadable.

'You live here?'

'Yes. Big, isn't it?'

'Sure. But it's filthy – and cold. What have you been doing?'

'Working.'

'Didn't you get any grieftime?'

'Yes, but I thought I had ages, then I didn't. You don't have to redecorate at once, you know.'

'Right. I'm going to get my things and I'll be right back. Will you be all right? Do you want to come with me?'

'Yes, I'll be all right. No, I don't want to come with you.'

The cleaning took less time than she thought it would. First she tackled the drifts of cobwebs because they were obvious, then she cleaned the carpets and stairs and piled up her paperwork. She'd already cleared the surfaces in the kitchen so she looked for other things she could do. Basically it was all fairly tidy but it was dingy at best. She hunted around and found some spray polish, which she used on the wood surfaces. The polish left smears. It still looked chilly and grimy. She tried to think how it had looked when Greg was alive. Not very different, she thought, but it had always felt more lived-in.

She began to hunt around and almost at once realised that

20

there were no plants. Greg used to bring flowers home some-times but they had all sorts of other plants growing: solemn ferns in the kitchen, decorative palms in the living room, odd-looking cacti on the window ledges. It didn't take a genius to figure out that the strange smell she'd been ignoring was mainly decaying and rotting vegetation. The windowsills were corroded with dead plants. Greg would have been horrified . . . she'd left vases of cut flowers un-emptied and she'd let all the rest die of thirst.

Her tag clicked to red.

When Mitch got back she was hunched over her computer link in the living room.

'What are you doing?'

'Working.'

'Come on, we've just got married. We can have an evening off.'

'Oh. Of course. Do you want food?'

'Have you got any?'

She looked up. It wasn't a joke. Outside it was getting dark. She couldn't think if there was any food or not but she thought probably not. 'What do you like?'

'Normal stuff. Pasta. Things with rice. Vegetables.'

Her eyes flooded with tears immediately. She was caught in this uncomfortable house with no food to offer her new husband and this was going to be it from now on. She would have to cook things and plan meals that he liked. She suddenly wanted Greg and his love of dining out, even though at the time she thought she'd have preferred the odd night in. If he was late he'd sometimes come in waving a box of pizza from the market saying, 'I know you don't cook but you still have to eat.'

She squared her shoulders. She'd have to go out to the food centre and it was late. There might not be much left. Oh well, she'd do her best. She reached for her jacket and felt his hand on her shoulder.

'Hey, it was just a joke. I know you don't cook – you used

to tell the girls in class that cooking wasn't everything. Anyway, I've brought some food and I'll cook.'

'You'll cook?'

'Well, yes. It's what I do.'

'I thought you were a mechanic?'

'No, you're confusing me with someone else. I was the one in the middle between Lucas and Kylie.' He walked out of the room and she could hear him dragging bags about, then there was some clattering from the kitchen. That explained the hot toddy incident then, she thought. She heard the fridge door slam. Oh, surely she hadn't hurt his feelings? He'd just have to get used to it. She saved her latest explorations into the world of emerald canyon and went after him.

The kitchen was already a fog of steam. Two glasses of red wine were on the table.

'More alcohol?'

'Yes, it's off my allowance. Once your balance is back to zero we'll work it out properly.'

She winced. 'How do you know what my balance is?'

'It was in your file.'

'Oh. Can I access your file then?'

'No, but you could have looked me up on centreinfo. It wouldn't tell you everything but it would give you an idea. Anyway, you should know this from the last time.'

Had Greg checked her file first? She didn't know. It had never occurred to her. She just thought that he fancied her but maybe it had been a bit more calculated than that. Certainly in those days she hadn't been much of a drinker and really she wasn't one now. It had just been the last couple of weeks. She still couldn't figure out how she'd gone over her allowance when Judith always used to tease her about being a lightweight. She sat at the table and tried to think about what she should do next.

'Do you want me to help?'

'What do you want to do?'

'I don't know . . . chop things . . . make a salad dressing?'

He spun round waving a spoon that dripped with sauce. 'Do I look as if I'm making a bloody salad?'

It was extraordinarily frightening. It was already going wrong and she didn't know what to do to make it right. Perhaps he'd just go crazy and kill her with a chef's knife . . . or a wooden spoon?

Immediately her tag clicked to red but this time it was flashing as well. She tried to pull her sleeve over it but then it started to emit a shrill squeaking like a budgie in pain. 'Oh, no – this bloody thing! I can't stop it.' She started to back out of the kitchen but he took hold of her firmly and shoved her towards a chair.

'Listen, Lyn, I'm sorry. Sit down and drink your wine and wait for the food. Come on, try to relax. I didn't mean to snap at you. God, that thing's annoying.'

She wanted to explain that it wasn't exactly his fault, she'd just overreacted, but she didn't have the energy, so she took a slug of wine instead. A sudden stab of pain in her side made her wince. She forced herself to sound normal but her voice was still wobbling. 'It'll stop in a minute I think. I haven't quite got the measure of it yet.'

'What's it for?'

'You don't know?'

He shrugged.

'It's a new centre thing – to monitor the emotional response of potential suicide risks among ladies whose grieftime has been abruptly curtailed.'

His expression was one of absolute horror. Too late she realised what she'd said. 'Oh, Mikey, I don't mean it like that. Obviously I'm not a suicide risk. Apparently it's just part of the new system . . . everyone gets one.'

There was an abrupt silence as the tag stopped shrilling and clicked back to amber. 'I'm glad to hear it.' He sat down opposite her and took a huge gulp of wine. 'No wonder you've turned to drink.'

But I haven't, she protested to herself, I really haven't turned to drink. I can't understand it.

8

I don't know what I'd expected really. I knew her husband had just died but he was old, so I supposed she'd miss the company rather than anything else. Then I was just so bloody excited when her name came up on the Bulletin. She looked much the same in her image file and just looking at the screen made my sixteen-year-old self want to be with her all over again. When I accessed her file I was even more excited. The boozing didn't bother me – in the restaurant trade everybody does it and I knew that her old husband would have been a drinker because in the old days they all were. No, it was the way her design career had taken off that impressed me. She had an open-ended contract with a huge games supplier based on her vivid imagination and her teaching experience. She was the unknown face behind Step Up Stones.

It meant she was on a medium scale salary, which was good for a woman but to me it was more significant that she was making a success of something different. She always used to tell us that we should aim high and all it took was confidence, and here was the proof.

Then here she was, in this ugly house, acting like a nervous wreck because I'd waved a spoon at her. OK, I'd shouted as well but she could take it at college. And I'm a chef, we're trained to shout. Mind you, she had almost finished her wine and you could see her calming down and, well, putting herself back together.

9

OK, the wine had steadied her. It was her kitchen, or was it? She had a nasty feeling that it all belonged to him now – she'd ask Judith tomorrow. In the meantime she ought to send in today's work and sort out a few things for tomorrow. Maybe she should take the time to decorate. Certainly she should do something about the heating and just make the place a bit cosier.

'So, chef, how long until we eat? If you don't need my invaluable assistance in here I can get out of your way and finish a few things off.' She sounded slightly mad, she thought, so she flung in a rueful smile. 'I think my nerves must be shot.'

'A while . . . say half an hour?'

'OK. I'll be around if you need me.' What was the matter with her? She couldn't find a normal tone to her voice at all. She went back into the living room and flicked on the screen . . . the emerald drop problem was still waiting for her but she'd completed most of the peripheral levels so she made sure they were saved and posted to the publisher. She needed about four days in total to finish the chapter, so was well within her time allowance. The screen flashed briefly with a thank you message, then died away.

What next? A truly horrible thought struck her. Mikey's bags were still in the passage but where was he going to sleep? Stupid question. He would obviously be expecting to sleep with her, and he'd be expecting sex since it was their first night. Well, she couldn't be awkward about it, she'd just better get on with things. The bedroom was a dingy tip. Since Greg died she hadn't changed the sheets or cleaned up. She couldn't make it look like a real wedding night but she could dust and sort out the cobwebs. She'd been planning to go through Greg's stuff when she felt better but now she'd have to face it, so she emptied his drawers and cupboards on to the spare room bed, piled his shoes and boots up in the corner, then closed the door on it.

When that was done and the bed remade, she ran a duster over the surfaces, drew the curtains against the evening and clicked on the table lamp. It looked better. Not exactly inviting but give it a few pictures on the walls and lighter paint. She felt her eyes filling again and turned away to go downstairs. Mikey was standing right behind her.

'It looks good.'

'Yes. It'll be better once it's decorated. I don't know what I've been thinking of really.'

'Food's ready.'

'Good.'

'Do you normally eat in the kitchen?'

'I have been.'

He'd set the table and there were flowers. She touched the bright petals, wondering where they'd come from.

'Mum got them for us . . . she's a bit sentimental.'

'They're lovely. I didn't notice them earlier.'

'I picked them up on the way back from getting my stuff. She wanted to know if you needed seeds and things for the garden. We've got a garden, haven't we?'

'Yes, out the back. I don't know what's growing out there though. We didn't spend much time in it. If you like we could grow tomatoes and things . . . and flowers.'

He handed her a plate of pasta with a vivid red sauce. 'Good grief, this is colourful. Whatever is it?'

'Tomato and peppers, mainly. Try it.'

It was hot but not too spicy. She was touched by the effort. 'What are the green bits?'

He stared across the table. 'The green bits are herbs – you must have had herbs before.'

'Oh, sure. I probably didn't take much notice of them.'

'Do you want some more wine?'

'I don't think so. There's some fizzy water in the fridge, that'll be fine.'

'So, do you like champagne? Because we'll be getting it on Sunday at Mum's.'

'Actually I've never had it.'

'Not at your last wedding?'

'God no! Greg wasn't a flash drinker, just a thorough one!'

'What do you mean?'

'He liked wine – well, you can tell that from the alco store. He didn't like me to drink much, though. It's only been since he died I've been drinking a bit more. I'll stop soon, it's not a problem.'

'I didn't think it was. I just thought you might want something else to take the edge off.'

'No – I'm fine.' She looked at him happily chewing his pasta and staring round the room, taking great gulps of fizzy water. He looked very vigorous and lively.

'What do you do in the evening usually?'

He considered. 'Go out with Luke and that lot sometimes, if I'm not working. Swim. Test recipes. Garden if the weather's OK. Play football. Muck about. You know. How about you?'

She vaguely remembered a class on structured conversation where you answered a question with a short statement and a question to keep the conversation going. It seemed easy in the classroom.

'Well?'

'Oh, sorry. Nothing much. Read, I suppose.'

'Hope that's not on the agenda for tonight!' She stared at him in pained surprise. 'I mean,' he carried on, 'it's our first night together and I thought we could take some wine up to bed and ... well ... have loads of sex.' She choked.

'Right, I see.'

He finished his pasta and grinned at her. 'I'll just give this a minute or two to go down, then we'll get on with it.'

'OK. I'll just stack the dishwasher,' she mumbled, clanging plates and forks together and nearly dropping the lot as she bent down to open the machine.

'Come on, Lyn, I'll do it or we won't have any china left. Why don't you go and put something decent on the entertainment screen and we'll relax for a bit.' She straightened up and looked at him. He was laughing at her.

'You bastard! I thought you meant it!'

'I know, it's the funniest thing that's happened all day. Your face! You should see yourself.'

'I'm so stressed I don't know which way is up, and you're laughing at me!'

'Not that I don't want loads of sex, but I want you to enjoy it.'

'Thanks, that's very thoughtful of you,' she muttered sarcastically as she headed for the living room.

The entertainment screen had a huge range of movies, opera and Shakespeare. She selected a particularly violent slasher movie just to be difficult. Mikey came in with two glasses of wine and smirked when he saw the titles.

'I didn't know you liked this sort of thing.'

'There's lots you don't know about me.'

'Hmm. Hang on while I light a couple of candles.' The room suddenly disappeared in a soft glow as candles flickered and the centre light was turned down. She felt a twinge of anxiety as the corners crept away into darkness.

'Sit with me.' She perched crossly at one end of the sofa and he passed over the wine.

'What are you doing with the cushions?' she asked suspiciously, as he tossed them behind the sofa.

'Nothing, babe, just kick back and enjoy the nice movie.'

She sipped her wine and watched the heroine walking

29

innocently into a darkened garden, calling for her pet cat. It looked like a cute little stripy creature with wide glinting eyes. The heroine reached up to coax it down from the fence. 'Come here, darling,' she was saying. 'What's the matter with you tonight?' The next moment Lyn gave a gasp of horror and covered her eyes. Ten minutes later she was still shivering in horror, although the plot seemed to have settled down into a no-thrills detective romp with a cute young female rookie searching a deserted garage and reporting into her walkie-talkie.

Mikey leant towards Lyn and whispered in her ear, 'Haven't you seen this one before? There's a really good bit coming up . . . look.'

There was a pause while another jet of blood hit the camera lens. 'Oh no! This is just vile!' She looked round for a cushion to hide behind, then remembered he'd moved them. She turned her back on the screen and found the remote.

'Oh, baby, don't switch it off yet.'

She twisted the other way, and gasped as he stretched over her shoulder and grabbed for the remote. There was a brief undignified tussle which he won easily.

'I'll turn the sound down if you kiss me.'

'Just turn it off, please, Mikey.'

He frowned. 'Are you hurt?'

'No – why?'

'It's your side, isn't it? You winced in the kitchen but then you seemed OK. What is it? Your ribs?'

'How do you know?'

'Football injuries and stuff. How long ago did you do it?'

'About six weeks ago. I'm so clumsy, I tumbled down the stairs. I'm OK really, it just sometimes catches me out.'

'Right. I'll be careful then.'

She had to admit he got top marks for kissing, even though he was irritatingly smug about it.

When she finally looked back at the screen he put his arm along the back of the sofa and inched in her direction.

'I'm not eighteen,' she muttered.

'Oh, definitely not,' he agreed, hitching a bit closer. On the screen another vapid looking teenager was walking down a deserted footpath. There was a crunch of gravel behind her and she quickened her pace. Lyn shrieked and buried her face in Mikey's chest.

'Please, please, turn it off. I know you think this is funny but I bloody don't.'

His arm closed round her. 'Worth another kiss, then?'

'Whatever.'

'I thought you said you weren't eighteen?'

'OK, yes. Worth another kiss – two if you want.' He smiled and clicked the remote. The screen died down to a pale glow and music flooded the room.

'What's this?'

'I chose something at random, don't you like it?'

'It's fine.'

He could tell that she was about to pull away and he started to rub her back with a circling motion.

'So, what do you really like to watch? I mean I like sport and spy things – typical stuff really. And I'm an expert on horror movies due to my misspent youth.'

'I like history and Shakespeare and dramas. We don't have anything in common.'

'Yeah, I remember you liked Shakespeare when we were at college. Guess I should have paid more attention.'

His hand slid under her top but he continued the circling thing on her back. Lyn supposed it was meant to be soothing and in fairness she thought it probably was . . . no, make that certainly was. The whole feeling of being cared for was strange. She shot him a glance from under her fringe. He looked quite intent and thoughtful.

'How about you choose one night and I choose the next – when we're in, that is.'

'When we're in?'

31

'Yeah. I'll be on lates at the restaurant sometimes and we'll be out and about exercising and things in the summer and ice skating and stuff in the winter, you know.' He looked down at her and laughed. 'You can teach me about Shakespeare.' She was starting to feel more relaxed.

'And what will you teach me?'

'Oh, this and that.'

He kissed her very gently then slid both hands round her waist and sat her in his lap.

Oh well, here we go, she thought, all roads lead to bed in this house, best get it over with.

10

She woke early in the icy bedroom with a solid warm body pressed against her. She carefully eased herself out of the bed and ran quietly shivering into the bathroom. The hot shower made her feel better and eased the nagging pain in her side. A brisk towel down brought her circulation almost back to normal. Pulling on her jeans, sweatshirt and thick socks and wrapping another towel round her dripping hair she trailed downstairs to the kitchen and flicked on the coffee breaker. A faint grey light was invading the garden when she pulled back the blinds. She peered through the window trying to make out the signs of anything growing.

'Mug needed. Mug needed,' insisted the machine behind her.

Back upstairs Mikey was glaring out from a huddle of bedding. 'How can you sleep in a room this cold?' He looked so completely outraged that for a second she forgot everything else and started to laugh. 'Don't the radiators work at all? What sort of system have you got?'

'How should I know?'

'You live here.'

'Have your coffee. The shower's hot, that'll warm you up.'

He scowled at her. 'We need to make some plans.'

'Sure, after you've had a shower.'

Back in the kitchen she was wondering if he was going to want toast or something when she heard the knocking at the door. It was Judith.

'What are you doing here so early, haven't you got work?'

'Yup – but I thought you might like some warm pastries for your first breakfast.'

'Thanks. That's really kind. I was just wondering how to make toast without any bread. Have you got time for coffee?'

'Sure. Are you OK?'

'Yes. He's complaining about the heating but I can't blame him, that bedroom is like Siberia.'

'Well, you'll have to get it fixed.'

The coffee breaker began muttering again. She got mugs and plates and unwrapped the pastries.

'There's something I need to ask you. Now I'm married again, does Mikey own all this?'

'The house? Yes, you know that, but you still have a moral responsibility for the heating.'

'Hi. Sorry, I didn't catch your name yesterday.' He paused in the doorway for a moment, then smiled. 'I see you've brought emergency supplies, so thanks.'

'No problem. I thought you probably wouldn't be too organised yet . . . first morning and all that.' She glanced between them and her eyes narrowed slightly. 'I expect your mind was on other things, Lyn, under the circumstances.'

Lyn frowned at her in surprise. 'Come on, drink your coffee.'

'Sorry. Better run actually. Catch you later.'

The door slammed.

Mikey looked at Lyn questioningly. 'Still didn't catch the name but she sure moves fast.'

Lyn shrugged. 'It's my friend Judith. We met at the dump – she's not normally as abrupt as that.'

He nodded, sat down, took a slug of coffee and began to make a list. Lyn pushed the pastries towards him and glanced at his notepad. She wasn't surprised to see that first on the list was 'fix heating'.

'I thought I'd get some decorating stuff today. Do you want to come?'

'No, I want to get the heating fixed.'

She perched next to him and rested her hand on his sleeve. 'What colours do you like?'

'You choose.'

He shivered violently. 'Your hands are like ice – we're going to freeze to death before you even get the paint on the walls.'

She grinned. 'You feel very warm, actually.'

'And I want to keep it that way.'

'We're insured. I'll dig out the forms. I don't suppose it's anything too drastic.'

'Probably not.'

She felt a spasm of irritation. It was only Thursday – he wouldn't be back at work until Monday. That was twelve meals to get through, minus Sunday lunch, of course, before routine claimed their lives.

'Do you want me to get food while I'm out?' Despite her best efforts her voice shook and he looked up at her with a sudden smile.

'What food would that be, then?'

She tried to look nonchalant. 'Fish? Or bread? Or . . .?'

His grin spread and he leant back.

'Come here.'

'Why?'

'Just come here.' He put an arm round her. 'Listen. I can deal with the food, it isn't a problem. I can get the heating fixed. You shoot off and get your decorating bits and we'll take it from there. We need to spend some time getting to know each other, that's all.'

She nodded and managed a smile when he hugged her.

She didn't look back as she left the house.

11

At the home place she swiped her card and was astounded to see the amount of materials she was allowed to buy. A smiling assistant walked over. 'Can I help?'

'I was just surprised at my home materials balance.'

'Oh, let's have a quick look. No, that's right. You didn't use your allowance from your first marriage and that's been added to your griefspend and now you've just got married again . . . lovely!'

Lyn wandered around the warehouse thinking about the house and trying to work out why she and Greg hadn't decorated when she moved in. It was only four years ago, so it must have needed something. Of course, she'd brought her stuff – cushions and pictures and throws – but they hadn't used many of them because they didn't fit in with the subdued colours that Greg preferred. Where had they gone? Even if the other stuff had been recycled, surely they'd kept her pictures? She had a vague idea she'd hidden most of it in the loft.

The paint charts were mainly pastels but if she opened up the spaces with them she could add some bright splashes with new curtains. She pulled out her pad and began working out what she could afford. They could do the living room, the kitchen and the passages upstairs and down. Perhaps they could do the bedroom as well, especially if they could find her old bits and pieces. But she wasn't going up in the loft, Mikey would have to do it. How quickly, she mused, she had gone from complete dismay to accepting that he was in the house.

'Hey, stranger! What are you going for? More mushroom and magnolia?'

'Judith! What are you doing here?'

'On my break, looking for cushions.'

'That's so weird. You're not checking up on me, are you?'

'No, I called Mikey to see if you were around for lunch and he said you were here, so two birds with one stone.'

'But we never meet for lunch.'

'We used to, especially when we had things to gossip about. No, I really wanted to apologise for being a bit off this morning. It was weird seeing you two together.'

'Well, you'll have to get used to it.'

'Sure, but it still seems strange. So, what have you chosen?'

'Colours actually. But why call Mikey and not me?'

'Where is your mobile?'

Well, thought Lyn, obviously not where it should be.

12

She used to lose her mobile all the time. She'd be in the middle of a presentation and she'd suddenly gasp, start fumbling in her bag, then groan, 'I've done it again.' Usually she'd already left it handy on the lectern or desk and we just wouldn't bother to tell her but sometimes she'd really lost it.

The thing with mobiles is that you're supposed to have them with you – little kids have them attached with elastic – but obviously older kids and especially adults are supposed to be sensible enough to keep hold of them. She'd sit down in despair and start telling us about how, in the old days, mobiles were just for calling people or looking on the internet and yes, you could track people with them but they were primarily a communication tool, not a tracking device, and if you lost one you could just get another. Then she'd click the screen and development of communication and intelligence devices would come up. Luke used to groan with disgust: 'She's done it again – you think you're just having a chat and it turns out she's trying to teach you something,' and she'd flash that grin and say 'Yup!' then give us an exercise while she tried to find out what she'd done with her mobile.

Once she actually left it on my desk after explaining something to me but I didn't dare touch it. All that information about her was right by my hand but I knew that if I even glanced at it I'd look too interested.

13

'Did Judith catch you?'

'Yes. I'm starting to feel paranoid. I think perhaps the centre have detailed her to keep checking on me until I get this bloody tag off. I just wish she'd tell me.'

Lyn left the paint in the passage and headed for the coffee breaker. The house was still cold but the kitchen felt warmer. She sniffed. 'What's that smell?'

'Oh come on, you know what that is.'

'It smells like bread cooking.'

'Exactly. Only technically, it's baking.'

'But that takes hours. It has to prove and stuff.'

'Well this was already partly there. I nicked it from the restaurant – nothing was going to prove in sub-zero temperatures, after all.'

'Didn't they mind? Was your manager OK with it?'

'No, they didn't mind and yes, he was fine with it.'

She reached for the coffee mugs and snapped them into the dispenser before the machine had a chance to remind her. 'You didn't tell me what colours you liked so I guessed.'

'What, for the walls?'

'Yes.'

'Something a bit cheerful, but I expect you've got better taste than me.'

'You can always say if you don't like it. Judith said I shouldn't have chosen it without you but I just wanted to get started.'

'No problem.'

'Right. Well, as soon as I've had my coffee I'll get on with it.'

39

She was aware that the manic actor tone was back in her voice as she fought to sound natural. 'I thought I'd begin in the living room. I'll do the kitchen when you're back at work. After all, you're not going to want to be knee deep in paint pots and . . .' She trailed off hopelessly.

'Lyn, like I said, we need some time to get used to being together. Let's just sit down for a minute and have a chat.'

A chat? Was he crazy? What could they possibly have to chat about?

'I expect you want to know about my family and work and things like that.'

'Oh, right, of course I do. Off you go then.'

He laughed at her. 'Of course you don't, not right now, anyway. I'm teasing you. Come here and tell me what you got at the home centre.'

She sat nursing her coffee. 'I got colours . . . Oh, I told you that.' He nodded encouragingly. 'I thought we could have yellows to cheer things up and I've got green for the living room. Two shades. I think I've got throws and things in the loft that'll go with everything. I hope you like it.'

'I'm sure I will.'

'Mikey, what you were saying last night about ice skating and exercising . . . you were joking, right?'

He frowned. 'No, actually I wasn't. What's the problem? You look pretty fit to me. Your ribs seem to be mending OK.'

'But I haven't done much sport as such. Obviously I carry the shopping and things but that's more stamina, isn't it.'

He snorted. 'Carry the shopping? You'd better get into training, woman. Tim's your man, he'll sort you out.'

'Tim?'

'My brother – he's an athletics coach – half way through his first year of pay back.' Lyn stared in appalled horror. 'What is it now? You look just like an owl when you do that.'

'I didn't know you had a brother,' she said faintly.

'Two, and a sister. You'll meet them on Sunday.'

'Is your sister a sporty girl, then?'

'No, she's a very girly girl – does a lot of pouting and can't stand football.'

Thank the Lord, she thought. 'Well, that's what I'm like too,' she declared firmly.

He snorted again and ruffled her hair. 'I'm not asking you to run a marathon, Lyn. It's just something we can do together. If you prefer cycling or bowling then we'll do that.'

'Good, thanks.' She sighed.

14

She woke with her heart pounding from a dreadful nightmare. Greg had died and she was married to a spotty student with green hair and piercings. She'd bought yellow paint for the passages and green paint for the living room. Greg would go mad – he'd be so angry – he hated anything that wasn't neutral, he hated her throws and pictures; she'd had to plead with him not to recycle them and in the end she'd had to hide them. She understood he just wanted to improve her and help her refine her taste. He thought she had a good brain but working at the college had coarsened it and he didn't like that. Now she'd proved him right – buying colours and even thinking of retrieving her stuff from the loft where it had been hidden away for four years.

'Why do you call it stuff?' he'd demanded furiously. 'That's a lazy, stupid way of speaking – I'd expected better from you.'

What could she do? She'd have to repaint the walls before he found out. And where was he? Where was he?

A shrill beeping made her gasp. On her wrist the tag was flashing red. She sat up, hands over her mouth, choking back sobs. She knew there was someone beside her but she didn't want to look.

An arm went round her shoulders. 'Hush. Is it your ribs? Do you feel all right?'

'I've put colours on the walls. I don't know what I was thinking of. Greg will be furious. I don't know what to do.'

'It's OK. You don't need to worry about Greg.'

'I do. You don't understand . . . I'm so stupid.'

'Lyn, look at me.'

'No. You've got green hair.'

'I haven't. You're dreaming. I've never had green hair, Mum would kill me.'

'You haven't? What about your piercings?'

'Nope. No tattoos either.'

She turned to look but it was too dark to see much. She tried a deep breath, then another. The beeping stopped but the tag still flashed red.

'I'm sorry, it was just a nightmare.'

'Lie down.'

She lowered herself back under the bedclothes. His arms went round her and pulled her against his body. 'I meant, lie down with me.'

She wondered how much sex he was going to want . . . after all, he was much younger than Greg. Oh Lord, she thought, perhaps it's just the novelty of having me available and it'll wear off in a few months.

It seemed only moments later that she opened her eyes to another grey morning. Mikey was sitting on the bed with a coffee.

'Want some?'

'Oh, yes please.'

She sat up, thinking vaguely how nice it was to have someone who brought her coffee in bed. She reached out for the mug and Mikey stared at her arm. 'What's that?'

Confused she glanced down . . . a pale blue bruise extended round her upper right arm. 'Oh, that. It's nothing.'

He pulled down the duvet to check her other arm. 'Did I do that?'

'It's nothing, Mikey.'

'Do you bruise easily or something?'

'No, I don't, actually,' she said crossly. 'It really isn't important.'

He put the mug on the bedside table and regarded his hands

for a moment then reached forward and fitted them exactly over the bruises.

'God, I'm sorry. Why didn't you say I was hurting you?'

'Because you weren't and anyway, it wouldn't have made any difference, would it?'

He recoiled as if she'd slapped him. 'Of course it would. I'd have been more careful. No wonder you don't enjoy it that much!'

'Don't start shouting at me, I've said it doesn't matter. And what do you mean, I don't enjoy it that much? It doesn't matter if I do or don't but actually I . . .' She faltered and looked down.

'Yes?'

'You know the rules.'

'Oh sure . . . the rules. Let me tell you something. I don't care about the rules. I want you to be brave enough to tell me what you like and don't like.'

'Well, right now I'd like my coffee.'

'Oh, good recovery. Here you go then.'

He passed her the mug and stalked out of the room. She heard him stomping down the stairs and lay back with a sigh. Only the third day, she thought. I'm going to be exhausted by Sunday if he carries on like this. She took a sip of her coffee. I suppose, she mused, that I've offended his male pride or something. She wriggled back under the duvet. I wonder if I'm allowed a lie-in now we're not speaking? Her eyes closed and she drifted off.

15

Well, it was obviously going to take us a while to settle down. I cringed at the thought of those bruises – they must have hurt but she should have said something. I got another coffee and started to plan the day but I just kept going back to what she'd said. At college we'd all thought she was a bit of a rebel yet somehow all that had been sucked out of her. I was wondering about her last husband now . . . somehow he'd undermined her, stolen her confidence, and left me to sort it out.

I didn't understand it. Why select someone, then try to change them? But wasn't that what I was doing? Trying to make her into what I remembered and imagined?

Hell, it wasn't her fault . . . she was probably upset so I thought I'd better go and check she was OK. We'd got things to do and I wanted to get going. I made her a fresh coffee and went back upstairs but she was asleep. Fast asleep. Snuggled under the duvet with just a tuft of hair showing.

'Time to get up.' She muttered something and wriggled further down the bed. 'No you don't. You've got to get up now.'

'No.'

'Yes.' I ripped the duvet away and pulled her up. 'Here – drink this.' She put both hands round the mug and sipped cautiously, then peered up at me.

'I can't believe you. One minute you're telling me off for not doing what I want and now I'm in trouble for trying to have a lie-in. You can't have it both ways.'

'That was different and you know it. We can't waste our days off just lolling around. We've got things to do.'

'Huh. I thought lolling around was pretty high on your list, actually.'

I huffed a bit. 'Drink your coffee, you'll feel better. Snap to it, wench, I want you up that step ladder in twenty minutes!'

To my relief she actually smiled. 'And what are you going to be doing?'

'Trying out the kitchen. But I'll do you some toast first, if you like.'

16

She could hear him on the mobile while she was halfway up the ladder in the passage. She was pleased with the colour: the mushroom was rapidly disappearing under a thick coat of pale marigold and she'd already decided which pictures she'd hang if she could find them. She was just hesitating over whether she needed to do the ceiling or if she could leave it this time. 'Listen to yourself,' she muttered 'as if you're going to want to do this again.' His voice so close made her jump and he grabbed the ladder with one hand as she wobbled.

'Steady. It's Mum. She wants to know if you'd like a cat?'

'A cat? Oh no, I don't think so.'

She noticed that he was holding his mobile and realised that Claire was probably still on the other end. 'That is, I hadn't thought . . . Do you want one? Do you like cats?'

'Yeah, it's good to have a pet. She thought it'd be company for you.'

'Well, in that case, of course . . . if you want one. How very thoughtful.'

He grinned suddenly as though he'd read her mind, and spoke into the phone. 'Yes, sure – no – honestly – she'll love it. Yup, Sunday, OK – I will.' He clicked off.

'She sends her love.'

'She does?'

'Yes – it's what the ladies of the family do.'

'Ahh, that would explain it then. I need to get my "How the Family Works" manual out.'

'I know from your file that you were dumped, but didn't Greg have a family?'

'No, he was an only and his parents were dead.'

'Better brace yourself for Sunday then.'

He disappeared back into the kitchen. What was he doing? They didn't need food for hours yet but she could definitely smell cooking. She finished the wall she was on then went into the kitchen – she could always pretend she wanted a glass of water. He was poking at something in a pan and keying notes into a data file.

'Umm, sorry. I just wanted a glass of water.'

'Yeah . . . Come over here and try this.' He waved a dripping spoon at her and as she drew nearer shoved it towards her mouth. She flinched but instantly controlled herself and opened her mouth obediently. The sauce was strong and fishy with a sharp tang of something unrecognisable and a salty aftertaste. He looked at her closely. 'You don't like it.'

'Nooo . . . it's fine.'

'That's not the point. You don't like it and I need to know why.' He took another spoonful himself. 'Is it the tarragon?'

'Not unless that's salty.'

'You think it's too salty?'

'Yes.'

'OK. Imagine it as a sauce over a white fish fillet served with potatoes.'

'I can't. Well, I can – it's still going to be too salty.'

There was a pause while she studied the table and he studied the hob. 'Well – that's tough because it's got to be tonight's dinner – I've just used most of the day's allowance on it.'

17

Lyn pushed her way through the crowds outside the centre and into the relative quiet of the atrium. As she went through the scanner, a guard looked up from the duty desk. 'How can we help?'

'I've had a tag recall. I don't know why, it looks fine to me.' She waved her wrist where the tag glowed placidly green. The guard passed his hand-held reader over the tag then nodded. 'If you'd take a seat in cubicle 6A, just on your left, I'll call a counsellor for you.' She found herself in a small, grey room very similar to the marriage registration venue. She looked at the tag – still green – and practised breathing calmly and slowly. She didn't want to set it off again.

'Breathing doesn't help – it's only one read-factor and a fairly minor one at that.' She jumped, looked up at the man hovering in the doorway, then glared as he eased his way into the seat opposite.

'Are you the counsellor? If so I can tell you now what I need is someone to repair this thing – or even better, get it off me.'

He sat back and considered her for a moment. 'Let's begin again. I'm sorry I startled you. I'm Dylan and, yes, I'm one of the counsellors. If you could just give me a moment to check your tag read-out.' He tapped on the on-desk screen and frowned. 'Do you know why you had this fitted?'

'Sort of. My husband died and I thought I had more grief-time due than I actually did, but then I got just 24 hours' notification that I'd been selected for marriage again, so the tag was a safeguard.'

'You only got 24 hours' notice? Are you sure?'

'Yes. It was probably my fault because I hadn't been checking my emails or calls, so it was all a bit of a shock. I was expecting months and I got six weeks.'

There was a longish pause. Dylan clicked a few keys then sat back and regarded her steadily. She was pale but she didn't look particularly unhappy, he thought. Obviously the tagging had upset her but she didn't seem aware that it should never have happened. If anything, she was starting to regain that lively demeanour that he remembered from when she was first married to Professor Langdale. He wondered how to handle the situation. Perhaps seeing her over a longer period would be helpful.

'Look, I know it sounds pathetic but that's how it was.'

'Were you overly upset when it happened?'

'What, when Greg died? No, I don't think so. It was a shock and I was miserable but I wasn't suicidal and I didn't try to bend any rules.'

He frowned again. 'It says here that you were treated for two broken ribs? How are they now?'

'Fine, thanks.' She lifted her chin and looked him in the eye. 'Look, umm, Dylan, I'm OK. This sort of monitoring freaks me out but I'm not any sort of risk. I'm a responsible adult.'

He nodded. 'Right. Let's run through the read-out so far, then.'

Despite herself she was interested, and leant forward across the table.

'This is the main emotional trace line across the last four days, from the moment you had the tag fitted, and this is the physical activity line. As you can see, they don't necessarily run in tandem. For example, this is a really serious peak on day three at about 04.00 hours – can you remember that?'

'Sure. I had a ghastly nightmare about my situation.' His eyebrows twitched so she went on. 'I dreamt that Greg, my husband, was furious because I'd painted the living room green and I'd married a student with studs and dyed hair.' This time his lips twitched and she sighed. 'I know it sounds ridiculous but it's just my subconscious trying to sort things out.'

'Hmm ... It was followed by some fairly strenuous physical activity but no further emotional trauma. Any thoughts about that?'

Lyn's head jerked up and her tag clicked to amber. 'How dare you! Isn't it bad enough that we've got no choices left? Why should we have to put up with grimy little men making insinuations about our private lives? I bet you were all fighting over this one, weren't you, slavering over who gets to find out the dirty on "physical activity" at 04.00 hours. Well, I'll leave it to your imagination.'

They regarded each other. She looked up at the camera in the ceiling and sighed again.

'OK, fine. Use that to prove that I need counselling and tagging and whatever. I can assure you that I'm perfectly fine considering the circumstances and I think we'd better end this session now.'

Dylan tapped the screen then looked up. 'Lyn, I'm extending your tag for an additional two weeks and I need you to come in for a review next week. Let's say the same day and time, so we don't get in a muddle.'

'Give me strength,' she muttered under her breath, as she stood up.

'I'll just walk you out.'

'I'm fine.'

'No, really. I'll walk you out.'

As they reached the doors of the centre, he extended his hand and she took it automatically. 'Next time,' he muttered, 'don't have an outburst in a room with a recorder.' Then he was gone.

18

She arrived home frozen almost to the bone but buoyed up with bad temper, her breath steaming in the cold air. Bouncing through the front door, she stopped in her tracks as a blast of warm air rushed out at her. She found Mikey in the living room peering out of the back window. 'You got the heating fixed. How did you do that?'

'Got a man in, of course.'

'But it takes weeks.'

'Not if you're a key worker, babe.'

'But you're a chef.'

He turned and pulled her towards him. 'Look out there – we've got enough garden for anything you want, plus vegetables. You've already got fruit trees down the end and raspberry canes. Oh, and a grape vine up the wall.'

She nodded. 'Will the cat like it?'

'Well, it can't go out to begin with.'

'Can't it?'

'No – it'll have a tray inside until it's used to us.'

She turned back to the window and her shoulders began to shake. Mikey stared then turned her to face him. 'What's so funny?'

'Greg would have gone berserk.'

He cupped her face in his hands. 'So?'

'So nothing, I suppose.' When he kissed her she concentrated on not stiffening and managed to slide one hand around his neck quite naturally. He didn't seem to want anything else, just put his arms around her and hugged her to him, then gazed out at the garden as though the barren lawn was already studded with a glorious abundance of herbs and vegetables.

'Can we have flowers as well?'

'If you like. I'll leave that up to you. I'm going to build some raised beds for the salad greens and we can get some frames for the cucumbers and tomatoes. Where have you been?'

'The centre.'

'On a Saturday afternoon?'

'Yes. I got a tag recall.'

'Why didn't you tell me?'

'I didn't think of it.'

'You forgot your mobile.'

'Sorry.'

His arms tightened. 'For someone who's so keen on the rules, you really struggle with the basics, don't you?'

'It wasn't as if I was doing anything wrong.'

'No – just let me know next time, huh?'

She pulled back a bit and looked into his face. He didn't look particularly annoyed or even concerned. 'Are you angry with me?'

'No, I just worry when you slip off without telling me. Especially when I call your mobile and it's on top of the fridge.'

'I didn't slip off, I just didn't disturb you when I left.'

19

Sunday lunch was looming and Lyn was bewildered about what to expect. 'Should I take something?'

He lay back in bed and watched her flicking through an array of clothes. 'What sort of thing?'

'I don't know ... A cake? A pudding? Flowers? She got us flowers.'

'That was different – that was for a wedding.'

'Right. Food then. How many people are there?'

'I don't know. It's going to be a bit of a wedding party, so probably lots.'

'Mikey, please help me. I've never been to a Sunday lunch, not with a family. I have no idea what to expect.'

'Oh, come on, Lyn, use your brain – it'll be people eating and getting to know you, that's all.'

'I know! I must have a huge chocolate allowance left – we'll get chocolates on the way.'

'Great, crisis averted ... how about you coming back to bed?'

'Should I wear a skirt?'

'If you like ... how about you coming back to bed?'

'Not so fast, young man. What should I do with my hair?'

'Come back to bed and I'll tell you.'

'Good grief. You're obsessed.'

'Sure ... I've had another idea about something you might like. Now get back here.'

She sighed. 'Please don't pretend this is all for my benefit. It's bound to be something you think you'd like.'

He grinned happily. 'It's all part of my continuing quest for maximum compatibility. Now just lie down, madam, and I'll give you a massage.'

20

It was damp, cold and slushy with a lowering yellow sky. Inside Claire's house it was stiflingly cosy with cushions and throws everywhere, photo frames rotating family pictures on every surface and a buzz of background music. There were flowers blooming in a mini greenhouse box on the windowsill, glasses of punch already set out on a tray and a large grey rabbit with enormous ears sitting up on the sofa. Claire followed Lyn's fascinated gaze and groaned. 'Krystal, take Dylan upstairs. I told you before.' A lanky teenager with huge brown eyes swooped down on the rabbit and bore it away.

Claire smiled. 'Sorry, that's Dylan for you – he always likes to know what's going on.'

'That's fine,' Lyn smiled back. 'I was just surprised because I know another Dylan – from the centre, not a rabbit, obviously. Here – these are for you.' She pushed the box of chocolates towards Claire.

'That's kind.'

'Oh no, it's nothing, I had loads of my allowance left so . . . well, I hope you like them.'

In response Claire passed her a glass of punch from the tray and said, 'Come into the kitchen and we'll have a chat.'

The kitchen was small and functional with a dining area at one end. Lyn sat on a pine chair nursing her drink. Outside was a long stretch of grass slippery with disintegrating snow. At the far end, two lads were kicking a ball around with Mikey. 'Ah,' said Lyn. 'I wondered where he'd disappeared to.'

Claire nodded. 'He's a good boy – always happy to kick about with the boys even though he's a bit older.'

'Is he your first?'

'Yes, by five years. I've got four altogether – Michael, Tim, Jack and Krystal.'

'And your husband?'

'Ray, he's on day work this weekend down at the station. He was sorry to miss you.'

'And what do you do, apart from looking after this lot?'

'Well, because of my age I'm exempt from the home-working regulations – they didn't come in until I was well past my probation. I work at the animal re-homing house part-time. There. That should have put you in the picture.'

'I'm so sorry, you must think I'm interrogating you.'

Claire sat down. 'Not really. It must be hard having to get used to so many people at once. Michael said you were nervous.'

Lyn flushed and took another slug of her drink.

'The thing is, I didn't have a family and Greg and I didn't socialise with his family because he'd fallen out with most of them, so although I was used to seeing lots of people when I was teaching I didn't have to worry about them knowing things about me.'

'Well, we're all quite normal so you've nothing to worry about here. Time we put the vegetables on. Do you want to give me a hand?'

'Of course. By the way, Mikey . . . er, Michael . . . has probably told you that I can't cook but I'm afraid that's not strictly true.'

'No?'

'No. I used to joke about it at college and then Greg liked to eat out a lot so I got out of the habit. I just let Michael take over because he's a chef but I'm going to have to confess once he's back at work . . . he won't want to work in a kitchen all day then come home to more of the same.'

'So you don't want me to show you how to chop a carrot then?'

'Not really, although I'm sure you're better at it than I am. But I'll willingly chop them for you.'
'Great – I'll get us another drink.'

21

The windows in the kitchen were steaming up but I could still see Lyn and Mum chopping and stirring. Mum wouldn't be anything but kind and Lyn was on her best behaviour so nothing could really go wrong but I couldn't stop trying to work out what they were doing. Jack gave me a smack on the arm as he dribbled the ball round me. 'Stop staring and concentrate, man! Are you playing or what?'

'Or what, definitely "or what"!' yelled Tim. 'Can't take his eyes off her. Bet he wishes he was at home right now having a lie-in!' I grabbed him around the waist and toppled him into the slush in one swift dive. For an instant I was humiliated and angry but only an instant. As he spluttered, a feeling of solid happiness shot through me because he was right: I did wish I was at home, in bed. I pummelled him happily and started to laugh. 'I am a love god,' I chanted, 'a beast in the sack!' Jack's side rush rolled me over easily and we rocketed round the garden, a mess of arms and legs. They needed showing who was top dog in this family. It wasn't until I saw my trainers that I started to slow down. 'Hey, guys, stop. Look at the state of us.'

As we pulled apart, the back door snicked open. Three faces stared out at us; two were glaring accusingly and Lyn was one huge grin. Her eyes were round and sparkling and she seemed to be enchanted with the whole scene. I heard Tim and Jack gasping beside me.

'Whoa,' Jack croaked, 'you are kidding me, man.'

'Nope, that's my lovely wife.'

'But she's lovely.'

'Yup – I did say that.'

Tim was completely silent. Krystal scowled at us. 'Uncle Martin and his lot are just arriving,' she spat. 'I suggest you get upstairs before they come in. You need to sort yourselves out. You are all pathetic.'

As we shuffled past, I glanced at them: Mum and Krystal with identical expressions of rigid fury and embarrassment, Lyn with her jaw dropping, her eyes glinting and her shoulders starting to shake.

'Can . . . can I do anything?' she muttered. I heard Mum saying, 'It would be lovely if you could chat to Martin and Sandra in the lounge for a few minutes while Krystal and I set the table.'

Oh my love, I thought, it would be lovely if you could come upstairs and help me get changed. I expect I've got some nasty bruises and I'm sure a massage would help . . .

22

Martin and Sandra introduced themselves as Claire's brother and sister-in-law plus little Emily, who was playing with a pudgy white and ginger kitten in one corner.

'So sorry we missed the wedding,' said Sandra, 'but Claire said it was very quick.'

'Yes, it was even shorter than my first and not at all romantic. You get an additional alcohol unit allowance but I think that's about it. I used to think that it was a good idea to have a general ceremony that suited everyone but this was absolutely basic.'

Martin coughed. Sandra's colour deepened. 'Martin's on the partnership registration development group at the centre,' she said quickly.

'Lord, it's a diplomatic minefield, isn't it? Have some punch before I say something else I shouldn't.'

'No offence taken. After all, we know how you ladies like the big frocks and floral arrangements. It's just we can't accommodate everybody. Claire never stops complaining about it.'

'Well, maybe she has a point. Perhaps you could just have a choice of music and a bouquet and a flower girl?'

'Or perhaps not,' Martin rumbled, as Emily chipped in with, 'I'd like to be a flower girl.' Martin gave Sandra and Lyn a grave look before he went in search of his sister.

'I'm so sorry,' said Lyn. 'I seem to spend all my time apologising at the moment.'

Sandra giggled, then glanced out of the window. 'Here come the reinforcements.' Lyn joined her and took another hefty slug of punch at the sight of five more people coming up the path.

'Who are they?'

'My sister Karen, with Lucy. And Claire's other brother Simon, with Amanda and James.'

Lyn had a confused impression of a wave of smiling adults and children pressing into the room, then she found herself squeezed on to the sofa with Mikey, a fresh drink in her hand, a babble of cheery conversation swirling around her.

Mikey was looking at her closely. 'How many of those have you had?'

'About four. Why? It's only punch – no alcohol.'

He retrieved the glass from her hand and took a gulp. 'Who told you it was non-alcoholic?'

'Well, no-one, I suppose. But punch isn't alcoholic, is it?'

'It is in this house. Don't panic – you'll just have to be on water for lunch, apart from the champagne toast, can't miss that.'

Too late she realised that the anxious, fuzzy feeling she'd been mistaking for nerves was actually the result of too much alcohol, too fast. The rest of the visit passed in a blur. Her amazement and delight at the kitchen table transformed with flowers and candles, her disbelief at how everybody crushed around it to eat, her hopeless embarrassment at the snow-white wedding cake (decorated by Krystal) washed down with glittering champagne and sparkling water – it all seemed to be happening at top speed to somebody else.

Suddenly everybody was leaving. Cold air flooded into the house and made her feel more awake. 'Oh look, Emily's left her kitten behind.'

'That's your kitten, Lyn, don't you remember?'

'Of course, but how are we going to get it home?'

'We've got you a carry box – Michael's got everything else at your place.'

There were kisses and hugs and then she and Mikey were slip-sliding down the path in the gathering dusk.

'Mikey!'

'What?'

'I feel most terribly sick!'

'Just hang on until we're home.'

'I don't know if I can.'

'You have to, otherwise you'll be arrested.'

'It's not my fault.'

He rubbed her back sympathetically. 'Tell that to the centre.'

She made it home and headed straight upstairs to the shower. Surprisingly she began to feel better almost at once and although her plan had been to fall into bed she decided to risk going downstairs for a glass of water. Mikey handed her a mug of pale green, steaming liquid. 'Whatever is it?'

'Mint tea. Go on, it'll settle your stomach.'

'I've never had it before. What's in it?'

'Mint and hot water. The best restaurants serve it as a *digestif.*'

'It tastes like mint but mainly hot water.'

'That's the general idea.'

'What have you done with the kitten?'

'It's just exploring.'

'I think I'll go to bed.'

'Me too.'

23

By the end of the semester we were all fluent in dictionary speak and could talk the hind leg off a donkey at interviews. She taught us not to sweat the hard stuff – if there was something interesting to be dragged out of what we were doing, she'd find it, and if not we'd just get through it as fast as we could. We didn't develop a love of fine literature or any particular writing ability but our presentation skills fell into shape and somehow we all passed the course, even Ryan.

The way the courses were structured, you spent most of your time in workshops learning a trade and after three years you were allocated a job. Smart kids were given a second chance after year one but the rest of us were slotted into the work-place. I ended up in a hotel kitchen plating up breakfast trays and chopping vegetables. Luke went straight into a bike factory. Ryan went to work in the centre park mowing the lawns and weeding the flower borders.

I hung out with Kylie for a while – nothing serious, but she was gorgeous with her red curls and tiny waist, not to mention her tiny skirts. Luke and Jolene went out with us sometimes and occasionally Ryan would bring Marie along. We'd hang out at the drink and dance bar if the girls were with us, or go somewhere a bit wilder if it was a booze buddies night.

Ryan was the first one to do really well. It turned out that he was a bloody good gardener, so good that the centre spon-sored him on a six-month design course and when he came back he was allocated to design a block of centre gardens. Pissed and excited he told us, 'It was because of that writing course –

I had to submit notes and I just remembered how Miss told us to do it.'

'That's good,' sneered Luke, 'because you wouldn't have been able to do it on your own.' Jolene gave him a slap and Marie shot him a nasty look.

'Actually,' she snapped, 'Ryan's right. I had to do some reports on my nursery placement and now I've been accepted on a fast track psychiatric course. She was a great teacher ... you just think you're so cool but really you're just up yourself.'

Luke sniggered but obviously felt a bit uncomfortable and slapped Ryan on the shoulder on his way to get another round of drinks in. Later that night Kylie rolled over in bed and said, 'You're very quiet. What's up?'

'Nothing, sweetheart, just thinking about college and stuff. But it's good about Ryan, isn't it?'

She sat up with an irate bounce and a pursed mouth. 'You're in bed with me and thinking about bloody college ...!'

After a moment I realised I should be saying something. 'Sorry, I've had a tough week at the restaurant.'

'Fine, but it's time you realised it isn't all about you,' she fumed. 'I can do better than this. There are still some men around who aren't obsessed with their English teacher, you know.'

She ended with a hiss and flounced out of bed, pulled on her clothes, grabbed her bag and made for the door. Then she looked back at me for one moment before swishing her lovely curls and heading for the stairs.

I lay in bed contemplating the ceiling. I was nearly twenty. I didn't need to think about selection for years yet. The love of my life must be, what? Twenty-seven, twenty-eight? She'd got married to some famous academic but he looked about a hundred and would probably drop dead in a couple of years. By then I'd have made it to chef and she'd be impressed. In the meantime I could hang out with Jolene for a bit if Luke was OK with it and if not, I'd seen Lucy a couple of weeks ago looking very sweet behind the till at the food centre. She'd improved a lot since college and she'd been pleased to see me.

24

Lyn was spooning canned tuna into a bowl for the kitten when he came into the kitchen already dressed for work, and held out his mobile.

'It's Mum – she wants to apologise.'

'What for?'

'For getting you pissed. Just don't take too long, I don't want to be late.' He clicked on the coffee breaker muttering, 'You could at least have made coffee.'

Lyn turned her back. 'Hi, Claire, I can't be too long. His lordship is getting grumpy.'

'Oh, Lyn, I didn't think about it until you'd gone but I should have warned you . . . I forgot you were still tagged and I thought a drink or two would loosen you up.'

'I made a complete idiot of myself, didn't I?'

'No, you were sweet. What I'm concerned about is your daily alcohol profile read-out. If you like, I'll ring the centre and explain.'

'No, no! Don't do that, it won't change my profile and it might lead to a general entry against you. There's no point. I tell you what, I'll have a word with my friend Judith, she'll know what's best.'

'That sounds OK. I'll leave it then, shall I?'

'Sure. And thanks for the lovely lunch. Bye then.'

She turned back and put the mobile on the table. 'What's the matter with you?'

'Nothing. I just don't want to be late my first day back.' He shot her a pained glance. 'I thought you might have made coffee or toast or something.'

'I can do you some tuna.'

'Very funny.' He knocked back a can of Coke from the fridge, grabbed his mobile and headed for the door. There was a weird moment when he almost hesitated and she wondered if he was waiting for her to say, 'missing you already', or 'take care', or 'have a good day'. Then he was gone and she hadn't even managed 'goodbye'.

'Well,' she said, and sat down, scooping the kitten on to her lap, 'our mornings are going to be pretty dismal if he doesn't cheer up a bit. You're happy though, aren't you?' The kitten purred. The coffee breaker soothed. 'Coffee ready . . . coffee ready . . .' He'd even remembered a mug for her.

'Well, OK, you're happy because you got tuna and he's unhappy because he didn't get coffee. Perhaps we ought to make Daddy a nice dinner for tonight. What do you think he'd like? It can't be anything complicated because we've got a lot to do today.' The kitten prodded her lap and curled up but didn't give her any further encouragement.

25

Mikey came home to a warm house smelling of paint mixed with onions.

'Hi,' Lyn yelled from the kitchen. 'Dinner in half an hour. Do you want a shower or something?'

'Nope. I showered at work.' He looked round the kitchen. 'Sorry, must be in the wrong house.'

'Very funny.'

'Then who are you and what have you done with my wife?'

'Look, I'm not going to apologise for this morning ... it didn't occur to me that you'd want a hot drink before setting out across the tundra to slay the odd mammoth. But I did think that you'd not want to cook when you got in with said mammoth so I've done a stew with mashed potatoes – OK?'

'We'll see. Any beer in the house?'

'I don't know. Greg was more of a wine man. Haven't you checked it out already?'

'Not particularly.' He swiped into the alcohol locker. 'Nope, no beer. Put it on the shopping list will you, honey?'

'What!'

'Well, since you've gone all perfect wife on me I assumed it was your job to look after my every need.' He took a closer look at the alco read-out. 'Oh dear, looks like your sign-out is still cancelled. Better take it easy or you could find yourself in rehab.' Before she could reply his arms were wrapped round her from behind. 'Don't get all upset – I'm teasing you.'

'I know.'

'No, you don't. Listen, I didn't select you for your perfect wifely qualities ... I wanted to be with you ... but you have to relax, we have to get used to each other.'

'I know, you keep saying.'

'Then stop trying to be someone else – just be yourself for a while.'

'What do you mean?'

'You weren't like this at college.'

'Well, no, but I was in front of a class of sixteen-year-olds. It was completely different. I was teaching, or trying to.'

'Oh, believe me, you were teaching all right.'

'Now you're making me sound like a pervert.'

'What?'

'Oh, come on, this has to be strange – you've married one of your teachers.'

'So I have. Thank God it wasn't old Matthews.'

26

She was doing what she thought I wanted. OK, some of it wasn't bad ... the house was already looking more comfortable and that weird, dead smell had been completely overtaken by drying paint with faint top notes of cat wee. The rooms were brighter, the cobwebs were gone and she'd lost that 'I don't know what I'm supposed to be doing' look. Something wasn't right, though. It was as if she thought she ought to be conforming to some standard of behaviour and was doing her best to measure up.

Each time we met it was almost like the first time all over again ... a bit of bantering, a bit of negotiation, then we were off. Now here she was making stew. It smelled OK ... mainly onions but not unlike the sort of thing Mum would make. I hadn't thought about what I'd do to eat when I got home so yes, it was a nice surprise, but why was she doing it? She obviously thought she'd made a dire blunder by not having my coffee ready in the morning. Anyone could have told her that I hate getting up early to go to work and I would have been mad whatever was going on but I suppose there was nobody to tell her.

I'd thought of apologising but it seemed a bit pointless. Maybe I'd be better off just telling her how it was going to be. I sat and watched for a while as she thrashed about cudgelling a pan of potatoes to death and generally flapping around. The kitten climbed on to my lap and watched as well. We were probably equally bemused but enjoying the show anyway. She'd tied her hair back but it was escaping and her lips were set in grim determination. 'I thought you told Mum you could cook?'

'Well, I can – the basics, you know. I didn't want her to think I was useless.'

'She wouldn't have minded – she likes teaching, like you, and Krystal and the others aren't really interested. But what are these basics, then?'

She gave me a vaguely hunted look as though it was a trick question but as usual, if it was about food, I was interested. I'd learnt to cook from Mum long before I went to college but Lyn didn't have a mum to teach her.

'What did they teach you at the dump?'

'Carrots mainly.'

'Carrots?'

'Yes, Mikey, carrots. And onions. How to cook stew, with meat. Umm . . . rice, pasta, sandwiches and potatoes . . . oh, and scrambled eggs.'

'I see.'

'What does that mean?' She poked viciously at the potatoes. 'Nothing . . . just if you use a fork instead of a spoon and add a knob of butter and a splash of milk – oh, and tip the water out first – then use your wrist more, you'll get a fluffier result.' She sighed and brushed her hair out of her eyes. 'Look, I'll show you.'

It was time for a drink.

27

Mikey slid the glass of red wine across the counter. 'Here you go.'

'Thanks. What's a knob of butter when it's at home, anyway?'

'First rule of cooking, relax; second rule, get your ingredients close to hand so that when I've got my arms around you I don't have to stretch too far to reach them; third rule, concentrate.' He drained the potatoes and positioned her in front of the hob. 'OK, turn down the heat for a moment so that they don't catch. Add the butter, add the milk – not too much – take the fork in your right hand and mash. That's pathetic.' His hand closed over her wrist. He was surprised at how small her bones felt sliding under the skin as he demonstrated. 'You are very bad at this.'

'Is that supposed to help?'

'Sure . . .' He turned her wrist, lifted it to his mouth and kissed it. 'You have small, weak wrists so you need to use technique, not brute force. Turn the heat up a notch, keep stirring and there you go. Heat off, give it a moment, then taste it and add some pepper if it needs it.'

'Thanks.'

'No problem. Want me to do anything else? Feed the cat? Set the table?'

Lyn gave him a slitty-eyed glance. 'You could empty the litter tray while I dish up.' She grinned as he groaned but had to give him points for nerve as he reached for the bin bags and went out into the passage. The kitten bounced around his feet and she could hear it christening the pristine tray immediately, accompanied by Mikey's grumbles. When he reappeared she'd set the table and was fidgeting with her glass of wine.

Her mobile cut into the silence. 'Hi, it's Judith, feeling a bit bored and wondering if you two needed any company?'

'Sure, Jude, where are you?'

'Just leaving work. Do you want me to bring pizza or something?'

'No, we've got stew. Loads for you if you want to risk it.'

'Great – see you in fifteen.'

Mikey stared. 'She's coming round now?'

'Yes.'

'Why? Are you two joined at the hip or what? How did Greg cope with this?'

'She didn't come round much when Greg was here. I don't know . . . perhaps she didn't like him.'

He nodded.

'What?'

'What what?'

'There's a shrug in your voice.'

'There is?'

'Yes.'

'Well, maybe I think it's weird that she's always around. I had plans.'

'Well, maybe she's checking on me – she works for the centre, after all.'

He scooped up the kitten. 'Have you fed him?'

'Constantly – he wants food all the time.'

'OK, good. Do you want me to taste your stew before Judith arrives?'

'Would you want me to taste yours?'

'Probably . . . yes.'

'OK then.' She stood back and let him dip a spoon into the pan. 'I'm getting onion . . . and onion . . . and, yes, onion. Yup – it's onion stew all right.'

'Very funny. What do you really think? Do you like it?'

Could she sound any more desperate for approval, she wondered?

'Fine. Is it beef?'

'I'm not sure. It's meat.'

'But you cooked it.'

'Point taken, but it all looks the same when it's in the freezer.'

'That's what labels are for. Here, you try it.' He held out the spoon and as she took a mouthful he hugged her. 'Listen, anything you do is OK with me.' There was a pounding at the front door and the kitten went into orbit.

'Let go. I've got to let her in.'

'Nope – we'll pretend we've gone out.' Lyn dithered for a second, then her tag clicked to amber. 'Oh hell . . . look at that.' She waved her wrist at him and headed for the front door, pulling her sleeve down.

'Hi, stranger.'

'Hardly that. Whoa. I can smell onions.'

'Good. It's tonight's key ingredient.'

'You mean you cooked?'

'Yes. I can cook, you know.'

'But you've got a trained chef on the premises.'

Mikey intervened. 'Who doesn't want to cook when he's cooked all day, and is happy to let his wife take over in the kitchen if she wants to. Hi, Judith, want a beer or wine or juice?'

Judith grinned. 'Hi yourself. Wine is fine, I'm off duty.' The kitten dodged under the table as she sat down. 'So, you two OK? I see the decorating is still in progress.'

'Give me a break. I've spent most of the afternoon chopping up onions. How about you? Anything exciting happening at the centre?'

'No, just the usual.' Mikey sat down opposite her and the kitten sprang on to his lap. 'What's that?'

'We've got a kitten, didn't Lyn tell you?'

'I've hardly had time,' Lyn said over her shoulder, as she prodded at the potatoes. 'Judith, how hungry are you?'

'Very.'

By the time she left, Lyn felt exhausted, and slumped on the sofa with the kitten on her lap. Mikey finished loading the dishwasher and opened the alco store to get another beer.

'How come your friend is such hard work?'

She was too tired to argue about it. 'I don't know, she must have had a bad day. Perhaps we need to restrict entertaining to weekends. I'm sorry – I shouldn't have let her come round.'

Mikey was standing in front of the open alco store looking puzzled. 'Lyn, your alco read-out.'

She sighed. 'What about it?'

'Well, where did you get it from?'

'It's on my data file, isn't it?'

'Come here.' He put his hands on her shoulders and pivoted her to face the store. 'Look in there – what do you see?'

She sighed again. 'Loads of booze, as befits an old soak like me.'

'No, you don't. That store is practically full and the last person to put anything in there apart from beer was Greg.'

'So?'

'So . . . your read-out is so high that you're banned from opening the store for a month. Yet we both know that you can't drink more than four units without keeling over. Plus the cupboard is hardly bare.'

'Perhaps we've had a burglar in reverse – someone who keeps topping it up.'

'Don't be silly. Far more likely that someone's tampered with your data file.'

'But what's the point of that?'

'To cause you some embarrassment and inconvenience, I guess.'

28

Dylan leant back and scrutinised her. 'So – a reasonable week apart from a serious alcohol intake on Sunday. What have you got to say about that?'

Lyn sighed. 'It was my responsibility. I was at a family party and I didn't realise that the fruit punch contained alcohol.'

'You mean that you weren't informed?'

'No, I mean that I'm an adult and I should have realised that it tasted good because it had alcohol in it.'

'Who prepared it? Who offered it to you?'

'I'm an adult. I don't see that this is relevant. It was my fault.'

The desk read-out showed that she was very tense but Dylan could see that anyway. He tapped a couple more keys and nodded. 'Your alcohol consumption for the rest of the period has been moderate and your protein and fibre intake has improved to good so I think we can take this as a minor blip.' He watched as her shoulders relaxed. Now, we need to explore a couple of other things. When we spoke last you felt that your grieftime had been cut short rather abruptly. I've checked the records and I tend to agree with you. I need to assess whether or not this has had an adverse impact on your new relationship.'

'No.'

'Sorry?'

'No. We're getting to know each other, but I'm sure you know all about that. My new partner is being very understanding.'

'He is?'

'Yes – why wouldn't he be?'

'Well, he's younger than you . . .'

'He might not perform so well in front of Judith but she just seems to make him nervous.'

'Judith?'

'Oh, come on – she works for the centre. She's a friend but she's been round every other day since this whole tagging thing started. You must have got her reports there.'

He tapped on the desk screen and frowned. 'No, there are no field reports on you or your husband. Are you suggesting that her behaviour is unusual?'

'No, I assumed that she was checking up on us officially but exercising some discretion.'

'Ah.'

29

This time he didn't walk her to the exit, so she was able to take a casual look round to see if Judith was about. She wasn't. Lyn picked up speed and went briskly down the steps. She needed to pick up food for the cat and beer for the boy before she went home and she had at least four hours work waiting for her when she got back.

From inside the centre Dylan watched her go. It was a bright day, the sky a clear, cold blue and her hair glinted and bounced behind her. She was, he supposed, attractive, certainly interesting and intelligent and there was no real reason that he could see for her to be tagged or monitored. Oh, there was no doubt that she'd been in a stressed condition initially but it would have been odd if she hadn't been. Someone with that level of sensitivity was going to need adjustment time and he couldn't really see why she'd been remarried so fast. He sighed . . . she really was a lovely woman, he thought. He glanced at the desk screen again, then back out of the window. She had reached the corner and for a moment he thought he saw someone following her but there were too many people about for him to be sure.

From the first floor of the centre, Judith was also watching. It was nearly time for her break and she was considering tracking Lyn and surprising her, then dragging her off for a sandwich and coffee. She pictured Lyn's initial discomfort followed by immediate capitulation, changing her plans at once for her dearest friend. No, it was too easy, and chances were Lyn would be doing something really boring like food shopping. Better wait until she was sure something significant was going on, something where any interruption would be extremely unwelcome. Meanwhile she'd just pull up the latest read-out. To her irritation it showed that Dylan was still updating the system following their counselling session. She should have thought of that. Even more irritatingly, the message system instantly flashed up: 'Hi, Judith, I'm a bit puzzled about something here – can you drop in? Dylan.'

No, she bloody couldn't, not until she'd thought about what to say. 'Sorry, Dylan, I've got a case conference booked. Catch you later. Judith.' She logged off quickly, blocked out the rest of the day on her calendar, then sat back for a think.

Lyn was queuing at the pet counter when a voice said, 'Hello, Miss.' She looked round and there was Luke grinning at her – older, taller, with his cynical scowl replaced by a quizzical look.

'Wow, Lucas, you're all grown up. When did that happen? What are you up to these days?'

'Designing . . . gizmos and gadgets.'

'That sounds very impressive.'

'All down to your sessions on how to write a CV and impress at interview.'

'I don't think so but it's kind of you to say so. So what are you doing in here?'

'Oh, it's my break and I spotted you coming out of the centre. By the way, congratulations! Mitch must be one very happy man.'

Lyn frowned.

'It was on the Bulletin.'

'Oh, yes, of course, it would be.'

'You know, if I'd spotted your profile on the selection list before he did I'd have snapped you up.' Silence fell for a moment and she buzzed her purchases through the reader, then turned back to him.

'Right, it's been great to see you, Lucas, but I really must . . .'

'Would you like coffee? Just ten minutes. After all, I don't know when we'll bump into each other again.'

'No, really. It's a nice idea but it wouldn't be appropriate and I am married. I shouldn't be socialising with an ex-student.' She smiled swiftly, hoisted her bag on to her shoulder and walked away.

30

The insistent beeping woke her. She sat up with a jerk. 'Oh nooo!'

Mikey rolled over. 'What is it? Another nightmare?'

'No, I don't think so. I can't understand it.'

'You're not upset?'

'I wasn't – though I am now.' The beeping slowed, then stopped.

'There must be something wrong with it. You'll have to get it checked at the centre.'

'Yes ... Oh hell, it'll show up as an episode on the read-out.'

'So?'

'I'm never going to get rid of this bloody thing.'

'Well, since we're awake now ...'

'No – no, we can't. It shows up as physical activity on the read-out and then I'm supposed to explain what I've been doing.'

'You mean the counsellor asks you?'

'Yes. It's humiliating.'

'Well, make something up – say you couldn't sleep and went for a run.'

'Now why didn't I think of that?'

'Not so smart as you pretend are you?' He stretched back against the pillows. 'Come on – I want my conjugal rights.'

'That's the worst line I've ever heard.'

'I don't care – it's the law.'

'Well you could stop looking so bloody smug.'

31

At the centre, Dylan was sceptical. 'You say you weren't having a bad dream and hadn't been disturbed by something that happened earlier?'

'No. I told you.'

'But it won't just go off – you need some kind of stimulus.' He frowned over the read-out again. 'It all looks fine up until it went off . . . then the usual activity following.'

'I went for a run.'

'Ah, of course. How have you been apart from this episode?'

'Fine.'

'Good – in that case I see no reason to extend your tagging again so you've just got three weeks to go and just three more counselling sessions.'

She beamed. 'Thanks, Dylan, I was really worried.'

'Not out of the woods yet but I can see you're feeling a bit more receptive so we need to start focusing on your psychological state and we do that by simply talking about what brought you here and how things have changed . . . that sort of thing.'

'But you know all that.'

'I know the outline but I would like you to examine how you felt about what happened . . . Perhaps we could use the rest of this session to discuss Greg and that will set the scene for next week.'

She lowered her eyes for an instant then looked up. 'I don't like to talk about Greg. I want to think about what's happening now.'

'All the more reason to get it over and done with. I've read up on the selection and he made a very good case at the time – obviously as a prominent academic he was looking for someone with similar interests and a high IQ. So I'm wondering what you felt about it.'

'Nothing. I mean I was pleased he liked me but since there was no choice I didn't really think about it.'

'I find that very hard to believe, Lyn.' He reached across the table and took her hand. 'You were, still are, a highly sensitive, intelligent individual. You had a good job and were popular with staff and students. Suddenly you have to give up your career to run the house of a man more than twice your age. Are you telling me you didn't feel resentful?'

'I knew it was going to happen sometime. I was just relieved that it was someone who had heard of Shakespeare.' She shook her head. 'I didn't think about his age at all. And he was happy for me to do homework – he encouraged me a lot. Step Up Stones – which coaches children through computer games linked to the national curriculum – was his idea.'

'Ah, yes. You're still developing those, I believe.'

'Yes. I'm on emerald now, I've just sent off the last proof.'

'Any more to go?'

'Just diamond, then it's all finished. Actually, there is something I need to speak to you about. Mikey thinks that my alco read-out has been falsified.'

Dylan raised a pained eyebrow. 'He thinks what?'

'That someone has changed the alco read-out on my data file to make a case for me being tagged.'

'And his reasoning?'

'Actually, Dylan, although it sounds mad, he does have a point. Our alco store is pretty much as it was when Greg died.'

He tapped the screen and nodded. 'Well, your tag read-out hasn't shown any abnormally high figures since that early blip, so he could be right. But perhaps he should leave this sort of thing to the centre.'

She flushed. 'I just thought I ought to point it out.'

'Dear lady . . .' He pressed her hand across the table. 'You can, naturally, confide in me about anything that is troubling you.'

32

'Were you at the restaurant today?' asked Mikey.

'Yes, I wanted to surprise you.'

'It was a surprise all right. Now you see her, now you don't. What happened to you?'

'Judith turned up.'

'At the restaurant? What was she doing there?'

'Following me, I think. Anyway, it would have completely ruined the surprise to have her there – I wanted to see in your kitchen and she . . . well, she . . .'

'She'd have been in the way. Come on, darling, this is just weird. Shouldn't you tell someone? Or do you want me to?'

'What did you just call me?'

'Darling . . . you know, it's a term . . .'

'Of endearment, I know. Actually, it's an archaic term of endearment . . . where on earth did you pick it up?'

'Mum and Dad. It's what they call each other. Don't you like it? Is there something you'd rather? '

'Rather what?'

'Rather I called you?'

'How about Lyn?'

'How about "unromantic pain in the arse"?'

'Oh, so now the boy wants romance . . . I don't remember that being part of the deal.'

'Actually, the boy wants a shower with his lovely wife.'

'There isn't room, it's too small.'

'Oh, I think you'll be surprised.'

'I'll be amazed – I'm not a contortionist.'

'We'll work something out.'

33

'How old is he, do you think?' said Lyn, holding the kitten.

Mikey shrugged. 'Mum said he was around twelve weeks when we got him, didn't she? That makes him four months old now.'

'He's very small. I mean, he's smaller than your rabbit.'

'Krystal's rabbit.'

'Yes, OK, Krystal's rabbit. But aren't cats bigger than rabbits? Do you think I'm feeding him enough?'

'My God, woman, you're obsessed. He's a kitten still – he won't be fully grown for about a year.'

Lyn scooped the kitten up and cuddled him against her neck. 'Do you think he's too fat, then? He feels a bit squashy.' The kitten stared at her with indignant green eyes, pushing his paws against her collarbone and struggling to get down. 'Do you think he understands what I'm saying?'

'Lyn, shut up, I'm trying to concentrate. We need to get this bloody oven serviced. When was the last time you had it done?'

'Never. Why would I?'

'The temperature control is all over the place – how can I test anything on it?'

'But it's just a basic cooker, Mikey, I didn't even know you could get them serviced.' She hesitated, put the kitten down and went over to him. He was fiddling with something on the hob, his back to her. After a moment she put her hand tentatively on his back. He leapt as if he'd been stung.

'What?' She stepped back hurriedly.

'Sorry. Never touch a chef when he's trying to cook.'

86

'I'll remember that.'

She picked up the kitten and went back to sit on the sofa. She could, she supposed, be working herself but she'd rather be in the kitchen although she wasn't sure why. After a moment she reached for her book and started to read. The kitten played idly with the pages, then settled down and began to chew the ends of her hair. Soon he was purring and his claws were scything in and out. She wasn't sure if he was meant to do that but she didn't want to interrupt Mikey again to ask, so she put up with it and tried to focus on her book. After a few minutes she realised that the various cooking noises had settled down. The air smelled of lemon and herbs and something she wasn't sure of. The oven door clanged shut.

Mikey came over and sat next to her. 'Sorry about that, it was a tense moment. Should be ready to try in about forty minutes.' He took the book out of her hands and glanced down at it. 'Oh, this is awful – how can you read this?'

'It's interesting – it's about Egypt. What have you cooked?'

'It's another fish recipe, plus Duchesse potatoes – they'll go in later on.' There was a silence. 'OK – you're not wild about recipe development and I'm not that keen on ancient history.'

'But at least we can eat the food.'

He nodded. 'Let's look at this squashy kitten then.' He pulled the fluffy bundle from her shoulder and bounced it in his hands. 'He feels just right, Lyn, though he's going to be massive – look at the size of his paws.' The kitten was drowsy and Mikey put him down on a cushion and turned back to Lyn. 'God, what's he done to your neck?'

'That's where his claws go in and out.'

'But why don't you move him? He can do that to a cushion or something.'

'He does it when he sucks my hair. I don't think he's attacking me or anything.'

'No, he thinks you're his mum. He's trying to get the milk to come down.'

She glared at him. 'Very funny.'

'No, it's true, it's an instinct with cats. Just don't let him get away with it, it's starting to look sore.'

He tucked her hair behind her ear and tipped her head to the side. 'I think it needs kissing better.' He ignored the nervous jolt that ran through her as he kissed her neck. After a moment, when he hadn't tried anything else, she looked round enquiringly.

'Umm . . . do you want . . . before we eat, that is?'

'Well, yes, but I've got to check on the fish and put the potatoes in, so I'll take a rain check.'

He got up, ran a hand through his hair and headed back to the oven. Lyn retrieved her book. The kitten heaved in sleep.

Outside it was raining fitfully. Judith stood in the garden, watching through the gauzy curtains. She felt resentful and angry – she couldn't see enough through the nets and she couldn't risk turning up the sound on her recorder to get a clear feeling for what was going on. From what she'd seen so far it looked as though they were the perfect couple – how the hell had that happened?

Lyn stood up and started to set the table and Mikey clicked open the alco store for beer. Lyn got fizzy water out of the fridge. Judith ground her teeth in bitterness and rage before slipping silently back across the lawn.

Lyn sat at the table sipping her water and watching Mikey doing clever things with food. She had a strange feeling that she couldn't quite work out but she was just starting to think that he was very kind to her. In fact he seemed to be affectionate. Oh God, she thought, please keep him this way for a little while longer . . . I know things will change but just for now let him be happy with me.

Mikey put a plate in front of her then stared. 'What is it?'

'Nothing, Mikey, this looks lovely. Thank you.'

'How about you making another guest appearance at lunchtime tomorrow? It'll have been a while.'

'Twenty-four hours.'
'Exactly – I miss you.'
'We'll see.'

34

Once again he watched as she left the centre. This time she was heading towards the park. The weather was milder and she was walking more slowly. He felt for a moment as if she was performing for him ... the sensitive, intelligent young woman reflecting on what he had said, and considering her feelings. He was, he realised, looking forward to their next session. With a sigh, he recognised some long dormant emotions.

A look at the on-desk screen showed nobody intrusively logged in this time and he quickly updated her records before logging off.

In the park Lyn was sitting with a coffee wondering if she could face going to the restaurant or if she just ought to go home. She had loads of time. She pictured the house: how it was now, how it used to be. The walls were all painted – she just needed Mikey to go up into the loft to retrieve her finishing touches. Perhaps she should go home and do it herself. The thought was enough to make her down her coffee and set off towards the restaurant.

Feeling ridiculous after the previous day, she took her time on the approach, checking both sides of the street for any acquaintances, looking back to ensure there was nobody behind her. Although she told herself she was being stupid, she actually went into a bookseller and watched the road for five minutes before buying a map and hurrying out. Crossing the street at a jog, she slowed abruptly at the restaurant door and scanned the occupants. The interior was dim and it took her a moment to adjust as she hovered by the door.

'Lyn, you made it then.' A young, smiling waitress was holding out her hand. 'Let me take your coat and get you a juice. I'll let chef know you're here.'

Lyn felt overwhelming relief. She allowed herself to be shepherded to a small table, accepted a prettily frosted drink, sat back and looked around. The restaurant was much more upmarket that she'd realised although she should have known that from the style of shops that surrounded it. An archway in one corner had a sign in scrollwork promising 'gardens this way' and the decoration in general was clean and comfortable – no skiddy banquettes or plastic tabletops. She picked up a menu and considered it carefully. This was an expensive place. Her heart sank. She'd eaten out enough with Greg to know that this was a cut above. Something else struck her. The waitress had referred to Mikey as chef – she was sure that meant he was running the kitchen but she'd assumed that at best he was one of the sous chefs and really she thought he spent his days peeling potatoes and making custard.

Her mouth suddenly dry, she took a gulp of her juice.

'Did you want to order anything?' She looked up at the smiley waitress.

'Oh no – I'm fine.'

'OK. Chef said to ask you to wait for him, he won't be long. He's just finishing off, then he'll be right out. Is it OK if I join you for a minute?'

'That would be lovely, if you're not too busy.'

'No, it's fine. I'm understudying front-of-house today so I just have to keep an eye on things and pitch in if it gets too busy. We're reasonably quiet at the moment although it's a bit manic in the kitchen.'

Lyn nodded, trying to think of an intelligent observation.

'I'm Jessica, by the way, and I've been desperate to meet you – my niece is a huge fan.'

'A fan?'

'Yes, of the Step Up books. She's just done amethyst and

she's frantic to move on to ruby but her teacher won't let her. She just loves the animation sequences. She spent hours doing choreography for the ballet show and designing the sets and everything. Her vocabulary is amazing, although it is a bit girly, I guess.'

'If she wants to try something else she could run the male gender option – that might balance out the girly vocabulary as well.'

'I didn't realise she could do that – it would give her something to keep her going in the holidays, I suppose, if she really can't step up?'

'Not until her teacher approves it – and since there's a month's break coming up, I expect she'll have to wait until she goes back.'

'I expect so.' Jessica looked a little downcast and refolded a pristine napkin.

'If that doesn't appeal, couldn't her mother give her a project? If she liked the ballet exercise, why not take her to the costume museum and get her to make up a ballet story based on what she sees there. They've got some beautiful clothes with materials you just can't find now, and wonderful embroidery. She could write a bit every day and tell her mother about it at bedtime.'

Jessica beamed. 'That's a great idea. You must have been a marvellous teacher. Are you and chef going to start a family soon?'

Lyn felt a wave of anxiety tinged with embarrassment flooding through her, so she took a steadying sip of her drink and smiled. 'We . . . well, it's early days.'

'I suppose so, but you can get the paperwork done, can't you?'

'Are you planning on children, Jessica?'

'Not yet. I'm up for selection next year so I'm making the most of things at the moment. Once I'm married, though, I can't wait.' She lowered her voice. 'I've started knitting already.

I've got some very smart patterns and I just couldn't resist . . .
Of course, nobody knows about it, it's my secret vice.'

'Well, your secret is safe with me.'

'Of course it is, I wouldn't tell you otherwise.' She beamed
again. 'So, how about you and chef? We all think it's so romantic
. . . he's so smitten, it's a miracle he hasn't chopped his arm off!'

'Oh no,' Lyn mumbled faintly.

'Oh, you've finished that. Can I get you something else? I've
been on a cocktails course so I could fix you anything you like.
I tell you what, I'll get you a strawberry daiquiri.'

She was gazing longingly at the door when Mikey sat down
opposite her. 'Just caught you, I see.'

'What?'

'Don't tell me you weren't thinking of doing another disappearing act, I know that look.' He glanced up as Jessica came
back with another frosted glass. 'Come on, bring your juice.
I'll show you round the kitchen then you can have some lunch.'
Jessica winked at her as she thrust the glass into her hand.

The kitchen was hot, very hot. There were banks of hobs
and ovens and pots and pans bubbling and steaming. There
was chopping and grating and stirring and blending going on
everywhere. And it was noisy. Lyn had been in the vocational
kitchen at college but that had been much smaller and generally quieter. This was hell. And the smells – acrid, sweet, searing
flesh, burning sugar, wafts of bubbling tomato and garlic mixed
with the tang of shellfish.

Then they were in a storeroom and he was showing her
shelves of dry spices and different kinds of herbs. There was a
huge cold store with vegetables in racks. Across the corridor
from the storeroom was another door that led to the staff
changing rooms and a small, very tidy office. 'Sit here and I'll
get you something. Anything in particular you'd like?'

'I don't want to be a pest – just some soup or a sandwich.'

He was back in minutes with a bowl of the tomato soup
and a small *niçoise* salad.

'Aren't you having anything?'

'Oh, we eat on the run usually. I'll get a coffee in a minute when it's a bit quieter. So,' he said, leaning against the door, 'what do you think?'

She stared at him. He looked eager and hopeful and anxious, as though it really mattered what she thought. She took a gulp of her drink and gasped as the rum hit. 'I'm very impressed. You didn't tell me you were in charge. It's amazing. I had no idea it was such a special place. You must be a brilliant cook to have got this far at your age.'

'OK, that's great, Lyn. Now what do you actually think?'

'That is what I actually think, but I'm really embarrassed that I didn't realise you were in charge.'

'That's all?' He was disappointed – she'd done it again. How could she get it right with everyone else and not with him? What was he expecting? What hadn't she said? The answer struck her almost immediately and she got up and went over to him, put her hand on his arm.

'I feel so proud I'm married to you, Mikey. I really wish I'd come here before.' She took another sip. 'And your juice selection is amazing.'

He looked down at her thoughtfully. 'Your soup's getting cold.'

35

The thing was, I could see she was astounded and impressed and quite in awe of the whole set up. The restaurant was very high quality and yes, I had done well to get so far so fast. I had wanted her to see it so that she knew I was successful in my world, not just the kid from remedial English who'd struck lucky with a safe career move. Yes, I wanted her to be proud of me and respect me and appreciate me.

There was a loud crash from the kitchen. 'Eat your soup, I'll be back in a minute,' I said and went to see what was going on. Nothing too drastic as it happened but it needed clearing up and it gave the team a chance to tell me I was a lucky guy and wonder how a boring cook like me had managed to find such a gorgeous woman and the rest. When I went back to the office she was flicking through my recipe notes and contemplating the computer screen.

'Hi, boring old cook. Your gorgeous wife was just wondering if you ever got round to putting all these notes on file or if you would like her to do it now she's in between proofs?'

Oh well, she hadn't heard too much of the kitchen chat then. 'That would be good. I don't really get time to do it here – too many interruptions.'

She grinned. 'I'll take the note file with me then – you can have it back tomorrow.'

We went back out through the kitchen and she waved goodbye to the team. I walked her to the restaurant door and took a breath. 'I'm so pleased you came in, Lyn.'

She glanced up at me, eyes glinting. 'Must be your animal

magnetism, sweetie . . . oh, and obviously you're a tiger in the sack. Got to go, the other boy in my life needs feeding.' And she was gone, bouncing down the street, hair flying – very like the woman I knew from college.

I must be doing something right . . . and if I just kept doing it, perhaps the woman I married would become the woman I fell in love with at sixteen.

Naturally it all went wrong as soon as I got home. She was still keying my notes into the pc, the kitten sitting glumly beside her. She wanted me to go up into the loft and get her stuff out so she could sort it tomorrow. I said OK, what was for supper, and she said, 'Oh, I hadn't thought – cheese on toast?' and yes, I got a bit annoyed and stamped upstairs to change and when I came out of the shower she was in the loft herself, banging things around.

I didn't know whether to go up and help, or go down and cook. In the end I made the wrong decision.

36

Lyn was opening boxes in the loft. She'd found not only her pictures and throws but also most of her old teaching resources – some books but mainly hard copies of lectures. She didn't remember storing them at first but then the fusty smell of her books reminded her. Greg had said she wouldn't need them as she was home working and she'd meekly packed them away. But why? 'Reason not the need' surfaced in her memory. She used to quote a lot, not just Shakespeare but other old poets and authors. Before taking on language classes she had been a literature specialist. Greg didn't like her quoting so she stopped.

Dylan wanted her to examine her relationship with Greg but she didn't want to. Why not? Her tag clicked to amber and she took a deep breath. She'd think about it later. She realised she was clasping a book to her chest like a Victorian damsel. She put it to one side and started sorting through a heap of throws – some were too vivid, collected to brighten a miserable, one-room apartment, but there were some mossy green and pretty pale blue shades that she thought would be fine in the living room. Also some cushions which would do on the sofa in the kitchen and a real bonus: completely forgotten, pale gossamer curtain material which would look great in the kitchen instead of the boring nets, even if it was impractical. Then she could wash the nets and maybe use them in the bedrooms. Maybe even dye them first.

A glance at her tag showed it was still amber. She took another breath and started on the pictures.

Mikey was just draining the pasta when he realised what

the beeping noise was. He ran up the stairs, called from the foot of the loft ladder then climbed the steps. In the gloom he made out Lyn instantly, bending over a box of canvases, crying. For once she hadn't even noticed her tag.

'Lyn, stop it – your tag's gone off. What's the matter?'

She shot round, crouched on the floor. 'I'm sorry. I should have left this. Don't be angry, please.'

'What are you talking about? Why would I be angry?'

'But you are!'

'No, I'm not – I'm worried.'

'It's the same thing . . . sorry, I'm OK now.' She wiped her eyes and smiled up at him. 'See – I was just being stupid.'

'Come here. Listen, what's this all about?'

He reached for her and she dredged up a smile. 'I'm OK.'

He held her, stroked her back and considered for a moment. It was quite obvious that she'd been bullied and threatened in the past. He suddenly felt a terrible rage that he had to cope with this. Lyn had stopped crying but she was looking at his clenched fists. He tilted her face up, found a smile and said, 'We can sort this lot out together when you're feeling better. We should just have some food first.'

There was a knocking at the front door. It was Judith.

Luckily, by the time he got downstairs, the beeping had stopped. 'Judith, hi, come on in.'

'I'm not interrupting?'

'Of course not. You hungry? It's pasta tonight. Lyn'll be down in a minute – she's just digging some stuff out of the loft.'

Judith followed him into the kitchen and noted the signs of abandoned cooking – pasta rapidly going cold in the sieve and sauce sticking to the pan. She had heard him coming down the stairs, not along the passage. Mikey was heating oil in another pan while he sliced mushrooms and onions, then tossed them in the oil and gave the sauce a stir. 'It needs to reduce a bit more,' he said. 'Like a beer?'

98

'I'd rather have wine.'

'OK.'

She watched him closely as he bustled about but he didn't say anything else. Lyn appeared in the doorway clutching a heap of fabric. 'Judith! Just the person. Come into the living room a minute, will you? I want to see how these look.'

The living room had been painted a pale green with darker touches in the alcoves. It looked a hundred per cent better, and when Lyn tossed the throws over the sofas it was transformed.

'Wow, you've done well with this. Perhaps you should take up design.'

'I don't think so. This is about the pinnacle of my decorating endeavours but I'm glad you like it.'

'So, what's up?'

'What do you mean?'

'You look as if you've been crying.'

'Oh, that's just the dust in the loft.'

'I'm not so sure. You would tell me if something was wrong, wouldn't you?'

'There's nothing wrong.'

They went back into the kitchen and watched Mikey quick-frying pasta with onions and mushrooms before tossing it in a reduced tomato sauce. It was very tasty.

37

'Lyn? I've run out of socks.'

'No you haven't, I did some earlier in the week.'

'Well, they aren't in the sock drawer.'

'The what?'

'The sock drawer – where we keep our socks.'

She ran upstairs and found him glaring at an empty drawer. 'Oh, they aren't in there – I think I put them with your vests.'

'Why?'

'Because that was the drawer I had open at the time.'

'But why change it?'

'I didn't. I've never had a sock drawer, I didn't think we needed one.'

'OK, we'll sort it out later. Where have you put my vests then?'

Her face fell. 'I'm not sure, you're confusing me.'

He opened a couple of drawers at random. 'Great – no socks and now no vests.'

'Perhaps if you looked for something else – like T-shirts. OK, OK, I'll look.' A quick hunt around the bedroom produced nothing. 'Oh, I know – they'll be with the pillow cases.'

'Why?'

'Because I dried them all at the same time . . . here you go.'

'They're all muddled up.'

'Well – socks go like that.'

'Not if you sort them.'

'But who is going to spend time sorting socks?'

'People who are organised, that's who.'

'I can't believe that you want me to sort your socks.'

'Well, believe it, darling, I do not want to spend hours every day hunting for my clothes before I can leave for work.'

38

'I've had an idea.'

'Yeah?'

'I thought we could adapt the Step Up Stones series into a Learn To Cook series. It would have a recipe set with it and start with the basics, then work up. It would have a game element for kids, but you could ignore that for the adults. What do you think?'

'It sounds like a lot of work.'

'Not really. You've already done most of the recipes and I've keyed them in so they just need proofing, and I can adapt the games from stuff I've already developed. In fact, there's loads of material I didn't use in Step Up Stones for the basic levels so apart from the overall design it will be original.'

'I dunno, Lyn, I still think it's too much work.'

'You'll get the credit for it.'

'It isn't about that.'

'What is it about then? You just want me waiting around for you to come home, cleaning and cooking and being allowed out every now and then to go to the food centre?'

His eyes lit up. 'Sounds good, little woman ... apart from the cooking.'

'Don't push your luck, you're just asking for a fight.'

'If you want to fight, darling, you can try.' He reached out, grasped her wrists in one hand and held them above her head, tipping her back against the pillows and smirking. 'Go on, have a go.' For a second she lay limply across the bed and then he bent to kiss her. Instantly she wriggled out from underneath him and twisted his arm behind his back.

'Think about it at least, or I'll break your arm.'

He snorted in derision. 'Somehow I doubt that very much. If you wanted to break my arm you'd have to hold it here like this.'

'Ow! How did you do that?'

'I'm a boy, remember, we know about wrestling and stuff. You're just a girl.'

He had her pinned hard against him, her wrist clamped in a firm grip and her nose squashed against the wall.

'Umm . . . Mikey?'

'Yes?'

'Would you like to let go of me now?'

'Sure, baby, as long as you're going to behave.' Her chest heaved with outrage and he let go immediately. 'Darling, I was only fooling around, are you OK?'

She gulped, then looked up at him. 'Yes.'

'Good. So let's talk about this recipe idea.'

39

The kitchen was bustling and Lyn was watching the sous chef fold egg whites into slightly warmed sugar before piping the mixture into circles on a baking tray.

'I could never do that.'

'It just takes practice.'

The sous chef reached out for another bowl of sugar, caught her sleeve and tipped it over the floor. 'Shit! Porter!' she yelled. Marvin raced up with his bucket and mop and had just started to swirl water round the floor when Mikey bellowed, 'What are you doing?'

'Cleaning up, chef.'

'And what do you get when you add water to sugar, huh? You get a very sticky floor, and if you use the mop you spread it everywhere. You've got five minutes to sort this out and if you can't . . . ' He didn't bother to finish, just stalked round the corner.

Marvin hung his head. He had the easiest job in the world at the best restaurant in the universe and he was going to lose it. This was his third mistake today. He pulled a cloth out of his pocket and sank to his knees, not looking at anyone. The floor was a blur and he blinked rapidly. There was a soft rustle beside him and a voice said, 'Hey, Marvin, this is a two-person job. Why don't you go and find the handivac and I'll sort this out.' When he got back, paper towels were soaking up the excess water and a heap of dry sugar had been pushed to one side. He crouched down and hoovered, making sure to angle alongside the unit. A sharp tang of vinegar hit his nostrils and he looked round.

Chef's wife was mopping up the sticky mess with a vinegar-soaked cloth. She ran over it with a paper towel and grinned at Marvin. 'Feel, go on.' He touched the floor and heaved a sigh of relief. 'So, next time something very sticky hits the floor you know what to do, right?' He nodded. 'Now, what else do we need to clean up before you do any more mopping?'

'The mop?'

'Right – give it a good wash in hot water and bleach or whatever you use and pop it out the back to dry. You've got another mop for emergencies, haven't you?'

He nodded.

'Great.' She stood up, gave him a wide grin and resumed her position at the sous chef's side.

Mikey reappeared, glaring suspiciously. 'OK, Marvin, good job. Get back to the sink.' He looked sharply at Lyn. 'Come on, we're going to the meat wholesalers.'

She smiled at the sous chef. 'Thank you so much ... umm ...'

'Nicola.'

'Thank you, Nicola, I could never do what you do.'

'Stop wittering, woman, and get a move on – where's your jacket?'

The sous chef watched the door swinging behind them. 'He's going to take her round the corner and kiss her, I bet.'

'He can't,' said one of the juniors, 'they'd be arrested for making prolonged personal contact in public.'

'Oh, I expect he'll find somewhere,' Nicola murmured, eyes glowing with the romance of it all.

Marvin was washing up. His heart was thudding and he couldn't stop a small grin. Of course he'd heard all about chef's wife; he'd even seen her a couple of times and ever since he'd been in the kitchen it seemed to be all everyone gossiped about. She'd been married to some famous lecturer on television, she'd been a teacher, she was writing some computer programme, chef had met her years ago and loved her forever. Well, Marvin could understand that, she was completely lovely. He tried to picture her but just had a confused impression of some sort of scarf and bright top, swinging hair and a kind face. She was years too old for him, of course, but that made it even better – he could just think of her without any of the complications. He clattered saucepans happily.

Outside Mikey was practically dragging Lyn down the street. 'What's the matter? Why are we going so fast? Slow down, Mikey.' He slowed slightly and adjusted his grip on her arm. 'For heaven's sake, speak to me.'

'Nothing to say.'

'Well, obviously you have . . . have I upset you?'

'If you don't know, there's no point in discussing it.'

'Mikey.' She was appalled. 'Stop right this minute. What on earth am I supposed to have done?'

He stopped and faced her. 'Sorry. I realise that you think you can do anything you like. Stupid of me.'

'Oh no . . . look, how old is Marvin? Sixteen, seventeen? Mikey, he was crying. You made him cry because he thought you were going to fire him.'

'I was, he was only on trial. I can get a porter anywhere.'

'That isn't the point. Someone has to train him, you can't expect him to know everything.'

'I expect him to know how to clean the floor. I don't expect him to sit back and watch my wife do it for him.'

'That's not fair and you know it. I showed him what to do so next time it'll be OK. Anyway, you didn't call him on it.'

'No – I didn't want to ruin your little conspiracy.' He was starting to lose steam. 'And he's not a bad kid, gets on with it, keeps quiet.'

'So you just thought you'd yell at me instead?'

He considered. 'I suppose . . . but it isn't just the kitchen porter, is it?'

'What's that supposed to mean?'

'Are you seriously expecting me to believe that you don't notice?'

'Come on, let's get to this meat place, I can't talk about this now.'

They crossed the road and continued in silence.

40

Judith was watching with interest. It looked as if they were having a row but then the cook had a very arrogant stance anyway so it didn't take much to make him look angry. Lyn was wearing a departure from her usual black or navy – a bright green top that matched her scarf. Judith scowled – her 'friend' was changing so fast. Then her brow cleared, because if she wasn't much mistaken Mikey was heading for a meat store and Judith knew exactly what was going to happen next. She settled down on a bench to wait.

Ten minutes later the door bounced open and Lyn shot out, hand to her mouth. Judith stood up and called out and Lyn swerved towards her. 'I'm going to be sick.'

'It's OK, I've got a bag – here you go.'

Lyn thought her insides were going to heave themselves to pieces but actually it only lasted a moment. She looked up with streaming eyes. 'Thanks. God, that was grim.'

Judith smirked. 'Your boy cook didn't bother to check whether a row of corpses hanging in a cold store would bother you then? Nice of him.'

'It wasn't his fault,' Lyn snapped back, 'he didn't know because I hadn't thought to tell him. And I didn't know that would be part of the guided tour. Anyway, it was the liver that did it although the whole pig thing probably started me off.' Judith passed her a water bottle in silence and she took a huge gulp, which made her cough.

When she'd finished choking she sat up straight and looked Judith in the eye. 'Why are you following me?'

Judith grinned. 'I like to know what you're up to – you and your cook – you seem to be getting very friendly considering how distraught you were at the time.'

'That's because he's very nice, Judith, and much easier to live with than Greg.'

'Oh well, then, better get back in the saddle.' Judith picked up her water bottle and lobbed the vomibag into a bin before strolling away.

Oh Lord, thought Lyn, I'm going to have to talk to Dylan about this. It's just too odd . . . please don't let it be some sort of lunatic compulsion thing where I end up chopped into pieces and distributed round the streets. A hand touched her shoulder and she jumped violently.

'Here, I've got you some mint tea.'

'Where on earth did you find that?'

'They've got a herb and spice store round the back – it saves having to trail all round the city. Oh, and they've got a kettle and a mug or two.'

She looked up at him. 'I'm so sorry, I really am. I hadn't thought about where we were going at all or I'd have warned you.'

'But you're OK at the restaurant, and at home.'

'That's because it doesn't really look like anything alive once it's cut up.'

'Hmm . . . maybe.'

'Do I have to go back in and apologise?'

'Not today – better not risk a repeat performance. Anyway, they're all fighting to apologise to you.'

She gave a slightly cracked laugh. 'Why?'

'Because they think they've offended your delicate female sensibilities, regardless of the fact that at least half of them are women. Finish your tea – I'll take the mug back and pick up the steak. By the way, did I see Judith out here?'

She nodded and looked at him anxiously.

'Too strange, darling. We'll have to register a complaint.'

41

Lyn had spent two hours finishing off section one of the diamond Step Up Stones and it had been tough. For the first time since she'd started the series she was struggling to find a theme and make it interesting. She was impatient and distracted, she didn't know what to cook for dinner, and the kitten was being a total pest. She pulled up Mikey's recipe file and flicked through it. Perhaps she could adapt a soup or something. She found a chowder recipe that looked possible. She would have to use canned tuna but she thought she'd got most of the other ingredients. She saved, submitted, clicked off and headed for the kitchen.

An hour later a pan of something was thickening on the stove. She peered at it dubiously. Huge bubbles were heaving and spluttering on the scummy surface. Should she turn it off? She sniffed . . . it just wasn't behaving like she thought it would. With relief she heard Mikey opening the front door. She turned down the heat.

'Super-chef, quick. I need your help.'

'Anything I can do, ma'am?'

'I'm not sure.'

'OK – suppose you start by telling me what this is supposed to be.'

'It's a fish chowder.'

'But we don't have any fish.'

'Well, I've adapted it to use canned tuna.'

'Hmm . . . Have you tasted it?'

'No – I've smelled it though.'

'And what did your nose tell you?'

'It smells a little odd.'

'It's burnt, that's why it smells odd. Anyway, don't worry. I'm out tonight.'

She turned on him. 'You're what?'

'I'm going out, it's a booze buddy night.'

'Since when?'

'Since forever – third Friday every month.'

'And I was supposed to know about this how? You didn't do it last month, or in January.'

'Well, no . . . We were only just married then.'

'So what am I supposed to do?'

'Lyn,' he answered, 'you can do whatever you like – have Judith round, watch your tedious Shakespeare, have an evening to yourself.'

'But I can't go out to a bar, can I?'

'Only if I say you can . . . you know that.'

Her eyes blazed in fury. 'Listen to me, Mikey, you can go out, have a fun time, I don't care what you get up to, but let me know first. I know that soup thing is rubbish but I spent time and effort on it because I was trying to make dinner for you.'

42

Well ... she had a point. I could have told her but I'd just assumed that she'd know. How could she though? She wasn't part of a family ... I guessed that Greg wouldn't have been out on the booze every third Friday in the month.

'Lyn, come on. It's not the end of the world, is it?'

She flounced off into the living room. I followed her. She was flicking crossly through the movie selection.

'Listen, OK, you didn't know about the Friday thing – it's only once a month – and next month you can plan something you want to do and it'll be fine.'

'So what time will you be back?'

'Early I should think.'

'And what am I going to eat?'

'Make yourself a sandwich. I'll get some wine out of the alco store for you. You can just relax and have a good time.'

'Sorry I was cross.'

I put my arms round her. 'That's OK, I was a bit thoughtless. I should have realised you wouldn't know.'

43

The sun was slanting through the billowing curtains when Mikey woke. He rolled over and frowned. Lyn wasn't there. He listened. She wasn't in the house. A small, solid warmth pushed against his legs. He squinted down the bed. The kitten squinted back at him. 'Geroff.' The kitten stared impassively. Mikey tried to sit up and felt bad. There was a cold mug of coffee on the bedside unit and a note. He tried the coffee but it was disgusting. He swung his legs out of bed and made for the shower.

Twenty minutes later he couldn't really say he felt better but certainly didn't feel worse. He'd found some Coke in the fridge and was swigging that while the coffee breaker whirred busily in the corner. He'd opened the French doors in the kitchen and the fresh air was doing its thing, although he was avoiding the bright glare of the sun. He looked at Lyn's note again. 'Gone food shopping for you and my baby. See you later. L xxx'

He simply couldn't work out if this was the note of a furious and outraged spouse whose husband had got very drunk or someone who was cool about it. He felt very guilty – he had a vague memory of being shovelled in through the door by his booze buddies and then heaved up the stairs by Lyn but that was about it.

The kitten padded into the kitchen, looked at his empty food bowl and jumped heavily on to Mikey's lap. 'Geroff, go on, geroff.' It stared at him intently. Lyn always said that he was an intelligent kitten but Mikey had never considered it before. Now he felt as if he was being examined and found very below standard. He took a breath and managed, 'Get down, come on now,' just as the coffee breaker murmured 'Coffee ready, coffee ready.' Then added helpfully, 'You requested extra strong blend, you requested extra strong blend.' He groaned.

Lyn's voice said, 'Now that sounds bad,' from the kitchen door.

He turned. She was loaded with shopping, smiling and looking unusually healthy. He groaned again and put his head on the table. 'I'm going to die.'

'Of course you're not. I mean, you are a bit of a strange colour but you look relatively undamaged.'

'I'm going to die of embarrassment.'

'Oh that . . . I don't think your friends will be telling anyone, they were no better.'

The kitten mewed pathetically and Lyn sighed. 'OK, you, you've got pretend rabbit or pretend mouse, which would you like?' She put Mikey's mug in front of him and filled the kitten's food station. 'Weren't we supposed to be doing something?'

'No – you were talking about setting up the barbecue but I've always thought they were over-rated so I wouldn't worry about it today.'

'I'm sorry, baby. I don't know what happened.'

'Mikey, you are making way too much of this. You went out and got drunk and came home and now you're hung over. End of. You're a very amiable drunk, you know, you even gave my baby kitten a cuddle. So, drink your coffee and relax.'

'Mum would be furious. She gets mad if Dad does this.'

'And your point is? You're not living with your mum. It's up to you, isn't it? Look, I'm not pretending I'm pleased that you got drunk and now you've got a hangover but it's not the end of life as we know it. You were fine when I got drunk at your mum's so why should I have a go at you?'

'It's different – I can't explain it. I just want you to know I'm sorry.'

Her mobile rang as she was drying her hair. 'Hello Lyn, it's Claire.'

'Claire, hello, how are you?'

'Fine. I just wondered if Michael had remembered it's Krystal's birthday at the end of the month?'

'He hasn't mentioned it. Do you want us to do something? A cake? Presents?' She tried to think about birthdays in the home but it was a bit of a blur – sometimes there were parties but mainly it was cake, but only up to eight years old. She was sure that families did it differently. 'How old is she?'

'She'll be sixteen – not a big birthday but we like to make a bit of a fuss.'

'Of course. What do you normally do?'

'Well, it's a bit cold still for a barbecue but I know she's dying to see your house . . . maybe a bit of a party?'

'Oh Claire, I'm still decorating, but if you think . . . I'd have to check with Michael but we've certainly got the space and I guess we could do the food OK.' Despite her initial panic, a flush of excitement was building. She could remember sitting with Judith planning the exact party they wanted: candles, music, balloons . . . and presents. 'Claire, what would she like as a present? What are you getting her?'

'Well, we'd thought one of those music earpieces that they all like.'

'That sounds like a good idea. Is there anything else she'd like? We could always give her tokens but if there's anything else?'

'She's keen on those big bags they all have at the moment.'

'Oh – a cargo bag?'

'Yes, she was showing me one on the trend screen the other night.'

'OK – we'll get her one of those.'

'Lyn, they are quite expensive.'

Of course they are but so what? Lyn had spent her entire youth not getting anything for birthdays. She hesitated – was she trying too hard? She realised Claire was still speaking. 'I'm sorry, Claire, what did you say?'

'I was just saying that maybe I could pop round after work one night next week and we could talk about it.'

'Great idea, I'll see you then!'

She knew that she'd been overly enthusiastic but couldn't stop her feet drumming with excitement.

44

I was knackered. Service had been a pain. Someone had plated up the wrong sauce on the steak and we didn't have enough to start again with all of them. Front of house panicked and couldn't remember what I told them to say. The complimentary fish course, which we threw in to keep the punters happy while we had another go at the mains, was average at best and cold at worst. There comes a point when shouting doesn't work any more – it just causes more panic. The moment I stopped shouting, the pastry chef chucked a pan of custard on the floor and the sous chef slipped in it and trying to save herself, knocked a knife off the bench which fell point down onto her foot.

While I was undoing her boot and hoping that she wasn't actually hurt – just scared – the head waiter came in ranting about missing profiteroles and cold sauce. The kitchen porter ran up with a bucket to clean up the custard and managed to slop half of it down the head waiter's waistcoat.

'Stand still, everybody!' I yelled. 'Let's do this one thing at a time. Marvin, mop the floor and dry it so nobody else falls over. Clio, bring me the first-aid chest. Alex, change your waistcoat. The rest of you, keep cooking.'

It was like some ghastly old comedy show, the sort Mum and Dad like. Luckily Nicola's boot had saved the day and she just had a slight scratch. Normally we review things at the end of service but I wasn't in the mood. I just wanted to get home.

'What do you mean, we're doing Krystal's birthday party? Are you insane? The place will be full of drunk teenagers shrieking and mucking about! Why didn't you ask me first?'

'I didn't realise I had to.'

'Of course you have to. What don't you understand about that?'

'I thought you weren't concerned with the rules – you say that often enough. Anyway, it was Claire who asked me and I couldn't really see that you'd have a problem with it. We'll do most of it.'

'God, sometimes you are just too much!'

'Do you want some food?'

'No. I'm going out.'

45

He thudded upstairs to shower and change then thudded back down again. Lyn was sitting at the kitchen table poking sadly at a dried-up plate of something unidentifiable. Curiosity brought him over to look. 'What's that supposed to be?'

'Mushroom and onion risotto.' Her tone was bleak; understandably, Mikey thought.

'You're not going to eat it?'

'I suppose not. Will you get something while you're out?'

'I'm not going out.'

'You're not?'

'No. I was just being bad-tempered, I don't really want to go out. I'm too tired. On the other hand I don't want to eat that either.'

'Oh God!' Lyn wailed suddenly. She put her head on the kitchen table. 'I can't do anything right.'

'Me too, sweetheart, it's just one of those days. How about an omelette? We've got some cheese, haven't we? And onions?'

'Loads of onions,' she sniffed dolefully, 'enough to feed the entire city, I think. But I don't know how to cook an omelette. You'll have to show me.'

He grinned suddenly and she felt her mood lifting. 'You start by breaking the eggs ... actually for this one we'll separate them but first we need to prep the filling – you can chop the onions.'

It seemed only minutes later that she was digging her fork into a light, fluffy omelette. 'This is very clever.'

'It's separating the eggs that does it.'

119

'Are you feeling a bit better now?' He sat back and nodded.

She reached across the table and took his hand in both of hers. 'I apologise for not asking you before I told Claire it would be OK to have Krystal's party here. I apologise for being a lousy cook. If we really can't have the party here I'll ring Claire and tell her that I've changed my mind but I don't want to.'

'No, I bet you don't. She'll eat you for breakfast.'

Lyn bit her lip. He was teaching her a lesson, she knew. 'It isn't fair,' she burst out. 'I was looking forward to it.'

'You were? Why didn't you say?'

'Well, it isn't about me, is it?'

'Oh, believe me, it's all about you as far as I'm concerned. No, don't run off – that's better.'

He brushed his thumbs under her eyes. 'Listen, I was just sounding off. If you want to do the party that's OK, I'll help you. Don't look so shattered.'

She pulled away, drew breath. 'Is this another joke – are you teasing me?'

'No, of course not. What do you mean?'

Her head drooped. 'I thought you were teaching me a lesson, keeping me in line.' She was startled when he laughed.

'You are a witch. It takes about two seconds for you to make me feel like a complete bastard. How do you do that?' He was holding her hands, kissing her fingers, stroking the insides of her wrists.

'Christ,' she murmured, as his teeth grazed her knuckles. 'Have you been taking extra classes?'

'Nope – just leading up to getting you into bed. You have lovely hands.'

She gulped. 'Mikey, this is lovely but it all feels a bit technical.'

'It's the training.'

'Pardon?'

'The training – the copulation training, you know, from school.'

'No, actually we just had some lectures on the practicalities and were told to let the men get on with it.'

'Oh. We were taught to explain clearly what was about to happen, with humour if we liked, but so there could be no misunderstandings. Spend time setting the mood. Oh, and then we're supposed to reflect on it afterwards in a drive towards good practice.'

'You're joking!'

'No, of course not.'

'So do you reflect on it afterwards?'

'If I remember to . . . usually my brain has turned to mush by then.'

46

'Oh hell! What's that?'

'It's a chocolate cake.'

'It is?'

'Yes! What's wrong with it?'

'Lyn, have you tasted it?'

'Of course not. I haven't iced it yet.'

'I tell you what – test it on the kitten.'

'Don't be so horrible. I know it looks a bit squidgy but it had ages in the oven and we can cover the cracks with icing.'

'My darling, it's burnt.'

'It can't be – it's still runny in the middle.'

'Sweetheart, you had the oven too hot. Come on, trust me – it'll taste disgusting. You can't serve this.'

'Well, what are we going to do?'

'Make another one . . . together.'

'Oh, Mikey, please don't make me do it all over again . . .'

He was already softening the rest of their butter allocation and sieving fine sugar. 'Darling, just beat some egg whites. Whoa, hang on. Better let me do that and you do the sieving. Lovely – now stir the sugar and the butter together.'

'I don't see why we can't just buy one.'

'But you were the one who wanted to bake from scratch.'

'Well, why didn't you stop me?'

'Have you ever tried to stop yourself doing anything? Now beat up these yolks . . . lovely . . . just a bit more so they look a bit frothy . . . that's lovely, just try to keep them in the bowl. Now, we need some more cocoa powder and some flour.

Come here and help me fold in the egg whites . . . there, that's lovely.'

'What's with all this "lovely" business? We're just cooking.'

He slid the cake tins back into the oven and adjusted the temperature. 'Twenty minutes should do it.' His arms were round her waist. 'What was that about just cooking?'

'All right. I am a complete failure in the kitchen.'

He ran a finger round the mixing bowl and held it to her lips. 'Taste.'

'But it isn't cooked.'

'Come on, Lyn, taste it.' She sucked obediently. 'OK – what does it taste of?'

'I don't know.'

'Yes, you do.'

'Well, it's sweet – so that's the sugar. And it's got a buttery taste. And there's something else – apart from the cocoa. You've cheated, what have you put in it?'

'You tell me.'

'I know, I know – it's cinnamon.'

He held out another finger of mixture. 'Anything else?'

'Not really – I suppose it's a bit eggy and floury under it all.' His finger traced the outline of her lips.

'What's going to happen after it's cooked?'

'I suppose it'll taste cooked.'

His hand slipped down to the neck of her blouse. 'Which means?'

'Umm . . . some of the flavours will stand out but it'll taste more like one thing.' He was undoing her buttons and she shivered.

'So, what was that about just cooking?'

47

Dylan scrutinised the read-out and said, 'A good week – nothing showing up on here anyway. How's it been?'

'It's strange.'

'How so?'

'Well, it has been a good week but Mikey and I have had a couple of arguments – not rows exactly but differences of opinion – and I half expected at least an amber warning, but there's been nothing.' She paused and frowned. 'I should be really pleased but it just seems odd that it was going off for nothing much then stopped when I was really anxious.'

He nodded. 'It could just be that although you were anxious that was a normal reaction to events so it didn't register. The tag is designed to pick up abnormal stresses, after all.'

Lyn looked up at him. His warm, kind eyes were creased with interested sympathy and he leant towards her. 'So you're starting to feel secure in this new relationship?'

'Yes. Mikey is very sweet and supportive. I've been to the restaurant a couple of times and it's great – he's done so well.'

'You're proud of him?'

'Of course.'

'Is that how you would expect to feel about a husband or are you pleased that an ex-student has done better than you expected? After all, although he made an excellent case for selecting you it's still a slightly unusual situation.'

'I honestly think we've moved past that, Dylan. I'll agree that I was anxious to begin with but his family has been so kind and he's so lovely that I've been able to relax.'

'Good. In that case I think that we really only have one area left to explore.'

'Which is?'

'You have a very strong connection with one of our security staff.'

'Oh, Judith. Yes – we were in a centre dump at the same time. We must have spent at least ten years together before we went off for training. She was selected for security and I went on to university then teaching.'

'I know, it's all on your profile. But you still see her?'

'Dylan, you know I do – I told you I thought she was reporting on me.'

He scanned her file. 'Of course – you reported it in week three. Is she still disturbing you?'

'Not as much, actually – perhaps once a week. She still turns up unexpectedly though.'

'Well, her visits to your home tend to coincide with peaks on your tag read-out. Is there something in your past which has led to this attachment?'

In the silence that fell, the click of her tag turning to amber echoed like a gunshot. Dylan's hand covered hers.

'Tell me. It's what I'm here for.'

'I can't.'

'You can. I understand that it's something you can't discuss with your husband. I know that that it could be something you're ashamed of . . . believe me, Lyn, I'm here to help and support you.'

'It's not what you think. We just agreed that since we didn't have a family we'd look out for each other.'

'And?'

'And she left me alone when I was with Greg . . . we just met occasionally for lunch and that was fine. Then as soon as Mikey selected me she was back in the picture and to begin with it was OK but she now just seems to turn up when it's inconvenient. It's not that we don't want to see her but it just gets a bit much.'

'Would you be surprised to learn that she's monitoring your movements?'

'Not really.' Her shoulders slumped. Dylan smiled at her. 'Don't fret. We'll keep an eye on it and if she becomes an issue give me a call. I suspect that Greg, because of the age difference, wasn't much of a threat to your "sisterly" relationship but she probably sees Mikey as more of a problem. I'm sure it will all settle down.'

Lyn's eyes narrowed. 'What do you mean? Why should it settle down? If you're saying that she's jealous then what could possibly change that?'

Dylan leant back happily. 'Beware the green-eyed monster.'

'Good grief! This is not a play! This is my relationship with my husband and my best friend!'

'Don't raise your voice, Lyn. Remember what happened last time.' Before she could react he leant forward again. 'I'm on your side.'

'Oh, please!'

'I am. I truly am. You are doing so well . . .' His eyes flicked to the session timer for an instant. 'Sorry – time's up!' He paused. 'I'm due a break, let me walk you out.'

48

From her office window, Judith watched in silent rage. What the hell was Dylan up to? He was bending close to listen to Lyn who was looking happy to be in the square and was nodding vigorously. As she stared down, Dylan stopped at a coffee vendor and Lyn carried on a few paces and sat at a table. It was another bright day and Lyn dug in her bag for her dark glasses. Dylan was back with the coffees. He sat. They sipped. They talked. Judith considered the possibilities. She could go out herself and interrupt. She could ring Mikey. She could complain to desk security.

Another figure came into view round the corner and Lyn waved. Mikey turned a chair round and sat down, his legs either side of the seat, his arms folded across the back. It was a pose she and Lyn used to deride as teen-boy macho – now Lyn was beaming at him fondly as he leant forward and stroked her hair.

Judith felt a spasm of fury that made her wince. At least she wasn't tagged so nobody knew her insides were churning.

Lyn was feeling increasingly uncomfortable. With no real reason to turn down Dylan's offer of a coffee and knowing that Mikey was meeting her outside the centre she had felt reasonably confident. Now stuck between both men she felt a nervous wreck. Mikey was pawing at her like some kind of proprietorial gorilla and Dylan was quoting Shakespeare completely out of context. At least now she understood why Greg had hated constant quotation – she thought she'd never quote again.

'Mikey, we'd better get going.' She smiled at Dylan. 'Thank you so much for keeping me company.'

'It was a pleasure, Lyn. You can call on me any time.'

They all stood, awkwardly. Mikey nodded at Dylan and put an arm round Lyn as though he thought she was going to make a break for it.

Dylan watched them until they turned the corner towards the shopping street then walked back to the centre. Judith stood back from the window but not in time to avoid seeing him look up in her direction and raise his hand in salute.

49

Claire settled back into the kitchen sofa and looked round her. 'Michael says you've done all this up in the last few weeks. It looks lovely.'

'Thanks, Claire. Actually, in here was the easiest because there was less paintwork to deal with. It just needed cheering up a bit and Michael put up the shelves and sorted the herbs out. I like it . . . it's different having a kitchen that somebody actually cooks in. Greg and I spent most of our time in the living room.' There was a faintly uncomfortable pause then Claire took a sip of wine and a breath.

'I wanted to know what you'd like us to bring for Krystal's party? I feel as if I've rather dumped it on you and you won't have enough food credits for all of it.'

Lyn looked at her. 'I tell you what – let's make a list of what we think we need and then see who can do which bits. Michael and I have done a chocolate cake which is in the freezer, which we thought might be OK for dessert with fruit or something but we haven't thought about a birthday cake. Would you normally do one?'

'Yes, I do my fruit recipe usually. Didn't Michael say?'

'No, actually he caught me murdering my first attempt at chocolate cake so it wouldn't have occurred to him that I might even attempt a birthday cake. Claire, I'm nowhere near the cook you are so I'll be grateful for any help or advice. I should have said before but I thought you'd think I was an idiot. Another drink?' she gabbled.

'Now you're getting your own back. Of course I don't think you're an idiot. When does your tag come off?'

'Next week, thank heavens. It's been absolutely horrible. I think it's designed to turn you into a nervous wreck. It goes off in the night for no reason half the time and you can be pottering about quite normally and it clicks to amber. I'm really lucky, though, my counsellor is very experienced and very helpful. He thought it was strange that I was tagged in the first place so that's made me feel more confident that I'll be set loose next week.'

Claire was watching her intently. 'It was your friend that tagged you, wasn't it? That must have been awkward. What was it for anyway?'

'It was ridiculous – because everything happened so fast and they cut down my grieftime, they decided that I was a suicide risk or something, but for this long it's just stupid.'

Claire looked appalled. 'But surely they could just have given you counselling?'

'I would have thought so.' She looked at Claire. 'I wasn't any sort of risk, you know, it's normal to have to adjust to a new relationship and Michael is really very sweet. You must be proud of him.'

She keyed open the alcohol store and grinned over her shoulder. 'Also, I'm back to normal with my alcohol units, so you don't need to worry any more. The centre accepted that what happened at the party was just a blip.'

'That's good.' Lyn came and sat next to Claire with a pad and pen. 'Oh, I thought you'd be all high tech and keying directly into your food account.'

Lyn laughed. 'Nope, I make too many mistakes. I like to have it all sorted out before I enter anything – I don't want to end up with a year's supply of ham and no bananas. We've already got enough onions to last until October.'

'Where is he?'

'Oh, he's on lates this month at the restaurant. I thought it was a bit strange that he never did evening service, then he just waltzed in one night and said he was back on evenings until May. Honestly, men send you crazy sometimes. I'd just got used to the early morning grumpies and now it all happens at midday.'

'He behaves himself though, doesn't he?'

'Oh, yes. He's lovely, Claire, don't worry.'

'I mean . . . he's not being too much of a nuisance?'

'A nuisance? No, he likes everything to be organised but so did Greg, although Michael's much more understanding when I get things wrong. Greg could be very charming but had an awful temper. Of course, I thought that was what they were all like at the time. About the worst thing Michael does is insist that I sort his socks and put them in a special drawer.'

'Oh, love, you girls have all been trained to be doormats.'

'What?' Lyn was genuinely amazed. 'I'm hardly a girl!'

'Yes you are, and you're obviously letting him get away with all sorts. When I asked if he was being a nuisance I meant in bed.'

Lyn gulped. 'I can't believe we're having this conversation, but no. I mean, he's young and very enthusiastic but I quite like that.' She looked at Claire appealingly.

'He's been brought up to be a gentleman . . . his father and I would be very disappointed if we thought he was taking advantage of different legislation.' She reached for Lyn's hand and held it firmly. 'I'm not going to refer to this again but if you don't want to have sex just tell him . . . he won't make you do it and he might respect you more in the long run.' She took a huge gulp of wine. 'Now, what about a rice salad?'

50

'Your mother wanted to know if you were pestering me for sex.'

Mikey choked on his onion soup. He stared across the table at her, waving his spoon and coughing.

'Please don't threaten me with that spoon, we don't want my tag to go off in the last week.' She beamed at him and carried on eating.

'What . . . what did you say?' His face was a picture of alarm and indignation.

'Eat your soup, we've still got half an onion mountain to get through. Actually, I offered to do cheese and onion pie for the party but I'm not sure how to do pastry. I've confessed to your mum that I can't cook much beyond the basics but I think her basics are more complicated than mine. Perhaps you could teach me . . . or give me a recipe?'

His eyes were watering. 'Oh, come on,' she added, 'it isn't that bad.'

'It's not the soup.'

'No?'

'It's Mum – what the hell were you talking about?'

'Oh, that. She was worried that you were having it all your own way, that you didn't respect me. I said you were lovely but she still urged me to stand up for myself and I thought it was good advice. How's the soup – really?'

'Truly?'

'Yes.'

'It's completely disgusting.'

'I thought so too ... we're just going to starve to death unless you do something. I can't understand it, I used to be able to cook when I lived on my own. I think you make me nervous. Perhaps you could leave me some easy notes.' She contemplated her bowl, stirred the contents. 'What do you think the lumpy things are?'

'At a wild guess I'd say onion.'

'Would it be better with croutons?'

'Have we got any?'

'No.'

'Then probably not.'

'There's some steak in the freezer. Or some eggs. Or cheese.' She tried another spoonful. 'While I think of it, when are the other birthdays in your family? When's your birthday for a start?'

'June 17.'

'Are you going to want a present and a party?'

'Not if you're doing the catering, no, but a present would be good.'

'OK, what do you want?'

'A surprise, darling.'

'What about the others?'

'Tim is November and Jack is December so we've got a while to go yet. Oh, and Mum's is September.'

'What about Ray?'

'December, so we normally do him and Jack together. Sorry but I can't eat any more of this ... what is it with you and soup?'

She ducked her head humbly. 'I don't know.'

'Don't you taste it as you go along?'

'No – it looks too horrid.'

He shouted with laughter. Then he got up and went to the fridge. 'How about a bacon sandwich?'

51

His bellow of rage brought Lyn downstairs at a run. 'Whatever is it?' The kitten came barrelling past as she shot into the kitchen.

Mikey was standing on one leg holding a dripping boot in his hand. 'That sodding cat has been in my boot! Look!'

'Oh dear.' She glanced once at his thunderous expression and her shoulders began to shake.

'Oh great! If all you can do is laugh! I've got a job to go to – these are my work boots, you know.'

'I know, sorry, it's just . . . Right, sit down and give me the boot. I'll get you a coffee and sort it out. It won't take a moment.'

'But the smell! I work in a kitchen!'

She set up the coffee breaker and took the boot over to the sink. 'Actually you're right. This does smell really grim – much worse than the litter tray. I wonder why that is? Is it your feet?'

'No, it's not my bloody feet! Find the basket and I'll drop him off at the animal hospital.'

She turned clutching the boot to her chest. 'No you won't! He just made a mistake – I won't let you do it!'

'Now what, Lyn? You want me to castrate him right here on the table with my sharp shiny chef's knife?'

'Castrate him?'

'Yes, unless you want the place to stink of un-neutered tom cat! Anyway, once he's had the chop he can go outside.'

'Oh . . . sorry. I thought you were going to have him put down.'

He rolled his eyes impatiently.

She rinsed the boot with the washer tap then hunted in one of the cupboards. 'Here we are – a quick soak in that while you have your coffee.' The coffee breaker intoned politely, 'Coffee ready. Coffee ready,' as she put the boot back in the sink. She put his coffee in front of him and smiled as beguilingly as she could manage. 'Hey, Mikey, don't be so grumpy.' She leant forward and kissed the top of his head. 'He's only a baby!'

'Not smelling like that, he isn't. Not any more!'

The not-so-small kitten crept back into the kitchen and took up a hopeful position by his food station. Mikey groaned, took a gulp of coffee and looked at her. 'Tell you what – I'll try not to be irritable if you'll give up the early morning flirtation.'

'Deal.'

'We still haven't talked about Judith.'

'Tonight.' She got up and shook out his boot, sniffed, frowned and shook some bicarb into it before popping it into the oven.

'You're cooking my boot?'

'Just drying it out a little. Don't want you catching cold.'

'I won't catch cold from a wet boot, give it here. Oh hell, that feels disgusting.'

'Give it another five minutes in the oven. I'll drop the kitten off at the animal hospital.'

'OK, but don't feed him – he'll be having an anaesthetic and it might make him sick.'

'Do you know absolutely everything?'

'Yes.'

52

Judith was hunched on the edge of the sofa drinking coffee and clicking idly through the diamond proof. 'How much more of this have you got to do?'

'Two sections, but they're the toughest. Then it's all over and I can concentrate on the recipe game.'

'The what?'

'Mikey and I are creating a recipe development series – I'm hoping my publishers will go for it.'

'But you've only been together a few months.'

'So?'

'He's taken over your life.'

'Jude, he's my husband – you're the one who's always banging on about centre regulations and I'd go mad if I didn't have some work to do but this way I can keep my hand in. Anyway, tell me about what's going on with you. Relax a bit, sit back — you look so uncomfortable, as if you're about to leap up and go.'

Judith looked pointedly at the other end of the sofa where a ginger and white bundle lay flat and apathetic. 'What's up with the cat? Is it ill?'

'He, Spike, has been castrated today and he's just getting over the anaesthetic.'

'Spike? Since when did you bother to give it a name?'

'Well, actually, since I had to register him at the animal hospital – Cat didn't sound very original.'

'And what did your lord and master think?'

'He's fine with it.'

Actually Mikey had been totally unimpressed.

'You've named him what?'

'Spike.'

'Any particular reason?'

'No – I had to think of something quickly.' She summoned up the animal hospital in her memory. She'd expected something cold and clinical, like a hospital in fact, smelling of blood and urine and disinfectant with grey walls and unpleasant staff in white coats. Instead it was quite charming ... pale peach walls and comfortable chairs, scrolling photographs of glossy, handsome pets and a charming receptionist who cooed over the cat in a manner that Lyn privately thought was totally demented.

'Oh, what a handsome little man ... and so brave. Look at his darling stripy tail, and those huge fluffy feet, and those eyes are to die for. Now, my big boy, what's Mummy brought you here for, I wonder?'

Feeling positively embarrassed Lyn muttered, 'He needs to be castrated. My husband was going to bring him in but I thought I'd better.'

The receptionist nodded sympathetically. 'We don't want a nasty, rough man around do we, little one? You want your mummy at a time like this, don't you?' At this point the cat had looked up at her and she could have sworn his expression was one of cynical exasperation.

'Have you got your animal care card with you?'

Lyn handed it over. 'Ooooh, you can have a thorough worming and flea and mite treatment on this plan. Excellent. We'll do it while he's sound asleep, then he won't know.'

Feeling she ought to enter into the spirit of things a little, Lyn smiled. 'But you just told him about it.' There was a pause.

The receptionist busied herself with the on-desk screen then looked up. 'Would you like an introductory grooming?'

'No, I don't think so.'

'Fine, if I could just have the name.'

'Lyn . . . Lyn Jones.'

'The name of the cat.'

'Sorry. Umm . . . it's Spike.'

'Take a seat, Mrs Jones, and we'll call you when he's ready to go home.'

Mikey had looked at her in bemusement. 'But why Spike?'

'It was the only name I could think of.'

Judith sneered. 'That's so like you, you can't even sort out a decent name for a cat.'

53

Lyn was perched on the bed holding a mirror in one hand and a make-up wand in the other. Spike was sitting on her lap. Mikey was drinking his coffee and thinking about nothing in particular. He wasn't going in until later so was in no rush to get up, and he watched idly as she stroked grey powder on to her eyelids. 'There we go, Spikey Spike, do you think Mummy looks pretty?'

'What are you doing?'

'Putting my face on.'

'OK, why are you putting your face on? Are you going somewhere?'

'Yes, I've got my last session with Dylan. He should be removing my tag and I want to make a good impression.'

'But you never wear make-up.'

'I do. I had make-up on when we got married, and at Sunday lunch at Claire's.'

'That was different . . . that was for me.'

'No it wasn't – it was to make me feel better.'

He huffed crossly. 'Does Dylan like you in make-up then?'

'I've no idea – it isn't for Dylan, Mikey, it's to make me feel more confident.'

'I don't like it.'

'You don't like me wearing make-up?'

'No. I don't like you wearing make-up for Dylan.'

She swivelled round and looked at him. 'I told you, it isn't for Dylan.' Anxiety started to flood her system; she could feel those bloody tears starting again. 'Please don't tell me to take it off, please.' I hate this, she thought, I hate having to beg for something this silly. He scowled. She forced herself to continue. 'I'm only wearing eye shadow and a bit of blusher . . . oh, and some lip gloss . . . it's hardly there. Please, Mikey, it just makes me feel better.'

His glare softened and he reached out to touch her cheek. 'You look lovely, sweetheart, I'm just not happy about you looking lovely for anyone but me. Tell you what, I'll come with you.'

She felt too jumpy to be witty about it and brush it off as if it wasn't significant. She ran her fingers distractedly through Spike's fur. 'You don't have to do that.'

'Why not? I'm going to anyway.' He stood up and stretched.

'No reason why not – just it's your morning off.' The shower began to run as she went downstairs.

54

Dylan gazed at her in appreciation. 'My word, you look lovely, Lyn. Are you going somewhere special?'

Her hackles rose and she tried to beat them into submission. 'No, Dylan, but thanks for the compliment.'

He smiled. 'I'm surprised Mr Jones has let you out on your own looking so delectable.' He glanced at the on-desk screen. 'Ah, I see he hasn't. Quite right too.'

Oh, let's just get on with it, she wailed silently, get it over and done with. She smiled sweetly and Dylan chuckled. God, she thought, he's an irritating man.

'So, how are things progressing?' Dylan beamed across the desk at her. 'This is our last session so I want to be assured that we've covered everything and that I can give you the all clear.'

Lyn felt a bit nettled. It wasn't as if there had been anything wrong really. She just wanted the tag removed so she could get back to normal. Mind you, she'd learnt her lesson, so she simply smiled back and tried to look as if there was nowhere else she'd rather be.

'We've finished the decorating, for the moment at least, and I've started on the diamond section of Step Up Stones. Mikey's putting together a recipe game programme. Oh, and Spike's started to use the cat flap.'

'Spike?'

'The kitten . . . well, cat. He had to have a name to be registered at the animal hospital.'

'Yes, I see, how very domesticated it all sounds.'

141

'Well, yes, perhaps it does but you did ask.' So much for keeping calm, she chided herself. 'I expect it sounds a little unadventurous to you, Dylan, but we like it.'

'Unadventurous? Not at all. I'm completely envious. But then I'm here all hours so don't have much time for the finer details of running a home. So now then . . . let's talk about how you are finding Mikey's family.'

'They're lovely. It was strange at first because there's lots of them and they tend to tell each other everything and there are aunts and uncles and cousins all over the place.'

'Do you find they interfere in your developing relationship?'

'No, nothing like that. We see them, obviously, but they're not camped on our doorstep.' Oh God, she thought desperately, that came out all wrong. 'I like them, Dylan, I don't have a family of my own so I like knowing that they're about.'

'Methinks the lady . . .'

' . . . doth protest too much. *Hamlet*. I know. But in this case it's hardly apposite. I'm just getting in a bit of a tangle trying to explain myself. Unfamiliar territory – no pun intended.'

Dylan laughed. 'I do enjoy our sessions together,' he said. 'Not wishing to flatter but you are an absolute tonic. You must have been an excellent teacher. Do you miss it?'

She knew the answer to that one at least. 'No. I remember it with great fondness but I wouldn't want to go back to it. I'm quite happy as I am.'

Dylan nodded and made an entry on her file. 'How are the mood swings? The nightmares?'

'All gone. I think I was just a bit anxious about all the changes.'

'Yes, probably.'

He smiled again then leant forward with his elbows on the desk. 'This problem with Judith . . .'

'There isn't a problem with Judith.'

'I think we agreed that there was.'

'I don't think so. I just acknowledged that she didn't seem all that happy about my marriage and she was crowding me a bit but that seems to have settled down.'

He grimaced sympathetically. 'I've had her on-desk screen checked and she has a lot of information about both of you.'

'But surely the centre security team has lots of information about everybody.'

'Not in their immediate access file. Not held by individuals.'

'Dylan, what are you telling me?'

'I don't know if you're going to accept it.'

'Just tell me.'

'She seems to have an unhealthy interest in you. She originated the tagging request, not the centre, and she's been setting it off. To begin with, that upset you, so then you generated a convincingly natural emotional read-out but once you decided it was faulty you didn't react when it went off, so she stopped doing it. Oh, hold out your wrist. I might as well remove it while I think of it.'

Lying on the desk, the tag looked small and fairly inoffensive. Lyn rubbed the pale band of skin left around her wrist. 'Thanks. But why would she do that?'

'Normally it's a sign of interest, wanting to be involved in events, sharing a secret with the subject. I expect you usually bumped into her quite soon after these episodes and she'd say, "Are you all right?" and you'd say "Yes". Then she'd know something about you that you didn't know she knew. In fact, I'm surprised it stopped there. It's common for people doing this sort of thing to use it to strengthen a dependent relationship. If that doesn't happen they usually raise their game.'

Lyn was a little pale but calm. 'Dylan, this sounds like psychobabble to me. You're saying that Judith set up the tag just to wind me up?'

'In a way, but I fear events could take a more sinister turn.'

'No, that's ridiculous, there's some error in the data.'

He rocked his chair back on two legs and nodded. 'Just as I thought . . . complete denial. Still, you can contact us when you need to make a complaint. Time's up, I'm afraid.'

55

The party was actually much more fun than Lyn had imagined it could be. Lyn pre-recorded a party selection for the entertainment screen and got Mikey to help with stringing up coloured lights and streamers, then made pizza, dips and non-alcoholic fruit punch, while Claire produced the birthday cake and rice salad and Ray brought beer.

Krystal arrived with a gaggle of hysterically giggling girl-friends and they took over the spare bedroom to check their hair and make-up, emerging with sparkly rainbow eyes and pouting lips. Tim and Jack brought a gang of mates and soon the living room was full of gyrating bodies. Lyn wriggled in and out, offering glasses of punch and suggesting food to begin with but it was quite obvious that they could all look after themselves so she retreated to the stairs with a glass of wine and sat watching the show.

'You all right, Lyn?' Tim perched next to her. He was a lankier, thinner version of Mikey with warm eyes and a genial expression. 'Why aren't you dancing?'

'Oh, I'm just enjoying it from a distance . . . and I'm hosting really.'

Tim nodded seriously but his expression was faintly sceptical.

'What?'

'Mum always says that a good host leads by example, so come on.' He took the glass from her hand and pulled her to her feet.

'Are all the men in your family this bossy?'

'Sure, we get it from Dad.'

He steered her into the living room, took her hand and there they were, dancing. After several fancy turns around the room he disappeared to get a drink, leaving her with an unknown youth who turned out to have a talent for jiving that far outstripped her own. Just when she was beginning to flag, Tim reappeared with a glass of punch. 'Here – got to keep your fluids up when you're dancing. OK, Aaron,' he added 'I'm not muscling in, just giving her a chance to catch her breath.' Aaron laughed and they set off round the room again.

At the next break in the music Lyn said, 'Aaron, I'm sorry but I can't do another jive without a bit of a break.'

Aaron sighed. 'But you're much better than the other girls.' He glanced round the bouncing bodies then brightened. 'Krystal's friend over there isn't bad though.' He slipped away.

Lyn gave a sigh of relief and leant against the wall. Ray handed her a beer and leant beside her. 'This is very nice, Lyn, Krystal is having a great time. As you know, we can't fit half as many people in our place, not if they want dancing.'

'You're very welcome . . . I never had a party when I was a teenager so this is almost as exciting for me as it is for Krystal.' The music paused then segued into a slower medley. 'Ah . . . one for the grown-ups.' Ray took her beer and placed it carefully on a window ledge, then held out his arms.

Lyn hesitated. 'How lovely – but shouldn't you be dancing with Claire? I mean, obviously you can dance with whoever you like but should I be dancing with you?'

Ray grinned, stepped forward and started to guide her round the room in style. 'Wow, you're good at this.' She was glancing around as they mingled with the others. She saw Mikey with his arms round a particularly pretty, fluffy friend of Krystal's. He gave her a happy thumbs-up as he shuffled past and she relaxed.

Ray looked at her. 'Is this some centre regulation I don't know about?'

She smiled. 'Yes – a married woman shouldn't fraternise with another male without specific permission from her spouse. I think I can count a thumbs-up as specific permission.'

Ray chuckled. 'Insecure lot at the centre, aren't they? Claire and I were together long before all this stuff started up so we don't worry about it. We dance with who we like.' They carried on in silence for a while then he looked keenly at her.

'Tell me, love, is it going OK with Michael? I mean, is he looking after you properly?'

'Yes – at least, I'm supposed to be looking after him but we're getting used to each other.'

'Good – it's just that it must be strange for you after your first husband.'

'Oh yes. Well, Greg was marvellous, of course – very intel-lectual – but not a terribly friendly man, so it was quite different. We went out a lot to dinner and academic events but we didn't have friends round very often or anything. He was very private.'

Ray nodded. 'Claire says that you seem a bit anxious some-times.'

Lyn sighed and he hugged her closer, inviting confidence. 'I suppose I am. I don't want to disappoint anybody and, without boring on about it, I was brought up in a dump home and so I know nothing about families. I lived on my own when I was teaching and then I lived with Greg who had no relatives at all either and so I don't know the rules – you know, what to wear, what I'm supposed to do. God, that sounds pathetic.'

'Not really. And there aren't any rules as such.' The music paused then quickened and he let go of her. 'Better sit this one out.' He gave her another look. 'I mean it, love, we couldn't be happier that Michael selected you – you'll be the making of him.' There was a sudden burst of cracking and shrieks from the kitchen.

'Don't worry,' Ray said, 'that'll be the popcorn going every-where.'

'What popcorn?' Lyn stuck her head round the kitchen door

and blinked. A shower of exploding white corn covered the hob and most of the floor. Jack and two lads she'd never seen in her life were filling bowls with syrup, salt and melted butter and the room was rapidly disappearing in a haze of blue smoke.

Mikey pushed past her. 'I said, no popcorn!' he roared as he pushed open the French doors. Jack grabbed a handful and pushed it down the neck of Mikey's shirt, then raced past him into the garden, jeering. Mikey shot after him and within seconds most of the party was crashing about on the grass, the boys wrestling each other to the ground, the girls teetering round the edges shrieking encouragement.

Claire pushed a glass of wine into Lyn's hand. 'Here, come and sit down a minute. We haven't had a chance to talk yet.'

'No ... Do you think they're all right out there?'

'Oh yes, it's just high spirits. Good thing we restricted the alcohol though.'

'I hope you didn't mind that I was dancing with Ray.'

'No, we dance with who we like.'

'That's what he said.'

They sat in silence for a while watching the outside antics dying down as the boys subsided. Then Lyn noticed lights beginning to flicker. 'Oh, how lovely.'

'Yes, the boys like sparklers – look, they're writing messages with them.'

'What messages?'

'Girls' names, usually. See if you can see yours.'

Lyn tried but couldn't make it out. It was cool in the garden and the kids began to drift back in looking for popcorn and leftover pizza. Claire yawned. 'We'll be making a move soon. Do you want a hand clearing up?'

'No, it's fine. It probably looks worse than it is and you've got quite a walk.'

Still, Claire found a brush and began to sweep the popcorn into a pile. 'You don't want this trodden in everywhere.'

Lyn started to hunt for glasses and plates which had been

abandoned all round the house. Krystal came up to her, beaming. 'Thank you so much. It's been really cool and I love my bag.'

Lyn was surprised at how pleased she felt. 'No problem, Krystal. Tell you what, we'll go shopping one day soon, just the two of us.'

'Really? This has been a great day. Michael, Lyn is going to take me shopping!'

Mikey groaned. 'You must be mad.'

More boys and girls came over to say goodbye and thank you. Tim gave her a hug and a kiss. Claire hugged her as well and Ray nodded from the doorway.

Everyone had gone. Lyn groaned to herself. It had been great but she didn't want to carry on clearing up now, she was too tired. Mikey came back into the living room and pulled her to her feet. 'I haven't danced with my wife yet, you know. In fact,' his arms slid round her, 'I've never danced with her.'

'Can you dance?'

'Let's find out.'

The entertainment screen obligingly started a slow number and they began to fumble their way round the room. 'Not bad, chef, not bad at all.' His arms tightened.

'Hey, you have to let your partner breathe.'

One hand slid down to her behind. 'You're supposed to be guiding me with a gentle but firm touch on my back.'

His other hand placed her arm around his neck then slid down to the small of her back. 'OK now, Miss?'

'Well, it's not exactly what I meant but yes, OK.'

He held her tighter and stopped shuffling.

'Oh, chef . . . are you trying to seduce me?'

'Who said anything about trying?'

56

The security office at the food place was located in the basement. It was grey and grim and filled with screens which covered every aisle. Lyn was sitting with a store security guard and the manager. On the desk in front of them was a packet of chocolate wafer biscuits which the security guard had just retrieved from her handbag. Lyn was feeling quite odd. Part of her was outraged by the entire thing. From the moment she'd left the store and been apprehended in possession of unscanned biscuits, it had taken minutes to have her booked and charged with shoplifting, a Code Four violation, which would remain on her data file forever with only a minor notation to say she was innocent. And then only if she was found innocent. Part of her was bitterly offended that the item she had supposedly stolen was something so ridiculous – why on earth couldn't it have been something slightly higher end? Part of her was naturally embarrassed. Part of her was completely bewildered – how on earth had the biscuits found their way into her bag? It was impossible.

'Come on,' the manager urged, 'roll back to aisle 23, there must be something.' He was young and anxious looking and trying to be polite. Lyn smiled at him encouragingly. It must be a horrible job, she thought. The screen flickered through shoppers moving jerkily backwards, hit a fuzzy patch, then stopped. 'That's me,' she said. At the top of the aisle she came into view and immediately disappeared. 'You see, I didn't go down there at all.' At which point the screen fuzzed and went blank. The security guard fiddled with the monitor, fiddled with the on-desk key pad, then shrugged. 'The camera went down – there's no evidence either way.'

Lyn sighed. 'I didn't take them . . . honestly.'

'I'm sorry,' muttered the boy manager, 'it'll have to be referred to centre for investigation. Without any proof either way it's a difficult one to call.'

At the centre things unravelled a bit more. Lyn asked to speak to Dylan but he wasn't available. Then she asked to speak to Judith who was, but arrived in a bad mood and seemed quite unable to grasp the truth.

'But why did you steal the biscuits?'

'Judith, I didn't. Somebody planted them in my bag.'

'Oh don't be silly, who would do that?'

'I don't know. I didn't see them do it. But I didn't go down the biscuit aisle – I never do. It's all home baking in our house, which is why there are never any biscuits.'

'Well, it sounds mad to me. You know you'll be tagged again, at least until this is sorted out.'

'So be it. As long as Mikey believes me I don't really care.'

Judith gave her a strange look. 'He'll be a very tolerant man if he does. I'll call him for you.'

57

The caramel brittle was just at the point of perfection when front-of-house rang through. As I spun a spider's web of pale gold across the top of the dessert I heard the sous chef say, 'No, he can't be interrupted,' and then, after a pause, 'What? No, I can't tell him that!'

The web hung, quivered, shattered. 'OK,' I said, 'we'll try again tomorrow. What is it?'

The sous chef shuffled his feet. 'It's Lyn, your wife, chef. She's been arrested for shoplifting and she's waiting for you at the centre.'

I blinked. Headed for my office and pulled off my whites. Grabbed my jacket. Went back into the kitchen and looked round. Most of the preparation for evening service had already happened. The team were busying themselves self-consciously with their backs to me. 'OK, guys, gather round. If I can't get back I'll ring Gareth to come in. Make sure all the prep is ready and check the dessert list. Hopefully I'll be in later.'

There were nods, and a couple of murmurs of 'Yes, chef.'

'Cheer up,' I said, 'it won't be anything too drastic.'

All the way to the centre I was picturing what could have happened. Had she just picked up something and forgotten to scan it? Had she been distracted by meeting someone and put something in the wrong bag? Would she be really upset? Had they frightened her? I raced up the centre steps and ran straight into Judith.

'Judith, hi.'

'Hello yourself. Come to bail out our favourite criminal, have you?'

I stopped and looked at her. I really didn't like that. She was supposed to be Lyn's friend.

'My wife isn't a criminal, Judith, you know that.'

'Well, she's in Room 1J, over there, having her tag fitted.' She turned on her heel and walked away. I went over to Room 1J and knocked on the door. There was no reply, so I pushed it open and went in. Lyn was sitting on a plastic chair and a smiling female security guard was tapping at the on-desk screen.

She looked up and her face brightened. 'Mikey, I didn't know if you'd be able to come.' She leapt up, flung her arms round me and buried her face against my chest. 'It's so embarrassing,' she mumbled, 'and it's not even as if it's something I'd want to steal.' She felt very small in my arms although her voice was steady and there were no tears.

'What happened?'

'I don't know. Honestly, I was just shopping and I was stopped on the way out and they found some biscuits in my hand bag.'

'Biscuits?'

'Yes, chocolate wafer ones. I'd never seen them before in my life.'

'What made them think you'd stolen them? Didn't they check the camera?'

'Yes, but it was all fuzzy.'

I thought for a moment. It all seemed a bit convenient. 'They must have a back-up system, surely?'

'They do.' The smiling security guard looked up from the screen. 'It just takes a while to unscramble – it's centre-driven and not local. And here we are.'

She beckoned us over: 'Look.' I had to smile. There was Lyn rushing about with her list and her trolley, pausing at the vegetables, the set of her back very serious. She picked up a very small cabbage, hesitated then put it back. Then there she was coming down the pet food aisle. Then she'd obviously forgotten something because she ran out of camera range and came back seconds later with a bag of Demerara sugar. And, of course, that was all it took. She'd left her handbag on top of the trolley and the camera quite clearly picked up a figure in a hooded jacket slipping something into her bag, then retreating out of range.

'Oh,' said Lyn, 'I am a fool.'

'Yes,' agreed the security guard, 'although this is very unusual. Normally people take things from unattended handbags, they don't leave things.' She glanced at us. 'If you can hang on a minute I'll see if I can get authorisation to remove your tag.'

Lyn held up her wrist so I could see the tag. 'The mark of a felon,' she murmured. 'I don't know why they just don't brand me.'

I sat down and pulled her into the seat next to me. She rested her head on my shoulder. I had a host of questions but asking them in the centre seemed a bit risky. It was stuffy in the room and I was tired.

'Right, give me your hand.' The tag clattered on to the desktop. 'You'll get a notification to come in for a more detailed interview but that's all for now.' Suddenly we were being ushered out into the atrium. Lyn flung herself down the steps and I realised it was dusk already.

'Stop, darling, I need a coffee.' I dragged her to a table and bought two coffees from the vendor. Her eyes were enormous in the fading light. She fiddled with her coffee, looked around and finally looked at me.

'I'm so sorry, Mikey, I'll try to be more careful. I can't think who would do something like that.'

'Can't you?'

'No.'

The coffee was muddy but still made me feel better. 'I'd better ring Gareth.'

'Why?'

'He'll have to stand in for evening service.'

For a second she looked pleased, really pleased, then she shook her head. She reached across the table for my hand. 'Mikey, I don't want this sort of thing to affect your work. Why don't I come into the restaurant with you? I won't get in the way.'

'What about the shopping?'

'It was confiscated. I can collect it tomorrow.'

Back at the restaurant there was jubilation. Jessica was on front-of-house and she hurled herself at Lyn, gave her a big kiss and yelled, 'What do you want? A cocktail? A brandy? I knew it was all some stupid cock-up! You must be exhausted.' Lyn allowed herself to be led to a chair and agreed that a small brandy would be nice. She glanced questioningly at me and I nodded, gave her a hug and went out back.

The kitchen was a mess, even though there weren't any orders in yet. Everyone was crowding to the door to peer at my wife. 'What are you doing?' I roared. Bodies scuttled back to pots and pans. Marvin looked as if he was going to cry. 'OK, guys, thanks for your interest but it was a false alarm . . . we don't have a criminal in our midst, so let's just get on with the job.'

One of the girls on the team muttered. 'Why can't he just tell us what happened? Do you think she's all right?' I glared at her until her gaze dropped to the potatoes she was supposed to be piping into intricate patterns. 'Lyn will come in after service and tell you herself,' I announced. 'She's fine but she needs some time on her own, and we need an hour or two of service!' Bang on cue the first batch of tickets came through the hatch.

I started to call the orders but was swamped in a wave of, 'That's great, chef!' 'What a relief, chef!' and from the kitchen porter, 'Can we cook her something nice, chef?' I opened my mouth to shout again, then thought, why not?

'OK, Marvin? What's it to be?' I asked, curiously. He looked at my boots but answered clearly enough. 'It needs to be light but balanced because she'll be upset and won't want anything too rich. Melon sorbet, only one scoop, beef consommé, omelette with fine herbs and . . .' there was a waver of hesitation, then he nodded. 'Lemon mousse without the cream.'

'And to drink?'

'Mineral water to begin with and a small dessert wine to finish off.'

I nodded. 'Sounds good. Write out a ticket for it and we'll get going.' I had to get my whites on so I walked away. The sous chef was hacking away at some chicken. 'Slower, more precision,' I said. 'It's not a massacre.'

He looked up, face flushed. 'Chef, Marvin really wants a chance to work with you. That menu he just made up . . . he's learnt all that stuff here. Can't you find him something if he does his LSQ certificate?'

'Later,' I said.

58

'I'm coming with you.'

'No, don't – it's your morning off.'

'Exactly, so I've got time.'

Lyn hovered in the bedroom doorway, holding Mikey's coffee and frowning.

'Please don't feel you have to. I'm quite capable of going on my own.'

'But you're not. I've made my mind up. Give me that coffee and go make some toast.'

She retreated back downstairs to the kitchen. Spike was a comforting presence around her ankles. 'I don't understand it, Spikey Spike, it's just shopping, that's all.' She shoved the bread into the toaster and went outside to look at the garden. Vegetables were beginning to come up – well, their leaves anyway. The flowers were easier to recognise, although she was alarmed to see that several of the shrubs were turning brown part-way up. She was just bending for a closer look when she heard a strange hooting from the kitchen. The toaster was on fire.

As she hesitated (should she throw a towel over it, or water? Should she put it in the sink?) Mikey appeared in the doorway clutching the fire extinguisher. At top speed he unplugged the toaster and sprayed the flames. Immediately everything went quiet.

'It's never done that before and I've made toast loads of times.'

'You weren't going to pour water on it, were you?'

'Oh no!'

'Good.'

She blinked at him. 'You look very under-dressed.'

'Well, sorry about that, darling, but I was in the shower when you decided to burn the house down.'

'Not that you don't look very nice.'

'Thank you. Perhaps you could scramble some eggs while I get dressed?'

Well, that told me, she thought as she hunted for eggs. Luckily the toaster lived far away from the hob so the powdery residue from the fire extinguisher hadn't travelled that far. The coffee breaker was a sorry sight though.

Mikey reappeared just as she was dishing up the eggs. He was looking quite smart in a dark shirt instead of his usual T-shirt.

'Mikey, we're only going to the shops – it's going to be really embarrassing as it is.'

'Not for us, it isn't. These are good, by the way. You sure know how to scramble an egg . . . sometimes.'

At the food store she felt really awkward. Yesterday had been quite surreal, lurching from one bizarre scene to another, but now she realised why Mikey had decided to come with her. There was a dismal queue of people at the service desk . . . people whose cards had been rejected and whose credit was too low. People who could only take a limited amount every day. She turned to Mikey. 'It doesn't matter, let's not bother.'

'Mrs Jones, I was looking out for you.' The boy manager shot from behind the counter holding out his hand.

Lyn flinched. Mikey put an arm round her and said, mildly, 'I'm Lyn's husband. I've got a few questions for you. Perhaps we could go somewhere more private?'

'Of course, my office, only too pleased.'

The office was cramped but certainly private. Lyn and Mikey took seats and the manager squeezed behind his desk. Mikey leant forward and smiled. 'Yesterday you accused my wife of shoplifting, a Category 4 felony. Is that right?'

'Well, yes, on the evidence presented . . .'

'My understanding is that there was actually no evidence apart from the biscuits in my wife's bag.'

'Yes, but . . .'

'Now, although you were easily able to convince my wife that you had to have her immediately arrested, in fact you were only too well aware that the centre camera system should have been interrogated prior to any such action.'

The boy went white, his eyes watering. Mikey leant further over the desk. 'I want to know what you have to say about that?' he asked, mildly. 'I have grounds for a serious complaint, especially since the centre camera proved that my wife was a victim and should have had support from your team. Instead she was publicly humiliated and illegally tagged. What have you to say?'

Lyn tugged at his sleeve. 'It wasn't his fault,' she muttered. Mikey shrugged her off and half rose to his feet. 'You haven't answered my question.'

'Mr Jones, I'm so very sorry. The inconvenience . . . your wife . . .' He rubbed his fists in his eyes. 'We can make you an offer, I'm sure, extra credit, vouchers . . .' He gave a yelp of terror as Mikey straightened up.

'You think we want extra credit?' he said. 'All we want is an apology.'

Lyn stopped him outside the store. 'Remind me never to upset you.'

'Come on, Lyn, he needed a talking to.'

'You terrified him . . . he was only a boy.'

'Sweetheart, if you'd gone on your own he would have fobbed you off with a few smiles. At least this way he'll be more careful next time.'

'I just don't like to see you bullying people.'

'Did I raise my voice?'

'No.'

'Did I threaten him?'

159

'Yes, not specifically but yes, you did.'

'Well, tough. I don't like to see you upset. Sometimes you need a man to sort things out. This shopping weighs a ton. Would you like one of those trolley things?'

59

'Tim does sport at the weekends, doesn't he?'

'Yup.'

'I was just wondering, Mikey, if he'd give Marvin a go.'

'Marvin?'

'Marvin who works for you.'

'I know who he is. What I don't know is why you should plan my kitchen porter's social life?'

'He's so nervous. I thought Tim might calm him down a bit. Get him used to new things.'

Mikey was dubious. 'Sounds a bit unlikely to me. It isn't even as if he knows Tim.'

'That doesn't matter. Just send him along anyway – he'll do what you tell him, won't he? I'll just give Tim a ring to let him know.'

'Hang on a minute . . . I don't remember saying yes.'

Lyn glared. 'I don't know what your problem is. Marvin works hard. He deserves some fun and if it makes him more confident, what's the harm? You lot are just so bloody full of yourselves that you've no time for anyone who doesn't measure up. He might not be the brightest bunny in the burrow but he's trying so hard and you never encourage him.'

'I don't need to with you fighting his corner of the burrow,' he snapped sarcastically.

They were eating a strange soup she'd concocted from what was available in the vegetable store, which was mainly cauliflower. Mikey was doing his best but Lyn's was largely untouched. Now she jumped up and flung her soup spoon into her bowl. A surprisingly lively tidal wave of greyish soup shot up and spattered everywhere. For an instant she shut her eyes. Then she looked across the table at him. 'Uh . . . it'll wash out, I'm sure . . .' She started to back towards the French doors.

Mikey stood up. 'Lyn . . .' She kept backing away, then she turned and ran across the patio and round to the side gate. 'Jesus, Lyn!' He caught her as she was fumbling with the latch. 'Stop it. Where do you think you're going?'

She twisted round and tried to duck under his arm. She looked very scared.

'Come back inside.' He pulled her back through the kitchen and into the living room. She flinched as he shifted his grip to hold her close. 'Don't do that. Don't run away from me. Ever.' He caught their reflection in the window and froze. He was actually looming over her as she cowered away. He drew breath. She struggled in his hands, turned her face away.

'Don't do it, Mikey, please, I'm sorry. Don't do it – it'll ruin everything.'

'What the hell are you talking about? You think I'm going to beat you, right? Are you crazy, woman? When have I ever hit you? Right – this ends now.' His hold tightened and she stood rigid. 'Right now.'

She swallowed and looked up at him. She was very pale and she shut her eyes and braced herself. 'OK, just let's get it over with. I won't run away.'

He swore. 'You cannot react like this every time we have a bit of a row. You should hear Mum and Dad sometimes. This is normal. This is what people do. We lose our tempers, have a bit of a spat, apologise and carry on. I'm going to be a nervous wreck at this rate and we're never going to get through our probation.'

'But you're shouting at me.'

He shook her and despite herself she struggled again. 'Lyn, I'm not letting you go until we sort this out . . . you have to accept that I won't hit you. The truth is that I adore you and yes, I get annoyed and exasperated but I'm only bloody human.'

She hung her head.

'Listen – if we can't sort it out ourselves I'll have to ask Mum to help.'

Her expression of horror was magical.

'Sit down.' She sat.

'Stay put.' She stayed. Spike wandered in. 'Spike, kill her if she moves an inch.' Spike jumped on her lap – well, someone had to do it. Mikey was back in seconds with wine and a cheese sandwich.

'What?'

'Just eat it, woman.'

'Good girl,' he murmured as she started to chew. 'I want you to tell me something. I want to know why throwing soup over me – and quite frankly, darling, I'm happier wearing it than eating it – made you think I was going to do you serious damage. Was it Greg – although I can't believe you threw food at him – or was it the dump?'

She nodded, still chewing.

'OK, next question. What did they do?'

Her eyes filled with tears, which she tried to swallow back. 'Tell me.'

'At the dump they locked us up in the coal shed, in the dark.'

He tried to sit still. 'And Greg?'

'He used to beat me when I made mistakes. He liked it.'

'Right. And why would you imagine that I'd be the same?'

She swallowed another chunk of sandwich and washed it down with a gulp of wine. 'Can I hold your hand?' He nodded and she took his hand and kissed the palm then held it against her cheek. 'I know you are a nice man. I knew it when I taught you and I know it now. So I know that you would feel bad afterwards and I don't want you to lose your temper and hit me and spoil things. I was scared.'

'But how could you think I'd do that? Don't you trust me?'

'I was frightened.'

There didn't seem to be any answer to that. He went and refilled their wine glasses and she stroked the cat. After a while he put a movie on.

60

Marvin was trembling in front of me, talking to the floor as usual. 'Chef, I want to ask you something.'

'OK.'

There was a long pause. He'd followed me into the store-room so there weren't any witnesses but even so he could hardly speak beyond a stammer. 'Chef?'

'Yes?'

'Chef, I . . .'

I was just drawing breath to tell him I hadn't got time for this when Jessica put her head round the door. 'Chef, Lyn's arrived.'

'Great.'

I made to leave but caught sight of Marvin out of the corner of my eye. He looked completely crushed. 'Just tell her I'll be there in a minute, thanks. OK, Marvin, what is it?'

'I want to do a course.'

I remembered the sous chef saying something about this. 'Great, so what's the problem?'

'They won't take me because I'm functionally illiterate – I haven't got any graded exams – that's why I'm the kitchen porter.'

I knew all this, of course, but it sounded very bleak in Marvin's stuttering mumble. 'So what do you want me to do about it?'

'Owen said . . .' He paused then looked up abruptly. 'No, it's nothing to do with Owen, I thought that Lyn, your wife, could help me. There's a thing called an LSQ Certificate. If I got that I could do the first course and that would let me start the training course.'

A jolt of rage shocked me . . . who the hell did he think he was? Then a burst of astonishment . . . where had he found the nerve to ask me? Then a completely strange feeling . . . I was almost ashamed because it had been so easy for me to get what I wanted.

'I see. Why my wife, though?'

'Because I know her . . . she won't make me feel stupid even if I can't do it. I just want to try.' A hot blush was spreading across his face. 'Please, Chef, won't you ask her?'

'No. She's got enough on her plate. Haven't you got something to be getting on with?'

His eyes flicked to the door. 'Ask me what, Marvin?' said Lyn.

'Lyn, this is nothing to do with you.' I had no idea how much she'd heard but I wasn't going to be manoeuvred into anything. 'Marvin, get back to work.' He shuffled away, gazing at the floor. She came into the storeroom and pushed the door shut.

'Mikey? He looked really upset. What was it all about?'

'Nothing I could help with.'

Her eyes were troubled. 'What did he want me to do? A letter or something? There's no reason why I shouldn't do that for him, surely?'

'Lots of reasons, actually. He's got a massive crush on you and he wants you to teach him for some certificate so he can start training. And you're finishing Step Up Stones and starting that recipe thing and . . .'

'Do you mean an LSQ Certificate? That's marvellous. But why didn't he ask me? Why bother you with it?'

I swivelled round. 'Do you know what you just said?'

'Look, I'm sorry, but he's hardly going to do anything . . . he can't even look me in the eye.'

I sighed. 'I've got to get on. What are you up to today?'

'Jessica's talking me through cocktails.'

'Right.'

'Mikey?'

'What?'

'Please reconsider.'

Something in her tone made me stop and turn round. She was just standing there, looking at me. Not trying anything; no joking, no flirting, no stroking my ego . . . she was just serious. Something clenched inside me. She was deferring to me. I took a step towards her and considered her for a moment. Her eyes met mine and I thought I saw resignation and hurt.

'It's my decision.'

'Yes.'

I could feel the refusal building in me and I could feel the disappointment welling up in her. I didn't like myself much but she had to understand that I was the boss.

'Marvin!'

'Yes, chef?' It was the usual terrified mumble. 'You've got ten minutes to talk to my wife about this, get on with it!' I went back into the kitchen before I could see any scenes of jubilation or hear any hushed cries of excitement. I didn't like anything about it.

61

The train had been a bit more exciting than Lyn had anticipated. It wasn't just that it was old and noisy – all the trains were prone to shrieking brakes and wobbly seats – but she'd forgotten that when she and Judith went out, Judith was already in uniform and carrying an impressive array of centre weaponry. Finding herself in a carriage with Krystal to look after was a completely different thing.

Krystal, wildly excited and wearing lots of shimmering make-up and a shiny top, kept drawing attention to them with her exclamations of delight, betraying her youth and innocence and attracting admiring looks from a range of dodgy looking characters. Lyn slipped her hand into her pocket just to check that her mobile was switched on, and then realised that she'd left it at home.

'Krystal, have you got your mobile?'

'Yes, of course.'

'Good, I've left mine at home.'

'Oh, do you want to call someone?'

'No, but it's just useful to have at least one between us in case we miss the train back or something.' Krystal nodded with the total disinterest of her sixteen years.

The train was racketing scarily over the city boundary viaduct and Lyn started to relax. The country market was only twenty or so miles away, built on what had originally been an out-of-city office complex with a high speed rail link. The offices had long ago been replaced by allotments and small craft shops but a lot of the building materials had been recycled into greenhouses and windmills and on a clear day you could see them sparkling for miles.

They juddered nerve-wrackingly into the station. The platform was boringly quiet and organised and they had to queue to scan at the exit. 'Remember what I told you. Keep your bag under your top so nobody can steal it.'

Krystal rolled her eyes at this boring adult advice. 'They wouldn't get much if they did, just my shopping credits and I could cancel them.'

Lyn rolled her eyes right back. 'Not before they've spent them and then where would you be?'

The first stop had to be in the rest area to check make-up and hair. The next had to be at a snack vendor to buy juice and pastries. Further down the first row Krystal spotted a scarf seller and entered into protracted negotiations over a turquoise silk number with peacock fringing.

'It's nice,' agreed Lyn 'but you should always feel the weight before you buy. It looks as though it might be too light to hang properly.'

'But I like it.'

'Then we can always come back if you don't find anything better.'

A few stalls on there was a leather and silver jewellery maker. Lyn stopped, looked, and chose a leather necklace with a silver bear.

Krystal was scornful. 'It's a man's leather tie ... what do you want that for?'

'It might have escaped your attention, little sister, but I am married to a man. I think he might like it.'

'Really?'

'Yes, don't you?'

'I don't know ... he doesn't usually wear stuff like that.'

'In which case I won't get the matching cuff this time ...'

'Will we be coming again then?'

'If you're good.'

They'd come to the end of the first row and turned up the next. This had several stalls devoted to woodcrafts, from beautifully detailed carvings to more solid pieces of furniture.

'Mum would love a rocking chair.'

'Yes, I'm sure she would but we'd never manage it on the train. We'll have to make do with some plants for her this time.'

The woodcraft was replaced by pottery and Krystal became entranced by the delicate vases and jugs with their liquid glazes. The afternoon wore on in a blur of beaded waistcoats, stained glass window ornaments and heavily scented candles.

Finally they reached the produce stalls and Lyn unfolded the bags she'd brought with her. Krystal, ecstatically chinking thirty thin silver bangles on her right wrist and fiddling with her new turquoise scarf, paid little attention, just nodding when asked. Lyn bought both cheese and honey syrup for Claire to go with the cuttings the plant vendor had sworn were celandines and honeysuckle. She bought juice, tomatoes, lettuce, onions and asparagus for Mikey, plus a pie made with something called aubergines and a different sort of cheese.

They were heading back to the station when someone called her name. She turned. 'Lucas, whatever are you doing here?'

Lucas smiled down at both of them. 'The same as you, it seems.' He was holding a bag of produce and another that looked strangely like fabrics. 'Here, let me take that.' He easily relieved Krystal of her share of the shopping and smiled down into her eyes. 'I can see that you're Mikey's sister. We haven't met but I'm Luke.'

Krystal melted. 'Luke as in Ryan and Luke and Kylie and Matt?'

'That's it.'

They'd reached the station and Lucas stepped back to let them scan in before him. He followed them on to the platform. 'I'd be very happy to ride shotgun for you ladies on the way back into the city.'

Lyn sighed. It would be a huge relief to know that somebody else would help her look after Krystal. She didn't need to tell Mikey, after all.

'Just one thing.'

'Yes?'

'Can I smell fish?'

Krystal burst out laughing.

62

'Where the hell have you been?'

Lyn stopped in the doorway, clutching her bags, eyes popping with surprise.

'What do you mean? I left you a note. I've been to the country market with Krystal. You know I promised to take her shopping. We had a great time and I've got a pie and some salad so we don't have to cook . . . and I've got you a present. Oh, and one for Spike too.'

'And just how did you get there?'

'On the railway . . . I've got loads of travel credit, so it wasn't a problem.'

'Fine. So you drag my baby sister out of the city on our lethally dangerous public transport system. Anything could have happened. Are you mad? I mean, have I married a complete psycho?' He turned away a moment and stared out of the window.

Lyn put her bags on the kitchen table and drew breath. 'It was fine. Claire knew all about it. Krystal had the time of her life.'

He spun round. 'Great! You know the rules! You can't just go running off whenever you feel like it, you're supposed to ask me first.'

'Get permission, you mean?'

'Yes! That's exactly what I mean! You can't just disappear, it's completely irresponsible!'

'Stop shouting, Mikey.'

'Why? Because you're going to cry and I shouldn't be upset-

172

ting you? Great . . . you do something mad and I have to put up with it so your feelings aren't hurt!'

'No, I'm not going to cry. You might not have noticed but I got over the crying phase once my tag was removed.'

'Oh, so no tag means you can do as you please, does it? And how would your precious Greg have put up with this?'

'He wouldn't have put up with it at all, but he didn't have a sister for me to go out with so it didn't arise.'

'You think you're so smart, don't you?'

'No. I just don't know what your problem is! You don't own me.'

He stepped across the room and grabbed her by the arms. 'That's just it. I do. You think you can do what you like because you're older but you can't. I'm not your sixteen-year-old student any more, I'm your husband and I have rights.'

'Sure, like the right to stay out all hours and come back and vomit all over the bathroom . . . that's very mature.' She glared into his face. 'Very adult behaviour.'

'I did not!'

'Yes you did but I cleaned it up and got you to bed and decided not to say anything in case your feelings were hurt. If you recall, you were embarrassed enough anyway.'

'So I suppose the great Greg never got drunk.'

'He did actually, on occasion, and I accorded him the same respect.'

Quite suddenly he slammed her against the wall. 'What respect? Keeping it all quiet until you could use it for ammunition? I don't think so . . . I think we both know how Saint Greg would have reacted to that.'

'Is that what this is all about? Do you want me to tell you? Or do you just want to see what it feels like to hit me?'

'You think I'm going to hit you?'

'No, Mikey, I don't.'

He tugged at her hair, knocked her head gently against the wall. 'I was going mad. I thought you'd run off. I didn't know

173

what to do. I saw your note but then Judith rang and it completely freaked me out.'

'Bloody Judith. I don't know what's going on with her these days.'

'She said you'd arranged to meet for lunch and you hadn't turned up.'

'Now that is plain weird. Of course I wasn't meeting her for lunch. And why on earth would you think I'd run off?'

'She said you'd done it before, with Greg.'

'That's not true. He'd have really murdered me for a start if I'd tried anything like that. OK, let's have a drink and I'll tell you about Greg. I think I'd better tell you a bit about him.'

'You don't have to.'

'I do. I should have done it before but I didn't want you to resent him.'

'But he's dead.'

'I had noticed. I guess I was just ashamed.' She went over to the alco store, then hesitated. 'Beer? Wine? Or juice? I found some organic apple at the market today.'

'Beer. But have wine yourself if you like.' She nodded, fidgeting with the glasses. Mikey sat at the table, waiting. Spike flopped through the cat door and jumped up for attention. Lyn sat down and passed the beer glass over, then stroked Spike absently. Mikey waited.

'OK. The thing is that there was quite an age difference and Greg selected me, I thought, because he wanted somebody intelligent but independent who he could have intellectual conversations with and I was stupid and completely wrong.' She drew breath. 'He kept telling me I was common and had poor taste and because of my background I believed him. I believed everything he said because I'd respected him for years. He was pleased that I had the design job because that reflected well on him but other than that he just wanted somebody to agree with him and run the house. He didn't expect me to cook, obviously, because he liked to be seen out and about, and on evenings

174

that we weren't dining out together he used to go to centre bars with prostitutes – licensed ones, of course. Although if he was pleased with me about something he'd come home with pizza sometimes and flowers.'

Mikey nodded but didn't comment.

'Actually we had a reasonably adequate sex life but what he really liked was to beat me up a bit first to get into the mood. He had to find an excuse, but it wasn't usually too difficult as I was always doing something wrong, contravening one or other of the bloody rules. He hit me where it wouldn't show and, in the end, it made me very nervous. I couldn't run away because I had nowhere to go and I had nobody to help me.' She ended on a bit of a squeak and took a breath.

'And that's it?'

'More or less.'

'Is that how you broke your ribs?'

'Oh, that was a bit of a departure. He . . . umm . . . I fell down the stairs. I told you that.'

'So is this what you've been talking to Dylan about? And Judith?'

'No, I've just been trying to forget it.'

'If he was here I'd kill him.'

'What, with a cleaver or a spoon or some subtle poisonous herb?'

'Probably with my bare hands.'

'Very heroic but unlikely. He was a completely charming man and you'd have enjoyed his company very much. He was wonderful in company – engaging, interested in people, just marvellous.'

'Why don't you hate him?'

'Probably because – as your mum would say – we girls are brought up to be doormats. In other words, I thought I deserved it even though I didn't like it.' He noticed that her wine was untouched. He took a slug of beer and looked her in the eye.

She wasn't giving much away. 'Actually,' she said, 'I meant to check with you about prostitutes.'

'What?' It was a bellow. 'What about them?'

'Well, when you use them you are careful, aren't you? I don't expect you to tell me anything about it but I just wanted to be sure that you only used licensed ones. It's only fair.'

'Christ, you think that after working all day in the restaurant and spending all night in bed with you I'd have the time or the strength or even the bloody inclination to go hunting for prostitutes? You must think I'm bloody superman or something.'

'Oh, OK, sorry, I suppose finding the time would be a bit of an issue at the moment . . . but you know, for the future. It is important, Mikey.'

'You mad woman . . . don't you realise that I haven't slept with anyone else since I selected you? And I never had any problems finding girlfriends before then, either,' he added in an annoyed grumble.

Before she could reply, Spike stretched up and batted her face with a big white paw. 'Oh, OK, Mister – you want your surprise, don't you?' She delved into one of the bags and pulled out a pack of mackerel fillets. 'Here you go.' Mikey leant over to look and took a deep sniff. 'You bought *fresh fish* for the cat?'

'Sure. If I'd known it would be that much of a hit you could have had some too. Instead you'll have to make do with this.' She pulled out the leather tie with the silver bear. The ends of the tie were silver as well. 'Look, you can slide the bear up to where you want it.' The leather cord was black and shiny, slightly stiff. 'Do you like it?' The silver felt solid and cold in his hand. He slipped it over his head. She leant forward and adjusted it, sliding the bear up slightly, patting it down against his T-shirt.

She smiled. 'There, now you belong to me.'

63

I didn't know what to think for a moment. She'd bought me a present, for no reason. I'd been so frantic, I'd shouted at her and nearly thumped her. She trusted me more than I trusted myself. I glanced at her, expecting to see the usual glint of amusement when she'd outmanoeuvred me, but she was just smiling and admiring her present. Then she looked up. 'I'm sorry, don't you like it?' A terrifying feeling surged over me. My heart began to thud – I could feel it, out of control, banging away somewhere in my chest. I thought I might cry. Or shout.

'Christ!'

'What? What is it?'

'Feel that.' I grabbed her hand and held it on my chest.

'Feel what?'

'You can't feel it?' It gave another huge lurch, as though it was actually going to burst out through my ribs.

'Oh, Mikey, what is it?' She sounded close to panic. Even Spike looked up from his mackerel.

'Well, I'm no expert, you goof, but I think it's my heart pounding. Like one of those bloody novels ... you've made my heart pound.'

'But how? What if it's a heart attack?'

'It isn't. I'm still breathing, aren't I?'

The thing was, I thought I knew what love felt like. I'd adored her from a distance. Then I'd married her. Then I'd had sex with her. But I'd never felt this. I was in emotional melt-down. I grabbed her and kissed her, very roughly, then I looked at her. I thought I could see a shadow of distaste or fear in her eyes and her mouth looked bruised but she smiled again. 'Is this make-up sex, then?'

'No, Lyn, I don't want sex. I just wanted to kiss you. To thank you for my present.'

'Thank goodness I didn't get you the matching cuff, then.'

64

'Come on in, Judith, Lyn's in the garden. Do you want coffee? It's time we had a break.'

Judith took in the kitchen, the sunlight filtering through the gauze curtains, the primrose walls, the rack of drying herbs, pots of parsley frothing on the windowsill, the bright cushions on the sofa which suddenly looked warm and inviting instead of lumpy and vaguely uncomfortable. She felt sick. Mikey had been working at the hob, a notebook by his elbow. Now he turned down the heat, took a quick look in the oven and clicked on the coffee breaker.

'This room looks amazing. However did you find the time?'

'Oh it wasn't me, I just hammered in a few nails and things. Lyn did all the work. Go on outside, I'll bring the coffee.'

Outside was reassuringly messy, with weeds and grass exploding everywhere. Lyn was fiddling about in what obviously used to be a flowerbed. She sat back as Judith approached. 'Watch where you put your feet – the lawn isn't as flat as it looks and there are some boggy patches.'

'What brought this on?'

'Oh, it's the first decent day we've had in weeks, so I thought I'd take advantage.'

'That's not what I meant. The house is starting to look like an ad for Centre Home Supplies and now you're gardening!'

'Hardly, but thanks for the compliment – I think. Upstairs is still a real chamber of horrors. As for the garden, we want to grow things so I've got to start sometime.'

'Why don't you get Mikey to do it?'

'He's working on a new recipe.'

'Oh please! I've stumbled into a hotbed of domestic creativity.' She sat down cautiously and wrapped her arms around her knees. 'Actually I came to speak to you about something else. Something that happened the day you missed lunch with me.'

'I didn't miss lunch with you.'

'OK ... if you don't want to admit it ...'

'Jude, you must have arranged to see someone else. Anyway, what came up?'

'It's a Code 19 violation.'

'What's that?'

'Transporting a minor across city boundaries without permission or supervision and exposing them to contact danger ... specifically, in this case, an unknown male. What were you thinking of? And who the hell was he? You were seen, you know.'

'Judith, don't be stupid. Of course I had parental permission to take Krystal out and neither of us had an assignation with anyone. Which reminds me – what's all this rubbish you told Mikey about me running away from Greg?'

'Don't change the subject. You were seen,' Judith repeated. 'You were seen at the railway station.'

'Oh that. That was Lucas. We bumped into him at the station and I was very pleased to see him. He helped us with our shopping. If we'd had to manage alone I'd have probably ended up with a hernia ... still, at least I managed to talk Krystal out of buying that rocking chair. I think that would have defeated even Lucas.'

'He's on the market camera records. He'd been following you for hours. Why do you think he ended up with a bag full of cushion covers and cheese?'

'I have no idea. Judith, you know that everyone follows the same route round the market – we went often enough when we were younger ... it's just a coincidence.'

'Sure. So who is he then, this Lucas?'

'He's a friend of Mikey's. He was in his class at college.'

'Another of your student conquests?'

'Don't be ridiculous. I don't have any student conquests. That sounds revolting.'

'Well, maybe it's too close to the truth.'

Mikey's voice cut in, sounding unusually grim. 'Judith, be careful what you're implying. Lyn has told you that meeting Lucas was a coincidence and I'm sure he'll back that up.'

'So you knew about it? She didn't just need parental permission, you know. She needed your permission as well. Did she get that? It would be just like her to leave a note when you weren't around and slip off forgetting her mobile.'

Lyn stared. Mikey nodded. 'It would be, but she didn't . . . she got the right permission and when she got back told me all about her day.'

'Including spending time with another man?'

'Including meeting Lucas, yes. Here, drink your coffee.' The silver bear hanging round his neck shimmered in the sun as he held out her mug.

Judith's eyes narrowed. 'You bought him a necklace?'

'Yes. It's great isn't it? Remember how we used to hang around that stall, and the one with the silk scarves?'

'Sure. Never thought you'd be suckered into spending at them, though. It's about time you grew up, isn't it?'

Mikey frowned. 'What on earth do you mean?'

'Come on, Mikey, she's running around with juveniles pretending she's a bloody teenager again. How pathetic is that?'

Eyes round with horror, Lyn went over to pick up her mug. She turned and opened her mouth but Mikey put his arm round her with a warning squeeze. 'Judith, I don't really know what's going on but I think you'd better leave.' Lyn started to stir in protest and his arm tightened. 'I mean it.'

'I'm just calling it as I see it.'

'Krystal is my sister, a member of our family. Lyn has a perfect right to take her out for the day.'

181

'But Lyn doesn't have a family.'

'She does. She joined my family when I married her.'

Judith paled, set down her mug and left by the side gate.

Mikey looked at the gate. 'I never thought of that. I'll pick up a bolt for it.' He looked down at Lyn. 'Why didn't you tell me?'

'About Lucas?'

'Yes.'

'I just forgot.' His arm dropped away and he started to turn back to the house. 'Wait! It's true. I got home, you were livid with me, we had that big row and then you had heart failure because I gave you a present.' She actually pulled at his arm, clutched at his sleeve. 'Mikey, it was so unimportant that I forgot all about it. Anyway, Krystal was there. She's bound to bore you to death about it.'

In the kitchen Mikey sat down at the table and put his head in his hands. 'It's just one thing after another with you,' he muttered. 'I think we got away with it this time because when she rang for you I just said you were out with Krystal but didn't go into detail. But Lyn, you've got to accept that there's something wrong here. It's obvious that she knew you'd left a note and your mobile because I reckon she had come round and looked through our window, though she can't say that because then we'd know. On the other hand we can't report her because then the centre would know that you'd gone out without your mobile.'

'But you do believe me?'

'Sure – but I want you to tell me about Judith. Why can't you just tell her to get lost?'

'You won't be pleased.'

'No kidding?'

'OK then – you know I've supposedly got this great IQ?'

'Hmm . . . shame it doesn't work in the kitchen.'

'Right, very funny. When we were leaving the dump I was chosen for an out-of-city two-year degree course and Judith wasn't chosen for anything. She applied for security training and she didn't get in, but they let her re-sit one of the entry papers and she passed that time, so she was OK.'

'You sat the paper for her?'

'Yes, it was all online. You just needed a computer link and a password. Nowadays you have to attend the centre and have a retina scan but it was different then. I was only sixteen, I didn't think much about it.'

'But she acts as if she's got something over you. Surely it should be the other way round?'

'Not really – we'd both be in trouble if we were found out.'

He sighed. 'It still doesn't really add up. How did she persuade you to do it in the first place?'

'Oh, she threatened one of the juniors in the dump – she was going to take her out in the dark and lose her.'

'What sort of threat is that?'

'Dump kids are never totally in the dark, even at night – we were all terrified of being lost . . . even more lost than we were. I slept with the light on until I married Greg.'

'So Greg cured you.'

'In a way. I was so terrified he'd hit me that I didn't tell him I was scared.'

'And are you scared with me?'

'No – surprisingly enough, I've got other things on my mind when I'm with you.'

65

The call from Dylan came two days later. Mikey was at work so Lyn sent him a text and left him a note. She was careful about taking her mobile with her to the centre as well.

Dylan looked rumpled and slightly bothered but got straight to the point. 'There's been an unattributed entry on your data file – a Code 19 violation apparently. Any idea what it's about?'

Lyn nodded. 'I took Mikey's sister out to the country market. I had all the appropriate permission but on the way back we met up with a friend of Mikey's from college. He travelled back on the train with us. That's all but somehow it's become a bit more sinister.'

'How do you mean?'

'Well, Judith came round and seemed to think that I'd had some sort of assignation with Lucas. I hadn't, of course, but she said she'd checked the market cameras and she thought he'd been following me.'

'And that worried you?'

'Of course it worried me. The whole thing's mad. I wouldn't have an assignation with anyone, especially if my husband's sister was with me.'

'It sounds unlikely. So you think Judith has made this entry on your file?'

'I don't know.'

'And what does your husband think about it?'

'He thought she was being very odd and he's banned her from the house.'

'So he didn't mind you going out of the city without him.'

Lyn sighed. 'He wasn't too pleased but he was OK about it.' She paused then smiled. 'Actually I got him a present.'

Dylan glanced up from the on-desk screen. 'You did?'

'Yes. It was just a little thing but it looks really good on him and I realised afterwards that I hadn't given him anything before.'

'Apart from your company.'

'Oh, that's not the same, Dylan, you know that.'

Dylan considered her for a moment . . . she looked pleased and somehow proud of herself. Good Lord, he thought.

'Lyn?'

'Yes?'

'Have you considered that you might be in love with him?'

She blanched in horror. 'No, of course not. Why ever would you think that?'

'I don't know . . . buying him spontaneous gifts, trying to please him, smiling when you talk about him. You've developed a crush at the very least.'

'No I haven't. I'm just doing exactly what the centre instructs – being compliant and adaptable, keeping my partner happy, remembering my place, etc.'

'Well, there's no harm in it as long as it doesn't get out of hand. Does he love you?' His voice was strange, Lyn thought, but when she glanced up he was smiling at her blandly.

'He says he does but he's from a family and they do a lot more of that stuff . . . it doesn't mean anything.'

'Right. This Code 19 violation will take six weeks to expire so no more shenanigans, please.' He tapped on the screen. 'Shouldn't you be submitting the diamond Step Up text in the next five days?' He frowned. 'No sign of it on your home computer.'

'I've just got to input it. As they get more advanced, they get harder . . . but I've never missed a deadline yet.'

'See you don't.'

66

I got home and she was in a complete frenzy, bashing away on the computer as though her life depended on it. Spike was sitting on the sofa watching her with a bemused expression. Pieces of paper littered the carpet.

'Hey, lovely wife, what's up?'

'I'm about to miss a deadline for the first time in my life! I completely forgot the diamond proof was due. Dylan reminded me.'

'What's Dylan got to do with it? I thought he was just counselling you? Why did he want to see you anyway?'

'Oh, it's all weird. I think he must be more senior than I thought because he had access to my home computer and he knew when the deadline was and he dropped a very heavy hint that I should keep my fingers to the grindstone. God, how could I have been so stupid!'

I could see that it was going to be another cheese on toast night so I clicked my fingers at Spike and we went to drown our sorrows in the kitchen. He chomped through a bowl of tuna and I had a beer. I wondered when she'd take a break and decided to knock up some soup so that it could be ready whenever she wanted it. Then I went upstairs for a shower, leaving Spike in charge. When I came down she was still pounding away so I tasted the soup and put the bowls to warm.

I thought about putting the entertainment screen on but it was still light outside so instead I thought I'd take a look in the garden and plan what we should be planting. Lyn had cleared a couple of flowerbeds but the rest needed to be dug

186

over before we could start any vegetables. I figured that Tim and Jack would help if I provided a barbecue and I knew that Mum would like it.

I nodded at Spike. 'OK, fella, where do you think we should put the barbecue?' He stared at me in disdain before continuing his own tour of inspection. Time for another beer. Back in the kitchen she was stirring the soup.

67

Mikey ambled in through the French doors and helped himself to a can of beer. 'I'm definitely going to set the barbecue up this weekend so we can have the family over to dig the vegetable patch.'

'Oh. Will they do that?'

'Of course they will. Then we can decide what to grow. What do you like?'

'I'm not sure. Just the usual things.'

She filled the bowls and dug out some spoons. 'Thanks for doing this. I lost track of the time.'

'No problem. So, what did Dylan want?'

She rested her spoon carefully in the bowl. 'I've got a Code 19 violation on my file.'

'What?'

'I'm sorry . . . it was that trip with Krystal. Someone's put it on my file. Fortunately it's only provisional and Dylan says it will expire in six weeks but I've got to keep my nose clean while it's in force. That's why he reminded me about the proof deadline.'

'You said "someone". Was it Judith?'

'I don't know, there's no way of telling.'

'It couldn't be anyone else, could it?' There was a difficult silence. 'Come on, Lyn, your soup's getting cold.'

The crash of the cat flap made them both jump. Spike was fluffed up and growling. Mikey looked out of the window. A small, skinny black tom cat was hesitating on the wall. 'Hey, fella, you need to defend your territory. Stop the bad guys getting in.' Lyn gave him an ironic glance.

He smiled. 'Look, do you want any help with your diamond thingie? After all, you have been spending time on my recipes.'

'Hmmm . . . and I suppose you'll be just about as useful?'

'Come on, let me have a go.' He stretched and looked at her consideringly. 'Two heads and all that.'

'And I suppose you'll want a reward?'

'Well, only if you're desperate – it's been a bit of a long day for both of us.' The cushion hit him with surprising force. 'Easy now, tiger, you're scaring Spike.'

Step Up Stones was a seven-stage literacy programme that coached children through a variety of artfully planned computer games linked in to the national curriculum. Or that was the idea. The final stage, diamond, was proving trickier than the rest put together, Lyn thought. It was supposed to lead the way seamlessly into the two-year school examination programme which itself tested different levels of literacy, from the basics to more creative output. The creative part was foxing her. She simply couldn't work out how the programme could be set to grade a variable input consistently.

Mikey sat back on the sofa and said, 'How did you do it at college?'

'We didn't use a programme.'

'No, I know. How did you do it yourself, when you were marking one of those descriptive things? How did you know if it was good or not?'

'Well, it was the feel of it.'

'That's like saying the taste, but it's still made up of things you can identify, isn't it?'

'I suppose so. It's use of vocabulary, grammar, style, complex structures, strong narrative if it's a story, similes, metaphors . . . I still don't see how you can grade it with a computer programme.'

'Why don't you have rules, like not having the oven too hot? You could have an exercise that has to be in sentences and use three similes – a programme could do that. Then you could feed in some examples of really good writing and get it to search for an equivalent and if it finds one they get extra marks.'

'Do you know what you're talking about?'

'No, but you've got to start somewhere. Sometimes all it takes is rubbing garlic round a salad bowl.'

'It just doesn't feel very creative.'

'Woman, you have no idea how to cook. You still think it's just stirring things together and hoping for the best. It's about tasting at every stage, knowing what you're aiming for, taking chances, using hundreds of different techniques. Why don't you sleep on it?'

'I'm too anxious to sleep.'

'OK, we'll think of something else, but staring at a blank screen isn't helping at the moment, is it?'

'Is this another pathetic attempt to entice me up to bed?'

'That's a very creative sentence: one adjective, a descriptive verb and a big chunk of innuendo.'

'How can you do that?'

'You taught it to us early on, I think.'

'You were never that smart in class.'

'I don't think, sweet wife, that we had that much opportunity to be smart, what with the curriculum and the class sizes, but I still believe that both Luke and I showed the odd flash of brilliance. And I also think that your problem is solved.'

She frowned, clicked, checked her database. 'Oh no.'

'What?'

'I hate to say it but I think you could be right – all the terms plus rules of usage are stored here, so I just need to refer them to the exercises and I've already written those. I just need to add the higher tier examples.' She clicked off the screen and joined him on the sofa. 'I'll finish it off tomorrow. Thank you, my genius.'

'Can we talk for a bit?'

'What do you want to talk about?'

'Let's get comfortable first.'

'Now that sounds ominous . . . do you want a drink?'

'Not really.'

'Shall I put the music centre on?'

'Woman, just relax.' He pulled her across him, tilted her back and without being sure how it happened she ended up lying with her feet up on the sofa and her head in his lap.

'Stop wriggling, woman, lie still for a minute.'

'But how did you do that?'

He grinned. 'It's just technique.' He stroked her hair. She lay as still as she could manage. Spike came and thudded on to her stomach. 'Ooof!' After a moment she began to stroke him. He started to purr and his claws flexed in and out.

'What do I have to do to make you purr?' He was staring down at her intently. She flicked her glance away. 'What did you want to talk about?'

'Starting a family.'

Oh, you are a cunning man, she thought; I can't move because you and Spike have got me pinned down tight between you. She studied the far wall where one of her favourite pictures hung in the alcove.

'I thought we ought to get the forms ready for our six-month probation review and it's one of the key questions. I didn't know what you thought about it.'

Oh no, her internal monologue continued, don't ask me, what should I say, I should have said something before . . .

'Lyn, come on, I want to know what you think. If it's too soon then just let me know – we can put it off.'

Her voice felt as though it was being wrenched out of her. 'You've seen my data file, haven't you?'

'Well, yes.'

'So you've looked at my medical history?'

His hands stilled in her hair. 'What are you saying?'

'I can't have children.'

'Of course you can . . . I checked.'

'I can't, I can't – there's something wrong with me.'

'The only thing that's wrong with you is an over-active imagination. No, lie still. I don't know where you got this idea from but the centre wouldn't have passed your selection if there was a problem.'

Spike huffed in apparent disgust and jumped heavily down from the sofa. Mikey tugged her up so that she was sitting in his lap and held her tightly. Her face was white and rigid.

'Darling, I can show you on-screen, you are perfect in every way. This is rubbish. A misunderstanding at one of your medicals or something.'

'No,' she croaked. 'No, it was Greg – he told me. And he was so nice, so sorry. It was one of the only times I thought he . . . he . . . How can I be so bloody stupid?'

Then she turned to him, put her arms around his neck and said, 'Thank you. I feel terrible, but thank you. Can we really look at my data file?'

'Well, I can and you can look over my shoulder. Come on, we'll do it now.'

The unfamiliar screen confused her for a moment, then she tensed. 'I can't believe you've got access to all of that.'

'Well, I don't have access to everything but I guess it's most of the things a husband needs to know.'

'Huh . . . I don't see that you have to know about me having foot rot when I was 10. And why can't I access your data file?'

'If it was up to me you could but I tell you everything, anyway.' He scrolled through a couple of screens then nodded. 'Look there – medical history, fertility – within normal tolerance.'

She gulped and snuffled a bit. He flicked the screen off and turned. 'Now that's settled can we go back to our original discussion?'

'I'm so gullible I can't believe you want to have a family with me. Don't tell Claire for heaven's sake. She'll think I'm a complete fool.'

'That, my darling, is because you are sometimes. But then it's not something people normally lie about, so it's hardly your fault.'

'Do you really want children, Mikey? This soon?'

'Right, here's the thing. I'm twenty-four and you're thirty-one.' She winced. 'It'll take around six months for all the licence paperwork and training, so even if we strike lucky at once it'll be well over a year before Michael Junior puts in an appearance. I'd like more than one as well.'

'I might have twins ... get it all over at once.'

He beamed at her. 'Hey, or triplets: two boys and a girl. Michael and George and Sarah.'

'George?'

'What's wrong with George?'

'It's horrible.'

'No, it isn't.'

'Anyway, we'll need lots of practice, Mrs Jones.' He was massaging her neck and she groaned softly.

'Mikey, what if it doesn't happen? Will you de-select me?'

'Never, you crazy woman. I love you and we'll just grow old and cranky together.'

'Good. Something we finally agree on.'

68

Marvin was waiting for Lyn at the back of the restaurant. Jessica had given him a coffee but he was shaking too much to drink it. There was a flurry at the door, then she was sitting next to him, unwinding her scarf, slipping off her jacket and beaming. 'OK, Marvin, let's just start with the basics and see where you're up to.'

He blushed horribly. 'I'm functionally illiterate,' he mumbled at the table.

'Technically maybe, but how long is it since you left school? Two years? Three? Things can change a lot in that time. You'll probably be surprised. Oh, before we start, do you think I could get a coffee?'

'I'll get it.' He shot to his feet and stumbled across the restaurant towards the bar. Lyn watched him and sighed ... this could be very painful. As Marvin headed back towards her, he slopped coffee into the saucer with every step.

She smiled encouragingly. 'Lovely. Just what I needed. Right, have you got your smart pad? Great. Let's start with the boring stuff.'

Marvin's hands were shaking as he started to key her instructions into his smart pad. He hadn't realised he'd be so nervous but now chef's wife was actually sitting next to him he was terrified. She was really kind and he'd thought that would help but now she was so close he could smell her hair and it was totally distracting. He was making one stupid mistake after another. He drew a wobbly breath and glanced round in despair. To his horror he saw chef looking at them through the kitchen door.

Lyn saw his glance and looked up. 'I'll be back in a minute, Marvin.' She slid out of her chair and went over to the door.

Mikey glared at her. 'What the hell are you doing?' he growled. 'Look at the state of him.'

'We're doing sentence structures and boring stuff like that. It's just an assessment at this stage. Actually, Mikey, he's so nervous it's like digging a trench with a teaspoon. I'm sure he can do much better but he's too scared to try.'

'He's bright red.'

'Well, I can't help that.'

'OK – I wouldn't normally do this but seeing as how he's not on shift . . .' Five minutes later a bemused Marvin was clutching a glass of beer and explaining what an adjective was used for. Lyn had a fresh coffee and Mikey was nodding encouragingly over a Coke.

Jessica sidled over with a pile of napkins and peered at the screen. 'That looks hard,' she commented. 'I was never very good at English.'

Marvin looked at her solemnly. 'It's remembering what all the things are called, that's the hard bit . . . I can do all the things but I can't explain why they're right.' He took another mouthful of beer and swallowed. 'You were right,' he said to Lyn, 'I can do things I couldn't do at school.'

She nodded. 'What we need to do is fill in the gaps where you're not quite sure, so that when you sit the exam you'll be good at everything.'

She slid a sheet of instructions across the table. 'I'm going to leave you to do this exercise for twenty minutes, then I'll come back and we'll go through it and that'll be enough for today. Jessica, you are not to help him.'

'Me?' said Jessica, starting to fold intricate shapes. 'Help with English – that'll be the day!'

Lyn followed Mikey through the kitchen and into his office. 'That was really kind, thank you.'

'I can do kind, you know.' She nodded and hugged him.

69

Lyn was planting a wobbly row of lettuce seedlings and thinking about the dump. In particular she was thinking about being with Judith at the dump and trying to sort out in her own mind what Judith could possibly be expecting now they were adults. Lyn had been at the dump since she was a baby but Judith had arrived when she was around six years old, after her mother had died. Each new child had been assigned a 'brother' or 'sister' to help them settle in. Judith had taken it literally and six-year-old Lyn had been proud to have someone to look after.

Now she sat back on her heels and thought about what had happened. Despite all her efforts all she could really recall was a succession of boring grey days spent in a never changing routine. Buzzers sounded to get you up, down to the canteen for meals, into class for education . . . no time was left unplanned although some sessions were for individual pursuits which you chose from the list for your age group.

There were no outings, no meeting other children, no external sporting events. Every room was monitored, even the bathroom, so there was no privacy, but nobody worried about it. At twelve, the boys began to attend some different classes from the girls and by fifteen they were completely segregated. It was a boring life but not a particularly unhappy one, she thought. They weren't beaten or abused, although they were sometimes shut in the dark. They were fed, educated and kept in a safe, healthy environment. She vaguely remembered Judith being keen to make solemn promises and pacts on a fairly regular basis

196

about never abandoning each other and looking back, she understood that Judith had always been unhappy about being in a dump, whereas she'd just gone along with it to keep her happy. But all the kids did it, she recalled, it was because we were on our own. It was accepted that once you were a grown-up in an adult relationship, these things didn't count any more.

At sixteen, equipped with all necessary practical skills (including how to chop a carrot and paint a wall) the girls were screened and despatched into the world to earn a living one way or another. Some were immediately put on the Bulletin for selection but the majority went off to training programmes of some kind. Most of these started with a year or two at college followed by real work. Lyn had been lucky enough, or so she thought at the time, to be sent away to university for two years, becoming an English specialist. Now she realised that perhaps a spell in her home city at college would have helped her socially, because that was where most of the ex-dump students found out about families and made new relationships prior to selection. It was against regulations to form attachments out of your home city and Lyn was pre-conditioned to follow the rules.

By the time she was back, Judith was a fully licensed member of centre security. For eight years, Lyn had to 'pay back' her time at university as part of the general city workforce before she could be put up for selection, and those eight years had largely been happy ones. She lived in a teacher's one-room flat. She and Judith went shopping and to cheap restaurants when their days off coincided. Their friendship had carried on just as it always had.

There must be something she thought, something that had made Judith change so much. She sighed and went to fetch another batch of seedlings.

70

Judith was sitting at the bar with a beer, watching the rest of the guys playing pool and joshing around. She knew that her presence was making them nervous; she could smell it, taste it, hear it in their slightly overloud jokes and see it in their slightly overdone manly punches. It made her feel good. It was better than being part of a team, even though it was her team, and by now they should have bonded closer than family. She was harder than them. She made more arrests. Her surveillance skills were beyond excellent. She was a sharp shooter in every sense.

She nodded cordially as one of the younger guys offered to get her a refill. She even smiled. He smiled back, soft kid. 'We're going on for pizza next, Judith, you coming?' She shrugged and he turned back to the rest of the team.

She took a drink and shifted on the bar stool. 'Hey, Sam.' He looked back ... he was nice looking with curls and dark eyes. 'If you're buying.'

He grinned and nodded. 'Sure.'

She held up her mobile to show she had a call and turned back to the bar. She keyed in her surveillance code to see what Lyn was up to ... surprise, surprise, she was in the kitchen flirting with her boy husband. It made her seethe.

She'd first met Lyn at the dump. They were the same age but Lyn was a couple of months older and half a head shorter. Lyn had been assigned as her 'sister', a role that she adopted immediately with kindness and consideration and surprising aplomb since everybody knew that she already had a best friend. Nevertheless, Lyn was determined to do her best to help

198

orphaned Judith through her transition period and happily admitted her to their little group. It hadn't taken Judith long to get shot of gentle Sophie – a few pinches and bruises blamed on Sophie, a few whispered comments about her, and the house mother had whisked her away to another dump. Lyn had enquired anxiously after her but the house mother had been kind but firm, pointing out that Lyn still had Judith to look after and Sophie had to learn to be kinder.

Judith didn't realise at first what attracted her to Lyn. Judith with long blonde hair and wide blue eyes was by far the prettier of the two but Lyn had huge enthusiasm and was obviously highly intelligent. She was also kind, gentle and had a sweet nature. It wasn't any of those things. What Judith came to realise was that, like her, Lyn was tough. It was a different sort of toughness – an ability to rise above slights and insults and disappointments, to bounce back.

Their ten years together had been too short. Their career choices were obvious. Judith went into training for a profession where her barely concealed aggression could be focused in the right place. Lyn went to be a teacher.

The problems started when Lyn married Professor Gregory Langdale. Judith loathed Greg but perversely quite liked watching him grinding Lyn into a subservient, occasionally beaten, woman who, although professionally successful, was a shadow of her former happy self. She enjoyed being in a position to pick up the pieces when Lyn started to go off the rails after Greg's inconvenient death. She was happy to see Lyn rushed into another ill-planned liaison, ably assisted by her IT skills. Stretching ahead of her she saw years of supporting Lyn and rattling Mitch Jones' chain.

What she didn't foresee was Lyn falling for an intellectually challenged ex-student who had a bit of a way with a spoon. She didn't foresee a bloody cook banning her from the house and Lyn standing by and letting him. To begin with she thought that a few hints would get Lyn running scared and being appreciative of her support. Lyn had turned to her husband.

'Judith, we're going now.' Sam was hovering.

She grinned and slipped off the stool. 'OK, Sam, I'm ready.' As her feet hit the floor she stumbled slightly and his arm shot out to steady her. 'Thanks.' She smiled up at him and tucked her arm around him for support. She might as well get something out of the evening.

71

'Mikey?'

'Oh no . . . What have you done now? Broken something?'

'Why on earth would you think that?'

'You're trying to get round me.'

'Well, yes, I am, but not because I've destroyed anything. I just wondered if I could call Judith, just to check that she's OK.'

'No.'

'Please.'

'No.'

'Oh come on.'

'No. I can't believe you're even asking me. That woman has caused you more grief in the last six months than everyone else at the centre put together. She's spied on you, had you tagged twice for no reason, incriminated you, put false data on your file – these things are never deleted, you know – and I dread to think what she'd do given access here again. In fact, I don't know why I didn't think of it before – what rooms has she been in?'

Lyn paled. 'Only the hall, the living room and here.'

Mikey nodded. 'No wonder she always knew where to find you, mobile or not.' He thought for a moment then went over to the alcohol store. The bug was behind the finger pad.

'How did you know there was a space there?'

'I was a boy scout.'

He put it on the table and went out into the hall. He was back very quickly with two more, which he lined up on the table. 'Drink?' Without waiting for an answer he poured them both two units of wine. They sat opposite each other drinking in silence. Mikey finished first but it was pretty close. 'I think we'd better have the other half of that.' Lyn nodded.

'What do we do?'

'Well, I think we need to assume that they're all still working and I don't know enough about them to dismember them without destroying them. We need to pass them over to centre security. It's all we can do.'

'But she'll say it wasn't her.'

'Maybe. But perhaps she'll just give up.'

Mikey's mobile rang. He looked at it. Lyn snatched it up saying, 'I'll answer it.' She walked over to the windows and said 'Yes?' There was a long silence while she held the phone close so he couldn't hear who was on the other end. Finally she turned and looked across the kitchen. 'Of course,' she said. 'Of course he's still here. Why would you think he wouldn't be? Anyway, how come you know we've found them? It's only just happened. Surely you don't listen out for us all the time? Jude, that's crazy.' There was another long pause. Lyn was starting to cry now but it didn't show in her voice. 'Jude, listen to me. It won't make any difference – of course I'll back him up, he would never hurt me and I'll tell them that.'

In the silence that followed her eyes widened and the blood drained dramatically from her face. Mikey crashed his chair back and grabbed for the mobile. 'She's gone, Mikey. She's not there ... Mikey, where's Spike?'

'He was asleep on the bed when I was changing.' They both dashed for the stairs. Lyn was faster and stopped so suddenly in the doorway that he cannoned into her.

'Ouch!' Spike looked up at them irritably, stood up, stretched and settled down this time with his back to them, paws firmly over his face.

72

OK, now that time I really did think I was going to have a heart attack. What a bitch. Lyn just turned round in my arms and started howling as though she was never going to stop. Mind you, I felt pretty close to it myself. It was the shock. You need carbs for shock – they calm you down. I shoved her towards the bed, sat her down and swung her feet up and tipped her on her side so that she was curled up with Spike.

'Stay there,' I said, 'I'm just going to make some toast.'

When I got back she was more or less where I'd left her but she was stroking Spike and she'd stopped crying. She sat up when I came in and reached for her wine glass. 'No, no, no. You have to eat your toast first.'

She eyed the plate of toast and marmalade dubiously. 'Is that the marmalade I made?'

'I'm afraid so . . . it was all I could find. Come on now, eat.'

'But why?'

'Carbs are good for shock – cake would probably be better, or biscuits, but strangely enough we don't seem to have any.'

'I meant why are carbs good for shock?'

'I have no idea – it's just one of those things that I know, OK?'

She rolled her eyes but obediently ate two slices of toast. I tried a slice as well. The marmalade did taste a bit burnt but it was OK.

'Now can I have my drink?'

'Not if you're going to start crying again.'

She gave me a kind of wonky smile. 'No – I'm good to go.'

Oh, my darling, I thought as I passed her wine over, I really need consoling as well but a gentleman never takes advantage. Still, who said I had to be a gentleman? I looked into her lovely eyes and she carefully put her drink on the bedside table and slid her arms round my neck. 'I'll save it for later.'

Spike gave a disgruntled mutter, jumped heavily off the bed and thudded his way downstairs.

'What was that?' Lyn said, a few minutes later.

'Just the cat flap.'

We consoled each other pretty thoroughly and it wasn't until I went downstairs to lock up that I realised that Spike hadn't come home.

73

Lyn shook her head. 'I just don't believe that she's taken him – last night was different – we were freaked out by the whole thing and she knew just the right buttons to press. Let's have a coffee before we do anything else.'

They were both slumped at the table, worn down by a sleepless night. 'I still think it's too much of a coincidence,' Mikey said. 'He's never stayed out all night before . . . in fact, he never goes out of the garden.'

She shoved a coffee in front of him. 'Come on, Mikey, you need to get ready for work. I'll have a quick look round while you shower and then we'll decide what to do next.' Nursing her coffee mug she pulled open the French doors and stepped into the cool early morning garden. She wandered through the long grass looking for clues knowing she wouldn't find any. Stop being such a pessimist, she told herself, he hasn't been gone for a day yet.

'He's over the back fence . . . in the lane.' There was a sudden burst of activity as Mikey galloped past her pulling his T-shirt over his head. To her complete amazement he scaled the back fence in seconds, leaving it swaying in his wake. She could hear him crashing about in the bushes on the other side. After a moment's thought she climbed carefully on to the compost bin, grabbed the top of the fence and peered over. Mikey was the other side of the lane in the dense undergrowth. He glanced up at her. 'He's in here but he won't come out. Get me a towel or something.'

Lyn whipped off her robe and hurled it across the lane. There was a brief tussle and Mikey emerged clutching a madly squirming bundle, which he passed up to Lyn. She grabbed it with both hands then squealed as the lid of the compost bin collapsed beneath her. Before she could even start to struggle out, Mikey vaulted back over the fence. 'Are you OK? What happened?'

She glared at him. 'What does it look like? Your crappy compost bin fell apart.'

'You're not supposed to stand on it.' He choked suddenly. 'Here – give me the cat.' He bent and took the furious bundle out of her arms and turned towards the house.

'What about me?' she demanded.

'I'll be back in a minute.' His voice was definitely quivering.

'You bastard! You think this is funny!' She managed to haul herself up and clambered out, brushing off grass clippings and vegetable peelings. Her slippers had vanished and her pyjama top had rucked up. She pulled it down, retrieved her coffee mug from the lawn and marched back to the kitchen with as much dignity as she could manage. Mikey was bending over Spike who was lying on the table looking sorry for himself. 'Close the door behind you and lock the cat flap – we don't want him getting out again.'

'Yes, sir! At once, sir!'

He gave her a quick glance. 'Don't be childish.' He continued to run his hands over Spike's coat. 'Get me some warm water and a cloth. He's been in a fight but it doesn't look too bad.'

Lyn felt incredibly annoyed as she ran water into a bowl and dug out a clean tea towel. 'Do you want some antiseptic with that?' she asked crossly.

'Good idea, just bung a splash in the water.' He was mopping Spike's ear now and the water was rapidly turning pink. Then he moved down to his back. 'OK, look here – he's been bitten and we need to keep this open. Cat bites can go really nasty if they heal over too fast. You'll need to keep an eye on it until you can book him into the animal hospital but he'll need antibiotics as soon as possible. If you're worried, call Mum. His ear's a mess and he's lost some claws and got a nasty scratch across his nose but it could be worse. I've got to get going.'

'Oh, little Spike ... come here.' She held out a finger for him to lick but he turned his back on her and gazed up adoringly at Mikey. 'Hey, Mister Cat – bet the other guy looks worse.' Lyn sighed. 'Come here, my hero – leaping fences at a single bound, saving cats in distress – how can I ever repay you?'

He snorted. 'Just have a shower before you leave the house – you've got potato in your hair.'

He was at the front door when she caught up with him. 'Mikey, thank you ... I would have been worried all day.' She reached up and kissed his cheek. 'Have a good day. By the way ... how did you get back over the fence?'

He grinned. 'Climbed on the meter box.'

'Oh, not a super-hero then.'

'Nope.'

74

The animal hospital had an emergency slot free in the afternoon. Lyn made a nest for Spike on the bed while she showered and changed so that she could keep an eye on him. As she combed her hair she tried to remember what she'd planned for the day. Well, it didn't really matter as long as she sorted out what they were going to have for dinner. She went downstairs for another coffee and looked in the food store . . .. then she looked outside. It was going to be hot, so a salad would do. They'd got most of it and she could pick up some cold meat while she was out. She put potatoes on to boil and went into the living room where she flicked on the computer.

Mikey's Diamond Drop recipes were logged in order but she needed to proof them before she sent them off to her editor for initial consideration. The educational game part of the programme was complete but the recipes needed to be added before it could all be tested. She took a slug of coffee and began to read. The battering at the cat flap made her leap in shock. She raced into the kitchen expecting to see Spike fighting to get out but the flap was still firmly locked. Peering out of the window she could see the edge of a bushy black tail. Immediately she yanked the door open expecting the visitor to make a run for it but instead he slipped past her and fled into the house. Slamming the door shut, Lyn darted after him only to find he'd gone to ground under the sofa. Twenty minutes later he was still under there. She sat back on her heels and groaned. Luckily Claire had a day off and was only too happy to be invited to help.

As Lyn pulled and tugged at the sofa, Claire waited to pounce holding a towel. It took seconds and she had the little black monster wrapped up and popped into a wire basket while Lyn was still straightening the throw on the sofa.

'Well, what have we got here then?'

'I've no idea. I think he's the cat that bit Spike but he's never come into the house before and this time he just shot past me as though something was after him.'

'Let's take him into the kitchen for a closer look then. The light's better.'

The kitchen was grey with steam. 'Oh no! That's the potato salad.' Lyn grabbed the pan off the hob and peered at the contents. 'Hmmm . . . they might survive as mash but I'm not too sure. Coffee?'

'Please, love.' Claire had flipped the lid off the cage and was feeling the cat cautiously. He stiffened and moaned. 'Was he limping when he came in?'

'Sorry, I didn't see, he was too fast.'

'Well, he's done something to his back leg – it's probably an abscess.'

'What should I do about it? Spike's got an appointment at the Animal Hospital this afternoon. Should I take this one as well?'

'No, I wouldn't do that. You're only licensed for one pet, aren't you? They'll take him off you and euthanase him.'

'But what about his owner?'

'I doubt that he's got one . . . he's an entire male and from the look of him he's been a stray for some time but he's not wild, so at some point he's been looked after. Look, I'll take him home today and into the animal house tomorrow. We can sort him out there and look for a new home for him. He stands slightly more chance if we do that.'

Lyn bent over the basket and looked into the wide green eyes. 'It's so sad . . . and why ever did he come in here?'

Claire looked out of the window. 'He must have felt safer

indoors than out.' Her eyes narrowed. 'What's happened to your fence at the bottom?'

'Oh, that was Michael being a super-hero.'

'But why would he take a fence panel out to do that?'

'What?'

Lyn straightened up and went to the window. The fence was drooping and one of the panels was lying across the lawn. She could see the lane and the bushes and a glimpse of fields beyond. 'Oh Lord – it's totally collapsed – too much excitement for it, I guess.'

'Coffee ready,' soothed the coffee breaker. Automatically Lyn found mugs and sugar for Claire. 'I'd better see if I can do something with it – I don't like it being all open like that. It was definitely standing first thing . . . it must have given up the ghost while I was in the shower. I took a while because I wanted to make sure I was totally free from vegetable matter.'

'OK. Now I'm completely at a loss. What do you mean?' By the time they'd propped up the panel and tied it to the supports Lyn had told the whole story and Claire was creased up with laughter.

'It's like one of those old sitcoms,' she wailed, 'the things you two get up to . . . God, I wish I'd seen it.' Lyn looked pained. 'Come on, Lyn, it must have been hilarious.'

'I suppose – if you weren't the one stuck in a heap of decaying vegetation.' Claire snorted with laughter again. 'Anyway, that should hold for the moment – the boys will fix it properly at the weekend. You do still want us to come over for the barbecue?'

'Yes, of course – Michael's pre-ordered the meat and I've got a shopping list that consists entirely of beer.'

'What do you want me to bring?'

'Actually, if you could do some punch or something for the ladies, and maybe some salad, that would be great. I'm going to make sure we've got juice and some puddings.'

Claire beamed happily. 'That's perfect, you sound very organised. Now, shall I take a look at Spike while I'm here?'

'Yes, please. And I wanted to ask you about Michael's birthday ... I thought we could do something as part of the barbecue because everybody will be around. Maybe some more fireworks or something.'

Claire beamed. 'Yes. I've already made him a cake so we can have that later in the evening. How about presents?'

'I've got him something for the actual day. I don't know what you normally do but if you do presents you could bring them to the barbecue couldn't you?' Spike blinked up at them from the bed.

'We only do small presents once the kids get older ... they don't expect so much once they're past eighteen but we still like to do something. What have you got him?'

Lyn blushed. 'I've got him a joke present – Tales from Shakespeare, because he doesn't know any of the stories and I love them. Then I've got him a real present which is a new rucksack which has all sorts of pockets and things.' She looked at Claire anxiously and stroked Spike's nose. 'What do you think?'

'I think you spoil that boy. I just hope he appreciates you. Now young Spike, let's look at this bite.'

75

Judith was leaning against the wall when Lyn came out of the animal hospital.

'Hi there. He survived, I see.'

Lyn jumped. 'What are you doing here?'

'Waiting for you, obviously.' Lyn turned down the road and began to walk briskly in the direction of home. Judith fell into step beside her.

'So, has your hero been to centre security yet? Because you know what I'll do if he has . . .'

'I shouldn't think he's had time. We had a busy morning and he had to get to work.'

'Well, just make sure he forgets all about it.'

The cat basket lurched suddenly. Judith glanced down at it. 'Just one cat in there?'

'Yes, it's Spike. We only have one cat.'

'No unexpected visitors then?'

Lyn stopped and faced her. 'Jude, what have you done?'

She smiled. 'Nothing, actually, but I saw you letting him in. I've checked and you're only licensed for one pet.'

'I haven't kept him, Jude, he's gone for rehoming. Where were you, anyway? I didn't see you.'

Judith nodded. 'You weren't looking though, were you? Or listening.'

'But you couldn't have . . . you work for the centre . . . This is mad. Jude, you didn't break the fence as well did you?'

'Well, no, not really. I think your husband did that – it just looked a bit wobbly and I gave it a shove . . . I was amazed when it came down completely.'

'But what on earth were you doing in the lane in the first place?'

Judith shrugged. 'This and that . . . there's a good view into the kitchen if you stand on the meter box. Now, I think we'd better have a chat over coffee . . . I'm on a break at the moment. Here's somewhere.'

Lyn popped the cat basket under the table and waited while Judith got the coffee. She was trying to sort out her thoughts but they kept flipping around – it seemed to have been an incredibly long day. She had to find a way to make this stop but it felt quite impossible. Judith put two coffees on the table. 'Right – this is how it is. Like I said last night, if your little boy husband goes to security I'm going to file a Section 23 against him.'

'What's that?'

'Domestic violence.'

'But it isn't true.'

'No one will believe that, you're complete victim material. I've got recordings of you crying and him shouting.'

'He's a chef – they shout a lot. He's never threatened me.'

'Sure . . . I've got the proof.'

'Jude, what makes you say I'm victim material?'

'Remember Greg?'

'Yes, but that was different.'

'Huh – he beat you black and blue.' She reached down and pulled a nasty-looking knife out of her boot. 'Look, I've got a new toy . . . courtesy of my latest male friend.'

'Jude, for God's sake, don't wave that about here.'

'Because I'll be arrested? Or maybe I'll give Spike here a trim.'

Lyn's hand shot out to grab Judith's wrist. 'Don't even think it.'

'Or what . . . you'll fight me? Or report me? Either way it'll be too late.' She twisted out of Lyn's grip and angled the knife at her face. 'How will your toy boy fancy you with a remod-elled face, huh?' Lyn pulled back out of range and Judith laughed and returned the knife to her boot in one swift, clean, flashy move.

They regarded each other. Lyn tried to get a grip on her thoughts. 'Why are you threatening me?'

'Just think of it as a friendly warning.'

'But what do you want?'

'Good question ... I think I want you to be available.'

'Available? For what?'

'Whatever ... when you were with Greg I know I didn't come round much but we still used to meet up fairly regularly. I didn't have to follow you about to see what you were up to.'

'Jude, we hardly met at all.'

'That's not how I remember it.'

Lyn drew a breath ... negotiate, she thought. 'OK, so do you want to come round for dinner? I know Mikey and you haven't hit it off ... '

'Oh – that little matter of him banning me from the house.' Judith snorted.

' ... but those bugs were out of line, you surely see that. Perhaps if you back off for a bit I can talk him round.'

'What, we can all be friends and play nicely?'

'Well, I think we should aim for civilised at least.'

'I don't think your boy would understand what that means. I don't think he likes me at all and I don't think he'd like you if he knew everything.'

'There isn't any "everything" for him to know.'

'That's your convenient memory speaking, sweetheart, and we both know it. Still, I don't suppose it'll come to that. I'm sure you can keep him off my back.' She drained her coffee and stared across the table. 'Remember – we agreed at the dump that we would be friends forever. I don't take disap-pointment well.'

76

Lyn looked down at her cold coffee. She's quite mad, she thought, she's gone quite mad and no one I know will ever be safe again. Her heart thudded and her eyes blurred. When she looked up Judith had gone. She reached for the cat basket then froze as a voice said, '"Ill met by moonlight, fair Titania". Although actually that should obviously be daylight. Maybe "What news upon the Rialto?" would be more appropriate.'

'Dylan!'

'The very same.' He eased himself on to the chair opposite and looked quizzically at her. 'So – you look as if you need a stiff brandy at the very least.' He produced a bottle and two plastic mugs from his briefcase. 'No, don't say anything until we've both had a drink.' Obediently she sipped and coughed. 'That's no good,' said Dylan, 'you have to knock it back . . . There, that's better.' Strangely it did seem to make her feel a bit better . . . certainly less shocked and less likely to burst into tears.

'Now.' He leant back and pulled a small black video cam from his pocket. 'On here I've got a fairly dodgy film but a very clear recording of your conversation with your friend. I need to clarify some things with you before I update the data file and this seems like the ideal time to do it. Especially since your friend doesn't know we're talking. She made reference to a Code 23 violation – I have to be sure that this has no basis in fact since she did say she had recorded proof.'

'No, it's not true. Mikey and I had a few shouting matches early on and I was upset that everything happened so fast but you know about that.' He nodded. 'But she did say there had been similar Code 23 violations in your previous marriage. Is that the case?'

'Not according to my file.'

Dylan grinned and finished his brandy then refilled both their mugs. 'You are a clever girl, aren't you? I am on your side, you know, Lyn. Tell me, how many bugs did your enterprising husband discover yesterday evening?'

'Three.'

'When you get home I suggest the first thing you do is have another look round.'

'Dylan, what can I do about Judith? If you heard what she said, you know she . . . she . . .' Lyn's voice choked on the words and she buried her face in her hands.

Dylan patted her arm. 'Let me take care of it . . .' There was an angry mew from under the table. 'Ahh . . . the lovely Spike is getting restless and I must move on.' He got up and carefully stowed his bottle and video cam away.

'But, Dylan, how are you going to take care of it?'

'That's up to me, I believe, Lyn.'

She put her face in her hands again.

'Just remember I'm your man.' He stood up then glanced back at her. 'Oh, Lord, apologies my dear, quite clearly I've given you too much medicinal brandy.' She raised swimming eyes to his face. He bit his lip. 'Come on, I'll escort you to your lovely home.'

77

When Mikey got home he found her huddled up on the sofa with the cat. 'Why are you sitting in the dark? What's up?' He sat next to her and put an arm round her then recoiled. 'You stink of brandy . . . where did you get it? Are you drunk?'

'No, Mikey, of course not. I got it from Dylan. Well . . . that's to say he made me drink it.'

'He did what? He had brandy at the centre? What were you doing there anyway?'

'It wasn't at the centre. It was outside the Animal Hospital. He said it was good for shock. I know . . . it should have been doughnuts or gingerbread but I don't think he had any of that.'

'But why did he give it to you?'

'He'd been watching me with Judith. No, don't get mad, it wasn't my fault, she was waiting outside the hospital when I came out. Dylan came over when she left . . . he'd recorded the whole thing. I was so scared . . . I didn't know what to think so I just did what he told me.'

'Which was?'

She waved a hand at the computer desk. 'They're on there. Oh, listen, a homonym.'

'You are drunk, you know.' He flicked on the light and stared in fascination at the shiny row of little bugs.

'That beats your collection, doesn't it? He told me to look and I looked but I don't suppose I've got them all. What do you think?'

'I think that Lucas has a gadget that can sort this out and I'll call him tomorrow.'

'Oh yes, Lucas . . . he's the only stalker I haven't seen today. Perhaps he's gone off me. By the way, Judith managed to kill our fence. You broke it but she killed it. Lucky she didn't get the cat.'

'Spike?'

'No, not little Spike – he's OK, aren't you, baby? No, the black cat. It was under the sofa. I think it liked me but Claire took it.'

'Mum was here?'

'Yes, but that was hours ago. God, I'm tired.'

'What scared you?'

'What?'

'You said you were scared . . . by Judith.'

'Oh, Mikey, she had a knife. I don't know, she said you wouldn't love me if she remodelled my face . . . it's all so confused.'

'Jesus! Have you reported her?'

'Yes . . . well, Dylan came, he said he'd do it.'

She focused on him suddenly. 'Hey, enough about me . . . how was your day?'

'Surprisingly dull by comparison.'

Spike abruptly leapt into action, clawed his way out of her arms and headed for the kitchen. 'Back in a minute, I'll just see to Spike.'

He spotted the antibiotics from the animal hospital on the kitchen table, glanced at the label and mixed two tablets in with Spike's food. 'No mucking around, fella, I've got enough to contend with, so you just eat those up.' He then rang the centre and left an abrupt message for Dylan before returning to the living room. 'Do you want something to eat?'

She frowned. 'No, but I'd like some of that green water – you know, the leaf drink that makes you feel better.'

'OK. Why don't you go up to bed and I'll bring it up to you?' She nodded, got up and headed upstairs.

Mikey was shredding mint leaves when his mobile rang. 'Yes?'

'Ah, Mitch, it's Dylan from the centre, returning your call.'

'Dylan, how much did you give her to drink? She's plastered! And what's all this about Judith?'

'Just a couple of brandies, all in a good cause. She had a serious fright, you know.'

'I'm surprised she made it home – she can't take her drink anyway. They must have been huge drinks.'

'Well, yes, they were very large, I suppose, but I made sure she got back safely. So, how many bugs have you found now?'

'She found about seven bugs plus the three I found last night.'

'Hmm . . . that sounds about right but if she was really drunk she could have missed some.'

'That's OK. I'll sort it tomorrow.'

'Mitch, has she told you what happened?'

'She tried to but I couldn't make that much sense of it.'

'Well, I expect she'll manage to explain it all tomorrow . . . I don't think you need to worry but there's an outside possibility that you'll be arrested for Code 23 violation – that's domestic violence if you didn't already know. I'll be in touch.'

78

She was sitting up in bed looking pale and uncomfortable. I sat down and handed her the tea. 'Thanks. I do feel terrible, Mikey. Don't let me get drunk again. I don't know why you men do it.' She sipped her drink then sighed. 'Who was it on the phone?'

'Dylan.'

'What did he want?'

What should I say? He wanted to tell me that he hadn't meant to get her drunk? He wanted to know how many bugs we'd got in the house? He was warning me that I was about to be arrested?

'God, I don't know, Lyn. The whole situation is completely mad and I don't think you're in any state to explain it to me tonight. Just tell me ... how big were the brandy glasses?'

'They were those plastic mug things.'

'OK.'

'Mikey?'

'What?'

'Can you stay with me, please?'

I stared at her. 'Where else am I going to go?'

She drew a deep breath and shook her head. 'Oh no ... everything's spinning. Look, I know I'm drunk but I'm not stupid. I know Dylan has said something ... something that he heard on the tape this afternoon. It's not true, it really isn't. I'll explain tomorrow but I just don't want you to leave.'

She was leaning heavily against my back and her arms came round my shoulders. I felt a sharp pang of disappointment

220

. . . she really only wanted me when she was out of it. She gave another huge, sighing breath. 'Please . . . please . . .' I turned round and carefully disentangled her.

'Lie down, Lyn, I'll be back in a minute.'

I went downstairs to lock up and check on Spike. He mewed hopefully so I collected his basket and took it upstairs into the bedroom and settled him in the corner. I went and took a shower. It didn't do much good. I went back downstairs. Later on I slid into bed and lay next to her. She wasn't crying but she was very tense. I switched off the light and lay in silence in the dark.

79

'Wake up! Wake up, Mikey! We need to sort things out.' Mikey blinked and rubbed his eyes. Lyn was waving a mug of coffee at him. 'Come on, Mikey, we need to decide what to do.'

'Hell, woman, why haven't you got a hangover?'

'I don't know. How can that be important?' She bounced on to the bed. 'Come on, drink your coffee. Wake up . . .'

He pulled himself up and took a gulp of coffee. 'What time is it?'

'Six o'clock. I thought we needed time to formulate a plan.'

'Huh, OK. Can you remember anything about last night?'

She looked abashed. 'Well, I have a very vaguely disturbing memory of pleading with you not to leave me – is that what you mean?' She fiddled with the bedcover.

'Maybe. Why did you think I would?'

She shrugged. 'The usual things. Umm . . . coming home to find your wife drunk and incapable, no dinner in the oven, the fence broken, knife-wielding stalkers roaming the streets . . . Oh, and the threat of arrest for wife beating. I just thought it might seem a bit extreme, that's all.'

'So what was it you thought Dylan had told me that I'd be so upset about?'

'Oh, you don't want to know.'

He reached out, pulled her down on to the bed and pinned her wrists. 'Oh, I do . . . now I'm awake, you've got me interested.'

'He recorded what Judith said to me. It wasn't right but I thought he might have told you.'

'What?'

'I . . . I sort of implied that I'd talk you round, that you weren't as difficult as Greg. Oh and she reminded me that we'd made an agreement when we were in the dump and she didn't take disappointment lightly.'

He stiffened. 'Is that true? What do you mean – an agreement?'

'No – I mean yes – we were children, we said we'd be together forever. All the dump kids do it. I thought she'd forgotten about it once we were grown up, then she was pretending that I'd seen her a lot when I was with Greg and now I'd dropped her, but it's all made up. She terrified me.'

'There's something you're not telling me.'

'What do you mean?' Her gaze slid away.

'Something about the dump.'

'No, really, Mikey. You and Dylan have got the same idea but it isn't true. Sure we used to get into each other's beds to tell stories and secrets and stuff but that was it.'

'So you didn't have any kind of physical relationship with her?'

'No, I bloody didn't. How can you, Mikey?'

'It's the shock of being threatened with arrest.'

'Yes, well . . . That's not likely to happen, is it? Dylan knows it's not true and you spoke to him last night, didn't you?'

'Sure. I expect it'll be OK. Mum doesn't know about it, does she?'

'No, it all happened after she'd been over here to help with the cat. I can't keep apologising,' she added, 'she was happy to do it – oh, and she said the boys could fix the fence when they came over for the barbecue.'

'But she doesn't know about all the other stuff?'

'No.'

He started to relax and ran his fingers down her face, then tilted her chin up towards him. 'Don't worry, I'm just going to kiss you . . . I'm too freaked out for anything else.' Lyn managed not to flinch too obviously. 'Right. You want to plan what we've got to do today?'

'Yes.'

'Has Spike had his medication?'

'Yes.'

'Good, then sort out his litter tray and keep him in.'

'Right.'

'Next, I have to go to work – we've got a centre restaurant inspector in today – so I won't be around.'

'Right.'

'I'll call Luke on my way into work and ask him to come round this evening with his gadget roll – he can make sure you didn't miss any bugs on your drunken trawl yesterday.' He paused. 'That means, beautiful wife, that you will need to find a dinner suitable for three – there is probably something excellent in the freezer – and make sure we have enough beers in the alcohol store for two.'

'He's coming for dinner?'

'I can't ask him a favour and not feed him.'

'No, of course not.'

'You might want to ring centre security and log a complaint against your friend.'

'Yes.'

'Good. I'll bring some garlic bread back from the restaurant. Maybe you'd like to make dessert?'

'Fine.'

He put his arms round her. 'Am I bullying you?'

'Yes.'

'Do you deserve it?'

'Yes.'

'Wrong answer, darling, I'm just in a bad mood.'

She looked up at him. 'I guess you won that round then.' She tensed suddenly. 'Oh no, what day is it?'

'Friday 10th. Why, sweetheart, what's the matter?'

'I've missed my proof deadline – I'll be tagged again.'

224

'No, you haven't.'

'But I have . . . and Dylan warned me.'

'I submitted it for you last night before I came up.'

'But it wasn't finished.'

'I finished it . . . it was only a proof and I knew what you were planning to do, so I finished it. You can tidy it up when they return it for the final.'

She grabbed at him. 'Mikey, I love you so much – you've saved my life. Thank you.'

Add an archaic term of endearment to that and I might believe you, he thought, but he didn't bother to say it.

80

'Oh my, oh my.' Lucas was leaning against the wall with a beer and a smirk. 'Sounds like marrying the teacher has caused you all sorts of grief, my man.'

Mikey shook his head. 'Nope, it's all good, apart from the crazed stalker bitch and the threat of arrest.'

'Yup. I can see that adds an interesting new twist. If anyone had an ex-girlfriend stalker I'd expect it to be you, not your respectable wife.'

'You saying I'm not respectable?'

'Mitch, we go back a long way . . .'

Lyn put her head round the door. 'I thought you two were supposed to be screening the house, not gossiping like little old ladies. If you don't get a move on the dinner will be cremated.'

Mikey looked round at that. 'You can't cremate a casserole.'

'Listen, mate, I can cremate anything.'

'OK, OK, we're going.'

Lucas bent down and retrieved a slim, shiny reader, flicked on the beam and began to run it across the walls and down the banisters. 'This shouldn't take too long – she wouldn't have had time to hide them anywhere complicated. You've probably got them all anyway.' He waved the beam casually in the direction of the understairs cupboard and it emitted a shrill buzzing noise. 'On the other hand . . .'

In the end they checked the entire house, including the loft.

Back in the kitchen, Mikey took over at the stove while Lucas emptied his pockets of small silver bugs. Lyn watched in horrified fascination. 'It's not as bad as it looks, actually,'

he said. 'These thin strip ones are standard centre issue moni-
tors – hardly ever used or listened in to. Most houses have got
a couple; normally I'd have left them but under the circumstances you can't be sure who's listening to what, so it's best
to get rid of them. Now these little beauties . . .' He nodded
at the ones Lyn had found. 'These are very state-of-the-art and
you really only need a couple for a place this size. Looking at
their registration dates, I'd say they've been purchased in pairs
over the last six months or so – the ones we found on the
outside windowsill are the most recent. But this is the really
interesting one: it's a centre-only camera, restricted issue. You've
been filmed.'

'Dinner,' said Mikey. 'Come on, sit down.' He took a look
at Lyn's horrified face. 'Here, have some garlic bread.'

Despite herself she giggled.

'Mitch, my man, give the girl a drink.'

'No thanks.' Lyn jumped in before Mikey could respond.
'I'm off the booze at the moment.'

'Hey, not pregnant by any chance?'

Good lord, Lyn thought, this is turning out to be the evening
from hell. Any moment now he's going to say, 'By the way, I
know you'd want to know . . . the camera was in your bedroom.'

'Did you just say that, Lucas, or did I just dream it?'

'Say what?'

'That the camera was in our bedroom.'

'Yes, I said that because it was. Probably been circulated
round the centre by now. Imagine, every time you set foot in
there . . . Hey, good salad by the way.' He crunched up a happy
mouthful and grinned. 'I can see I'll have to get married – it
must be great to come home to this every night. An extensive
range of non-cooked meals.'

Mikey flinched and looked at Lyn. She was staring at Lucas
as though he was a venomous snake. 'What's come over you?'
she said. 'You were always a bit sarcastic in class but I never
thought you were mean.' Lucas shifted slightly but carried on

eating. 'Don't pretend that you don't know what you've just said – you've insulted my cooking, or lack of it, you've asked if I'm pregnant when we haven't been married long enough to get a centre licence and you've implied that our sex life has been drooled over by centre security staff. Fair enough, we're just acquaintances – but Mikey is your best friend.'

Mikey put his hand over hers. 'Lyn, Luke is always like this – he didn't mean to be personal, he's just making fun of us.'

Lucas nodded. 'Sorry, Miss . . . I mean Lyn. I wasn't trying to make you uncomfortable. I suppose I just find the whole thing a bit strange. Any more beer?'

Lyn went over to the alco store and got two more beers. 'There's a crumble in the fridge if you want it. Lucas, thanks for your help with all this. There's loads more beer as well. Sorry if I was a bit cranky. I'm off to bed.'

Mikey looked Lucas in the eye. 'You were totally out of line, Luke, what were you thinking of?'

'Sorry, mate, I was just joking. I forgot how smart she is . . . I think the world of her, you know that.'

'Sure. But she's my wife and I don't want her upset.'

'Of course not – she obviously thinks a lot of you.'

'And your point is?'

'Well, it's an unusual relationship, isn't it?'

'Because of the age thing or the teacher thing?'

'No, my man, because you're black.'

81

'I forgot to ask earlier – how did your inspection go?'

'OK. The food quality was rated seven, kitchen practice got eight – it would have been nine but some moron put fish on the meat shelf – overall cleanliness got eight and front of house got nine, which was down to Jessica. All in all we got eight – half a point up on last time.'

'That's good, isn't it?'

'Yes, it's OK.'

'Are you disappointed about the food score?'

'No – I think it was fair.'

'So what's wrong?'

'Nothing.'

'Are you mad with me about Lucas? I thought I was defending you.'

'I don't need defending.'

'Oh, now you sound about five years old.'

'You saying I'm immature?'

'No, I'm not saying you're immature. Are you trying to pick an argument with me?'

'That wouldn't be much of a challenge, would it? I just want to get some sleep.'

Only I couldn't sleep. I'd been so dense, so wrapped up in my dream of what it would be like to have Lyn to myself that I'd forgotten the most obvious stumbling block. Forget the age difference. Forget the different backgrounds. Forget that her last husband had been a mean bastard. We'd worked through most of that. I had thought we were building a strong, secure partnership. I thought she would come to love me in time, simply because I loved her. And I did. Even though she wasn't the Lyn I'd loved when I was sixteen, the differences just made her more lovable to me. I couldn't stand the thought of her being with someone else.

But I couldn't stop thinking about what Luke had said. He was right. It had simply never occurred to me. Acknowledging difference in race or colour was not allowed. It never came up because if you were caught you'd be arrested. The centre couldn't read my mind, though, and the fact was that my entire family was black. White families were entirely white. Orientals married other orientals. Without anybody ever saying a word about it, mixed marriages were very unusual. Not unheard of but very unusual. Somehow an attempt to ensure communal inclusivity had resulted in nothing changing.

I looked at Lyn sleeping next to me . . . she looked very sweet when she was sleeping, and very white. Her pale hands were tiny compared to mine. Her features were small and neat as well. She wasn't spectacularly beautiful although I thought she was lovely. Her skin was very light and she had a few freckles. I felt a very real stab of pain. I couldn't recall a single moment when she'd mentioned race or colour in any situation. She loved Krystal, she loved Mum and they loved her right back. But then she knew how to make people feel comfortable. I needed to talk to her about this but I was scared . . . what if Luke was right and if I pulled it out into the open it would turn out to be true? A deep swell of anguish rolled through me.

I turned on my side with a groan . . .

'What is it?'

'Nothing . . . go to sleep.'

'Mikey, speak to me, what's happened?'

'Go to sleep, woman, we'll talk tomorrow.'

She didn't say anything else but I felt her arms slide round me as she nestled against my back. I could feel my breathing was all wrong and I concentrated on not giving anything away. Perhaps that was how she felt all the time, though.

82

It had rained in the night and the early morning garden was a dazzling glitter of crystal. The sun shone, the birds sang, some of the flowers had come out. Lyn sat on the patio nursing her coffee and considering. Mikey had gone off early to get the meat for the barbecue so that it could marinate for hours before cooking. When he got back they were going to tidy the garden, sort out dessert and set up the living room for the boys to watch the sport. It all sounded very organised and well thought out. She supposed it was. Earlier in the week she'd been looking forward to it. Now it didn't feel the same at all.

Despite her reputation for sensitivity Lyn wasn't much given to examining her own feelings – she just let them get on with it. Maybe, she thought, maybe the last two days had been too much of a strain on them. Maybe Mikey was fed up with all the drama ... he had a busy enough life without all this stuff going on. She'd thought that she was keeping him reasonably happy but perhaps it wasn't enough. Oh stop that, she instructed herself, of course he was happy, we both were, up until the bugging, stalking, threatening stuff happened. She sighed. Good lord, now I'm sighing, she thought. In a moment I'll be cuddling one of his T-shirts or sniffing his boots. At least, she added, I'm not crying ... all that crying had to stop ... it didn't achieve anything.

She had a bad feeling all the same. She'd called the centre yesterday while Mikey was at work and asked to speak to security but had been put through to Dylan's office instead. He wasn't there and she'd left a voice mail then tried security again, and the same thing had happened. Dylan had called back later and reassured her that he'd already logged a complaint on her behalf. He had been helpful over Mikey's potential Code 23 violation and had checked his file at once – nothing had been reported to date. He was very interested in the final tally of bugs and chuckled amiably when she told him about the camera in the bedroom. When Lyn said that Judith had never been upstairs so couldn't have planted it, he simply pointed out that she'd no doubt gone up to use the bathroom at some point and could have easily done it then.

She realised now that what she'd been expecting was some dramatic centre action, such as Judith being arrested and flung into a dungeon, where the only question would be how many years she should languish in chains. Instead Dylan had talked comfortingly of internal investigations, monitoring and restricted postings, which meant that Judith was still out and about with all her weapons intact. Somehow Dylan's repetitive tones had left her feeling quite calm but now she was starting to feel anxious again.

'What are you doing?'

He was back. She could tell from his voice that his mood had shifted but not much. She had to stop herself from flinging her arms around him. As it was, she bounded to her feet so fast that she slopped her coffee. 'Nothing ... just worrying generally.'

'Has Spike had his medication?'

'Yes. What meat did you get? I mean, did you find what you wanted?'

He looked at her more closely. 'Come here.' She shuffled over, looking at the ground. He rested his hand on her shoulder and she jumped. 'Has something else happened?'

'No – I'd tell you if it had. I've just been fretting a bit too much. Do you want me to help with the marinade thing? What shall I do?'

'Stop acting so weird for a start. You're behaving like you were at the beginning. All nervy and that.'

'I'm not ... I've never been nervy in my life!'

'That's clever ... you're avoiding the issue. Now, suppose you tell me exactly what's got you all wound up like this.' He sat down on the patio and pulled her down next to him. 'Ouch. That's really uncomfortable. Haven't we got some garden furniture anywhere?'

'Probably in the loft ... shall I go and look?'

'No, Lyn, we've got to talk about this.'

'I don't like arguing with you.'

'What? We argue all the time ... I told you, it's normal.'

'No, this is different. You've barely spoken to me since Lucas was here.'

'So it's my fault.'

'No, that isn't what I meant. Mikey, did Lucas say something after I'd gone up? What did he mean about ex-girlfriends?'

'That? Oh, that was nothing. We used to go out with loads of different girls after we left college, though there wasn't anyone special.'

'Then he must have said something else. You haven't been the same since, really. He's put you off me.'

Mikey laughed bleakly. 'Don't be daft – how could he do that? Look at me – I'm putty in your hands.'

'Now who's avoiding the issue?'

'OK, point taken. There is something. How well do you think we're getting on?'

'I thought we were fine. I was worried to begin with because we're so different but that doesn't seem to be a problem. I thought we'd settled down. I know we've had issues with Judith and my cooking and that but I thought everything else was going well.' She shuffled unhappily. 'If there's something you want done differently, in bed or anything, then just tell me ... I know I can be a bit opinionated but I do want us to get on.'

'What do you mean by "so different"?' She glanced up briefly at his tone.

'Everything I suppose – you've got a trade, I went to university; you hadn't been married, I had; you've got a family, I was dumped; you hate Shakespeare . . . you're younger . . .'

'I'm black.'

'Pardon?'

'Come on, Lyn, you are such an operator.' Despite his best efforts his voice was rising, grating with fury and frustration. 'I'm a big, black guy and I scare you rigid!'

'Shout that a little louder, why don't you? They probably didn't quite catch it five streets away!'

'You never tell the truth! It's always a joke with you, isn't it? Constant ducking and diving and not telling me what you really think! Well, I've got wise to that game and I know what you really think of me!' She was silent, looking at the ground. 'It's obvious. Look.' He grabbed her hand. 'You're bloody shaking!'

The first punch took him completely by surprise. 'Of course I'm bloody shaking, you moron! Is that what he said? You'd better not let me get my hands on him. That's the most revolting thing I've ever heard! Didn't he do any inclusivity classes – probably thought he didn't need to, the bigoted little smart arse!' She paused. 'As for you! How dare you! How can you imagine for a moment that I care one iota what bloody colour you are.' Words failed her temporarily so she smacked him hard on the chest. He stared at her in bemusement.

'I don't scare you then.'

'Scare me . . . huh! You wait until Claire hears about this, she's going to skin you alive!'

'Oh hey, don't tell Mum, she'll kill me.'

'And you'd deserve it. And don't come that little boy act with me. She thinks the sun shines out of your backside. It's like some great sodding conspiracy to make me feel inferior. You think I'm a liar . . . well, you're spoiled rotten!' The light caught the silver bear dancing on his chest and she grabbed it with some vague idea of taking it back and hurling it into his precious organic compost. 'How can you think that, even for a moment? I've tried so hard to make things OK and it just takes one remark . . . one tiny comment . . . and you suddenly think I'm someone totally different. I expected better of you. I thought you'd grown up.' There was a very difficult pause. Mikey drew breath to speak but she got in first.

'Anyway, you should know though that even when you were a pathetic sixteen-year-old in remedial English – and pathetic is what you definitely were, and I had no inappropriate interest in you or anyone else, you were still the best looking boy I'd ever seen.'

'I was?'

'Indeed.'

'So why do you jump practically every time I touch you?'

She looked up at that. Her gaze was quite truthful but he could see something else there. Then she smacked him again, hard, but this time he was ready for it and caught her wrist. 'Lyn, what are you thinking?'

'I'm not sure why, but you jump when I touch you some-times . . . it must be hormones or something.'

He smirked . . . he couldn't help it.

'Mikey, I think it's because I like you and I think about you and . . . and . . . I thought you might not come home this morning and it made me feel terrible. I thought Lucas had said some-thing about me . . . and he had. How could he? What was he thinking of? And how could you believe him?'

She stopped and looked him in the eye. 'I'm sorry I hit you. You must know I'm not like that. I think a lot of you.' She stroked his chest then reached up and kissed him. He ran his hands down her back and she wound her arms around him and kissed him again, harder, then pulled back. 'Oh, I'm sorry – now I'm initiating sex. God – I don't know what's wrong with me!'

He grinned delightedly. 'Nothing – you just want sex . . . and I'm your man.'

Oh well, she thought, he's still a boy really, and it would be quite comforting. Then she remembered Dylan – he'd used the same words. She dismissed the thought as Mikey stood up and pulled her to her feet.

83

The knocking woke them. Mikey struggled out of bed and went into the spare room to look out of the window. 'Christ! It's Mum! What time is it? I haven't done the marinade. She really will kill me.'

'Oh, don't be daft – just go down and let her in.' She opened the window and leant out. 'Hi, Claire, hang on – Michael's just on his way down.'

Mikey thundered down the stairs struggling into his jeans, a clean shirt flapping open. 'Hi, Mum. Come on in.'

Claire nodded, her face unreadable. 'The boys will be over soon to see to the fence. I thought I'd come early to help Lyn get ready.' She glanced round the kitchen and sniffed the air thoughtfully. 'You haven't got too much done then?'

'No – I was just going to sort out the meat, then I thought I'd mow the lawn.'

'Claire, how lovely, I was just hunting around for garden furniture in the loft.'

Claire smiled. 'Hello, love. That's a good idea, we ladies could do with some chairs in the shade while the boys watch the game.' Lyn nodded. She looked flushed and slightly self-conscious. Claire put her bags on the table, started to unpack the salad she'd brought with her then turned round suddenly. 'Michael Jones – take your hand off Lyn's bottom this instant. Don't you know how to behave in company?'

'Oh, Claire,' said Lyn, 'it doesn't matter when it's just us, surely.'

'I happen to think it does – he'll get sloppy and then let you down when you least expect it.'

'Oh, well if you put it like that. Although he has had one serious telling off today already, so I think he'll toe the line for a bit.'

'Why? What's he done?'

Lyn grinned. 'I can't tell you ... that way I can blackmail him for months. I'll put the coffee on and then we'll get started.'

Mikey stuck out his tongue behind Claire's back and started grinding herbs for his marinade. Claire shook her head. 'You shouldn't let him get away with it. He can't upset you, then think he can make everything OK by sleeping with you.' Lyn snorted.

Mikey spun round. 'Mum!'

'Careful, lover,' said Lyn, 'you're dripping olive oil down your jeans.'

84

Lyn and Claire found four canvas chairs and a couple of patio tables in the loft. 'I'll give these a clean while you do the puddings, if you like,' Claire offered.

'Thanks. I thought I'd do a pavlova but Michael pointed out that you had to cook the meringue thing so I'm doing fruit salad and trifle.'

'What are you putting in the trifle? It won't have time to set if you use jelly.'

'That's OK, I've got some custard mix stuff and I cooked some dry sponge for the base. Actually, it's the only sort of sponge I can cook – I seem to burn everything.'

She wandered over to the sink to start peeling the fruit. Outside, Mikey was cutting the grass with the ancient mower – he'd stripped off his shirt and was going up and down the lawn in very straight lines.

'Lyn, I said what have you got beside meat for the barbecue?' Claire came up beside her. 'What's so interesting? Surely you've seen a man mowing the lawn before.'

'Hmm . . . but not this man.'

'Lyn?'

'Yes?'

'Has it occurred to you that you might be in love with him?' Lyn jumped, yelped and clutched her fingers.

'Oh, what have you done? Let me see? Under the tap with it.'

'Ow! It hurts!'

'Of course it does, you silly girl.'

'Look at all the blood.'

'It probably looks worse than it is – let me take a proper look.' As Lyn, feeling like a very silly girl indeed, held out her hand for inspection, there was a loud knocking at the door. 'Here – wrap it in this tea towel for a moment.'

Claire went to the French doors. 'Michael,' she bellowed, 'get your shirt on and answer the front door. Lyn's cut herself.'

Mikey grabbed his shirt, dashed into the kitchen and looked at Lyn for a second then went to the front door. Lyn heard the babble of voices hush, then start again on a rising crescendo. Ray's voice broke through. 'Get out of the way, you lot, I'm a trained first aider. Leave her alone, Claire, let me have a look.'

Claire bristled but stepped back. Krystal ducked under her father's arm for a good look, then backed away. 'Gross, it looks as though you've slaughtered a goat. It's all down your front.' Jack and Tim hovered for a moment, then grabbed a beer each and made for the garden.

Ray had got Lyn's hand in a firm grip and straightened her fingers under the tap. 'Good lord, girl, what were you doing?'

'Peeling a banana.'

'With a cleaver?'

'I thought it would be quicker.'

Mikey gave a huge guffaw of laughter.

'It's not funny,' she said crossly. 'You used one on those peppers the other day.' Claire began to smile and even Ray permitted himself a dry chuckle.

'OK – we need three plasters and some antiseptic. I think you'll be OK without stitches. Come on, sit down at the table and we'll get you sorted out.'

Mikey passed over the antiseptic and some cotton wool and Ray dabbed it on liberally. 'Right,' he instructed, 'I think you'd better sit there until the bleeding stops, then we'll stick the plasters on. That's right,' he refolded the tea towel, 'just apply pressure for a couple of minutes then it'll be fine. Now, where's this fence?' Lyn felt like pointing out – snarkily – that strangely enough it was in the garden, but just then Mikey rubbed her back and she started to feel better.

He sat down and put the cleaver on the table. 'Is this it?'

'Yes.'

'For future reference, I never use cleavers for chopping vegetables – what you saw the other day was some fancy work with a large vegetable knife.'

'Oh, I'm sorry.'

'And whatever made you think you should peel a banana with a knife anyway?'

'I thought it would be like a carrot – I'm good at those.' His shout of laughter made her jump.

'Michael, behave yourself,' said Claire. 'It was my fault really. I distracted her while she was staring at you in the garden and she forgot what she was doing. Silly girl . . . but it's nice to see it all the same. I remember with your dad . . . it so rarely happens these days.' Claire beamed fondly at Lyn, who for once was quite unable to think of any tactful remark to stop the romantic flow. 'Mind you, I think she's been a bit reticent – no doubt it's because of all these centre regulations.'

Lyn's eyes were like saucers as she gazed at the table. 'Come on, Lyn, you're going to have to tell him at some point.'

Mikey looked at her. Claire looked at her. Spike appeared from under the table and looked at her.

'What's happened? Why are you sitting there like a paralysed rabbit?'

She put her face in her unbloodied hand. 'I'm too embarrassed.'

'About what? Am I going to have to beat it out of you? What are you embarrassed about?'

Lyn glared at him. 'I hope your friend did a thorough job bug-finding the other night, else you are in dead trouble.'

Claire heaved a gusty sigh. 'I'll just go and see if Ray wants a coffee . . . or a beer.'

242

'Well?'

'Mikey, this is just so awkward. I was watching you mowing the lawn and Claire thought . . . she thought . . . well, she was right really – I fancy you.'

'What?'

'You know . . . I think you are very . . . appealing. There, I've said it.'

Mikey shook his head. 'I don't quite understand you.'

'Oh, come on, you know exactly what I mean.'

'Is this because of what happened earlier?'

'Nope.' She was getting into her stride now. 'This is turning into another ghastly day – do you think three cut fingers are enough to let me go back to bed?'

'No, and I can't get my head round why my beautiful, articulate, brainy wife can't just relax and tell me the truth for once.'

'I am telling you the truth.'

'Not all of it.'

'Greg never did this.'

'He probably never felt the need.'

'OK, I think I might be in love with you . . . or at least, have formed an emotional attachment to you. Well, everybody else seems to think I have, but I don't do darlings or sweethearts and I'm not going to start.'

'That is the most graceless declaration I've ever heard, and you an English teacher.'

'Have you heard a lot then?'

'Enough.'

'Shall I get on with the trifle then?'

'Let me just get these plasters on.'

She held out her hand and he examined the cuts carefully before applying the shiny blue strips. He kept hold of her hand and bent and kissed it. 'All better now.'

She nodded. 'All better now.'

He ruffled her hair and grinned. 'Actually, although it's nice to hear it, I already knew.'

Conceited bastard, she thought. You weren't so sure this morning, were you?

85

'Claire?'

'Hi, Lyn, are you all right? There isn't a problem with Spike, is there?'

'No, it's me actually.'

'What do you mean?'

'I just need a bit of advice. My fingers are really sore and throbbing. I've taken the plasters off and, well, the cuts are sort of oozing.'

'Didn't they teach you anything at that home? You need to pop down to the medicentre and they'll clean them up and probably give you some antibiotics.'

'I can't – I've lost my medicard.'

'Oh, Lyn, how can you have done that?'

'I don't know but I've been all through the drawers and it isn't there.'

'OK – why don't you pop round and I'll take a quick look. Mind you, if it's really bad you'll still have to go to the medicentre.'

'Thanks.' She grabbed her holdall and pulled on a jacket.

At Claire's it was unusually quiet. 'Just me, I'm afraid,' said Claire. 'Everybody is at work or college. Come on, sit down and I'll take a look.' Lyn winced as Claire flexed her fingers then reached for the antiseptic.

'They look horribly sore and I've no doubt they hurt a lot but I'll give them a good clean and then you should soak them in a bowl of warm salt water a couple of times a day.'

'But what is it?'

245

'You've just got a bit of an infection – that's what the oozing is about. Clean them twice a day and change the plasters. Michael should have told you that. Oh, and use this antiseptic cream – it should help them heal faster.'

Lyn yelped as Claire pushed her hand into a bowl of salt water. 'There you go. If it was really serious you'd have red streaks going up your fingers.'

'I didn't tell Michael – I thought he'd think I was being pathetic.'

'Well, you don't need to tell him if you don't want to but being a chef he knows all about cutting himself.'

'He never cuts himself.'

'He doesn't now but it used to be like an emergency centre in here when he was training. You have to remember when he's teasing you about knife skills that he wasn't born knowing how to do it, he had six years training and working his way up before he became a chef.' She found two mugs. 'Camomile tea?'

'Oh, can't I have ordinary tea?'

'No, love, camomile is better for you.'

'So was Michael always good at cooking or did his things turn out wrong sometimes?'

Claire beamed at her. 'Just ask him about the time his mobile rang when he was boiling mint jelly – we were sticking to the floor for weeks and he burnt the skin off his fingers trying to mop it up. But mostly he was very good ... he just had to learn about keeping things tidy, not grating his knuckles on the cheese grater, that sort of thing.'

'I haven't done that yet – it sounds painful.'

'Oh it's horrid – everybody does it at some point.' She grinned. 'I just get Ray to do any grating or chopping if he's around.'

86

'Happy Birthday to you . . .'

'God, woman, what time is it?'

'Mikey, it's your birthday – wake up.'

He groaned and rolled over, burying his face in the pillow.

'I've cooked you a delicious birthday breakfast . . . Come on, look.'

He rolled back, pulled himself up and stared. 'What is it?'

'Kedgeree . . . I got it off the history net.'

'But, darling, what is it?'

'Eggs and fish and rice . . . they used to eat it all the time at house parties in the early twentieth century.'

'Is it supposed to be that colour – or is it just that old?'

Her face fell. 'Well, I've done toast and bacon and orange juice as well.'

'Darling, it all looks amazing, just let me wake up a bit and I'm sure it will be great.'

She brightened. 'I'll get the coffee.' He took a cautious taste while she was out of the room . . . actually, it wasn't too bad. He leant back with another groan. The problem was that he had a monumental hangover. He took a huge slug of orange juice and headed for the bathroom. Lyn was waiting when he got back. 'Come on, into bed. Did you have a good time last night?'

'Do you do this on purpose?' he grumbled.

'Of course. Now, try the kedgeree . . . what do you think?'

'I'm not sure what it's supposed to taste like but it seems very nice.'

She gave him a hug and took a forkful herself. 'Oh.'

'Oh what?'

'It's very fishy.'

'And your point is?'

'You can have mine and I'll have your bacon.'

'No deal, woman.'

'I'll arm wrestle you for it.'

'You must be desperate.'

'How about my toast for your bacon?'

'How about I do some scrambled eggs?'

'No, this is ridiculous. It's your birthday and you deserve a treat.'

'Hmm ... let's just eat the bits we like and have a lie-in.'

'Nice idea, chef, you have the fishy stuff and I'll have the toast ... Ow! I thought you had a hangover.'

'No putting one over on you, is there?'

'Come on, drink your juice and we'll just lie down for a while.'

87

She was sitting at the end of the bed when I woke up for the second time. 'Darling, I've got a present for you.'

I felt wrecked and now I had to be enthusiastic again. 'Sweetheart,' I managed, 'that's lovely – what is it?'

'You have to unwrap it.' I was learning something here; going out with your booze buddies the night before your birthday was a poor idea once you were married. She was holding a large, shimmering parcel. 'Thank you.' I sat up and started pulling at the tape. Nothing was working. I struggled with the ends, pulled at the middle.

'Have I done it wrong?' Her face was anxious.

I abandoned the parcel and held her tightly. 'Darling, how could you do it wrong? What do you mean? It's beautiful – I've always been rubbish at opening presents. Tell you what – we could just leave it as it is.'

'What if you don't like it?'

'You could give me a turnip and I'd like it.'

'What?'

'It's the thought that counts.'

'But I wanted to give you something you'd like.'

I pulled at the tape again. 'Good grief, woman, this is a very thoroughly wrapped present. Don't panic, I'll get in there.'

She was quivering, with her face in her hands, when I finally wrenched it open. It was a rucksack. It was great. It had special pockets for flasks and maps and inside compartments for mobiles and wallets and all sorts. It was waterproof. I loved it.

'You don't like it.' Her voice was low and defeated.

'I love it.'

'You don't – it's boring and unimaginative.'

I held her very close. I remembered Dad giving me some advice about women; they needed constant reassurance and just stating the obvious didn't cut it. 'My love, look at me. It's great, we can go hiking to try it out . . . We can go to Wales or somewhere, borrow a tent – you'll love it. We can go up Snowdon.'

'Snowdon?'

'It's a mountain, but it isn't too steep a one. There might even be a railway or something.'

'You really like it?'

'Of course I do.'

'Spike's got you a present as well.'

'He has?' She thrust another carefully wrapped gift into my hands. It was obviously a book. 'Spike went to a bookshop?'

'Yes.'

'OK – I see – Tales from Shakespeare . . . I didn't realise he was so intellectual.' I kissed her gently . . . sometimes that's more effective. 'Can we have a bit more of a lie-in, darling, or do you have anything else on the agenda for this morning?'

She slithered into bed with me, pulled up the duvet and I dozed off again.

88

Nicola was leaning against the counter watching Marvin slicing bread for croutons. Lyn was making notes. 'There is no point in making them too small,' instructed Nicola, leaning over to adjust the angle of his knife, 'they'll end up like bullets if you do that – that's if they don't disintegrate. Remember you've got to fry them off, they'll shrink a bit then.'

Marvin frowned, deep in concentration. 'That's better,' Nicola said. 'Lyn?'

'Yes?'

'Do you want to come out with Jessica and me next week? We've got tickets for the theatre – there's a spare because her friend can't come.'

Lyn stared at her. 'Umm . . . I'll have to ask chef but yes, I'd love to come.'

'Good. We normally go for a drink afterwards so you'll need to tell him it could be a late night.'

Good Lord, thought Lyn, faintly, I wonder if he'll let me go. 'Will there be other people. Men, I mean?' she muttered.

Nicola grinned at her. 'I wish. No, I'm not that daft, I know that it'd be hard for you to get out if it was a mixed group. Let's just build up to that gradually.'

There was a splutter from Marvin and they both looked at him curiously. He was pink and faintly shiny but determined. 'Where do you go afterwards? I mean, won't there be men there?'

'Well, we won't speak to them,' said Nicola firmly. 'You need to get out more, Marvin – we'll be quite safe, you know.'

He shook his head and reached for the garlic crusher. 'If you were my wife I wouldn't let you go out without me.'

'Just as well she isn't then.' All three of them jumped as Mikey leant over the counter. 'Go easy on the garlic, Marvin, and don't waste much more of sous chef's time. She's got vegetable prep to sort out.' Marvin's neck turned scarlet as he began to rub garlic across the pan.

'So this is what you get up to when I'm not around,' Mikey added, giving Nicola and Lyn a glare.

'I did say that we'd be doing it,' Lyn replied. 'We've just about finished but it's really important that Marvin logs his progress as part of his entry portfolio.'

Mikey rolled his eyes. 'OK, OK – I just didn't realise the entire kitchen would be getting in on the act. Marvin, I'm just borrowing my wife for ten minutes . . . you can have her back then. And make sure you've got the pan hot enough to fry those off, I'll be checking.'

He grabbed Lyn's wrist and headed back out of the restaurant to the street. 'Where are we going?'

'Round the corner for a coffee.'

'But I've just had a coffee.'

'Humour me for once. I just don't want to have this conversation in the restaurant. Here we are. How about a milkshake?'

The café was quite pleasant with bright paintwork and check curtains. Lyn watched as Mikey strode over to the counter and chatted to the girl manning the drinks station. He was looking very big, she thought, very athletic. She was still thinking about this when he sat down with a coffee and a pink frothy concoction. 'Are you still growing?' she asked. He looked completely baffled.

'Am I what?'

'Still growing – you look very big in here.'

Despite himself he laughed. 'I think it's got low ceilings . . . you wouldn't notice because you're petite.'

'Maybe . . .' She was doubtful. 'Did you start going to the

gym or something? You look very muscly.' He shook his head and a flood of horror shot through her. 'I'm sorry, Mikey, I don't know what I'm thinking of. What was it you wanted to tell me? Is it about going out?'

'No. I know Jessica and Nicola want you to go somewhere with them – they were whispering about it last week but I pretended I hadn't heard them. No, it's about the recipe book/game idea. Your publishers have been on to me and they're very keen, apparently. I just wanted to check that you still wanted to do it. I don't want you taking too much on.'

She beamed. 'This is turning into a great day – of course I can do it.'

'Good. Drink your milkshake.'

'It tastes odd.'

'It must be rough if you think it tastes odd.' He took a cautious sip, then a larger one. 'No, it tastes like a milkshake, Lyn, have you never had one before?'

'No, I suppose not. Is it supposed to be so thick then?'

'Yes – that's the ice cream.'

'Then it's too sweet.'

He shrugged and swopped her milkshake for his coffee. 'How much more has Marvin got to do?'

'Three more practicals and an extended piece on any aspect of his chosen career. Then he's got the examination of course but he'll pass that, no trouble.'

'So,' he leant back and stretched out his legs, 'what's all this about you going out?'

'Nicola's invited me to the theatre with her and Jessica.'

'Sounds OK – what's Marvin's problem, then?'

'They go for a drink afterwards.'

'Ah.' He looked at her thoughtfully – she obviously wanted to go but she was being careful and not pushing it. Lyn tried to read his expression. She realised he was watching her very closely and that made her feel a bit pressurised. She dropped her eyes then realised she was staring at his chest.

'Mikey, I think I've shrunk your T-shirt.'

'No . . . this one's always been a bit tight. Hadn't you noticed?'

'No.'

'I normally wear a shirt over it – it's more like a vest really – but it's hot today.'

'Oh.'

'Come on then, back to work.'

He left so abruptly that she was taken by surprise. Outside she was just breaking into a run to catch up when he stopped suddenly and turned round to face her. Unable to stop herself she ran into his chest. 'God, woman, take it easy.'

'Sorry.' She tipped her face upwards, swallowed and licked her lips.

'Stop it – we'll get arrested.'

'But I . . . I wasn't . . .' A very odd feeling was washing over her. She stifled a giggle.

'Lyn, stop messing about. Marvin's probably burnt the kitchen down.' He tugged her briskly back round the corner and into the restaurant. An ominous cloud of smoke greeted their entry.

'It was my fault,' said Nicola, 'we've just put the extractor fan on and we'll air the dining area as soon as the smoke's cleared.'

'It was my fault,' said Marvin. 'I was trying to make notes at the same time and I forgot what I was doing.'

'It was my fault,' said Lyn. 'I should have been here to help.'

'Anyone else want to claim responsibility?' Mikey yelled. 'Good. Thank you. Clear up.' He strode through the kitchen still towing Lyn behind him. She shot an astonished and apologetic look at the room in general as she disappeared through the door to the cold store.

'What on earth are we doing in here?'

'Checking the courgettes for tonight.'

'What?' She was mystified.

'What the hell do you think we're doing in here?' He walked her round to the back of the racks and began to kiss her. She mumbled, 'But what's come over you?' into his mouth.

'You have, Lyn. You arrive here looking all cute with your top undone and turn my kitchen upside down. And I decide to let you off, take you out for a coffee and you keep staring at me and licking your lips . . . and this is the result. You've turned me into a bloody adolescent.'

'Oh God.' She looked down in horror. 'Oh! It's only two buttons but you could have told me.'

'It's too late now . . . no wonder Marvin burnt his croutons. I'm amazed he managed to chop his fine herbs without losing his fingers. From now on you check that you're fully dressed before you set foot in my kitchen.'

'Right. Sorry about all that but that T-shirt, vest, whatever is positively indecent. I don't think you can talk.'

'Talking isn't on the agenda right now.'

'Mikey, we can't . . . What if someone comes in to get some carrots or something?'

There was a tentative knock on the door.

'What?'

'Sorry, chef, I need to start prepping the celeriac and we need more cabbage.'

'Well, get it then.' Footsteps echoed across the floor; there was a rustling, more footsteps and the door closed softly. Lyn giggled helplessly. 'Do you only have vegetables beginning with c? It's like that word game we used to do.'

He sighed and fingered her hair. 'OK, just a quick snog and we'd better get on.'

'What's that?'

'What's what?'

'A snog.'

'This is a snog, darling. It's probably Anglo Saxon or something. You should know.'

'It doesn't sound Anglo Saxon, not really. I'll have to look it up.'

'Now who's being technical?'
'Mikey ... I thought you said a quick snog ...'
'I changed my mind.'
'Oh, in that case ...'

89

'What time are you off out?'

'We're meeting at the restaurant around seven to give Nicola time to change after her shift. The theatre starts at 7.30. Are you still OK with me going out after?'

'Yup. I'll walk you round to the restaurant – I want to check on the mains.'

'Aren't you going out then?'

'Maybe – it depends who's around. Don't forget your mobile – you can ring me when you've had enough and I'll come and collect you.'

'Are you sure? I'll be OK on my own – I'm not a child.'

He rolled his eyes in despair. 'No – and you're not single either. And it'll be late and dark.' He dug his spade into the earth and turned round to face her. 'Do me a favour ... get me a beer, will you? I don't want to track muck all over the kitchen.'

'He's positively anal,' Lyn grumbled to herself as she trotted obediently into the kitchen. 'I couldn't have found a more organised, controlling, patronising man if I'd advertised.'

'Here you are, honey.' She held out the beer with a sweet smile.

'Thanks, you having one?'

'No – I've got a juice somewhere about.' She perched on a heap of planks that he'd dragged across the lawn. 'Anything else I can do for you, sugar?'

'Yes – you can get the tape measure – it's in the small toolbox

257

under the sink. I'll need the pegs and string as well so you might as well get those – they're in the second drawer down.'

Trying to control her breathing – well, she had volunteered – she stomped back to the house. By the time she'd found everything, Mikey had stripped his top off and was hauling planks about. 'Give us the tape . . . OK, hold that end there.' Very efficiently he began marking lengths of planking, ruling lines with chalk and finally he propped the planks on the barbecue, dug around in his tool bag and pulled out an autosaw.

Lyn gazed in surprise as he rapidly built three rectangular shapes, which he fitted into the border and started to fill with soil. 'Do you want me to do anything else?'

He paused for a second. 'You could connect the hose up – we'll need to get this watered down a bit before we do the planting.'

Right, she thought, connect the hose – something the little woman can't possibly get wrong. She pulled the hose out from a corner and looked at it dubiously. 'Mikey, this isn't our hose.'

'Yes it is. I got us a new one with a proper tap fitting – yours was disintegrating.' She looked thoughtfully at the jumble of fittings that lay under the bench beside it. Well, it couldn't be that hard. Mikey had filled one raised bed and was starting on the next. She screwed the fitting on to the outside tap and gave it an experimental turn – she was expecting the fitting to fall off immediately but it didn't. Instead the hose groaned and shuddered. 'Good,' she said, going to take hold of the end.

Mikey glanced round just as the hose reared up, flinging a jet of water round the garden. He grabbed for it automatically, missed and was caught full in the face with a drenching spray. Dashing the water out of his eyes he yelled, 'Turn it off!' Lyn hesitated, trying not to laugh, then skipped back out of the way as the hose focused on her. Water was cascading across the lawn. The hose gave another writhe and spun round again. This time Mikey grabbed it. For a moment he stood there, pointing the hose down at the grass, blinking and shaking his head. Silvery drops hung in the air around him. Lyn turned and made for the tap. Halfway there a jet of water caught her in the neck.

'Stop it, Mikey, that isn't funny.'

'No?' He aimed the jet at her feet. She shrieked, skidded on the slippery grass and sat down with a thud. He stood over her and played the water through his fingers for a moment, then sighed and went to turn it off. 'We used to love playing with the hose when we were kids.'

He held out his hand and pulled her to her feet. 'My, Mrs Jones, you're very wet.'

'And whose fault is that?'

'I think it's probably yours, but you were going to change anyway, weren't you? Let me help you, we don't want you catching cold.'

At the French doors he kicked off his boots and pulled the curtains across behind them. The kitchen instantly felt cooler and more mysterious than usual. Lyn stiffened as he reached for her, then relaxed as he ran his fingers through her wet hair. 'Mrs Jones, you need to take your punishment with good grace. You can't run about looking like that without severe repercussions.'

The cat flap rattled as Spike went to explore the garden. 'Mikey – do you think that Spike will use your raised beds as a toilet?'

'Probably.'

'Don't you care?'

'Not at this precise moment, no.' He tugged her T-shirt over her head, walked her to the sofa, sat her down and shook his head. 'I don't know how you do it but even a cold shower can't put me off.'

90

The bar they went to was one of the drink 'n' dance chain that boasted cocktails, beer and a reasonably sized dance floor. It was fairly busy with a mid-week crowd. Music was courtesy of a looped surround sound system – nothing too exciting, but several youngsters were already dancing and a table of older ladies was sitting watching with motherly approval. Lyn felt about 100 years old.

Jessica fought her way back to the table with three different cocktails. 'Lyn, you try the daiquiri, Nicola the pina colada and I'll take the mojito. Points for taste, alcohol content and presentation.'

Lyn grinned. 'Do you never stop working?'

'Of course – it's just you need to check out the competition and you might learn something.'

Nicola nodded. 'Quite often it's just the garnish that makes all the difference. Not that we eat out often. You used to dine out everywhere, didn't you? Do you miss it?'

'Oh, with Greg, you mean.' Both girls stared at her. 'My first husband.'

'Yes,' said Jessica, 'it's just that I can't imagine being so casual as calling Professor Langdale by his first name. Not with him being so important and well . . . famous.'

'Believe me, it didn't feel like that being married to him. And no, I don't miss dining out – it gets quite boring after a while.'

Nicola looked up. 'What we really want to know is what's it like being married to chef?' She took a gulp of her cocktail and started to splutter.

Lyn smiled. 'We're still getting used to each other – he's very organised and very tidy and I'm not.'

Jessica leant forward. 'Come on, Lyn, you know what she means. He is our boss and we want details.'

Lyn laughed outright. 'He's great – that's all I'm saying. He's kind to the cat and he's teaching me to cook . . . slowly.' The girls pouted but she shook her head. A bunch of young men suddenly pushed their way in.

Jessica stared. 'Isn't that chef's brother?' Lyn twisted round in her seat and waved. 'Yes, it's Tim – that must be his football team.' Tim appeared at her side.

'Can I get anyone a drink?'

Aaron popped up next to him. 'Lyn, do you remember me?'

'Hi, Aaron, of course I do. This is Jessica and Nicola.'

'Right,' said Tim. 'From the restaurant, yeah?' The noise level was steadily creeping up as more young men appeared at their table. 'We've been training,' explained Tim. 'Just stopped off for a beer.'

Aaron turned to Lyn. 'Do you want to dance?' he asked. Lyn shook her head. 'Sorry, Aaron, I really can't, but I'm sure that Jessica or Nicola will be happy to.' Aaron nodded and looked at the two girls enquiringly. 'He's very good,' Lyn whispered behind her hand.

Tim smirked. 'Nicola, how about it?' Seconds later, Lyn was deserted. She didn't mind at all, just sat back with her drink and relaxed. It wasn't very late and she supposed she ought to give it another half an hour before making a move but perhaps she should ring Mikey to let him know. She was just reaching for her bag when Lucas slid into Jessica's seat.

'Well, well, well,' he drawled, 'all alone?'

'Not really,' said Lyn, 'the girls are dancing.'

'And you aren't?'

'No, Lucas, I'm married.'

'So you keep saying, yet I keep bumping into you without your husband. He's getting pretty careless, isn't he?' Across the dance floor she could see Tim staring in her direction. Lucas leant forward and grabbed her wrist. She shot Tim a glance of desperate appeal.

'Oh, Lyn, Mitch won't mind if we take a turn together. After all, he trusts both of us . . . he's a very naive man.'

'Let go, Lucas, you're hurting me.'

He increased his grip. 'Then come and dance with me.'

'No. Let go – bullying me isn't going to help you get what you want.'

'And what do you think I want, pretty lady?'

'Hey, Luke, what are you doing?' Tim sat down suddenly. 'You don't usually hang out here.'

'Nope – I was just passing and I saw Lyn all alone. Thought I'd ask her for a dance but she isn't interested.'

Tim grinned easily. 'Of course not, man, you know better than that. She can't dance without specific permission and Michael isn't here yet.'

'Oh, is he on his way then?'

'Sure – give it ten minutes and you'll be able to dance her feet off, although there's a bit of a queue building.' He glanced down at Lucas's hand. 'You'd better let go of her, man.'

Lucas shrugged and stood up. 'I'll leave you to it.'

Lyn gulped. She felt a bit tearful. Tim sat down and groaned. 'For an awful moment I thought I was going to have to fight him.'

'Oh no, Tim.'

He laughed. 'Don't worry, I'd have won but it might not have been very pretty.'

She reached for her mobile.

'It's OK – I rang Michael before I came over.'

'Tim, I am grateful – it was just so difficult.'

He patted her arm. 'You know, you look very lovely tonight. No wonder he wanted to dance with you.' They sat in silence for a couple of minutes then he started to tell her about their training session and she told him about Mikey thinking she might like to take up something sporty and they were both laughing when Mikey strolled through the doorway. Lyn blushed as he looked at her but he simply held out his hand, took her in his arms and began to dance.

91

She had a forced smile on her face and was laughing at some joke Tim was telling her but I could see at once that she was unhappy. I scanned the crowd in the bar and spotted Tim's football buddies. Jessica and Nicola were dancing with some of them; the rest were hanging out at the bar, looking across at Lyn and nudging each other. They were harmless enough.

Lyn looked beautiful. Her hair was slightly ruffled and her skin was very pale. Her eyes were enormous. Time to make an entrance. I headed for the door, then heard a scuffling behind me. I stopped and looked back – there might have been someone in the shadows, there might not.

I pushed the door open. Lyn gazed at me with her paralysed rabbit expression. I held out my hand as I reached the table and she took it, smiled and said, 'I thought you were hanging out with your booze buddies?'

'I figured you might like to dance with your husband and I didn't want to let the side down.'

92

They swung round a corner quite elegantly. Lyn sighed. 'Mr Jones, you lied to me about your dancing ability. You are a very smooth mover indeed.'

'Well, thank you, ma'am, I aim to please.' He manhandled her through a pivot turn. 'Follow me . . . relax . . . that's better.' The music shifted down a gear and he tugged her closer.

'Is this a shuffly one?'

'I suppose you could call it that.'

'Great – I'm good at those.' She smiled to herself and let her head rest on his shoulder.

Mikey looked around the crowd and saw Tim dancing with Jessica. As he watched, Tim glanced in their direction and raised his eyebrows. Mikey nodded but something made him tighten his grip and Lyn immediately looked up. 'What is it?'

'Nothing.'

'I haven't been dancing with anyone if that's what you think – ask Tim – he looked after me.'

'Have you enjoyed yourself?'

'Yes, the theatre was wonderful. I haven't been to anything like that for ages.'

'What was it?'

'Ballet. Only extracts but it was still lovely. Not what I'd expect Nicola to choose but I'm not complaining.'

Back at the table, Aaron was chatting to Nicola and watching Lyn. 'I was hoping to get a dance with her but I guess that's not going to happen.'

Nicola grinned. 'Nope, I think you're right.' She looked at

Aaron consideringly . . . not her type, she decided, but Tim was another matter.

Mikey figured it was time to take his wife home . . . it was clear that all the attention was making her nervous. 'Are you ready to make a move, sweetheart?'

'Don't get sloppy in public, for heaven's sake.'

He sighed. 'Are you ready to leave yet?'

'Yes, please.' The music abruptly moved up a to a faster pace and he automatically shifted his grip and began to jive. 'Just this one, then.' She groaned.

Tim waved at Nicola and Aaron and they got up and started to dance. 'This is bizarre,' said Lyn. 'How come all these footballers can dance?'

Mikey changed his grip again and she found herself moving from side to side with his hands on her waist. 'You're stereotyping,' he breathed in her ear. 'We all do dance at school nowadays. It came in when I was fourteen. Right – cross hands.'

'Oh God, don't spin me round.'

'Oh, OK then.' He steered her over to the table. 'You're very good, Lyn, honestly.' While she found her bag he waved goodbye to the others. Moments later they were outside.

'How tired are you?'

'Not particularly. Why, did you want to go somewhere else?'

'Yes – I want to show you something.' They walked slowly down the road. At the park he led her down the path to the lake. She stopped suddenly. 'What is it?'

'It's only switched on at night. They have to run it to keep the system clean, I think. Then last week they put the lights on.' The central fountain, which Lyn had always thought of as derelict and filthy, assumed a strange grandeur at night, water cascading through it and lights flickering through the streams and rivulets.

'Is it a mermaid or what?' she thought aloud. 'I just thought it was some classical goddess but it looks different in the water.'

'It looks like you . . . it's got those huge, anxious eyes and little snub nose and it's very pale.'

She could feel herself blushing. 'I haven't got a snub nose.'

'I'm not going to argue with you about it.' They passed the fountain and continued across the park. 'Just tell me what's upset you.'

'I'm not upset.'

'Lyn, I got two calls to come and rescue you. I just want to know who it was that was bothering you.'

'You don't know?'

'Marvin described him but it wasn't very clear.'

'Marvin?'

'Yes – he was lurking about outside the bar. You know he was bothered about you. Then he was too anxious to go in. Then he rang me . . . you're right, he's an absolute nervous wreck. Anyway, that doesn't matter. He said it was someone thin and nasty, wearing a black shirt.'

She had to laugh. 'It was Lucas, if you must know. He wanted me to dance and I wouldn't and he got a bit difficult but Tim scared him off. It wasn't really that important. I expect I over-reacted.'

'Maybe, but I guess both Tim and Marvin have pretty good instincts. What did he do?'

'He wanted to dance with me and I said I wouldn't and he held my wrist and wouldn't let go. I told you I'd overreacted.'

They were approaching the canal basin and a soft breeze ruffled her hair. There were all sorts of craft rocking gently – some with lights and some just dark shadows. Mikey took her hand and walked to the centre of the bridge. 'Look at them.'

'It's lovely – I haven't been down here before.'

'Look down there – there are swans and ducks under the bridge.'

She peered into the water, finally making out some glimmering white shapes. 'We saw a bit of Swan Lake tonight, the bit with all the cygnets in a row.'

Mikey grinned at her. 'Darling, I know nothing about ballet. I believe it's a girl thing.' He lifted her up so that her feet were on the railing and held her tightly. 'Lean over . . . you'll get a better view.'

'Oh, Mikey, they're lovely.'

'I thought you'd like them.'

He lifted her back down and leant beside her. 'I thought I'd get a travel pass for next year . . . What do you think?'

For a moment she felt her heart stop. 'If that's what you want.'

'Well, once the training is sorted out at the restaurant and your publishers have actually paid us, we'll have a bit of time and some cash. I thought I could do a mid-European module. And I'd like to take a look at Paris and Naples and maybe Venice.'

'Venice?'

'Sure – before it sinks.'

She couldn't repress a violent sniff. 'What now?' His voice had a thin edge of irritation.

'I'll miss you.'

'What?'

'I'll miss you. How long will you be gone?'

'You think I'm going without you?'

'Well, yes.'

'What would be the point of that?'

'What do you mean?'

'Well – I'm sure the food is nice but I don't think Venice rates that highly on its international cuisine. I thought it could be like a honeymoon thing. You know, just us, having an adventure.'

She sighed. 'I think Venice probably has excellent cuisine, chef, and I would love to come.'

93

She was lying on the grass pretending to read but really listening drowsily to the sound of men trying to light the barbecue. Next to her, Krystal was texting rapidly and huffing irritably to herself. Claire was in the kitchen making iced tea. Krystal gave an extra loud huff and flopped down on her back.

'What is it?'

'Everyone else has gone to the fair.'

'Everyone?'

'Everyone from school.'

'Oh, I see . . . and you?'

'I'm not allowed to go without a responsible person.'

Lyn sniggered. 'Well, there's no point in looking at me . . . Michael thinks I'm completely irresponsible.'

'But he'd go if you asked him, then I could come with you.'

'Krystal, he's in charge of the barbecue.'

'Well, he could tell Tim to go with us.'

Lyn looked towards the house. The men folk were hotly arguing the merits of various barbecue techniques. 'It's all about control,' Mikey was protesting vehemently, 'we just need a consistent heat.'

'It's physics really.' Jack was prodding at heaps of barbecue briquettes. Ray was just generally shouting and waving his arms about. Only Tim was silent, staring down the garden towards them. Mikey shrugged suddenly, looked at Tim for a moment then started in Lyn's direction. 'Ask him, please,' whispered Krystal.

Mikey took Lyn's hand and pulled her to her feet, wrapped his arms round her and kissed her. 'Mikey, let go,' she murmured into his neck. He looked into her eyes and smiled. 'Sorry, darling, I just couldn't help myself. What does Krystal want you to ask me?'

'She wants to go to the fair. Apparently all her friends are there already.'

'It's not for me, really,' exclaimed Krystal, 'it's for Lyn. Imagine – she's never been to the fair before.'

'Ah . . . so it was just a kind thought then.'

Krystal looked down at the grass and wriggled. 'I thought Tim could go with us,' she muttered, 'but Lyn needs permission and all that and you're doing the barbecue . . .'

Claire came bustling towards them. 'You're all looking very serious . . . what is it?'

Lyn sighed. 'Krystal wants to go to the fair but it's got a bit complicated.'

'Krystal, we've talked about this already today,' huffed Claire. 'We're having a nice family afternoon relaxing together.'

Krystal nodded. 'It's just that Lyn's never been.'

Claire looked at Lyn with interest. 'And you want to go, do you, Lyn?'

Mikey put a firm arm round her waist and pulled her against him. 'Say what you think, darling.'

She drew a breath. 'OK, I've never been but it's never really appealed to me. I'm sorry, Krystal, but perhaps Tim and Jack could go with you for an hour?'

Claire laughed. 'She's got you twisted round her finger all right, hasn't she? No, Lyn, it wouldn't be polite to you and Michael – we're your guests.'

'How about,' said Mikey, 'Lyn and I accompany Tim, Jack and Krystal to the fair while Dad lights the barbecue. Then we'll come back after thirty minutes and they can stay on for another hour, by which time I'll have cooked everything.'

'The planning capacity of Napoleon and Machiavelli combined,' Lyn murmured, gazing at him with admiration.

'Lyn needs the exercise,' Mikey added, without a flicker of a smile.

The fair was in the school playing fields. The centrepiece was a very pretty, jangling carousel with traditionally painted horses and fluttering ribbons. Lyn was entranced but thought it looked very dangerous. Jack laughed at her. 'Of course it isn't – the floor's padded and they don't start it until you're strapped into the safety harness ... in the old days you just had to hang on where you could.'

'How do you know?'

'Oh, there's an educational exhibition tent somewhere – tells you all about it.' Krystal was shifting from foot to foot.

'Tim, put Krystal out of her misery, will you? Here, take the door key.' Tim grinned and led the other two into the hubbub. Mikey looked at the crowd and looked at Lyn. 'Think of it as being like the country market – very busy, quite scary if you haven't been before, but fine once you get to know it. Look, we'll sit down and I'll point things out to you.'

They perched on the fence. 'Over in that corner they have some ponies who give rides to the little ones ... see ... they're trained to be very careful. We've got pictures at home of Krystal on one. Then there's the plastic duck pond – that's for the little ones as well – they hook a duck and win a prize. Then there are the junior swing boats – they have to wear helmets and be strapped in. Jack was sick on one of those. This side, there are the food stalls – ice cream, fruit, burgers, juice and coffee. They used to do toffee apples, and candyfloss in the old days but it's unhealthy and unhygienic so they banned it. Then there's the big stuff – the big wheel, which has a great view from the top, the flying saucers, and the giant teacups. Then you've got the side shows: bowling, shooting, darts, that sort of thing.' He paused for breath.

'So what do you like to do?' asked Lyn.

'Bowling and the big wheel, I guess. I haven't been for a while.'

Lyn slipped off the fence and tugged him after her. 'We'd better get going then. I think I can cope with that.'

94

They wandered back down the road, sharing a lemon crush cornet, Lyn clutching a large pink bear under one arm and clinging to Mikey with the other. 'I still feel sick.'

'Don't think about it.'

'It was the teacups.'

'I know, love, just don't tell Mum, OK.'

Claire took one look at Lyn's sticky, white face and rushed her into the kitchen. 'Cold towel on your forehead, feet up, sips of iced water,' she pronounced. 'I suppose that stupid boy took you on the teacups?'

'Yes, he lied to me. He said we'd just go on the big wheel but after he'd won the bear for me he got all macho and we had to do the swings and the teacups . . . God, I hate him.'

Claire laughed and patted Lyn's hand. 'As long as you didn't do the flying saucers.'

'Oh God, I feel sick – do you know, Claire, they went up and down and twizzled as well as going round.'

'So you never went to the fair when you were a child?'

Lyn shook her head. 'They said it wasn't suitable – I suppose taking forty kids would have been a bit of a struggle.'

'So what did you do for entertainment?'

Lyn considered. 'That's an interesting question. I don't want to sound pathetic but apart from the odd walk or trip to a museum we didn't do much. I haven't thought about it before – maybe it was a funding problem. When I was older I was studying all the time anyway so I didn't really notice. And then

I got my two-year degree scholarship and that was that – my life was sorted.'

Claire was chopping apples for the fruit salad. 'Sorry, Claire, I should be doing that, I'm the hostess.'

'You just relax for a few more minutes – you can do the rice salad in a moment, then we can sit in the garden while the men make idiots of themselves.'

'Claire, what are toffee apples? Michael said they used to sell them but they'd been banned – oh, and candyfloss? I've heard of them in novels and things but I suddenly realised I don't know what they are.'

'Oh, love, I was a child ... toffee apples are a real disappointment but they smell wonderful and look so tasty – they're apples on a stick dipped in toffee.'

'They sound lovely. Why are they disappointing?'

'To keep them, the toffee has to be the hard kind and the apples are hard too, so if you don't break your teeth on the toffee, the apples are sour. But you just had to buy them.'

Lyn sat up and sipped some more water. 'And the candyfloss?'

'Ahh, now you're talking. It used to be just pink but before they banned it you could get all the colours of the rainbow and flavours too. It's pure sugar, heated and spun around. If you licked it too fast you could cut your tongue. When I was small they were already putting it in plastic bags but my mother remembers getting it wrapped round on a stick – a cloud of pink – and as soon as you touched it, it melted all over your face.'

'Mum, it must have been disgusting – all colourings and e-numbers – and in the open like that.' Mikey was hanging in the doorway. 'Feeling better?' he asked Lyn. She nodded but her stomach grumbled loudly and Claire rounded on him.

'Idiot boy, she'd never been before and you take her on the swings and the teacups and the flying saucers – what were you thinking?'

Lyn began to laugh at Mikey's face. 'You said you wouldn't tell,' he mumbled.

274

'I didn't – Claire tortured me to get to the truth.' She giggled. 'Anyway – I've got to get on with the rice salad. Who's going to show me what to do?'

She was just draining the rice when Jack appeared beside her. 'Hi, you're back then, and almost on time.'

'Not exactly.'

She spun round in a cloud of rising steam. 'You've not lost Krystal?' He nodded, eyes on the ground. 'Jack, for God's sake.' She grabbed his arm and shook it. 'Where's Tim?'

'He's still looking for her. I thought I'd come back and check that she wasn't here.'

'You'd better go straight back – I'll get Michael.'

She ran into the garden then slowed to a walk as Ray, Claire and Mikey stared at her. 'Have you cut yourself again?' Mikey said anxiously.

'No – it's probably nothing drastic but the boys can't find Krystal.' She expected pandemonium to break out but although Mikey frowned and Ray pulled on his jacket, nobody started to rant and rave. She felt like doing both.

Claire sighed. 'Lyn, if you could go with them that will be good – I'll stay here.'

They hurried back up the road. 'It isn't the first time and it won't be the last,' said Ray. 'We have a system. One of us stays by the entrance in case she turns up there and the others search. We've used it since Michael was a toddler and got lost at the football club.'

At the fair, Lyn was stationed by the entrance. 'Just ring if she turns up,' instructed Mikey.

'Can't we just ring her?'

He rolled his eyes at her. 'It's turned off.'

'But surely we could track her?'

'The centre can, but we don't want to report her if we can avoid it – once she's been missing for two hours we'll have to but it'll go on her data file.'

'Oh, right.' She watched as he disappeared into the crowd.

For once she really wanted to see Dylan. Krystal was sixteen, not a child but not an irresponsible girl either.

The fair was starting to empty and a crowd was leaving the field. Lyn craned her neck and suddenly spotted a familiar face. 'Ruthie, isn't it?'

The girl stopped then beamed. 'Lyn – you did Krystal's party, didn't you? How are you?'

'Fine, thanks. Ruthie, have you seen Krystal? I was supposed to meet her but I think I might have missed her.'

'She did say she had to go because she didn't want to be late. She was heading this way.'

'So where did you see her last?' Lyn tried to keep the urgency from her voice but Ruthie faltered and looked worried.

'We should have stayed with her . . . we normally do at things like this but I wanted another go on that stall with the rings. It's in the end tent over there.'

'Don't worry.' Lyn smiled. 'She's probably just got distracted. I'll get her to call you later.' Ruthie nodded and moved away.

Lyn took a few paces into the crush, then moved to the edge. She could see the fluttering tents which held the smaller stalls. She glanced behind her and was surprised to see how far she'd come. She'd just take a quick look, she decided; after all, she had her mobile. It was a direct route from the stalls to the entrance along the side of the field. Krystal wasn't in any of the tents. The crowds were thinning by the second. Lyn considered . . . she couldn't still be in the field, they'd have found her by now. She walked around the back of the end tent and studied the fence. There was a gap leading into a deserted industrial unit. She tried to visualise her map of the area. They were the opposite side of the field from the footpath and as far as she remembered, this was just a storage facility.

She opened her mouth to call, just as a hand closed on her arm. Her breath caught in her throat and her heart thumped terrifyingly. 'Sorry, Lyn, you're a nervous wreck. I just wanted to stop you going in there – there's rusting wire and all sorts. It's not really very safe.'

She looked over her shoulder into Tim's reassuring eyes. 'Have you found her?'

'Yes. Actually, your Marvin found her – she'd dropped her mobile and he was helping her look, then he bought her a juice. She says she forgot the time.' He shrugged. 'No harm done.'

Lyn turned away from him so he couldn't see the abrupt rush of tears.

'Hey . . .' His hand ran up and down her arm. 'It's all right.' She gave a choking sob then another. He turned her against his chest and stroked her back. 'Come on, Lyn, nothing bad happened.'

She lifted her eyes to his. 'Don't tell Michael I cried . . . it's just that being lost frightens me. I thought something had happened to her.' When Tim looked up, Mikey was standing right there.

'Don't be daft,' said Tim, 'he's right here – he's bound to notice the wet patch on my T-shirt if nothing else.' Lyn flung herself into Mikey's arms with a soft wail.

'Woman,' he whispered in her ear, 'stop your crying and tell me what's wrong.' She snuffled against his chest and he jerked his head at Tim. 'Right, there's nobody here but me . . . what's the matter, dear heart?'

'I suppose everything. I didn't stay at the entrance. I thought Krystal was lost . . . I mean really lost. You won't understand . . . Then Tim startled me and then you caught me and him . . .' More tears choked her voice. He picked her up and carried her across the waste ground to a scruffy area of grass and over-grown shrubs. 'Listen, Mikey, it was my fault . . . he was just trying to comfort me.' He looked at her with resignation.

'Darling Lyn, you are my wife, I trust you. You look very sexy when you cry. Unfortunately I have a barbecue to cook, so all we have time for now is some basic comforting.' He dug out a water bottle and handed it to her. 'How's your stomach?'

'Better, I think.'

'Good.' He kissed her eyelids and her nose. She reached up and kissed him passionately and he laughed. 'Stop, sweetheart, you'll get us arrested.'

She pulled back immediately, dug out a tissue and blew her nose. 'OK, business as usual.'

95

'It's our six-month review today.'

'I know.'

'I'm going in to work for a couple of hours so I'll meet you there – 11.15 OK?'

'Sure.'

'You all right?'

'Of course.'

'OK then, Lyn, I just wanted to say that if anything comes up that you're not sure about, just let me deal with it, OK?'

'What sort of thing?'

'Anything. Remember, I'm the husband.'

'Fine. Do you want some more toast?'

He smirked. 'Do you know that your mouth goes all squashed in when you're annoyed?'

'I'm not annoyed.'

'Good.'

Actually she was terrified and when he'd gone she sat at the table drinking her coffee and frowning over the possible questions. Her review with Greg had been over in a flash – they'd discussed compatibility and household management and it had all been quite unalarming. She supposed the questions would be much the same this time. It just seemed more serious.

At the centre, Mikey was waiting for her in the atrium with a big smile and a hug. 'OK, sweetheart?'

'Of course.'

He held her hand and gave her a reassuring grin. 'You can't be as nervous as I am, I hate things like this.' Their

279

appointment flashed up on the screen before she could reply. 'That's us.' He steered her into a cubicle and introduced himself to the young man in a suit who was already sitting there staring at the on-desk screen. With incredible speed the interview was in progress. They covered the basics in minutes, Mikey answering with an easy confidence while Lyn sat and fidgeted. Under the desk his hand found hers. The interviewer was clicking the screen while watching both of them – obviously a knack, she thought.

'Now . . . that's fine so far. If we could move on to house-hold management. Perhaps, Mr Jones, you could let your wife handle this section of the questions?'

Mikey smiled blandly. 'Yes.'

Lyn coughed and sat up straighter.

'Now . . . Lyn. You live in a house? That's right? With a garden at the back?' He didn't give her a chance to comment but carried straight on. 'Who looks after general maintenance?' This time there was a pause and actually it was quite easy to explain that she did the decorating and cleaning and looked after the garden and Mikey handled heavy or complicated things such as mending the washing machine and mowing the grass.

'I see.' She knew immediately that there was something wrong with her answers but she couldn't work out what and anyway the questions were still coming. 'And the cooking?' She hesi-tated. 'Lyn? The cooking?'

'I . . . I shop and, of course, I cook . . . it's just that . . .'

Mikey squeezed her hand. 'Sorry to interrupt . . . I'm a chef so sometimes, if I'm working on a recipe, I cook.' Suddenly he grinned at her. 'She's not the best cook in world, are you, sweet-heart?' Lyn shook her head, shamed. 'But I tell you what,' Mikey continued, 'she makes an onion stew to die for.'

'Onion stew?' murmured the young man. 'I don't think I've ever had that.'

And suddenly it was all OK. Lyn glared at Mikey and said, 'I'm sorry – he thinks he's being funny. In a minute he'll tell you about how I tried to peel a banana with a cleaver and the chocolate cake I cremated. But I handle the shopping because he's at work and I can do the basics like eggs and I'm good at carrots.' Mikey actually laughed and the young man smiled politely.

'Good, that's cleared up then. What about relaxation, Mr Jones?' And so it went on for a further thirty minutes, nothing too awkward and certainly nothing they couldn't answer.

'Nearly there now . . . just one other thing. I see you've applied for a family licence.'

'Yes,' said Mikey, 'we thought we'd get things moving.'

'Good idea, it can take a couple of months to come through. Lyn . . .' He suddenly stared at her disconcertingly. 'How do you feel about that?'

'We're both very keen,' said Lyn, firmly.

'It's just that obviously Mr Jones has a very strong family base with experience of younger siblings but you have no experience at all.'

'I know that but I'm happy to take any centre recommended training and I really don't want to wait.' There was more clicking on the screen then he studied both of them. 'Mr Jones, Lyn, I see no reason for not starting the licencing process at this stage but I have to warn you that there may be a number of interviews to follow. You can collect the Stage 1 paperwork from reception on your way out. Lyn, just let me take a look at your medicard to make sure it matches what we've got on file.'

Lyn gulped. 'I'm sorry, I don't have it.'

'You knew you were supposed to bring it with you?'

'Yes. I'm afraid I've lost it.'

Another glance at the screen. 'But you haven't applied for a new one?'

'Actually,' said Mikey, 'she has. Well, I have. We had a break-in and both our medicards and passports were taken, plus a few other bits and pieces. If you check my data file it should be on there.'

There was a pause. 'Ah, yes, here we are. Well, you'll be relieved to hear that everything has been cleared and you should have your new "bits and pieces" in the next couple of days.' His gaze switched to Lyn. 'You weren't aware of this break-in?'

'It was when the fence came down, Lyn,' said Mikey.

'Well, I knew the fence had been damaged . . . it happened while I was at the animal hospital with Spike, our cat, but no, I didn't know we'd lost anything.' She looked at Mikey. 'Why on earth didn't you tell me?'

'I didn't want you to worry – I've sorted out improved security but I didn't want you to feel nervous while I was at work.'

'That's ridiculous! You've just made me look a complete idiot!'

The interviewer interrupted. 'Well, I think that wraps it up for now. You obviously have a mutually supportive relationship, so best of luck with your family licence.' They all stood up. 'Just one other thing. Curiosity really. You seem very compatible which, under the circumstances, people could think unusual?'

Lyn smiled broadly across the cubicle at him. 'Oh I know.' Mikey tensed and swore under his breath. 'On the face of it,' she paused, 'on the face of it, I'm the one with the near-genius IQ and Mikey had to take additional studies at college to get his diploma.' She smiled again. 'But he's definitely the one with all the brains.'

'I see. Well, I think we can say that you've certainly passed your probation – both of you.'

Dylan was waiting for them. 'How very well done, you two,' he observed. 'Mikey, you are a very quick thinker, Lyn is quite right. However did you slip through the centre intelligence net at Year 10 screening?'

'I wanted to be a chef.'

'Hmm . . . odd. Still, if you fancy a change of scene we can certainly use those quick reactions in the service.'

Mikey nodded.

'And Lyn, good lord! I thought poor young Adam was going to faint – a "near genius IQ"! You are a smart girl, aren't you? Most people simply go to pieces at that question, especially in your circumstances.'

'And what circumstances would those be, Dylan?'

He laughed and patted her on the shoulder. 'Like I said, you're a smart girl. Now, I must press on but just remember, if you need anything, I'm your man.' He walked back into the depths of the building.

'Come on, let's go home.'

'Don't you have to go back to work?'

'No. I've taken the rest of the day off to celebrate our first six months.'

They left the centre and he dropped an arm over her shoulders. 'What did Dylan mean, he's "your man"?'

'It's just something he says, he doesn't really mean anything by it.'

His grip tightened. 'You've got me to take care of you.'

'Yes, I know. But what was all that about our passports going missing?'

'I thought it sounded more authentic if all our documents had been stolen, not just your medicard, which wouldn't really be any use to anyone but could get you into trouble.'

'But how did you know it was missing? I thought I'd lost it.'

'I was just checking that Judith hadn't helped herself to anything that could cause a problem.'

'So where are our passports?'

'Like I said, they were stolen. Now, where shall we go to celebrate?'

96

'Judith, baby, are you awake?' Something in his tone made her suspicious. She stretched languorously, sweetly enough to encourage any young stud to try his luck, but kept her eyes shut and breathed deeply. After a pause she heard him leave the room. She had been with Sam for a couple of months and he was adorable in his youth and energy. No wonder Lyn liked her cook . . . young skin and all that. Still, it was probably time to get shot of him . . . he was a bit of a distraction and, now she came to think of it, he had lasted longer than her usual.

She supposed that he'd gone out for coffee and pastries but why did she have to be asleep for him to do that? She sat up and looked around his room. His holster was slung over the chair, so obviously he was coming back, but the coffee place was only across the street so what was taking so long? She got out of bed and looked out of the window. He was nowhere in sight. She dived for her uniform then turned her attention to his holster.

Sam clattered back up the stairs five minutes later with coffee, pastries and a newspaper. He froze in the doorway. Judith was sitting on the bed, fully dressed, pointing his gun at the door.

'New game, baby?' he asked but his voice gave him away.

Judith sighed. 'It's a shame . . . I was going to dump you and then I found this.' She tossed his intelligence ID pin on to the floor in front of him. 'What I'd like to know is why you're investigating my team . . . or is it just me?'

He didn't reply, simply reached out slowly and put his purchases on the chair. His soft brown eyes gazed at her. 'I wish I could have told you, Judith, but I simply couldn't. This has nothing to do with you ... with us. You know how I feel about you.'

She ran her fingers up and down the barrel of the gun but kept it pointing towards him. 'Oh, Sam, you've been very careless, haven't you?'

He took another step forward and gave her an appealing shrug. 'You're wasted in security,' he smiled. 'I knew you'd find me out in the end. Come here ... forgive me?'

She smiled back and sighed. 'Oh, baby boy.' She could see that he wasn't fooled any more than she was.

He took one more step forward and she blinked up at him. 'Hey,' he whispered, 'you had me worried there for a moment.' His hand went out for the gun and she shot him in the leg.

'Christ!'

'Like I always say, trust your gut instinct – you should have run. You know, Sam, there isn't any point in killing you and I don't think I've hit anything major but you'll have your hands full, stopping the bleeding and calling for back up.' He was struggling on the floor and as she stepped over him he grabbed her sleeve. 'Oh, please don't try and pin a trace on me.' She flicked the silver bug on to the floor and dug his mobile out of his pocket. She placed it on the windowsill and gave him one last glance. 'Interesting, isn't it? Should you sort your leg out first or go for your mobile?'

And she was gone.

97

Have I made a mistake? Everyone in the family adores her. They think she's funny, clever, kind, hopeless in the kitchen and great to have around. Dad flirts with her, teases her and treats her like a slightly older version of Krystal. Mum thinks she's her new best friend, shares recipes with her, helps with plans for the garden, advises her on a thousand unimportant things about running the home and gets her to help out at the animal house when they're pushed. Jack talks to her about college and girlfriends and asks when he's stuck on an essay and Tim is always hanging around her, offering to help carry her bags and make her coffee.

As for Krystal, she thinks that Planet Cool originated in our house. She's always up in the loft finding more stuff of Lyn's: cushions and throws and bits of material and odd little ornaments. She's started wearing scarves and boots and bouncing around instead of doing that teenage girl loafing thing.

And I just don't know any more. I was understanding at the beginning – she'd had a shock and Greg had obviously been a complete bastard to her. Basically I suppose she'd had the stuffing kicked out of her. So I was comforting and I looked after her when she got upset and that stage passed pretty quickly. But she still wasn't like she was at college – it was as if that had all been an act and now she was all dependent and silly and couldn't do things. But that wasn't right either because it turned out she could do quite a lot, so she was just playing at being a young married. Well, of course she was! She'd been married before, hadn't she, and she was hardly young.

Then all this stuff with Judith. I could tell immediately that Judith was barking mad, possessive and obsessed with a nasty streak a mile wide, so why couldn't Lyn? Because she didn't want to? Because she was lying to me about what had really gone on in that home? And what about Dylan? Why is he always in the picture?

Even the team at the restaurant are always asking after her or sending her cakes home. If she drops in I hardly get to speak to her these days. But didn't I want a wife who was popular and interested in what I did?

Christ! What is my problem? She's attractive, compliant, says she loves me, tries to please me, and isn't afraid of a good argument now she's got used to them. Just, since the six-month review, I don't believe in her. I've married someone who just turns into whoever she thinks I want her to be at the time.

98

Dylan was annoyed. 'Your bloody woman has shot one of my team and done a runner.'

The head of security nodded, lined up for the next target and fired. 'Not bad.'

'Hmm . . . it sounds to me as if your lad made a bit of a mess of things.'

'A mess of our flat anyway – it looked like an abattoir. Actually, he did pretty well. He's only young which is why I chose him for it – she likes them young – and he managed to get two traces attached to her before stopping the bleeding and calling for back-up. Three if you count the decoy.'

Dylan lined up and fired.

'Impressive,' said the head of security. Dylan nodded. 'I keep in practice.'

'So, did he find anything out? Anything useful, that is.'

'Apparently she is spending most of her time off stalking my girl and her husband. The problem is that even if you transfer her she'll keep making her way back. Oh, and she's very good in bed, so she finds it easy to win friends and influence people. On the plus side she's not that bright, so although her skills are good she doesn't hide her tracks very well.'

The head of security nodded, lined up for the next target and fired. 'Better, I think.'

Dylan looked and nodded. 'Excellent, I'd say. So, what to do next?'

'What is your interest here?'

'Painfully obvious, I'm afraid. I find Mrs Jones of special

interest and I want to keep her in one piece. If your team let me down there could be a problem.'

'Hmm . . . have your people located her?'

'Yes. She's under close surveillance but I think we need to decide what to do with her before we bring her in.'

Dylan lined up and fired.

'Oh Lord,' said the head of security. 'Drinks on me I suppose then?'

'Undoubtedly. And our . . . problem?'

'She'll have to go down. Shame but there it is. I'd suggest maximum security and some serious therapy.'

'Fine.'

99

It was humid. The air was heavy with heat and damp. Lyn was sitting on the kitchen sofa with Spike and a cold can of beer. The French doors were open but there wasn't a breath of air. Spike stretched and thudded to the floor. He sniffed and headed out into the darkness of the garden. 'Don't be long, Spike,' she called after him. She'd pulled her hair up off her neck but was still unpleasantly warm. Mikey was due home soon and she ought to be thinking about a snack for him but she couldn't face the thought of cooking. Anyway, she told herself, he's probably caught something on the run at the restaurant or maybe he'll bring a salad.

She wandered over to the sink to splash her face with cold water then opened the fridge. Lemonade, she thought, I can make lemonade, no problem. She dug out a jug and found the citrus juicer. Seconds later she had lemons and sugar assembled. Without thinking about it she prepared a basic syrup, combined it with lemon rind and juice, tasted it – added water and ice cubes and set the jug in the fridge. Good lord, she thought, I've made something without an injury and it tastes fine. Whenever did I learn to do that?

She sank down on the sofa and opened her book. There was an abrupt flash of lightning and roar of thunder that made her jump, then a hissing cascade of rain. She jumped up. 'Spikey-Spike,' she called, 'come in now.' The raindrops were enormous, splashing up from the patio and soaking her jeans as she hovered half in and half out. She could see Spike huddled under a shrub halfway down the garden. Bloody cat, she thought,

290

doesn't want to get his fur wet. She ran out into the storm, grabbed him and ran back to the house.

Spike growled and struggled but as soon as she put him down went and sat by his food station. Lyn sighed. Her shirt was soaked, her jeans were soaked and her bare feet were cold and muddy. On the plus side she felt cooler than she had for hours. 'Listen, Spike, if you count between the flashes and the noise you can tell how far away the storm is.' Spike looked totally disinterested. She went and stood looking out across the lawn – there was a splintering flash of blue light followed by a huge roll of sound. Then all the lights went out.

Lyn took a pace back. She pulled the French doors closed and locked them. She took another pace back. The lightning flashed again. There was a shape in the garden. She felt her heart thud against her ribs. She slid further back into the darkness of the house. Her mouth was completely dry. She slipped through the kitchen door and stopped to listen. Nothing.

Upstairs she approached the window with caution. The lightning was flickering and exploding almost continuously. She flattened herself against the wall and peered out. The garden was empty. She drew a deep breath of relief. Honestly, she thought, your imagination is just running haywire. She glanced out again and stiffened in shock. A figure was suddenly outlined on the back fence. As she watched, it dropped out of sight. She flew downstairs and double-locked the front door. Then she sat on the stairs.

Minutes later she heard rattling at the door followed by an irate yell. 'Open up, sweetheart, I'm drowning out here and I've got a *niçoise* for you.'

She leapt for the door and flung her arms round him.

'Hang on, what did I do to deserve that? Oh, darling, I forgot – you don't like the dark, do you? Half the city's out but at least it's a bit cooler.' He wrapped her in his arms and grinned. 'You're soaked through, sweetheart – come on, let's find some candles then you'll feel better.' He shepherded her into the kitchen. Moments later the walls were glowing in candlelight and he'd found a torch. 'There you go – hang on to this.'

'Mikey.'

'In a moment, just let me get some plates and . . . hey, what's this? Lemonade – great.'

'Mikey . . .'

'Right, here we go – can't do any garlic bread but I'm sure we'll survive.'

'Mikey . . .'

'What?'

'There was someone in the garden.'

'Who?'

'I don't know – they left over the back fence.'

'When?'

'Just before you got back. When all the lights went out.'

He regarded her thoughtfully.

'Don't you believe me?'

'I believe you all right, I just can't think what they were doing.'

'Watching.'

He nodded. 'Nothing we can do tonight . . . we'll check for any damage in the morning and report it.' He rubbed her back. 'You think it was Judith, don't you?'

'Yes.'

The thunder rumbled on, moving away across the city.

100

Dylan sounded cool and efficient on the mobile. 'Just calling to update you on the situation re Judith,' he announced. 'I thought you'd like to know that centre security have reviewed her case load and her secondment to North Division has been extended so you won't be seeing her about.'

'How long is she seconded for?'

'Now, Lyn, you know I can't go into centre security arrangements.'

'I'm just asking for an idea.'

'I understand that but I can't tell you. It would be a breach of security. By the way, I see that you've been spreading your gifts among the catering community.'

'I have?'

'Oh, Lyn, it hasn't gone unnoticed that a certain kitchen porter has done exceptionally well in his LSQ Certificate – another three marks and he could well have qualified for an exemption. Now don't tell me you had nothing to do with it.'

'No, I won't tell you that, but we haven't had the results through yet.'

'Ah well, I have friends in high places.'

'Dylan, what exactly is your job? You seem to be involved in everything.'

'You don't need to know. Now – are you planning to tutor him through his entry to basic training? That will be a much longer commitment you know.'

'Yes, I know, we've agreed that I can do it.'

'And which "we" are we talking about here?'

'Mikey and me, naturally. You must know, Dylan, that I can't agree anything without prior permission from my husband.'

'Put those claws away, my dear, I was just checking that you understood a separate permission is required for each new qualification.'

'Dylan, you know what I said about Judith killing Greg?'

'Hmm . . .'

'She told me she'd done it.'

'Really?'

'Well . . . it was a very strong hint. She thinks it puts me under an obligation.'

'Lyn, listen to me. It was all very thoroughly investigated at the time and I've reviewed the records. There is nothing to suggest that it was anything other than an accident. Remember that we have the meditech's report as well. Also, my dear, we have their report on your condition.'

'Oh. Well, I'm so clumsy.'

'Lyn, it takes a particular kind of clumsy to end up with a black eye, cracked ribs and a split lip, not to mention all the other bruises.' He paused. 'Perhaps you ought to come in for a chat . . . you sound anxious.'

'No, I'm probably just being silly. I think Judith rattled me.'

'Lyn, I'm not asking you to come in, I'm telling you. I think it's important. I'll put it on your data file.'

101

It was late when Lyn heard him fumbling with the door. She hopped out of bed and ran down to let him in, only to find Lucas on the doorstep leering at her.

'Hi, babe, want to join us in a nightcap?' He pushed past her and headed for the kitchen. She peered outside. Mikey was propped up against the wall staring at the stars.

'Mikey, come in at once.'

'It's beautiful . . . like velvet with holes. Why should I come in?'

'You can see it better from the garden, that's why.'

He pushed himself upright and swaggered past her. 'Hey, doll, you'd better get some clothes on if you're planning on entertaining us.'

'I'm perfectly OK, thanks.'

'You're in your night clothes . . . it's . . . umm . . . suggestible. I don't like it and I'm . . .'

'The husband. OK, I know. Give me a minute.' She left him making his way along the hall and galloped upstairs to pull on jeans, a long sleeved T-shirt and trainers. On the way out of the bedroom she paused, shot into the bathroom and tied her hair back severely before splashing her face.

The kitchen was empty but the French doors were swinging open . . . four steaks were lying on the worktop and she heard the distinctive noise of charcoal hitting the barbecue.

'No, Mikey, it's the middle of the night, we can't barbecue in the dark.'

'Says who, pretty lady?' Lucas lounged towards her.

'Why don't you stay out here and I'll fix you something in the kitchen?' she said, trying to find a smile but failing dismally. 'How about a toasted cheese sandwich with extra bacon and mayo?'

'Are you saying you can cook that?'

'Yes, Lucas, I can cook that.'

'How about a beer with us first?'

'How about you two have the beer out here – quietly – and I'll get on with the cooking.'

He looked at her quizzically. 'Never had you pegged as the domestic type.'

'Fine, Lucas, you've had your fun. Just sit down, have your beer and shut up.'

She stomped into the kitchen, took out two beers and turned. He was right behind her and grabbed her waist. 'I'm not as loaded as you think.'

'I couldn't care less how you are. Take these and keep out of my way.'

She watched him slope back out into the garden and then she put the steaks back in the freezer. They'll probably kill us when we do eat them, she thought, they've been in and out so many times.

Carefully she chopped lettuce, cut bread, grilled bacon and dug out some ready mixed mayonnaise. So far, so good. She made the toast, only slightly charred, then hesitated . . . What was she supposed to do with the cheese? She grated it over the lettuce that she'd already piled on the toast and stuck it under the grill for a few minutes. Then she added the bacon, a generous splodge of mayonnaise and popped another slice of toast on top.

The boys were lying on the grass naming constellations and giggling. 'Here you are, guys, toasted sandwiches.'

'Hey, looking good, Lyn.' Lucas smirked at her.

Mikey sat up, frowned, took a bite and frowned some more. 'What? Oh, I get it. Why have you cooked the lettuce, darling?'

'You're out of your skull and you're still a food critic? I don't believe you sometimes. Lucas isn't complaining.'

Lucas gave her a knowing smile. 'I'd never complain about you, baby. Now come and sit down with us for a minute. The night is young and beautiful.'

'Just for a minute. Once you've eaten that you're going to have to go home. We have plans for tomorrow.'

'Hey, I get the message but if you want me to go you'll have to persuade me.'

'I'll let Mitch do that.'

'He's in no state.' He edged towards her and put a hand on her knee. 'No state.'

She ignored him. His hand slid up her thigh.

There was a deep silence then Mikey erupted, scattering lettuce and bacon. 'Let go of her, she doesn't like it!'

Lucas instantly withdrew his hand. 'Sure, man, guess I'm drunker than I thought. Lyn, sincere apologies, really.' He stood up, dusted down his black jeans, grinned at them both. 'I'll catch you soon, my man.' He was gone.

Mikey lay back and groaned. 'Thank God I didn't have to fight him. I feel grim.'

'And you bloody deserve it. You didn't even let me know you were going out.'

He reached for her. 'Darling, I didn't mean to but I felt bad and I thought a drink would make me feel better, so I called Luke and we went to that western theme bar and I did feel better, for a bit.'

'Why did you need to feel better?'

'I'm not happy about you and Marvin.'

'Mikey, it's a really short course and you won't even know it's happening.'

'It's not that.'

'Then what is it?'

'You have to do what I say.'

Lyn looked away, head bowed. 'I know that, but you said it was OK.'

'I don't feel good about it.'

Her head came up and she smiled. 'But you will – it's going to make such a difference to him and that'll be because of you.'

'But I've realised that I don't like you being with any other man. I've turned possessive.'

'Thank goodness . . . my virtue is safe in your hands. Look – why don't we lock up and you can take a shower and we'll talk some more tomorrow.'

'Sorry. I've got another agenda.'

'Mikey, it's late – we're both tired.'

'Don't argue with me. You have to do as I say.'

'I . . .'

'You nothing, woman, just shut up.'

102

It resonated round her head. 'You nothing, woman, just shut up.' Of course he didn't mean it . . . he didn't mean that she was nothing but he was *in vino veritas* – he was just like Greg, really. They probably all are. Claire said I could refuse him and it would be OK but obviously not. She felt a dreadful, demeaning sorrow . . . she had thought she'd got the measure of him and suddenly he'd become someone else.

Someone who tore at her clothes in the middle of the night in the garden.

Someone who ignored her protests – although they had been pretty pathetic.

Someone who didn't care what she felt.

She had been right to be cautious.

'Lyn?'

She looked round and saw Judith.

'Lyn, what are you doing out here on your own?'

'On my own is the point, Jude. How did you find me?'

'Oh, I just tracked you on your mobile.'

'You could have rung me.'

'Sure, but you might not have picked up. Come on, I've brought coffee and doughnuts. Now what's the big trauma?'

'There's no trauma.'

'You look as if you've seen a ghost.'

'Well, I didn't think you were around. I haven't heard from you for ages.'

'No, I know. I got a posting to the north. It's great, actually, but I'm on leave this week so I thought I'd drop back and see what was going on.'

'Judith, why are you tracking me?'

'What do you mean?'

'Come on, you know we found the bugs, you've made dodgy entries on my data file at the centre. You've threatened my cat. Threatened me. Taken my medicard. What's it about?'

'Oh dear, has it been bothering you?'

Lyn stared out across the woods. She was sitting on a swing in the playground that was next to the dump. It was on the edge of the city and had a great view of the surrounding countryside, or that was what they'd always been told. She broke off a piece of doughnut and chewed thoughtfully.

'Yes, because I don't understand it.'

Judith leant back on her swing. 'I've told you before, I don't take disappointment lightly.'

'But what are you disappointed about? Why can't you leave me alone?'

'Why should I? I'm your best friend.'

'Not any more, you're not.' She was unable to stop herself glancing round the deserted play area.

Judith shrugged. 'There's no one around to save you.'

'Jude, just think about what you're saying. You're acting as if you're obsessed with me . . . '

Judith's eyes narrowed and she took a noisy slurp of coffee. 'You think I'm obsessed? What about that husband of yours, that cook – he won't let you out of his sight.'

Lyn shook her head. 'I'm out of his sight right now.'

'And that's because you've run away. Oh, I know it's just for this morning. If you scurry back home he won't even realise you've gone.' The bitterness in her voice was startling. Lyn turned to look at her.

'Jude, what is it?'

'You owe me, don't forget. Or is this another one of your convenient memory lapses?'

'Jude, I genuinely don't know what you mean. What do I owe you?'

Judith looked up at the sky. 'He's hurt you, hasn't he?'

'No, of course not. Mikey would never hurt me.'

'Yes, he has. I can see it. Don't panic, I don't know exactly what he's done and I don't want to. I can still get rid of him, you know, one way or another. I've done it before, as you know.'

Lyn stiffened. 'What are you talking about?' she whispered.

Judith smiled. 'Darling Greg – you don't really think he slipped in the bath?'

After a moment Lyn looked up. Judith's empty swing was swaying in silence.

103

Lyn staggered to her feet and looked round. Judith had definitely gone, her discarded paper coffee cup the only sign she'd ever been there. Automatically Lyn retrieved the litter and binned it. The sky was still pale blue, delicate clouds bouncing across the surface, the trees rippling in the wind. She felt completely alone and totally exposed. Abruptly her legs wobbled and she dropped to her knees and threw up violently. She wanted to scream but was afraid somebody might hear her so she shoved her knuckles into her mouth instead.

Greg had drowned in the bath. He'd sent her downstairs to start dinner and while she was cooking, Judith had arrived. She'd helped Lyn and settled her on the kitchen sofa with a drink. Lyn had started to worry that Greg hadn't come down to see who was there, so Judith had gone upstairs to check and come down with the terrible news that he was lying in the bath, dead. The post mortem had shown that he'd had a considerable amount to drink and there were signs of a slight blow to the back of his head consistent with striking it on the rim of the bath.

But that couldn't be right ... Judith wouldn't have gone upstairs, she would have gone herself. She searched her memory. No, she hadn't seen Greg dead in the bath, she was sure of that. What had happened?

Unhappily she got to her feet and walked over to the edge of the playground where she leant on the wire fence. She looked across at the woods and began to reconstruct what she could.

She had made a big mistake that day. Unusually, Greg had

302

decided that they'd stay in and he wanted fish for dinner. The fish at the food place hadn't looked good so she'd got chicken but she hadn't told him when she got home with the shopping. He'd discovered it later in the fridge. At first he'd seemed OK about it. He'd had one drink, then another, then he'd started to beat her. It had taken a while but in the end they'd gone up to bed and afterwards he'd literally kicked her down the stairs.

Although she was more bruised and frightened than seriously hurt, she had looked dramatic with a swelling eye, sluggishly bleeding nose and a puffy split lip. For once Greg had really lost his temper. She'd been wondering exactly what to do with the chicken when she felt a truly awful pain in her side, so bad that she started to feel faint. That scared her more than anything. In panic, she rang Judith for help.

Judith had been brilliant. With a muttered, 'That bastard,' she'd come round immediately, taken Lyn into the kitchen, wiped away the blood, reassured her that feeling faint was quite normal under the circumstances, found her some aspirin and finally tucked her up on the sofa. She must have slept because when she awoke Judith was on her mobile requesting a medivan and a security unit. She had jerked up and taken a nervous gulp of the wine Judith held out to her.

'I don't need a medivan, Jude, I'm fine. Please don't – Greg will be furious.'

And Judith had turned with a strange expression on her face and said calmly, 'It's not for you. It's for Greg. I think he's had an accident.'

The wire fence was digging into her hands. She straightened up and began to jog back home.

104

She felt completely alone as she hovered in the kitchen doorway. She'd hoped that Mikey would have still been in bed but now she'd have to explain her absence and why she was shivering. 'I'm sorry,' she started. 'I didn't want to wake you and I haven't been very long.'

He shook his head. 'Don't – it doesn't matter.'

Lyn studied him – he looked hungover and depressed. He hadn't actually looked at her. 'I just went for a walk . . . and a think.'

'Sure.'

'I fed Spike before I went out.'

'Lyn, did I hurt you?'

'Yes, you did.'

'What can I do?'

'I'm not sure. Telling me you didn't mean to might help.'

He took another gulp of cold coffee. Looked back at her. 'I made a mistake. I apologise. It's not been a problem before.'

'I've never said "no" before.'

'True enough. I can't say I didn't mean it, though. I was just making sure of you. But I am truly sorry.'

'Making sure of me? Are you crazy? Don't you know what you did?'

'Woman, don't you know what you are to me?'

'I sincerely hope you're not expecting me to answer that.' She turned away, suddenly feeling completely exhausted.

'OK, let's cut the crap,' he burst out. 'I'm not a bloody saint. I was annoyed. Then I was drunk. Then my best friend made a pass at you in front of me. Forget the rules, forget what should and shouldn't happen. I'm sorry I made you do it when I knew you didn't want to. End of. Now stop sulking.'

'You think I'm sulking?'

'Yes! I want to get through all this. I don't want you moping about the place. I want you to be happy with me. I thought you were.' He shook his head. 'It's not as if I hit you. I love you.'

'I'm not moping!' she spun back. 'Or sulking! I'm tired and I'm a bit fed up and that's all. If this is your idea of an apology you'd better think again, because it's rubbish. You think you can get round me with a few sad looks from your big brown eyes and no doubt in a minute you'll be suggesting a quick cuddle and some make-up sex and it'll all be over. Well, you can just sod off until I've calmed down. I'm fed up with everyone at the moment and you are top of the list.'

He stood up and caught hold of her. His hands cupped her face. 'I've apologised. If it happens again just kick me where it hurts. I mean it.' He pulled her forward and kissed her. He caressed her throat, stroked her neck. 'I selected you because you mean a lot to me. I'm jealous, but that's the way it is.'

She was boiling with rage. 'Let go of me – you have no bloody idea!' She pushed him away, gritted her teeth, kept her mouth shut. Something was wriggling to the surface of her mind, something to do with Judith who had had a mother for her first six years . . . a mother who had always believed her partner when he said he wouldn't ever hit her again.

'Oh God. I've got to call the centre.'

'What?' He was stroking her hair now, running his fingers through it, tugging gently on the ends.

'Stop fiddling about with me, Mikey, I've got to call the centre.'

'Wait a moment – are we OK now?'

'Not until you've worked on that apology.' She took her mobile into the living room.

105

Dylan rang back. 'Even counsellors have days off, you know,' he complained gently.

'Sorry, Dylan, it's just that Judith is back. She says she's on a break and she tracked me down this morning. Anyway, I thought of something about the dump – when we were there, I mean – and I didn't know if it was important.'

'You're going too fast for me, Lyn. Did you report Judith to the centre?'

'I tried but the autosystem just puts me through to you all the time. It needs checking. Anyway, it's not as if she isn't allowed to be here, is it? And she didn't really do anything. And I think I know what her problem is.'

'Oh yes – and what's your diagnosis?'

She frowned at the faintly sarcastic tone of his voice but pressed on anyway. 'She was only left at the dump when she was six. Up until then she lived with her mother.'

'And your point is?'

'She missed the early training modules but she was too young for the catch-up courses. She's not been properly socialised.'

'So?'

'Well, I don't know. I just think that's had a bad effect on her. She thinks she doesn't have to follow the rules. Dylan,' her voice shook, 'I think she might have killed Greg.'

His booming laugh made her jump. 'Lyn, my dear, leave the psychoanalysis to the experts, please. Let's just deal with the facts. Judith is still stalking you and that's what we have to deal with. I'll alert her team leader who will take the appropriate steps. I suggest you just carry on as normal and just let us know if anything untoward happens. As for killing Professor Langdale ... I believe the post mortem proved that he was drunk, slipped and drowned in the bath. And a good thing too,' he added.

'What did you say?'

'I said he was a great loss to society as well as you,' he replied smoothly and hung up. She thought she might explode with rage and terror.

'Bloody men!'

Mikey was hovering with a coffee and an appealing expression. She scowled. 'Just go away.'

'How long will you be cross for?'

'I don't know. I'm out of practice but judging by how I feel now it could be days.' She took a gulp and choked. 'My God! What have you done to the coffee?'

'It's a treat – Gaelic – I've put Scotch in it, and sugar.'

'It's bloody disgusting. I hate Scotch and you know I don't take sugar. Why didn't you ask first!' He went to hold her and she leapt away.

'Keep off. I don't want anything to do with you.'

'Darling, what's going on?'

'Nothing you want to know about – just get back to your bloody kitchen.' She lay back on the sofa and reached for the remote.

106

I'd seriously misjudged the situation. I felt genuinely terrible about my behaviour but from past experience Lyn would quote the rules at me and make it her fault and that would somehow get me off the hook. Plus she'd gone out again without telling me and that gave me the upper hand. I thought about what she'd said and an icy feeling suddenly flooded through me. I'd thought that just her feelings were hurt but now I thought about what had actually happened and I felt like a complete asshole.

She flinched every time I touched her, and she was right – I'd made a pathetic excuse for an apology and she had every right to be angry. She could even report me, although she probably wouldn't get very far with it. She hadn't struggled much but I'd been too rough all the same.

Then I thought a fancy coffee would calm her down. I was crazy. I winced – I'd been really crass. She could read me like a book.

I wanted to call Dad to see what I could do but then he'd want to know what I was apologising for and it would get back to Mum and all hell would break loose. I had to solve this for myself.

I stuck my head round the living room door. Part of me was still indulging in a hopeful fantasy of female apologies and snuffles. Oh well, forget that then. The entertainment screen was showing some hideous thing where a beautiful woman was trying to write in the sand with a stick but both her hands had been cut off. As I watched, the camera zoomed in on her face and her tongue had been cut out as well. I hesitated for a moment – it sounded like more Shakespeare but surely not . . .

'I'm going out.'

'Good.'

'I won't be too long.'

'Take as long as you like.'

'Will you be OK on your own?'

'What do you think?'

'Right, I'm off then.'

I was going to buy flowers, lots of them. I knew she liked them and I thought I'd get some things in pots for the front as well.

When I let myself back in, it was quiet. She was asleep upstairs, tightly curled up with a throw pulled over her shoulders and her face buried in the pillow. I watched her for a while then went back downstairs to sort out the flowers and see about something to eat. I thought about what Marvin had said: 'If she's upset she won't want anything too heavy.' I knew she wasn't keen on too much seasoning but she liked courgettes and soufflés and salad. I dithered about, slicing and separating and tasting and leaving things to rest under foil. I unearthed the steamer then put it away again. I found frozen raspberries and made a coulis, then didn't know what dessert to make to go with it. I decided to arrange the flowers instead and made a genuinely ham-fisted mess of them, so put them all back in the bucket on the floor.

I sat at the table. Spike came and sat with me. We waited.

About an hour later she came downstairs.

107

'What are you doing?'

'Waiting for you.'

'What are these?'

'Flowers for you.'

She looked at the work surface. 'What's happened here?'

'Oh, that – trying to cook dinner.'

Alarm flickered across her face. 'Are you ill? Have you cut yourself?'

'No, darling, I just couldn't decide what to do so I stopped.'

Lyn slipped into the chair opposite him and took his hand. 'Perhaps you're more hungover than you realised.'

'No, I don't think so. I feel a bit strange but that's shame, I think.'

She held his hand to her cheek. 'You were the one who said normal people have rows and then get over it. I've every right to be angry. You know that I don't like being dominated and bullied.'

He was hot with embarrassment. 'I don't know what to say.'

'Let's just leave it for the moment.' She got up and went to feed Spike, who was regarding them both with a jaundiced eye. She went back to the table and pulled him to his feet. 'Let's go and sit in the living room for a while.'

They curled up together on the sofa. Mikey felt terribly tired and closed his eyes. Lyn snuggled up closer and waited until she knew he was asleep. She spread her fingers open on his chest and felt its rise and fall. She rested her head against his ribs and felt his heart beat. She thought he was probably still her kind, handsome, uncomplicated husband but she wondered how she could ever trust him again. Perhaps, she thought, I just have to live with things as they are. After all, he's usually very good. Or perhaps I could just try to be less subservient. Can you be obedient without being subservient? God, it's difficult.

In sleep, his face was that of the boy she remembered, the male arrogance and experience blotted away. She thought about Judith being mad. She thought about Greg being murdered. For a moment of true panic she wondered if she'd murdered him herself and then she remembered that she'd been barely able to move for the pain in her ribs. She thought that she might feel better if she made herself some tea but when she tried to get up, Mikey's arm tightened around her. 'Don't go,' he murmured, 'don't leave me.' Well, thought Lyn, if you only knew, sonny. It won't be me doing the leaving. As if.

'Don't leave me.' She reached up to kiss him and saw that his eyes were open. 'I know you think make-up sex would be too obvious but maybe we could try it anyway?' She shuddered at the mere thought . . . it was the last thing she wanted. She pulled away, considered him . . . had an idea.

'Now, I know that I'm not supposed to do this but for once in your life why don't you settle back down and see what happens next.'

108

'Where on earth did you learn to do that?'

'Come on, Mikey, you know you liked it – you were whimpering at one point.'

'That's because I was terrified.'

She smiled coldly. 'Good.'

'Seriously, I had no idea what you were going to do next. It could have been some hideous revenge attack.'

'You watch too many horror movies.'

'No, I don't – it was that awful thing you had on earlier if you must know. Anyway, if it wasn't in the training, how could you even think of it?'

'I'm very well read, as you know. All the great writers cover these things in enormous detail.'

'You're kidding.'

'No, my little mongoose, it's one of the perks of a university education.'

He sat up and frowned at her. 'You mean you've done it before?'

'No! Certainly not. I saved it for someone I thought would appreciate it.'

'How about Greg? He was very well read, wasn't he?'

'I don't think Greg would have enjoyed it. Anyway, what's for dinner?'

'I'm not sure. I started all sorts of things but I couldn't concentrate.' The hangdog expression was back in his eyes. 'Have you forgiven me yet?'

'No. I'll see what dinner tastes like first.' Her tone was caustic.

He snapped immediately. 'Come on, Lyn, I've apologised, we've had sex, enough is enough.'

She laughed in his face. 'Actually, Mikey, you've had sex, not me. And now I'm going to have a shower – alone – and then eat a delicious dinner specially prepared for me. Then I'll think about it. Oh, and another thing, it isn't always all about you, you know. Go on, get off me.' She slithered away, marched upstairs to the bathroom and slammed the door.

109

The table was properly set with a lace cloth and napkins. There were candles flickering and champagne on ice. There were blinis with flaked salmon and soft white cream cheese. A salad. A plate of melba toast. If it hadn't been for the flowers still languishing in their bucket she would have thought that she'd strayed into another dimension. It was a cliché waiting to happen. Speechless, she sat down and fingered the tablecloth, stared at the napkins.

'Champagne?'

She nodded. Mikey shoved the salad in her direction. 'Go on, eat something. I'm going to do soufflés but they can't go in until we're ready for them and I'm starving.'

'Souffles?'

'Yes – courgette and ricotta – and then I've done individual mushroom risotto with hot tomato salad, and miniature lemon tart with raspberry coulis.'

'But I've only been half an hour.'

'Well, I'd done most of it earlier. I just had to decide what to do with it.' He topped up her glass and forked two blinis on to her plate. They were delicate and wonderful. The champagne was dry and frothed enticingly.

'Mikey, are you trying to get me drunk?'

'Yes. By my calculations it should only take three glasses before you're well on the way and then everything will be much easier. How are the blinis? And the salad?'

'All very clever and delicious. I don't know what you've done to make it all taste so lovely.'

'It's the flavour combination. And the texture. If you try a bit of the salmon mix on some melba toast you'll see it's quite different.' He forked some on to the toast and held it out to her. 'Go on, try it. Then chase it down with the champagne – it should be just as good but different. Right – now which do you like best?'

She considered. 'I don't know – I like the texture of the toast but there's something about the flavour of the blinis.'

'OK, try a forkful of salad – that should be a great contrast.'

She sat back and held up her hand. 'Mikey, stop a minute. This is all wonderful but I don't understand what you think you're doing.'

'I'm treating you to a romantic experience I'm sure you've never had. I'm trying to get you relaxed quickly, then I'm going to make you drink fizzy water so you don't get a hangover. You'll enjoy the rest of the meal much more if you're not completely sober.'

'You're incorrigible. And it's not going to work. And where did this tablecloth appear from?'

'I thought we could use it for special occasions. I bought it this morning. Time to put the soufflés in, I think.' He jumped up, slid the tray into the oven and grabbed a second bottle of champagne on the way back to the table.

Lyn held her hand over her glass but before she could say anything he'd seized it and kissed it. Then he turned it over and kissed her palm. She looked into his eyes and felt ridiculous. 'I feel ridiculous.'

'That's because you're not relaxed enough . . . come on, Lyn, what was it you said? Just sit back and see what happens.'

Her soufflé was light and her risotto was slightly spicy, which made her drink more champagne. She switched to water for the dessert course. Mikey cleared the plates and handed her a cup of mint tea. He pulled his chair round so he could sit next to her and ran his fingers up and down her spine while she sipped her tea. Finally she twisted round to look at him.

315

'OK, I'm impressed . . . it was a lovely meal and I feel much better.'

'Good. I wanted to do something different that was just for you. I know you think it's just a particularly elaborate form of seduction but actually it's to set the scene.'

'For what?' She thought she could feel her bruises starting to throb as she tensed.

'This.' He reached into his pocket and produced a tiny black velvet box. 'Go on, open it.'

She clicked it open and stared.

'Do you like it?'

'It's very pretty . . . is it old?'

'Yes – they don't often make them now. No point, I suppose.'

'But what made you do it?'

'I went out to get you flowers to say sorry. Then I realised that I've never given you a present. I just selected you and married you and I was so excited I expected you to be excited too. It's all back to front but this is to say, will you marry me? I know,' he added hastily, 'I know you think that's nonsense because we're already married and you had no choice but this is about our feelings. I want to know that if I'd dated you first and all that then asked you to marry me, you'd have said yes. And I know it's still about what I want but I just can't seem to help it.'

'My God, you are romantic, aren't you?' She reached out and picked up the ring. 'So does this mean we're formally engaged?'

'You haven't answered me yet.'

'You haven't slipped the ring on to my finger against a background of swelling violins.'

He took the ring from her hand and slid it on to her finger. 'Sorry – no violins.'

'How did you get the size right?'

He frowned. 'It just looked the right size.'

'Hmmm . . . well then, it's a bit of a gamble but yes, I'll marry you.'

'And will you tell me the truth?'

'About?'

'About last night . . . and earlier this evening.'

She twisted the ring on her finger. 'You don't want to know – anyway, it's complicated. Like I said, it isn't all about you.'

'You said I'd hurt you – I want to know how much damage I've done.'

'Damage?'

'Lyn, I'm not an idiot. I know I hurt your feelings but it obviously isn't just that. You don't want me to touch you and I won't.' He looked down at the table. 'I don't know how to say this. I didn't mean to hurt you physically . . . you know. I didn't think. It's no excuse but I want to know if it's bad.'

She sighed. 'You let me down, that's the main thing. I've been through worse but not from someone I trusted. That's the difference. I'm disappointed in both of us.' She groaned. 'I need to tell you something else as well and I don't know how you'll react.'

'What?'

'I saw Judith this morning . . . that's why I rang Dylan. She's still following me.'

'Oh, baby.' His arms went round her. 'I'll have a word with him tomorrow, if you like, and see what the centre are doing about it.'

She was quiet for a moment – it all seemed quite useless to keep explaining the situation.

'I have this feeling of dread,' she said as clearly as she could. 'She's very dangerous.'

Mikey smiled and gave her a squeeze. 'I'll sort it out, darling.'

He was back in control and all was right with the world, she thought, glumly.

110

The sun was slanting through the curtains, dancing across the kitchen. Lyn sipped her orange juice and squinted across the lawn.

'Spike's doing something strange.'

'Huh?'

'No, really, look – he's running about, then flopping down and wriggling and jumping.'

'Lyn, you plank, he's playing. Well, actually he's practising hunting.'

'But what?'

'Something on the lawn . . . probably bees after the clover.'

'Won't they hurt him?'

'Only if he catches one. Now sit down and finish your breakfast . . . if you can call it breakfast,' he added under his breath.

'It said on the packet just add an egg and milk and whisk – I thought it'd be a nice change.'

'How about I knock up some real pancakes? It'll only take a minute and we'll be able to eat them.'

'Lovely. I'll just get some more orange juice, shall I?' Seconds later the floor was awash. 'Oh lord. I started this marriage able to cook all sorts of things and now I can't even get juice out of the fridge.'

'What happened?'

'The bottom's come out of the carton.'

'That probably isn't your fault, then. Anyway, lovely wife, what do you want to do today?' She looked blank. 'We're having a day off, remember? So what would you like to do?

OK, what did you do with Greg on your days off? There must have been something.'

She thought for a while – they had been an erudite, educated couple. 'We . . . we went to galleries, museums, things like that.' She thought about those trips . . . she was interested, all right, but something always seemed to happen to her brain when Greg began explaining things to her. He knew such a lot and he'd start talking in his measured, cultured tones about painterly technique or Eastern influences and she'd feel all the facts sliding out of her mind faster than she could capture them. Then she'd feel the faint stirrings of panic, knowing that he'd be disappointed when they got home and she couldn't remember everything, and he'd use that as an excuse to slap her around a bit.

She jumped when Mikey put an arm round her. 'Well, I can see that those trips were a big hit with you. What did he do – test you afterwards?'

'You're burning your pancakes.'

'No, I'm not.' Still, he turned to check and she carried on mopping the floor.

'Sorry. I know you don't like to talk about it. I just thought you might have gone swimming, or played badminton or hired bicycles or something like that.'

'Oh, sure,' she snorted. 'I can just see Greg on a bicycle or playing badminton. Enjoying himself. What he liked was attracting an admiring crowd as he lectured me at an exhibition. Then, flushed with success, he'd bring me back here and if I couldn't remember every little point in the correct order he'd beat me with the catalogue. He cracked a rib once. If it was a big catalogue I was in real trouble. The only time he let me off was because he'd forgotten to pick one up and couldn't find anything else in his collection that looked like a suitable replacement.'

She realised what she'd said and groaned. 'I know, it sounds completely insane.' She had a picture of Greg muttering furiously as he ransacked his collection for something close to the work of Lalique in order to force her to the floor and batter her with it. She sniggered. 'He even made me help him look for articles on glassware in case there was anything appropriate . . . I don't know what I was thinking.'

Mikey put the pancakes on the table. 'You'd better eat these before they go cold.'

'Thanks. I suppose I should have reported him, shouldn't I?'

'I'm too frightened to comment. How do you like the pancakes?'

'Delicious – you could take this up as a profession.'

'Very funny. If you haven't got any favourite diversions in mind, perhaps we could start off gently by going for a walk.'

'A walk?'

'Lyn, don't pretend you don't know what I'm talking about.'

'But where?'

'Along the river.'

'I can't swim.'

'You won't have to, although if I get fed up with you I can throw you in.'

'How will we get to the river – through the park?'

'No – according to that map you picked up there's a footpath more or less opposite our back fence. We'll just nip round to the service alley and back along the lane and there should be a stile. Come on, don't look so dubious – you'll like it.'

111

'You knew this was going to happen, didn't you?'

Mikey looked up from the kitchen table and stared. 'No, I swear ... does it hurt?'

'Yes.' She slumped down opposite him, tears in her eyes and moaned. 'It's so sore I don't know what to do with myself.' She put her head in her hands.

'Oh, darling, come here ... let me look.'

'No!' She shoved her chair back. 'No, don't touch me. I've been under a cold shower for twenty minutes and it still hurts. If you touch me you'll probably regret it for years! And don't laugh – there's nothing remotely funny about it.'

Her face was an interesting shade of pink but the back of her neck and her shoulders were bright red. 'I won't touch you but I think you need to put something on that – in the kitchen we'd use a wet tea towel.'

'OK.'

'Then you need to lie down.'

'Mikey, I can't possibly at the moment.'

'No, I meant just that: lie down.'

'That's what caused all the trouble in the first place.'

They'd been for a gentle saunter along the riverbank. Mikey had discovered a footpath that led from the lane behind the house across the fields down to the river and they'd wandered along until they found somewhere to sit and watch the ducks and the occasional boat passing by. The warm day had relaxed them both and inevitably she'd fallen asleep while he sat watching nothing much and making the odd note in his recipe pad. It had been almost an hour before he glanced over at her to see her shoulders turning a gentle pink. 'Lyn, wake up, you're burning!' By the time they'd made it home, the gentle pink had flushed to a dull red and now it looked even worse.

He handed her a cool, dripping tea towel and she winced as she draped it around her shoulders. 'Ohhh . . . I think I'm going to die!'

'Do you want me to call Mum? She might have some ideas.'

'No. I'm living on borrowed time with her already after the finger thing. Anyway, she'll only tell me to bathe in the blood of a virgin or drink nettle tea or something.'

'Christ!' He reached over and touched her forehead. 'I think you're delirious – you'd better have some aspirin and then go to bed.'

'I don't want to go to bed.'

'OK – come into the living room and lie on the sofa while I do some work on the recipe book.'

She trailed unhappily into the living room and lowered herself carefully on to the sofa. Immediately Spike appeared from nowhere and thudded heavily on to her legs. 'Get him off me.'

'Hush, woman, take your aspirin. Now let me get on.' He sat on the floor with his back against the sofa and flicked on the coffee table screen. Lyn drew a huffy breath . . . she thought she was actually sulking, which was something she never did although maybe she'd never had cause to before. As he started to tap away with one hand, he reached back with the other and clasped her ankle, rubbing his thumb over the bone. She found it surprisingly soothing and enormously aggravating at the same time. For a while she tried to puzzle this out but only got as far as thinking the ankle holding was rather like her stroking Spike at best and at worst was another sign of her complete capitulation before she dozed off.

Absorbed in writing about aubergine soufflé, Mikey registered that she was asleep and removed his hand, settling more comfortably into his work.

112

I needed a beer . . . in fact I needed several. Spike needed a can of tuna. 'OK, big fella, where's Mummy got to, huh?' Spike looked distant, as though my question was beneath him. I fed him anyway, because I am considerate like that. I found a beer and checked the time again. Where the hell was she? Admittedly I'd arrived home early but now it was way past my usual time and she hadn't said she was going anywhere. Why hadn't she left me a message? Was she doing something she thought I wouldn't like? I grinned to myself . . . like what, then? I decided to get dinner on the go, so began knocking up a clam sauce. The champagne at work had made me a bit sentimental and I was remembering the first time I cooked for her when I heard her keys rattling in the front door.

I bounded into the passage, pushed her against the wall as she came in and waved the wooden spoon in her face. Her eyes widened, 'Oh, Mikey, no!' she whispered. It was sexy as hell. I leant closer. 'No, really!' she hissed, looking over my shoulder. Pinning her to the wall, I glanced round. Krystal and Jack were standing frozen right behind me. It wasn't the most embarrassing moment of my life but it was right up there.

There was a silence for a second or two, then Jack dropped his rucksack, leapt at me and bellowed, 'Let go of her, you bastard!' Krystal added insult to potential injury by kicking my shins with her pointy shoes. I struggled to free myself without actually hurting anyone.

Lyn moved carefully to one side, then said, 'Relax, guys, it was your big brother's idea of a joke.' Nothing happened. Krystal carried on kicking and Jack carried on trying to get me in an arm lock.

'Lyn, say something!' I shouted. Instead she just started to laugh. 'Oh, great, that's really helpful. Stop it, you two!' We tussled round the passage a couple of times dislodging pictures and tripping over shopping, then Krystal gave Lyn a closer look.

'Is it hysterics? Should I slap you?' she enquired in helpful tones that just cracked me up. Lyn fended her off and retreated into the kitchen. Seconds later she was back with a handful of ice cubes that she thrust down Jack's neck.

'You're lucky it wasn't a bucket of water. I just didn't want to have to clear it up,' said my wife, severely. 'Now behave, both of you – there's something burning on the stove and we could all do with a drink. Juice for you,' she added pointedly, in Krystal's direction.

113

Jack was still bristling. He stared moodily at them over his beer. 'So what's so funny about pretend domestic violence?' he asked solemnly.

'Yes, what?' chimed in Krystal.

Lyn and Mikey, hovering at the stove, exchanged a guilty glance. 'Nothing, really,' Lyn said, 'it was just a silly thing.'

'That's right, mate, it's a private joke. I've got some good news so I thought I'd surprise Lyn.'

Lyn looked at him in amazement. 'So why not surprise me with flowers or something? Why attack me with a wooden spoon?'

'I was being romantic . . . you know, remembering our first meal together.'

'He hit you with a spoon on your wedding day?' gasped Krystal in awe. 'But why? Dad will go mental. So will Mum.'

'No, he didn't – like I said, it was just a silly joke. Now come on, guys, what did you come round for?'

'Oh yes, we're going to try out your recipe game.'

'Right, I'll just set things up and then I'll help Mikey with the supper.'

Jack gave her a tolerant smile. 'I think we can manage, actually.'

'Fine, then, off you go.'

The door closed behind them and Lyn looked at Mikey. He had his back to her and was busily stirring. She went over and leant against him, her arms round his waist.

'You were a big help,' he grumbled.

'Don't sulk, have we got enough to feed them as well?'

'Naturally.'

'Because if not I've got some cheese and tomatoes and potatoes.'

'Oh yes, and what will you make with that?'

'Cheese and potato pie with tomatoes.'

'You don't say.'

'Well – what would you make?'

He turned. 'Let's see – I'd skin the tomatoes and marinade them in a light dressing for thirty minutes.' His hands slid down her back. 'Then I'd grate the potatoes to make a rosti.' He trailed a finger up her spine. 'You're not paying attention.'

'Uh huh.'

'Then I'd knock up a cheese and herb soufflé – *et voilà* – soufflé *avec* tomato salad and rosti.' He walked her towards the table, sat down and pulled her on to his lap. 'But I won't be doing that.'

'And why not?'

'Because I'm doing this.'

A burst of laugher came from the living room. Lyn pushed him away. 'We'd better not – they're already scarred for life. Anyway, you don't want your linguine to go soggy.'

He gave her a thoughtful look. 'You are a hard woman.'

'I'm a hungry woman. And you haven't told me your news yet.'

He was gratified that she'd remembered to ask. 'It'll keep until later.' He hesitated. 'Lyn, would you really have liked flowers?'

'Ask your mum, we women always like flowers.'

'Rather than jewellery and things?'

'Why?'

He delved in his pocket. 'Well, I got you this.'

'This' was a very smooth, polished piece of translucent pink stone.

'Rose quartz,' she murmured, running her fingers over it.

'I don't know what it is,' he admitted, 'but I thought you'd like it.'

'It's a palm crystal,' she said. 'It's to hold if things get bad because it's soothing. Where did you find it?'

'In the jewellers – at the back, not in the window.'

'You are very surprising sometimes,' she said.

114

They were lying in the garden under the apple trees. The sky was unusually blue with bright white puffy clouds scudding about overhead. Lyn had her eyes shut against the glare. Mikey was carefully unplaiting her hair and teasing it out through his fingers.

'You haven't told me your news yet.'

'No. We've hardly had a moment alone since it happened.'

'So, we're alone now.'

'We've been given a training contract for the restaurant.'

'I thought you trained your team anyway?'

'Yes, but this means we can take on outside students from other restaurants as well as training our own. Lyn, it means that we can develop courses and award our own qualifications. It means more funding from the centre. It means we can train people like Marvin in-house. It's a huge boost to our reputation.'

She rolled over. 'You are so smart. How did you do it? It can't have just happened out of nowhere.'

'Your incredibly smart and good-looking husband toiled away in his lonely office compiling a bid for the funding. Developing the recipe book really helped as well. It meant we could offer a range of training levels from the basics right the way up.'

'Does this mean that you will be training Marvin once he's got his entry qualification out of the way?'

'Yeah, sure.'

'Oh God – he's terrified of you.'

'Well, he'll have to learn not to be – all chefs are the same, you know.'

She sat up. 'I don't think so.'

Mikey pushed himself up on his elbows. 'How many chefs do you know?'

'Umm . . . one, actually.'

'Exactly. You're hardly qualified to comment. We have to be loud so the kitchen can hear us and firm so they know what to do.'

'Only during service, though, surely.'

'Stop quibbling and tell me you're proud of me.'

'Here.' She slipped a daisy chain round his neck. 'One of my girlish fantasies used to be doing this sort of thing. Then I grew up.' Her hands lingered round the back of his neck. 'Then I met this loud, opinionated, arrogant chef. I'm so proud of you I could spontaneously combust – what shall we do to celebrate?'

His eyes widened and he grinned. 'I can think of loads of things that don't involve going up in smoke, darling.' He put his hands on her waist and rolled so she was beneath him.

'Oh, and can I help?'

'I guess. What do you want to do?'

She put her hands against his chest. 'I can do their log books with them . . . you know what a pain they are. They'll have to submit folders and things – I can put them on the right track with the written requirements. It'll only take a couple of mornings a week at most but I think it could push the standards up, and I'd like to do it.'

'It'll be boring for you, won't it? And I've already said you can tutor Marvin for his entry certificate.'

'But we're already halfway through that and he's so keen it'll only take another four weeks. You won't have started by then. It'll be useful, I'll be helping.' Suddenly she wound her arms round him. 'Please, Mikey, you know I'd be good at it.'

'I dunno, you've got things to do at home.'

'Claire works . . . it won't be every day. Say I can, please.'

'I'm still not sure. Hey, what are you doing?'

'Lie still, you'll like it.'

'Ow! You nearly had my nose off!' She smiled as she tossed his T-shirt over the rhubarb and began to run her fingers across his chest.

'Come on, Lyn, stop it.' She licked her lips and bent her head. 'Now I'm really scared . . .' His voiced tailed off in a croak and his eyes closed.

She paused.

'Don't stop.'

'I thought you didn't like it?'

'God, woman. OK, you can help with the teaching.'

'Great.' She sat up and his hands shot out and grabbed her wrists.

'Not so fast,' he said, pulling her back down, 'just pick up where you left off. I don't know what you think you're up to but it's . . . well, unusual.'

Lyn smirked. 'It's all to do with erogenous zones, poppet. Didn't you study those in copulation classes?'

115

Christ! I had no idea . . . it was as though all the training had been crap and all the other women had been just going through the motions. And I thought I was such a stud. The blood was practically fizzing in my veins. I felt heavy and helpless. Her hair trailed across my face. Her thumb grazed my mouth and sent me crazy. I could feel her teeth at my neck. Jesus! I'd married a vampire.

Then she started to kiss me and suddenly I could breathe again. No major damage done then. I realised that my arms were locked firmly round her back and her hands were cradling my head. I heard an embarrassingly faint moan and realised it was me. She looked at me enquiringly. 'Oh, chef, too much for you, huh?'

'How could Greg refuse you anything?'

'Greg?'

'Yeah, when you did this sort of stuff.'

'I didn't do this sort of stuff with Greg – this is specially for you.' Her head dipped again and her lips parted.

'Wait,' I mumbled. 'I can't just lie here. It's not . . . Oh Christ!'

'Why don't you roll over?' she murmured in my ear. So I did. It was like no massage I'd ever had and certainly like no massage I'd ever given. I felt as though my nerve ends were being shredded. Her nails delicately scraped my skin and her hair tickled my neck. Her fingers fluttered against the top of my jeans but went no further. I groaned again.

'Patience,' she whispered, and then all sensation stopped for a moment. I gathered myself to turn back and she ran her thumbnail down my spine. I was lost. 'Boy down.' She curled against my side with a sigh.

'What the hell was that?'

'You didn't like geisha massage, Mr Chef?'

I swallowed. I felt very unsophisticated and faintly silly, as though she'd played a trick on me. I twisted round to look at her.

'Mikey, what is it?'

'You swear you've never done that before?'

'Never . . . I was just seeing what happened and you seemed to like it, so . . .' She looked away.

I swung round and pulled her to me. 'Darling, it was incredible – and you are sensational.'

I could feel her doubts swimming to the surface like a shoal of marauding sharks. 'Lyn, my lovely wife, you might not be too great in the kitchen but you are infinitely better than me in the sack.'

'You're just saying that.'

I stretched and grinned. 'Nope – as far as I'm concerned you can try out anything you like, but only on me.'

'Mikey, you think I did it to get round you, don't you?'

'So?'

'That was my excuse but it was the other way round. I enjoyed it because I was in control. I'm sorry.'

'OK, I know I'm going to regret this at some point but I don't have a problem with that, as long as I'm allowed a turn sometimes.'

I thought I might have gone too far but then she started to laugh.

116

'Mikey!'

He came running. 'What?'

'There, under there . . . quick.'

'Ahh, right. I see.'

'Well, do something.'

'Like what, my love?'

'Trap it – that's what you do, isn't it?'

'Sometimes – but then what? Do you want me to cook it for you, or skin it and make you some very small boots?'

'Be serious, it's vermin. We've got vermin.'

'We've got a cat.'

'No. You don't think . . .'

'I certainly do think . . . It's a big day for Spike. Not only has he caught a very small field mouse but he's brought it home for you in one piece. Where is he anyway?'

'I'm not sure. I thought he was outside.'

'I guess he's just collecting more provisions for the hard times ahead. You should be honoured that he's brought you a fresh mouse to eat.'

'Mikey, please, be sensible for a moment. What can we do?'

He was hunting around in the cupboard. 'There we go. Just pop the bucket over it, slide a bit of that box under it and turn it the right way up.'

'But then what?'

'Take it back to the field.'

She nodded. 'OK – as long as I don't have to kill it with a shovel.'

'Darling, that would be horrible.'

'But it's . . .'

'I know – what they used to do in the dump. Then I suppose you turned them into a nourishing stew.'

117

She hesitated at the top of the alley, her shopping digging into her shoulder. She rearranged the bags and took a step forward. Two days ago she'd been looking at the map, hoping to find another local walk across the fields, and she'd spotted a foot-path that went from opposite the food centre to the top of their street. It ran straight between small industrial units and the back of a chapel, then it crossed another road and took a more curved route between gardens and the local school before finally emerging on the corner.

She'd wandered up the street to take a closer look and, although a bit derelict and overgrown, it looked perfectly usable. It would cut nearly a mile off her trip with the shopping. She'd been pleased with her discovery and told Mikey that evening. Of course, he'd said she couldn't use it.

'Don't be daft,' he'd snapped, 'it isn't safe.'

'But it'll be broad daylight, Mikey, and I'm not a child. What on earth is going to happen?'

'Nothing – because you won't be using it. Look, I can see that the top bit looks OK – you can probably see from one end to the other – but once it starts winding about, you could run into anything. And that's a very long stretch . . . I doubt that it's covered by cameras, either. There's a reason that it's not signposted and that's because it's not a centre-recommended route.'

Now she was thinking about it again. She took another step. Mikey was right – the first stretch was completely safe and the alley was completely empty. He won't know anyway, she thought,

335

and set off at a good pace. Once she'd crossed the road and entered the second part of the alley her progress slowed. The enclosed gardens on either side were fenced off but trees swept low across her path and patches of nettles lined the sides. It was a narrow, twisting route that seemed more isolated than it looked on the map. She plodded on, battling the strange feeling that the city around her had disappeared. It's just because I'm not used to it, she thought; once I've done it a couple of times I'll know what to expect. Her pace slowed as she followed a tight turn, which she thought would lead to the school boundary. Instead it just led to another stretch of overgrown bushes and nettles; the path had almost disappeared. God, she thought, perhaps I'd better go back. She glanced behind her and that was when she heard it.

Immediately she began to jog, forcing her way through the nettles, her shopping banging her side and legs uncomfortably. Round the next bend the path finally opened out past the school. She paused for a moment, listening, then dropped her bags and fled. Despite her fright she managed to keep breathing and as the path flattened out her speed increased so that she erupted on to the street zig-zagging madly to keep her balance. In seconds she was fumbling at the front door.

She raced in and slammed it behind her. The house settled and closed round her. She sat on the floor and considered the carpet in enormous detail. She was surprised and alarmed but not terrified. She supposed that somebody at the centre was even now watching a grainy film of her bursting out of the alley and sprinting up the street. She wondered what to do about her shopping. Perhaps, she thought, they'll find it and bring it round.

She sniggered at the thought and then frowned. Oh Lord, don't let Dylan find out. Spike appeared and sat next to her with a serious expression on his face. 'Oh, Spikey Boy, I've lost your shopping – what will you do?' Spike patted her knee with a large paw and she scooped him up for a cuddle, rubbing her nose against his. After a moment he struggled to get down. Leaning back against the wall she thought she heard a very faint rustling but couldn't work out what it was. Slowly she got to her feet and worked her way down to the kitchen. Nothing. So if there was anything it was in the living room, she supposed, or lurking on the upstairs landing. Suddenly impatient, she made for the living room, only to see that the front window was slightly open and the curtains were moving about restlessly.

She didn't know if she'd left them open after cleaning the windows or not. It was a reasonable day and she could have left the living room to air. What was it Mikey had said? 'The only thing wrong with you is a galloping imagination.'

She'd have to go back to get the shopping. She opened the front door and saw Dylan on the step, hand raised to knock.

'Christ!'

'Sorry to disappoint you.' He beamed. 'Can you spare a moment?'

Eying him warily she nodded and backed into the hall. 'Coffee?'

'Please.'

She led the way into the kitchen. 'Have a seat.' To her surprise he chose the sofa and sat with Spike on his knee gazing thoughtfully out at the garden.

'Here you are.'

'Thank you. Are you all right?'

She smiled. 'Of course, why wouldn't I be?'

'Well, according to our records you've just run most of the way from the food centre and you appear to have lost your shopping en route.'

She snorted nervously. 'I just got a bit spooked. Silly, I know.'

'You were on an unauthorised pathway.'

Abruptly all her assumed calm fell away. She rubbed her arms. 'I know. I just thought I'd try it – it's a short cut but it was a bit overgrown.'

'You must have been a sprinter in your youth – you covered the last hundred metres in seconds. Most impressive.' He was looking at her enquiringly. She concentrated on not spilling her coffee and trying to avoid eye contact.

'Sit down,' he said. 'Sit down here and we'll talk for a moment.' Eyes round with horror she perched on the edge of the sofa. Dylan ignored her body language completely. 'Let's just focus on the facts, Lyn. You dropped your shopping in the alley somewhere and ran flat out to get home. Quite evidently you believed someone was pursuing you. Can you explain that to me?'

'I heard a motorbike coming up behind me . . . at first it was slow, but then it began to get closer and I thought I'd be run over at the very least. I had to drop the shopping because it was slowing me down. I was just going out to get it back when you arrived.'

He pulled out his infopad. 'Where did you leave your shopping?'

'Where the path runs beside the school field – just after the last bend.'

He tapped, nodded to himself and tapped again. 'Right. That's one thing sorted out. Security will retrieve it for you and bring it round. Now, tell me why you thought you'd be run over . . . surely any sane person would have tried to avoid you once they saw you up ahead? The path is very winding and until you reach the final stretch, there isn't a clear view. They probably didn't even realise you were there.'

'I just had a feeling. I told you it was silly, but I wasn't going to wait to find out.' She took a gulp of coffee. A thought struck her. 'Why don't you check the cameras?'

'Ah, dear lady, contrary to popular opinion the entire city is not under surveillance. That alley is being allowed to fall into decay like a thousand others. It isn't signposted because we don't want people using it. In the end we'll block access entirely. In the meantime, tempting short cut though it is, it isn't safe even in daylight.'

Her heart sank and she gulped at her coffee again, looking unhappily down at the floor. 'Dylan,' she muttered, 'I'm a total nuisance and I do apologise. You must have much more important things to do than run about after me.'

When he didn't respond immediately she braced herself for the worst: tagging or an entry on her data file, she supposed. It was with a true sense of horror that she felt his arm across her shoulders. Without effort he pulled her towards him so that she was leaning against him. She didn't dare to move. Spike was purring happily. Dylan continued to look at the garden. 'Your raised beds are looking very productive,' he said. 'Do you spend much time on them?'

'Not much. Mikey does the vegetables. I do the flowers and shrubs.'

'I see. The tubs and other colourful features are your handiwork then?'

'Yes.'

'A most rewarding pastime, I imagine. What are the bright red ones just there?'

'Busy Lizzies.'

'And the blue things?'

'Lobelia.'

'Have you always been a gardener?'

'No. I'm not really one now, I'm just learning.'

His eyes narrowed in amusement as he glanced at her averted profile. 'Oh well, delightful though this is I must make a move. Duty calls and all that.' He drained his coffee, tipped Spike off his lap and stood up. 'We will, of course, check for signs of a motorcycle in the vicinity but you must behave with more caution, young lady.'

When she opened the front door for him her shopping bags were sitting outside. Dylan courteously lifted them into the hall and smiled. 'Don't look so tragic, my dear, no harm done.'

118

Krystal was perched on the kitchen table examining her nails. 'So you think I should narrow my options for next year?'

'Yes,' said Lyn, 'I really do.'

'Well, Mum wants me to go into medicine. That way if I don't make it as a doctor or surgeon I can be a nurse or a dentist or a physiotherapist. But the training's really long.' She sighed and started fiddling with her hair. 'I'd like to be a receptionist.'

'Aim high, why don't you!'

'What?'

'I mean there's nothing wrong in being a receptionist but you could probably handle something more challenging.'

'But what's the point?'

'Krystal – just listen to yourself!'

'How many female doctors do you know?'

'OK, I suppose there aren't that many, but if you do well you can get a reserved occupation licence and stay single – like my friend Judith in security.'

She frowned. 'But I don't want to stay single, I want to get married and have a family like you and Michael. I don't see why I can't do both. If I do medicine it's a year's preparation, then three years for the degree, then two years vocational training on top – that's six years! I'll only have two years before I have to register for selection and I won't even have finished payback. Anyway, I'd quite like to do design – bags and things.'

'Krystal, you really have to try and focus. Have you completed the centre careers questionnaire?'

340

'Sure – it said I could be a doctor, a librarian or a teacher.'

'Good lord. What would you teach?'

'Oh, mathematics I suppose, that's what I'm best at. When you were teaching, what was it like?'

'Very nice . . . hard work but very satisfying.'

Krystal peered up through her newly cut fringe. 'What was Michael like?'

'He was shorter . . . he was only 16. He was quiet and his work was fine, so the class was probably a bit of a waste of time for him and Lucas as well. But it was part of their vocational course, so they had to do it. If you opt for a receptionist type job you'll have to do that course and the maths one as well. You won't like it.'

'Michael thought it was great. Of course, that was because they all thought you were so cool. Most of the teachers at college are very dull but he said you never followed the curriculum so they never really knew what was going to happen. Anyway, that isn't what I wanted to know.'

'No?'

'No, I wanted to know if you liked him back then.'

'I liked all of my students.'

'But did you like him specially?'

'Krystal, you know as well as I do that that would be completely unprofessional and against all the rules.'

'Oh well, it was worth a try. I expect that really you liked him and when he selected you it was as if all your dreams had come true.' She hugged her knees in silent satisfaction.

Lyn turned back to her vegetable stew and gave it a stir. Her memory had abruptly shot into sharp focus; she could see the classroom, smell the musky odour of slightly unwashed males mixed with *eau de toilette* and hairspray from the girls. Some of the staff hated that smell but she quite liked it. It reminded her of the dump, she supposed. Krystal had made her think of something that was teetering on the edge of her memory, trying to force its way in. Her imagination toured the classroom looking at the faces, adding names where she could. Mikey was stretched out next to Kylie, flicking her ginger curls with an idle finger while she smiled sideways at him. On the other side, Lucas was leaning forward, elbows on the desk, his expression blank. Then he glanced up, indicated Mikey and Kylie with a sardonic tilt of his head and gave Lyn a smile, genuine, amused, right into her eyes. 'Young love, Miss,' he murmured, holding her gaze. 'I like them slightly older.'

Had she responded, she wondered? Not that she could remember – she'd probably ignored him and carried on round the room checking the work. Her memory gave her another jolt. Back at the teacher's station, looking round the class and thinking to herself that Lucas had the cheek of the devil when he looked up and nodded at her. No wonder he thinks we're friends, she thought miserably.

She turned back to Krystal. 'Come and look at this – it's changing colour.'

Krystal bustled over and shrieked affectedly. 'It's turning grey – what have you put in it? God, what are those?'

'Mushrooms, I think.'

'That's it then – I thought they were slugs. Mum always does them separately, then adds them at the last minute. It'll still taste OK – you'll just have to blindfold Michael first.'

'Krystal, why on earth would you think I'd be cooking slugs?'

'Dunno,' she shrugged, 'different habits? I don't know what you had to eat in that home, do I? I know, why don't you use the whizzer and make it into soup, then you can add some food colouring and do some garlic bread.'

'Krystal, you are a genius. You will be wasted as a receptionist. What colour shall I use?'

'I dunno, you decide – it's your soup . . .'

Mikey frowned dubiously into his bowl. 'What did you say this was?'

'It's soup.'

'I can see that but what kind of soup?'

'Carrot and mushroom.'

'Unusual colour.'

'They were unusual carrots.'

'And the floating black things?'

'Croutons – as you very well know. I was going to do garlic bread but it over-cooked itself. Go on – taste it at least.'

He took a spoonful and gulped. 'Have you tried it?'

'No, I thought I'd let you try first.' He scowled and she hastily took a spoonful. 'Oh – how strange.'

'Strange? It's horrible!'

'No, it's just that the texture is a bit odd combined with the flavour. Try it with your eyes closed.'

'Hmm … I'm getting overall mushroom and something starchy like carrot or parsnip, and a massive amount of e-numbers – mainly 160 but some 120.'

'You can taste that?'

'Not particularly – you left the food colourings on the side. I haven't dared try the croutons yet – they look like pure carbon. We could save them for the next time you have a hangover.'

He opened the fridge and looked in. 'Right, it's scrambled eggs again. I'll do them.'

'Mikey, you know I can do scrambled eggs – I'll do them.'

'OK.'

He leant back against the work top and watched as Lyn dug out the butter, cut bread for toast, loaded the toaster, set the pan on the hob, broke the eggs and started frantic beating. After a moment she said, 'I do wish you wouldn't just watch me like that, you're making me nervous.'

He raised his hands in a gesture of surrender. 'Sorry, do you want a beer?'

'Please.'

He swiped the alco store and added, casually, 'Did you make any shortbread or anything?'

Her back stiffened. 'No – I was making soup and giving Krystal career advice.' The toaster pinged and she grabbed plates and buttered the toast. A gentle smoke started to drift from the eggs. Mikey reached over and lifting the pan from the hob, tipped the runny eggs into a clean pan, leaving the brown goo undisturbed in the original pan which he put in the sink. Then he turned the heat down, waiting a moment before sliding the new pan on to the hob and giving the eggs a quick stir.

'OK, over here with the toast, Wonder Woman.'

'Oh, you are a God in the kitchen, aren't you?'

'Don't get sarky just because I saved your eggs – you had the heat too high to begin with, so as soon as you stopped stirring they caught. That's all. The toast is great.'

'Krystal thought we ate slugs in the dump.'

'She what?'

'What I mean is that she thought the mushrooms were slugs and seemed to think it was quite reasonable to assume that I was cooking them because that was what I was used to.'

'How were you cooking them?'

'Boiling them with vegetables as a base for the soup. The mushrooms, that is.'

'That's a relief. I wouldn't like to think we'd been eating slug, however briefly.'

'But do I seem that odd to you? I mean, like the sort of demented person who'd cook slugs?'

He looked up. 'No. You look to me like the kind of woman who needs a cookery book. You can't expect to know how to cook if you haven't been taught. What was it you told Luke? You wouldn't try to plaster a wall without a trowel or something? This is the same – you're trying to make a soufflé before you can boil an egg.'

'I can boil an egg!'

'Only to be used as a lethal weapon.' He finished his eggs and chewed the last piece of toast reflectively. 'Why don't you do some of the recipes from the book? They're fairly straightforward and it'd be a good way to test them out.'

'Yes, of course, if you like. But about the slug thing?'

He reached across the table and took her hand. 'This is really bothering you, isn't it? It was just Krystal being daft as usual.'

'Well, yes. I know it was silly but do your family think I'm that different?'

'Of course not. They all love you. Mind you, they don't know that you've lied to me again.'

'What about?'

'The shortbread – I found it in the bin when I was sorting Spike out.'

'Ah.' Lyn shot out of her seat, round the table and on to Mikey's lap. 'The thing is . . .' She shifted to get more comfortable and put one arm round his neck. 'The thing is, I was ashamed about wasting the food allowance and . . .' She fiddled with the silver bear, sliding it up and down the leather tie, then looking him full in the face, 'And I thought I'd just try again another day. Or perhaps you could show me how to do it . . . when you have time and you're not so tired?' She shifted again and looked down.

Mikey laughed and she started to get up indignantly but he held on to her. 'Woman, you are such a piece of work.'

'Well,' she said, knowing that she sounded cross, 'it was worth a go.'

'It certainly was, I have no argument with that.' He stroked her hair, kissed her. 'Listen, darling, you had the oven on too high – remember the chocolate cake? That's why you burn things. And you should check once they've been in for five minutes to see how they're doing.'

'I'm sorry about lying to you.'

'Oh, that. I was just trying to get you to tell me about the shortbread so I could tell you what to do next time.' He kissed her again. 'I don't expect you to tell me everything. Just the important things.'

'So how important is shortbread?'

'In this house it's a priority, right up there with keeping my whites white and looking after Spike.' His hands moved round to her back and he ran a thumbnail down her spine. 'And this, of course.'

119

She was struggling at the food depot, juggling her list and hesitating over wholemeal spaghetti or semolina linguine when a dry voice murmured in her ear. 'He won't like either of those . . . he makes his own, you know.' For a second she thought she'd literally jumped out of her skin; she'd felt her feet leave the ground and her heart was thudding uncomfortably.

'Lucas, what are you thinking of, creeping up on me like that?' she said, managing to stop her voice from trembling.

'Just thinking that buying a great chef dried pasta is a big mistake.'

'Not when I'm going to cook it – everybody seems to think that he wants to cook all day but he doesn't. Nor does he expect me to create pasta from scratch. He's fine with this, although I don't think he'd like me to buy the flavoured stuff in pots where you just add water.'

'Oh, right, I stand corrected.' He grinned at her, looked her up and down and grinned again. 'Looking good, if I may say so.'

'Lucas, what are you doing here?'

He indicated his basket with a shrug. 'A guy's got to eat.'

'Fine, well, I've got to get going so . . .' She started to turn her trolley and he stepped in front of it.

'Lyn.'

'Come on, Lucas, get out of the way.' He grabbed the trolley.

'Just listen for a moment, OK. I haven't seen you since the sandwich night and I just wanted to apologise. I know I was rude and intrusive but I never meant to offend you, either of you.'

'Fine, apology accepted. Get out of my way.'

'No – Mitch is like my brother and I don't want there to be a problem between us.'

'Perhaps you should have thought of that before.'

He started to look impatient. 'What do I have to do to be friends again?'

'Lucas, you were never my friend, you were my student. Look, I'll forget it, but we're never going to be friends. You're just one of my husband's booze buddies from way back.'

'Please, Lyn.' She looked up at him. He was pale and intense and looking tragic.

'Oh, OK, let's agree to take it one step at a time. I'll tell Mitch I've seen you and perhaps you can go out or something. Now let go of my trolley.'

He smiled, nodded and fell into step beside her as she went to swipe her card. She took her time loading her bags and when she'd finished he'd gone. Feeling a bit confused and anxious, she swung her knapsack over one shoulder and hefted the holdall on the other side so she was at least balanced. It was the cat food and the beer that made it all so heavy, she thought. In comparison, shopping for Greg had been a pleasure.

As she rounded the first corner Lucas was there, and loaded down with shopping she couldn't move fast enough to get round him.

'Let me.'

'No, there's no need.'

'Of course there is.' He looked at her intently. 'You look tired, Lyn, there are a few shadows under your eyes. Actually, they suit you, but there's no point in wearing yourself out if there's someone to carry your bags for you.'

She looked around but there was never anybody about to help when you needed them. 'Go away!'

'Now you look as if you're going to cry.' To her horror he

reached out and ran a finger down her cheek. She backed up as fast as she could. 'Relax. Let's go for coffee.'

'No, let's not.' Although she thought at least half the centre regulations were ridiculous, this was one she was happy to use. 'I can't. I'm married. I have to have specific permission. Otherwise it's a Code 19 violation.'

For a second he paused. 'You never struck me as a lady who'd be scared of taking a risk.'

'And you never struck me as a boy who'd try to take advantage but I guess we all make mistakes.'

He laughed in her face. 'Ah, the same old Lyn; that's why we all loved you in class. I tell you what,' he said, leaning closer. 'If Ryan and Matt and Simon were here they'd all be harassing you as well.'

She stood like a statue as he took her bags and he set off down the street with an easy stride. In the end she had to follow him – he'd got her shopping after all. When they reached the corner of her road he stopped, turned and handed the bags back to her. She was pleased to see that he was breathing more heavily than before and had a light sheen of perspiration.

'Don't I get a thank you kiss?'

'You are unbelievable!' she spat. 'Just leave me alone.'

120

At home she made sure the door was locked, dumped the shopping in the kitchen and had a long shower. Then she put all her clothes in the machine, pinned her hair up and pulled on her gardening outfit of ancient jeans and T-shirt. She had weeding to do and plants to water. As she trudged to and fro with the watering can, she tried to blank the images from her mind. Why hadn't anyone noticed what was happening? In fairness, she supposed, because there had been nothing much to notice. A conversation in the food depot with neither of them doing much to attract attention. Then a kindly friend waiting for her and carrying her bags.

But it hadn't felt like that. 'Well, of course not,' she muttered to herself. He'd touched her, touched her face and she'd let him. She felt tears rising and stopped them. Remember, no more tears, they are useless. She'd let Mikey's best friend stroke her face and behave in a personal manner and she'd gone along with it. Because she was embarrassed. A wave of shame flooded through her. And what had he said? That more of the boys liked her? Oh, that couldn't be right – he was just trying to upset her. She thought about how he looked. Pale and definitely interesting in his dark shirt and black slim fit jeans with that leather jacket. Surely he had a girlfriend.

She attacked another patch of weeds with unusual venom.

'Whoa, ' said Mikey from behind her, 'what did they do to you?'

'Lord, are you back already?'

'Well, yes, evidently.'

'Sorry, I didn't realise it was that time.' She stood up and stretched ... her back felt cramped and her shoulders were tense. Mikey reached over and pressed on her shoulders.

'My God, what have you been doing? You're stiff as a board.' He kneaded her shoulders, probing with his thumbs and spreading out his fingers. 'This needs a proper going-over. Come on, you, let's get you sitting down.'

Lyn followed him meekly into the kitchen, sat in a chair at the table and let him get to work. It was very painful but she thought she deserved it – in a way he was driving out the devil – and then it started to feel warm and finally soothing. In the end she was groaning as the tension was stripped from her muscles.

'Where did you learn to do that?'

'At college, studying bread making. It wasn't all useless, you know. Anyway – what's for dinner?'

'Oh no! I haven't started anything.'

'Good, because I have.'

'I can't smell anything.'

'That's because it's a delicious chilled asparagus soup followed by lightly poached fish which I haven't cooked yet and green salad followed by a light sorbet nicked from work for dessert.'

'You are so good to me.'

'I know.'

'Do you need me to do anything?'

He sniffed. 'You could take a shower.' She glared.

'I could help?'

'Oh, that sort of a shower?'

'Yes, darling, that sort of a shower.'

'Right. Will it be too decadent if I get us some wine to be going on with?'

'Hmm ... probably not.'

As she dried herself off, Lyn reflected briefly on how relaxed she felt. Remarkable, she thought, one minute I'm so fraught I could be powering the city lights on my own and the next, I

351

don't think a bomb going off would bother me – and all it took was a massage and a very friendly shower. She pulled on her bathrobe and went downstairs to set the table. Mikey was unpacking the shopping.

'What the hell is this?'

'What?'

He waved a package at her. She frowned. 'I have no idea, what is it?'

'It's a pot of dehydrated instant pasta Italiano – just add boiling water.'

'What's that? I've never seen it before.'

'So what is it doing in your shopping?'

'I didn't buy it, Mikey, why would I?' And even as she spoke she realised. 'Oh no. Mikey, I bumped into Lucas at the shopping place and he was teasing me about buying you dried pasta. He must have planted it as a joke or something.'

To her amazement, his face cleared at once. 'That's just the sort of stunt he'd pull. He knows that I hate these things. Sorry, darling, I didn't mean to bark at you. How was he anyway?'

She paused for an instant. This is the friend, she thought, who tried to convince you I was racist, who has tried to pick me up twice, who is patronising, sarcastic and unpleasant and frightens me. This isn't a message for you, it's a message for me.

'He wants to meet up with you for a drink so you'd better give him a call. He looked fine, very trendy and he carried my bags most of the way back.'

Mikey nodded. 'Here we go, asparagus soup *avec* croutons.'

'Aren't you going to call him?'

'What, now? Love, we're having a romantic dinner . . . I can call Luke any time.'

121

Dylan looked at Lyn gravely. 'You've missed two appointments.'

'I'm sorry. I didn't want Mikey to know.'

'But he only has to look at your data file.'

'He won't, Dylan, he's got no reason to.'

His fingers drummed on the desk. 'Lyn, why don't you tell him about Judith?'

'There's not really anything to tell, especially now she's back up north. I don't want to worry him.'

'OK – so what's bothering you then?'

'I just have this feeling . . . as though she's coming after me. It doesn't make any sense, I know, but I have this dreadful sense of foreboding. Dylan, I can't explain it to Mikey, he'd just think I was being nervous but I think she's jealous.' She finished on a squeak. Dylan took her hand and squeezed it. It didn't make her feel any better.

'My dear, in my experience female instincts are seldom wrong but I can assure you that Judith is happily engaged up north in a new training programme. What I'm interested in is why you think this unhealthy relationship has developed.'

'We've been through this, Dylan, it's just the dump system – learnt dependency or something like that.'

'But what interests me is how you've apparently escaped unscathed while your erstwhile best friend is mired in the past.'

She studied the desk. 'I do know what you mean but I think you're over-complicating things . . . Judith just doesn't like Mikey because I like him. She hated Greg but she thought I hated him as well, so that was fine. She just wants to be my best friend. She doesn't want to share me.'

He nodded. 'As I said, the female instinct is rarely wrong. I think you are an astute, intelligent woman. However, in practical terms she is hundreds of miles away.'

'Yes, Dylan.'

122

It had been a very cloudy day and night had fallen abruptly. Lyn was about to start on her third attempt at shortbread. Mikey had assured her that success lay in preparation, so she was putting everything ready in advance. She rummaged through the top cupboard but couldn't find the sieve, although she did find a lost vase and three glasses. She dropped to her knees and was delving at the back of the bottom cupboard when her phone rang. She ignored it for the moment because she was reaching into the furthest corner.

The phone cut off and immediately rang again – two rings, then silence. It rang again – three rings, then silence. She shot out of the cupboard and rocketed to her feet. The pain when she hit the open door of the top cupboard was extraordinary. Her vision blurred and streaks of light dashed across her eyes. She groaned and shook it off, grabbed her mobile. 'Message from Judith' it read. She was immediately drenched in icy sweat. She ran upstairs, grabbed the cat carrier and stuffed an amazed and dozy Spike inside, then ran down as quietly as she could. She put Spike under the kitchen table, positioned herself where she could see the front door and dialled Claire.

'Hello, love.'

'Claire – has Krystal left yet?'

'No, she's just about to. Do you need her to bring something?'

'No – tell her not to come. Get centre security, there's somebody trying to break in.' The front door latch was moving up and down.

'I'll send Ray.'

'No. No, don't send anybody – just get security.' She clicked the mobile off and slid back into the kitchen. She grabbed Spike in his carrier, left the mobile on the table, opened the French doors and clicked off the light. Yanking the key from the lock, she stepped onto the patio and locked the doors behind her. There was a soft thud from inside the house and she froze, listening. She'd left the upstairs lights on but now another thought struck her and she crept around the side of the house and unbolted the side gate with clammy fingers, leaving it swinging open. Turning, she nearly fell over the cat carrier but kept her footing and made a stumbling dash down the garden to the shelter of the fruit trees.

Trying to make no noise, she wriggled through the trees, bent low, convinced that Judith had seen her, was aiming, squeezing the trigger. She felt rather than saw the compost bin and, shaking all over, pulled herself on to it, then up on to the fence, which quivered and moaned under her. Spike was a solid weight at the end of her arm – she began an unstable wriggling progress along the fence until the meter box was more or less beneath her then she lowered Spike cautiously down. His carrier slithered on the narrow surface, then held. She was just wondering how to follow him when the lights burst on in the kitchen, flooding the top of the garden, followed by a splintering crash as the French doors blew open.

Instantly she rolled off the fence, ripping a flap of skin from her palm and banging her head on the metre box. She grabbed the cat carrier – Spike was now completely silent, pressed flat with his eyes shut. She crouched in terror, trying to think. All her instincts were screaming at her to run up the lane towards the service road; centre security would be coming and there would be lights and people. But Judith would expect her to do that, would catch her, would catch Spike, would make her watch while she dealt with him first. But there was nowhere else to go . . .

She looked across the lane – the fields were completely black. Dump children were afraid of the dark. They would never go away from the light. She made three giant strides across the lane and flung herself at the hedge. There was no time to look for the stile. On her hands and knees she found a gap and thrust Spike through it then began to fight through herself. Brambles clawed at her. Bindweed dragged at her feet. Bushes ripped through her hair. She sobbed in terror and just as she knew it was hopeless she tumbled into the field, into the long grass. She rolled over and felt around for the cat carrier. Had she lost him? Frightened to move too far until she had him safe, she began to pat around in ever-widening circles. There was the flicker of torchlight in the lane – the beam filtered through the hedge and bounced off plastic. She wormed on her front towards the cat carrier, grabbed the handle, worked her way backwards and when she was out of the faint circle of light, stumbled to her feet and began to run again.

She thought she remembered where the trees were from their walks to the river but after only a few steps, she tripped and her ankle gave way with a terrifying crunch. After she'd fallen twice she realised that trying to run was a waste of time. Her ankle was throbbing, blood was trickling into her eyes and she needed to get used to the darkness. She sat down in the long grass, then began to inch forward, dragging the cat carrier. Just look for the trees, she thought, just find the trees.

The dark made her struggle to catch her breath; she couldn't make out anything in front of her. Spike mewed softly and she sobbed. He mewed again louder. 'Spikey Spike, don't,' she whispered, 'it isn't safe to make a noise.' She thought she could hear sounds behind her and struggled to her feet. Her ankle gave way immediately so she rolled on to her hands and knees and started to crawl. The next time she paused to wipe the blood from her eyes she could see the blurred outline of trees – a darker darkness. She thought she could hear the river but it was all muddled up with her heart pounding and her drag-

357

ging fight for breath. She crawled some more and found a tree. She sat against it with her back against the trunk. 'It's all right Spikey, we're just going to sit and wait for Daddy to come.'

Tears and blood ran down her face as the silence grew around her.

123

She was still sitting behind the tree when Tim found her. He was swinging a torch and calling, and he loomed up, a tall, frightening shape but recognisable. She tried to call out but only managed a croak. He turned and flashed his torch at her.

'Lyn ... thank God!' He stepped closer and gasped then gathered himself. 'It's OK now. Centre security are at the house and Dad's there – we just need to get you to the medicentre. Can you stand up?'

She tried to speak but only managed another croak. He stared. Crouched down with her. Stroked her hair. Looked at the blood on his hands. 'Lyn, Lyn ... it's all right. Do you understand?' She nodded. 'Do you think you can walk?' She nodded again, so he tried to pull her to her feet. The cat carrier bumped between them awkwardly. She couldn't stand on her own and leant against him.

'Lyn, I'm going to get help – you sit down and just wait here.'

She began to shake, clutched at his arm, tried again to speak and finally put Spike down and clung to Tim with all her strength. He looked at her again. She tried to calm herself. Shook her head and nodded towards the lane. 'You don't want to be left alone?' She nodded. His arms closed round her and she thought she felt his lips on her hair. She wrapped her arms around his neck and shuddered. Her eyes were stinging and she could taste blood on her lips. She pulled away and retched. The field spun around her.

'Then I won't leave you. It'll take as long as it takes. Nobody's going to hurt you, Lyn, not while I'm here to look after you.'

He drew a deep, quivering breath and it occurred to her that he was as scared as she was. His hand tilted her face towards him; he wiped the blood from her mouth and gently kissed her. 'Sorry, I couldn't help it. Right, put your hand on my shoulder ... that's it.' He slid one arm round her waist and held her tightly then bent for Spike's carrier and straightened up. 'Can you hop if I hold you?' She nodded. They began the painful progress back to the flashing lights and the noise.

To begin with they had to stop every few paces but then they achieved some sort of rhythm and managed a run of several yards before stopping again. Lyn was struggling for breath and he paused to brush the hair from her face. 'We'll give it a moment,' he said, 'then we'll have another go.' His hand slid down her back and she snuffled against his chest. Spike began to wail in complaint. 'He's bored now,' said Tim. 'We'd better try again.' This time they managed to cover more ground before she staggered to a halt. 'I'll give a yell – they might hear us now we're closer.'

They paused and he shouted in a strangely cracked voice, 'I've found her, it's all right!' then they carried on struggling through the long grass. Finally torches wheeled in their direction and Tim stopped and turned her to face him. 'We'll be able to carry you the last bit.' His breathing was ragged. 'Lyn, you know I'd do anything for you. If you need me, just let me know.' She shook her head, tried a wobbly smile and put a bloodied finger to her lips. He took her hand and kissed it and she pulled away and nearly toppled over. He caught at her just as there was a rush of feet behind her and Ray took her weight.

'Steady, love, mind how you go. Bring the cat, Tim.' He looked around and waved impatiently. 'Over here, mate, we need to carry her.'

The meditech came carefully through the grass. 'It's pitch black out here – how did she get so far from the lane?' He shone his torch over the group and faltered a moment. 'We won't get a stretcher over here in the dark.'

'No need,' said Ray, 'we'll chair lift her. That's all right, isn't it, love?' Lyn nodded. Tim looked at Ray. 'She can't speak, Dad. I don't know what's happened to her but she can't speak at all.'

The meditech shrugged. 'Shock, I should think – we'll sort her out once we can see what we're doing. Can't think why she had to run into the fields anyway ... enough to spook anyone.'

'Best place to hide then,' observed Ray.

124

Still in his whites, Mikey strode into the treatment room. His eyes widened and he stared. 'What the hell have you done to your hair?'

Ray scowled. 'Don't speak to her like that – they had to shave her hair off to glue the cut together.' There was a neat, two-inch-wide strip running from the front to the back of Lyn's scalp – it looked like a bowling green.

'But why cut so much off?'

The nurse tutted. 'If we didn't, the first time she used a comb she'd scalp herself because of the glue. Then it would never grow back!'

'Good grief,' murmured Lyn. 'I didn't think you cared about my hair that much.'

'I don't care how you curl it or tie it up and all that, but I expect it to be there! You look ridiculous!'

'Don't speak to her like that,' Ray repeated. 'She's had a nasty shock.'

'So have I.' Mikey went closer, touched her cheek, took in the bloodied hands and the scratches, looked at her ankle. 'My God! What have you done to yourself?'

The nurse glared at him. 'Your wife thought she was going to be attacked – it's a miracle she isn't badly hurt.'

'That's right,' added Ray, 'she could have been killed.'

Lyn stared at him and her lips began to twitch. 'I'm so sorry,' she spluttered. 'I know I'm a nuisance.'

'A nuisance?'

'OK, a terrible nuisance.'

'Can you manage a straight answer to a straight question or
are you full of painkillers?'

'Well, yes . . . I'm full of painkillers but they're really good.
I've already done my security statement.'

'Right. What exactly happened?'

'Perfect timing . . . that's just what I want to know as well.'
There was a sudden hush as Dylan appeared in the doorway.
His pale face was impassive and his mouth was set in a grim
line. He looked stern and assertive, not at all his usual avun-
cular self. Their eyes met. Lyn felt a stupid impulse to fling
herself into his arms but instead she burst into tears. She half
sat up as he took a step towards the bed. At the same instant
she realised that Mikey was looking at her with an expression
of horrified amazement. She looked at him. She looked at Dylan
who'd stopped in his tracks. The room tilted.

'Lie back, Mrs Jones,' said the meditech.

'No,' she choked, 'no – I feel sick.'

'You'll feel better if you lie down.'

'No.'

Mikey put a hand on her neck and shoved her forward as
he looked round for a vomibag.

Dylan barked, 'Is anyone going to treat this patient or are
you just going to look at her?'

Lyn threw up just as Mikey thrust a bunch of paper towels
on to her lap.

Eyes streaming, she reached for him and squeezed her eyes
shut. When she opened them everyone was still there. 'Sorry –
that was a surprise.'

'Telling me, darling.'

She coughed and attempted a smile. Dylan nodded at Mikey.
'We still need some information. Now, I've seen the initial statement and security are extending their search but it would help
if you could run through everything you can remember.'

Lyn sighed. 'OK, I was looking in the cupboard for the sieve
and I heard something outside the front door. I stood up too

fast, hence the cut on my head, although I didn't really notice it at the time.'

'Lyn,' said Dylan, 'the doctor said that cut was from some kind of blunt instrument.' Mikey rolled his eyes.

'Well,' she said, 'I suppose it was. I stood up under the cupboard door – I hadn't closed it. Anyway,' she hurried on, avoiding Mikey's eye, 'I went into the passage and someone was trying to open the door. I ran back into the kitchen, got the cat, ran down the garden, climbed the fence and went across the lane into the field to hide.'

'And your other injuries?' Dylan persisted.

'I think I did most of them getting over the fence, but I ripped my nails getting through the hedge and I guess that's where the scratches came from as well.'

'Your ankle?'

'I knocked it on the fence but I turned it properly when I fell over in the field – I couldn't see where I was going.'

'That's enough,' said Mikey. 'Lyn's been through enough tonight. I'm taking her home as soon as she's been tidied up.'

'You can't quite yet, your house is still a crime scene,' remarked Dylan. 'And I need a few more details filled in.'

'Anyway, you're coming back to ours,' said Ray. 'Spike's already there and the ladies want to look after Lyn.'

'You need that ankle strapped up properly,' added the nurse, 'and we'll want to take some more X-rays in two days' time – it isn't broken but it's dislocated, and we need to be sure that it stays where it should be once we've put it back.'

Lyn pushed herself up the bed. 'I'd quite like a word with my husband without an audience.'

'Two minutes,' said the nurse, 'then I'll be back to strap you up.' Everybody trooped out, leaving Mikey staring out of the window.

Lyn looked at his back in despair. 'You can leave me, you know. I wouldn't blame you. It's just going from bad to worse.'

He was silent.

'Please speak to me, even if it's just to tell me you've given up.'

He turned. 'Darling, you must have been terrified, and you ended up ripped to shreds – don't tell me it isn't that bad because you haven't seen a mirror yet – and you managed to do it all to yourself. You must be the clumsiest person I've ever known.'

The bed was too narrow for him to sit on so he pulled a chair up and rubbed her shoulder.

'Is it that bad?'

'Lyn, you look as if you've fallen into the mincer. It's all superficial and Mum is probably creating a miracle cream out of rat's testicles and earwigs even as we speak. Just let's get through Dylan's interrogation as fast as we can so that we can go home.' He paused. 'You can cry if you want, it's OK.'

'I'm never going to cry again.'

A doctor came in with a set of X-rays under one arm and stared at the screen on the wall for a moment. 'OK, Mr Jones,' he observed, 'we just need to dress the hand injuries and sort out your wife's ankle, then we can discharge her.'

'Like that?'

'How do you mean?'

Mikey looked at him with disfavour. 'She's covered in blood.'

'It'll wash off. We've already glued her scalp wound.'

The nurse then clattered back into the room with dressings. 'Normally I'd ask you to hold her hand, but that would probably cause more damage. Just distract her because, painkillers or not, this is going to hurt.'

Lyn looked at the nurse . . . her head was still spinning but she knew that this was going to be bad.

'Listen,' said the nurse, 'young James is going to help me with this. We just need to lift your knee up and I'll keep it there, and he'll deal with your ankle. You'll feel some sharp tugging but it shouldn't be too bad. We just need to do it sooner rather than later – we don't want you compromising the blood supply to your foot.'

A nervous looking youth was suddenly there clutching her ankle.

'Mikey?'

'Yes, love?'

'Hold my hand anyway.'

'OK. You are a piece of work . . . you know that, don't you?'

'I was making shortbread for you.'

'God! You didn't leave the oven on, did you?'

'Nope. I hadn't got that far.'

'Good. Chances are the house won't have burned down, then.'

'No, but I forgot to put the butter back in the fridge.'

'Woman, you are hopeless.'

'I know, I'm sorry. What were you doing at work?'

'I was working on a vegetarian option for the boeuf bour-guignon.'

'Couldn't you just leave out the meat?'

'And produce one of your onion specials?'

'Oh, I see what you mean.'

'I ran into your problem with the mushrooms though.'

'Oh – grey food?'

'Yup – not too appealing.'

There was a horrible crunching noise and Lyn felt her stomach clench. 'Uhh . . . I'm going to be sick again.'

'Not yet, please,' said the nurse, 'we just need to . . .' There was another crunch and Lyn felt a rush of cold sweat. She fell back against the pillow, coughed and closed her eyes.

The nurse looked at Mikey. 'You did OK. I guess you have nervous patients all the time?'

'Not really, I'm a chef.'

'Oh . . . all that white, I thought you were a dentist.' She was busy with the strapping. 'Right – she's been very lucky. It's most unusual to have a dislocation without a fracture, which is why we want to do another X-ray. She's torn the ligaments but it doesn't look as if she's lost circulation to the foot at any stage.' She straightened up and smiled. 'I've fixed a splint and nobody is to touch it until she's been re-examined. Right, let's clean these hands up.'

Lyn yelped as the nurse sprayed her hand with a high-pressure, antiseptic wash. 'God, that hurts.'

'You can't have any more painkillers for two hours, you're up to your limit. Give me your other hand.'

'Mikey.'

'Right here . . .' Her eyelids fluttered and she collapsed against him.

'Good – I'll get these fingernails off while she's out.' Mikey winced.

She was in a haze of pain . . . every time she closed her eyes, she saw Dylan staring at her in anguish and Mikey glaring in suspicion. I've gone mad, she thought, I don't want Dylan, I don't. At the thought, her eyes shot open again.

'Hush, darling.' Mikey's voice was gentle but he was looking very bleak and she shivered in terror. The nurse bent forward and began to dab at her face. She could feel very little but the antiseptic cream stung. The nurse looked up at Mikey. 'I can't do much here – it's clean enough but if I do anything else she'll just start bleeding again. You'd better take her home and let things settle.'

Lyn opened her eyes. 'Sorry. I was a terrible coward.'

'Brave as lions and tigers, sweetheart. I was proud of you.'

Her eyes were enormous. 'I wasn't brave. I was absolutely terrified the whole time. I thought Spike was going to be dismembered in front of me, I thought I was going to be shot in the leg and immobilised, then dragged off somewhere and chopped up inch by inch. Mikey, I thought I'd never see you again.'

Dylan walked in before he could respond.

125

Definitely one of the worst moments of my life – her ankle was huge and already purple; her face and arms were scratched to blazes, some of the cuts still bleeding; her hands were a mess. Her hair just looked ridiculous – apart from the enormous shaved patch, there was a jagged wound filled with glue and the rest of it was bushed out and filled with leaves and all sorts.

I didn't know where to touch her without hurting her.

And the room was full of people asking her questions and talking over her . . . she must have been hating that. She looked as if she was OK so they just kept badgering her but I knew she needed to go home. I needed her to come home with me.

When the nurse came back in I felt like killing her, then when her junior started wrenching Lyn's ankle about, trying to get it into a good position for the splint, I thought I'd definitely kill both of them, but Lyn put out a hand to me so I had to hold it. She didn't cry but her lips went completely white and her eyes closed tightly.

Dylan came back in, took one look and disappeared again.

The nurse handed over an instruction sheet and more painkillers.

I picked her up, still wrapped in a blanket, and carried her outside. I was going to call a taxi but Dad had already done it.

'Is she all right?' he asked. 'Lyn, darling, are you all right?' He'd been his usual bossy self in the medicentre but now he was all over the place. Lyn didn't say anything.

'They hurt her putting her ankle back in position,' I explained. 'Let's get her home and then we'll see.'

We drove home in silence. As soon as we pulled up at the gate, Mum shot out of the front door, followed by Krystal. 'Where's the wounded soldier? Let's take a look at you.' Then, as I carried Lyn into the living room and sat her down on the sofa, 'Oh, darling, my darling, look at you. Oh, my sweetheart . . .' Her voice faded away.

Krystal sat next to Lyn with her eyes full of tears, stroking her arm, kissing her hair, patting at her.

'Tea!' said Mum. 'Camomile I think – we all need it.'

'Rubbish,' said Dad, 'we need a real drink.'

Lyn raised her head. 'I . . . I . . .' Everybody went quiet. 'I know that camomile tea is a good idea but personally I would like a large brandy to start with, if you've got one.' Dad rushed off and Mum went to put the kettle on.

Lyn looked at Krystal. 'Don't cry, honey, it's not as bad as it looks although I understand that my hair's a bit of a mess.' Krystal gulped. 'Is Tim around?'

'He's upstairs,' Krystal sniffed, 'with Spike. Shall I ask him to come down?'

'If you could, love, I must have really scared him and I want him to see that I'm all right.' Krystal nodded and went out.

I put an arm around my lovely, kind wife. 'Darling, now do you understand about archaic endearments?'

She glared. 'Don't take advantage. I've never said they were demeaning in a family setting, even though I'm not used to them.'

'So, my darling, can I take it that your brain is unimpaired despite your attempt to bash it out?'

'Yes.'

'So, understand this: I have no intention of leaving you. I don't know how you've got hold of this idea but it's not going to happen. I'm the husband and what I say goes.'

'Is that supposed to reassure me?' she muttered.

369

'Depends on your point of view, I suppose.'

She put her bandaged hand against my cheek but didn't say anything because at that point Tim came into the room. He looked shattered.

Lyn looked up. 'Tim, come here. You are such a hero, thank you so much. See, it's not as bad as you thought. Is Spike OK?'

'You've got your voice back.'

I stared. 'What's this about your voice?'

Lyn glanced at me, then at Tim, obviously gauging what to say, how to make light of it. 'I lost my voice – when Tim found me I couldn't say a word. Apparently it was the shock. They just sprayed some muscle relaxant stuff down my throat and it came back.' Her eyes were fixed on Tim . . . don't say anything.

I sighed. Now all of my family were keeping secrets. 'I'll see what's happened to the brandy.'

126

The room was dim, with a soft pink light coming from the windows. Lyn shifted uncomfortably on the sofa and squinted. Her face felt oddly stiff and her eyes were swollen almost shut. She was wrapped in a soft duvet that she didn't recognise and she started to struggle up. Immediately a shooting pain from her ankle made her groan. She tried to raise her hands and saw that they were bandaged. A painful weight lay on her chest and she began to panic in earnest. Then she heard purring and squinted down her body. 'Spike.' Her voice was creaky and thin. 'Spikey Spike – you're too heavy.' Spike turned his head and widened his green eyes, then stretched and moved towards her face. She tried to shift him but couldn't get a grip with her bandaged hands. 'Spike.' He purred into her face and patted it with a soft paw then started to lick her chin. She felt caught between laughing and crying . . . it was so uncomfortable but so sweet of him at the same time.

'I thought I heard you.' Claire came into the room with a mug.

'What's that? Eye of newt and toe of frog?'

'Very funny . . . it's valerian and lemon balm to relax you.' She scooped Spike away with a practised hand. 'Once you've drunk it we'll sort out some breakfast for you and then Krystal and I will give you a bath.'

'What?' Her face flamed.

'Lyn, you need a bit of a wash and brush-up and some cream for your cuts and bruises. And Krystal has some ideas for your hair.'

'Oh God.' Lyn lay back and closed her eyes. I'm never going to cry again, she reminded herself. She struggled back up and reached out for the mug. 'Thanks, Claire. I don't want to be a nuisance. Where's Mikey by the way? I mean Michael.'

'He's had to go to work. Here, you need to take your painkillers now. He'll be back later. Now, what would you like for breakfast? Don't tell me you don't want anything because that won't help you. We've got toast, eggs, orange juice and Krystal can run out if you fancy bacon or pastries.'

'Toast will be fine, Claire, honestly.'

'You'll need protein so I'll scramble some eggs – unless you like them boiled – or an omelette?'

'Claire, please . . . I mean, scrambled will be fine.'

Claire nodded and smiled. 'Lyn, we're not going to boss you around, it's just that you need to be cosseted a bit, that's all. Try to relax and let us look after you.' She paused. 'I know it's awkward but you'll be here for a couple of days at least and Jack will be home for the weekend later on so you'll have to put up with everyone making a fuss of you.'

'You must think I'm very ungrateful and I'm not, truly.'

'Darling girl, I know that. I'm on shift later on but Krystal will be here to keep you company.'

Lyn nodded. Her eyes welled up but she blinked the tears away firmly and smiled.

After her bath – with her foot wrapped in two plastic bin bags and draped over the side of the bath tub – she did feel better. Then Claire left for work and Krystal started on her hair.

Krystal had lots of ideas, mostly involving distracting purple and turquoise dyes and shiny hair slides, but first her hair had to be combed free of debris and washed. It was agonising. Krystal, normally sweet and sympathetic, had absolutely no mercy.

'You're not planning on hair styling as a career, are you?'

'No, not really. It's number seven on the list.'

'Well, you're supposed to be gentle with your clients.'

'Most clients don't have half a bush in their hair. You'll thank me when it's done.'

'If I'm still conscious.'

The combing and washing over, Krystal went and made some camomile tea and found the next round of painkillers.

'I really don't want colours, Krystal, Michael won't like it.'

Krystal sat with her head on one side, considering. 'OK, I'll try a sort of stylised comb-over, although personally I don't think you should pay any attention to him. What does he know? It's your hair.'

Actually, reflected Lyn, it isn't – it all belongs to him, and I don't really mind. But that can't be right. I should be allowed to decide for myself.

Krystal looked at her closely and said, 'You look really exhausted, Lyn. I'm going to leave you to have a nap for a little while then I'll come back and finish your hair off and start on your face.'

Lyn tried to muster the energy to say something but went to sleep instead.

She woke to a face peering into hers at close range and sat up with a shriek.

'Oh, Lyn, sorry, I'm sorry, I didn't mean to frighten you.'

She shook her head. 'No, I'm the one that's sorry, Jack. I think my nerves are still a bit jangled up.' She tried to sit up but floundered in the cushions. Jack put his arms round her and scooped her upright, propped cushions behind her, shoved a footstool under her feet and sat down next to her. He took her hand gently.

'What have you done to this one, then?'

She sighed. 'I'm so clumsy – I ripped some fingernails off getting through the hedge.' She waved the other hand. 'I cut my palm on the fence on this one. I can still use my hands, it's just a bit awkward.' She sniffed, and he put an arm round her, patted her shoulder and somehow she found herself leaning on him.

Krystal stomped through the door. 'What are you doing? I told you not to wake her – I haven't done her face yet!' She was carrying a tray of tea things and looked completely exasperated. 'Lyn, you are impossible – I can't leave you alone for a minute. And you're such a flirt as well. Mum would be furious!'

Despite herself Lyn smiled. 'Oh, Krystal, he was just trying to comfort me. I was feeling a bit wobbly.'

'Of course you were. Now drink your tea and I'll sort the rest of you out.'

Jack frowned. 'Don't I get tea?'

'You'll have to get your own – this is camomile. You hate it, but it's good for Lyn.'

'I bet she'd rather have a drink. Do you want a beer, Lyn?'

'Not at the moment, thanks. Maybe later.'

'Right, I'll be back in a minute.'

She sipped her tea while Krystal bustled about with cotton wool and a bowl of steaming water. Her face felt horribly stiff.

'Right.' Krystal was consulting a list of directions with a frown of concentration. 'Sprinkle the mix into the bowl of water and leave to steep for four minutes. Soak the cotton wool and use to swab the injuries. Don't forget the tweezers and plastic gloves.'

'It all sounds very medical, Krystal.'

'Oh, sure. Mum knows all about this sort of thing – she doesn't want you going septic.'

Jack wandered back in, just as Krystal was advancing on her patient. 'Do you want me to hold your hand, Lyn?'

'No, I'll be fine.'

The next instant she was clutching both his hands as tears of pain ran down her face. The water in the bowl was turning red. Even Krystal looked a bit startled. 'It'll stop in a moment,' she muttered, 'I'm sure it will – it's just the . . . er . . . dried blood coming off.'

Lyn looked at Jack and he smiled as reassuringly as he could. 'She's right, Lyn, it's stopping now. There, now we can see what's happening.'

Krystal applied some clean cotton wool. Jack squeezed her hands. Lyn sniffed. 'OK,' announced Krystal. 'I just need to get the cream Mum left in the fridge and you'll feel loads better.'

'Jack?'

'Yes?'

'Do I look as awful as I feel?'

He regarded her with a faintly judicious eye. 'Worse, I should think – don't you know how you look?'

'No – I haven't seen a mirror since it happened.'

He nodded. 'Best not really.'

'But Michael said I looked as if I'd fallen into the mincer.'

'Hey – that's pretty accurate.'

She leant back with a sigh and murmured, 'He won't love me any more.'

Jack put his arms round her again. 'Lyn, darling Lyn, you're not making any sense. Michael loves you for loads of reasons, he has since he was sixteen and used to bore us to death about it, but I promise you that your looks are the least of it. And if he goes off you I'm happy to oblige.' Before she could muster a reply the front door banged and Mikey walked into the room.

'Woman, why are you cuddling my brother?' he demanded.

Krystal hovered behind him clutching another bowl. 'Oh, Jack, not again!'

Lyn looked up at Mikey with immense relief. 'You've got some stiff competition, chef, but take your place in line and I'll get to you.'

Jack leapt up and muttered, 'I'll get you a beer,' before disappearing into the kitchen. Mikey took his place on the sofa and ran a finger down her face. 'That looks so sore, baby. Hasn't Krystal applied the bat gizzard and saliva ointment yet?'

'Bat gizzard?' shrieked Krystal.

'Little sister, it's a joke. Why don't you leave it with me and I'll see to it?'

'OK. Here, do you want the plastic gloves?'

'No – I'll risk it.'

'What time is it? Why are you home?' asked Lyn, anxiously.

'I've got to go back later – I thought I'd nip round between service.'

'Thank you. I missed you so much. I mean – Krystal's been marvellous but I feel so dreadful.'

'And Jack?'

'Oh, yes, Jack's been great as well, and Tim was last night.' She groaned. 'When can I go home?'

'Once the French doors are fixed and we think it's safe.'

She nodded. 'Spike wants to go home too.'

'Where is he?'

'I think he's under that chair – he didn't like all the blood and gore, or the screaming.'

'There, all finished. Did it hurt a lot?'

'Not really. I feel much better when you're here.'

'Aw, shucks, ma'am, you're just saying that.'

'No, really.' She tried to pull him closer but her bandaged hands couldn't get a purchase. 'Mikey, I really mean it.'

He dug in his back pocket and produced a silky green scarf. 'Here, Jessica thought this would be easier to handle than fiddling about with your hair all the time, at least until it's grown back a bit.' He pulled her head forward, looped the scarf over her scalp and tied it firmly at the back. Then he pulled out a few tendrils of hair around her face. 'That's my girl.'

She stared. 'Is it really better like this?'

'Yes, sweetheart, it really is. And it won't be for long.'

'What about my face?'

'Do you want to see?'

'Yes.'

He reached behind the sofa and pulled out the mirror that

usually hung on the wall. Lyn drew breath. 'Well, it's much worse than I thought but I'm sure it will wear off in a day or two.' She took another look. There was a long deep gash across her nose, one eye was pink and puffy, her forehead was a mass of scratches and her chin was raw. Her cheeks were scratched but not too badly. Everything glistened unattractively beneath a layer of ointment.

She gazed at Mikey appealingly. 'It will get better, I swear.'

She licked her lips nervously. 'Perhaps your mum's got some hemlock stowed away for this sort of emergency.'

He nodded. 'Or rats' bane or something . . . do you want me to check?'

'I know this isn't what you bargained for.' She gave a shuddering laugh. 'Judith said she'd remodel my face.'

'It's hardly what anyone would bargain for. You need to rest some more. I'll see you later.'

'Don't go, Mikey, I can't bear it. I know I look disgusting but it will get better.' She struggled to get a grip on his sleeve.

He looked down at her for a moment then dug out his mobile. 'Gareth, can you cover? Sure, it's all prepped. Owen's been in all day – he'll update you. Thanks, mate, I owe you one. What? No, she's OK – a bit battered but OK. Will do.'

'I'm sorry,' she moaned. 'I'm just being feeble but I feel so terrible.'

'Gareth sends you lots of love. Oh, and Nicola and Marvin are making some sort of dessert for you.' He sat down and she groaned. 'Hush, darling, just go to sleep, I'll sit with you.'

'Hold my hand.'

'Are you sure?'

'Yes. I don't care if it hurts, I just don't want you to go anywhere.' Her eyes closed.

A noise at the door made him look round. Claire was standing there looking exasperated. 'So you were planning on going back to work, were you? Have I raised an idiot?'

'It's OK, Mum, Gareth's covering.'

'Sure, after you'd got her all upset again. When she wakes up you'd better be here and be good and ready to reassure her that you still love her.'

'She knows that.'

'Well, that's just where you're wrong, she's already told Jack you won't love her any more.'

'Jack?'

'Yes – he's only seventeen and he's more mature than you.'

'Mum, I'm not the bad guy here. I didn't do any of this.'

She glared at him. 'You have no idea, do you?' she grumbled, heading for the kitchen.

Mikey looked down at Lyn. 'You'll always be my girl, sweetheart. You don't need to worry but the sooner we get out of here the better.'

127

Dylan sighed heavily. 'My dear girl, you don't look at all well. I'm sorry about this but I do need to check some things on your statement.'

'It's OK, Dylan, it looks worse than it is – a couple more days and the bandages will be off my hands, then I can sort the rest of me out.'

'Right. Let's press on then. You didn't actually say who attacked you?'

'I didn't actually see anyone – I was too busy running away.'

'Yet we both know it was Judith.'

'Well – I don't know how you know but yes, I know it was her because she was humming.'

'Humming?'

'Yes – it's a bit of a cliché but when we were in the dump playing hide and seek she didn't like the dark, so she used to hum. When she got older she used it as a threat to say she was coming to get you. The little ones were terrified of her.'

'She rang you when she was outside – did she speak?'

'No, that was another sort of message, a code: three rings, then a gap, then two. That sort of thing.'

'You were very precise about the nature of the threat when you were speaking to Mikey at the medicentre. You thought she was going to immobilise you, kill Spike with you watching and then ... now, what was it? Ah yes – drag you off some-where and chop you up. What made you think that?'

'When she joined security she was doing the administration on a case where that happened. She thought that it must have

379

been the worst kind of torture to see something you loved destroyed in front of you. She knew I didn't like her telling me details but it didn't stop her.'

'Why did you choose to hide in the field and not seek help from your neighbours?'

'She would have caught me – she runs faster, she's stronger and I had Spike to carry. I knew she wouldn't look for me in the dark. Dump children are all scared of the dark, Dylan. She thinks I'm a terrible coward, so she'd have looked for me closer to home first, which gave me time to hide.'

'And you're not afraid of the dark?'

'Absolutely petrified, to tell the truth, but it turned out I was more afraid of my best friend.'

'With very good reason. That's it really – I wanted to tie up the loose ends.' He smiled. 'Mr Jones is right – you are a brave woman, albeit a clumsy one.'

'Dylan, what is happening to Judith? Has she been charged with anything? Will I have to see her in court? Did you catch her?'

'Yes, we tracked her through her mobile, as you'd expect. It's a very clear case and we can handle it under centre security rules. Nothing for you to worry about.'

'But is she still around?'

'Oh, you mean have we locked her up and thrown away the key? Something of that nature. You really don't need to know.'

Lyn sighed heavily. 'Really, my dear, you must leave it to us.'

Mikey was waiting for her outside, his face taut. 'Are you OK? Why wouldn't they let me come in with you? What happened? Was it Dylan? Or someone else? Do you need a drink? Do you want to sit down?'

She stared. 'Whatever's the matter? You're burbling at me. I'm fine. I'd like a very expensive coffee and a cream cake. Followed by a lie-down with my favourite cat.'

He didn't even smile. 'Right – we'll go over there.' He shepherded her into a cafe, deposited her on a squashy sofa and shot off to the counter. She sank back slightly apprehensively. She'd seen a movie where somebody got eaten by a sofa and this one felt particularly deep. She was trying to wedge a cushion behind her back when Mikey sank down opposite her.

'What are you doing – don't you feel well?'

'I'm fine,' she repeated. 'I'm just trying to make sure this big sofa doesn't eat me.'

'Eat you?'

'Like in that horror movie.'

'I have extensive experience of horror movies and I've never seen one where the furniture ate people.'

'Perhaps it was an old one – anyway I don't want it to happen here.'

'Love, do you really feel OK?'

'Well, a bit sore and bruised but nothing other than that. Why?'

'Our family licence has come through.'

'But we haven't finished the application.'

'They've changed the process – I checked while you were being interviewed in case they'd made a mistake. We have to take a family parenting course before we do the final part of the application and you can only do that if you're licensed because they don't want to waste training on couples who aren't going to pass – so basically we've done it.'

'Good grief, Mikey, that's astounding. When do we go on the training course?'

'There isn't one for two months, so you should be better by then.'

'Yes, but don't let me forget I've got that X-ray this afternoon. They won't let you in for that either,' she added with a faintly malicious grin. 'You can't have it all your own way, chef.'

Two coffees and a pinkish mound covered in cream and strawberries appeared on the table between them. Momentarily distracted, Mikey sniffed the coffee, then tasted it. Then he peered at the dessert. 'It's supposed to be a bavarois but it looks like a pile of . . .'

'Mikey, for heaven's sake, get over yourself.'

He sat back. 'This little jaunt of yours has done you the world of good.'

'I wouldn't say that. Whatever do you mean?'

'I thought you'd be upset but actually you seem fine . . . better than fine really.'

'Well, I could tell you that I'm putting on a brave face and inside I'm a quivering jelly but that wouldn't be true. Maybe I'll wake up tomorrow completely traumatised but I don't think so.'

'Tim seems more upset than anyone.' He gave her a questioning look.

She shook her head. 'Nothing happened. It was just a lot for him to deal with at his age. His sister-in-law covered in blood and speechless with terror, clinging to him for dear life and refusing to be parted from a cat carrier. I was a mess.'

He nodded. 'OK, point taken. Drink your very expensive coffee, darling, then we'll nip home and check on the French doors.'

'There's a problem.'

'There is?'

'I can't manage these slidey mugs and forks and things. Sorry – I hadn't thought of it.'

Completely unembarrassed, he moved round the table and sat beside her. The sofa sagged dramatically. 'See what you mean about the man-eating sofa. Here you go.' He held a forkful of pink goo to her mouth. 'How is it?'

'I'm not sure yet. I'd better have some more to check it thoroughly.'

'Try the coffee.' She smiled and took a loud slurp. 'Sorry, that wasn't very elegant.'

'If I'd wanted elegant I'd have married Kylie or Jolene.'

128

The bridge spanned a broad stretch of water where the canal finally met the river. It was quite pretty at dusk, Lyn thought. There were some lights on the opposite bank, and a couple of boats, and it was very quiet. She pulled herself up on the railing so that she could see over properly. She'd fed Spike and made some soup that just needed reheating. She thought she could hear a muted splashing and peered at the water below her trying to make out what it was.

'Lyn!'

Her entire body jerked in shock. 'God, Dylan, you scared me. I was miles away.'

Dylan put out a hand to help her down from the railing. 'Miles from home, certainly. These railings aren't for climbing on – they're a safety feature designed to stop people falling in.'

'Oh, sorry, I was just trying to spot the swans.'

'What are you doing here in the dark on your own?'

'Nothing ... I mean I was just taking a walk and it wasn't dark when I started. Still isn't, really.' She faltered to a stop. 'Is there something wrong?'

'No, only that I get the feeling that you're out and about without your husband's permission again.'

'He won't mind, Dylan. I sent him a text and if he finishes early he'll join me. I just needed some exercise and we come here sometimes at the weekends. It's not so far from home, you know.'

Dylan shook his head. 'It isn't safe. I'm going to walk you

back now and we'll say no more about it but if it happens again I'll have to tag you.'

They started to walk back across the bridge. Lyn was hunched with anger and fright. Dylan took her arm as they stepped back on to the pavement and matched his pace to hers.

'Listen, Lyn, I'm sure you think this is an over-reaction but you have been having an exciting time of late and while it's fine for you to stick to your normal outings in the day, you simply can't wander about like this at night.'

'But how did you know I was wandering about?'

'Lyn, you're an intelligent woman. It must have occurred to you that I hold a range of responsibilities in addition to my counselling role. You've been coded "special interest" for some time now, so anything out of the ordinary is flagged up immediately. Obviously it takes time to find you but the centre does pride itself on its coverage of the city. Once you'd been located I just came out to get you.'

'You mean you knew when I'd left the house?'

'In a way – we knew when the house had no human occupants because it's on a fifteen-minute sweep at the moment. Although we didn't know precisely when you'd left, we started a search scan at once.'

'Oh God!' She tried to pull away and was surprised at the strength of his grip. 'What if I'd just been going round to see the family? Would you have turned up there? And what do you mean, "special interest"? Does Mikey know about this?'

'The family? Oh, Mitch's family. Probably not, once we'd identified the address. You shouldn't think of them as your family, you know, there's no blood connection.'

'They treat me as one of the family.'

'Of course, they're good people, but if Mitch ever decides to de-select for some reason you won't have anything to do with them from that point on. It isn't fair to either party for you to get too attached.'

'He's not going to de-select! We've passed our probation! We're fine!'

Dylan stopped walking and pulled her round to face him. 'I'm just spelling it out for you – your only connection with this family is through him and once he's gone, they've gone. It's the rules. It saves unnecessary complications.'

She hung her head. 'I understand.'

'Good. Don't be too downcast, I know it's unlikely to happen, but it's best to be prepared. And as for that husband of yours, he's obviously giving you a little too much latitude, so try not to take advantage.'

'Dylan, I want to know why I'm coded special interest. I haven't done anything.'

He glanced down at her. 'It doesn't mean you've done anything against the rules, although you do sail a bit close to the wind on occasion. It means that the head of centre finds you of special interest, so we keep an eye on you.'

'But why?'

'Because you are exactly that – special and interesting.'

They walked the rest of the way in silence. Lyn turned miserably outside the house. 'Do you want to come in?'

Dylan nodded. 'I think I'd better, just to check things out. Don't worry, I'll be gone long before Mitch gets back.'

For some reason this made her feel more anxious. Inside, she offered coffee and led Dylan into the kitchen. He waved a small monitor at the downstairs doors and windows, then took a seat. 'You're looking well, my dear. Not much of a limp and your face is healing well. How's the scalp wound?'

'It still itches a bit sometimes but that's all.'

'Good. Come and sit down for a minute.' He smiled at her and patted the sofa. 'You've made this house very inviting, Lyn, something I fear it never was in Professor Langdale's time.'

'You knew Greg?'

'Only casually. I came to an Arts Trust evening here once, just before he selected you. It was all very serious and quite dull, although he did have a fascinating array of house plants. He must have been quite an interesting husband even though he was so much older.'

'Dylan, stop fishing for information. I've told you before it was an honour to be selected by Greg.'

His expression hardened and instinctively she gulped in fright. 'And I've told you that I don't believe you.' She tried to stand up and he put a firm hand on her arm. 'Listen, dear lady, things would be considerably less complicated if you just told me the truth.'

'About what?'

'About Professor Langdale, about Judith, about your young friend in black . . . how can I protect you if you don't tell me everything?'

'Everything?' She tried hard not to make eye contact but failed dismally. 'Dylan, there isn't any everything.'

'You expect me to believe you live this perilous, dramatic life quite accidentally?' His hand tightened on her arm and she gave another gulp of fear.

'I don't know what you mean. I don't know what you want. I don't need you to protect me, I've got Mikey.'

Dylan paused as if considering how to proceed. 'Lyn, I want you to understand that whatever happens you can always come to me.' He leant towards her and she hurled herself out of her seat and shot behind the table. Dylan looked bemused and irritated. 'Believe me, my dear, if I was about to make any inappropriate or unwanted advances you'd need to move a lot faster than that.' As he spoke he took two paces towards her and grabbed her shoulders.

She gazed into his suddenly cold face. Her voice trembled. 'Dylan . . .'

He shook his head and took a step towards the door. 'Apologies . . . I shouldn't have said that. It's been a long day and I'm wanting my supper and a stiff drink.'

He stood behind her and patted her shoulder. 'Remember,

no more nocturnal wanderings. Thanks for the coffee. I'll see myself out.'

When she heard the front door close she sat down with a thud. 'Oh, Spike, what's going on?' A dull throb of unease ran through her. 'I'm fed up with all these men, that's for sure.' Spike mewed unhappily. 'OK, Mister Cat, what would you like? Salmon? Caviar? Tough, you've got pretend pheasant tonight.'

129

They were at the market together. Mikey had one arm slung possessively across Lyn's shoulders as he steered her through the crowds. 'Where do you want to go first?'

She smiled. 'I'd like to get us a coffee and a pastry before we do anything else.'

He nodded. 'OK, you got it. After that?'

'Normally I would go to the jewellery stalls and scarves and things like that. I'd leave the food stalls 'til the end.'

They followed the usual route through the market, sipping their coffee and chewing on pastries. 'Do you like this junk?'

'No, Mikey, but it's all part of the experience.'

At the stall where she'd found his leather tie, she stopped. There were a number of cuffs and pins in the same style. She chose a cuff, paid and insisted that he wore it immediately.

'I won't be able to wear it at work.'

'Maybe not, but you're not at work now so behave yourself.' She limped off to the next stall then looked back at him. 'It definitely suits you.' Above their heads the cameras whirred and recorded.

'Shall I get you something?'

'If you like.'

'What do you want?'

'Surprise me.'

She flicked through the filmy scarves heaped on the stall and picked out two, in rose pink and sky blue. 'What do you think?'

'Too girly.'

388

She nodded, riffled through the pile again and came up with a rich midnight blue and shimmering dark gold scarf.

'That's better.'

They moved on, examining carvings, enamel boxes, glass animals, wind chimes . . . Finally, Lyn stopped. 'Sorry, I've got to rest my ankle for a minute. Do you think we could sit down here?'

'Here' was one of the alcoves reserved for cafe customers.

'Do you mean you'd like an ice cream?'

'What a lovely idea.' Her eyes shone. 'I've hardly ever had ice cream.'

'You're kidding, right?'

'No, we didn't have it in the dump so I never really thought of it and Greg didn't like desserts so when we went out we just used to have coffee after dinner.'

'No wonder Krystal thought you ate slugs!'

'It's not that big a deal . . . I thought I didn't like dessert either. It was always rice pudding in the dump.'

He groaned and rolled his eyes. 'Tomorrow I'll teach you how to make ice cream at home. Today you can have a scoop of strawberry and a wafer, if you're very good.'

They sat in the sunshine with their ice creams and coffees. Lyn sighed.

'Are you getting tired?'

'A bit. Perhaps we should just head to the produce section and leave the rest for another day.'

Mikey didn't try to suppress his grin of relief. 'Great – I can't take much more cute stuff. Oh, this found its way into my pocket.'

He handed her a screw of tissue paper. She shook it open and a crystal pendant fell out. He slipped it round her neck. 'Rose quartz, I believe.' She nodded.

'You didn't tell me that it had a therapeutic meaning.'

'Well, I thought you'd think I was deranged.'

'You know what it is then?'

'Yes.' She was embarrassed. 'Unconditional love.'

'Right.' He grinned at her. 'The boy wants romance in his marriage.'

'He's going the right way to get it.'

'Good – let's go and see what sort of cabbages they've got.'

130

It was suspiciously quiet when I got back from the wholesalers. I wasn't in the best mood because their fish selection was abysmal. I'd had to go for cheap and cheerful to get the volume and the freshness but they'd need a lot more preparation to get the flavours right. I'd have to change the menu as well. Thinking hard, I flung open the kitchen door to find the entire team clustered in a huddle, chattering over a small mountain of recipes.

'Why is nobody working?' I bellowed. 'Why haven't you started the vegetable prep? Look at the state of this floor!'

Predictably, everybody jumped and started to get to work.

'It's my fault,' said Lyn, as the crowd around her thinned. 'I just called in to see if you'd got an ice cream recipe. You did promise.'

'And it took how many of you . . . nine people to help?' I glared round the kitchen but nobody met my eye.

'How many chefs does it take to find an ice cream recipe?' murmured my beloved wife, unhelpfully. I swung back round and glared at her. She was holding her pendant up to the light admiringly. Then she shot me a slitty-eyed, laughing look.

'Oh, that's very pretty,' breathed Nicola looking up from her chopping block. 'Where did you find it?'

'The farmer's market. Mikey bought it for me.'

'Right!' I barked. 'Enough! You, in my office, now!' Into the startled silence that followed I added, as caustically as I could manage, 'There's half a ton of distinctly average fish over there. I want suggestions for this evening!'

391

In the office Lyn was perched on my desk looking about twelve years old. 'What are you playing at? My team are paid to work, not to entertain you.'

'I know. Actually, I hadn't been here long and they were just trying to help.' She swung her legs idly. I glared. Her lips started to quiver and her shoulders to shake. I glared some more. She looked down. She looked up.

I pulled her off the table and gave her a shake. 'It isn't funny – a kitchen runs on discipline.'

'Yes, chef.'

I meant to sit her in a chair out of the way but somehow my grip tightened instead and I started to kiss her. Her hands slipped up my back inside my T-shirt. My hands shot down to her bottom. 'Whoa,' I mumbled, 'we'd better stop right now because it's unhygienic.' There was a muted crash as a heap of files cascaded off the desk.

'Not to mention health and safety,' she replied. We were heading for the carpet when I managed to take control and we ended up sitting against the wall. Still very entangled but no real harm done.

'OK, if you'd just stop kissing me I think I ought to get back to work.'

'I like that – it's you that was doing all the kissing, as I recall. I was just doing a bit of incidental fondling.'

'Oh, I wondered what that was called.'

Five minutes later we went back through the kitchen. Lyn had a couple of ice cream recipes and a suitably chastened expression. I was looking stern. I accompanied her to the pavement outside the restaurant where I took her in my arms, swung her round and gave her a firm pat on the bottom to send her on her way.

I went back into the kitchen just in time to hear the sous chef saying, 'I think it's very sweet. They're obviously crazy about each other.'

I decided to let her off. I felt ludicrously happy but I scowled as I looked round the kitchen. Took a taste of the soup and shouted, 'Who is responsible for this? Check the seasoning! It needs more tarragon! And where are those menu suggestions?' Then I strode back to my office. I thought I'd been pretty convincing but when I heard the babble of rising comment I realised I hadn't.

131

Lyn was fiddling with her headscarf. Krystal had given her some feathery earrings in green and gold and they swung lightly as she moved her head. She sighed. Her hair was beginning to grow back but it looked tufty, and reddish patches of scalp showed through. Most of the glue had peeled off but a solid residue remained embedded in the scar tissue and she just didn't know when, if ever, it would lift away. She fought the temptation to give it a sharp tug – she couldn't stand the thought of having to go back to the medicentre if she did any damage.

She shifted her attention to her face. The scratches had faded to nothing and her chin looked pink but not too bad. It was the gash across her nose that was taking ages to heal – she rubbed in the antiseptic cream and sighed again. Spike clambered on to the bed next to her and batted at her earrings.

'Stop titivating, woman, it's time to go.'

'Be patient. It takes me longer to sort myself out at the moment. My head's all itchy and I can't get the scarf right with one hand.'

'Let me do it then.'

'No, you know what happened the last time you tried to help me get dressed.'

'Come on . . . we haven't got time to waste fooling around.' He untied the scarf and smoothed her hair. 'Sit still.' He held her shoulders and straightened the scarf before sweeping it up and over her hair. As he bent forward to tie it at the back he groaned. 'What?'

'Nothing. There – you're done.'

She straightened up and patted his cheek. 'Thank you, kind sir.' He groaned again. 'It's no use – it must be the smell of that antiseptic stuff.'

'Oh dear. Try reciting Shakespeare.'

He toppled her back on to the bed. 'Mikey, we haven't got time.'

'It's OK – I'm just going to kiss you.'

'That's what you said the last time.'

At the restaurant, Jessica was impatiently shifting from foot to foot. 'Good – you're here. Have a drink. Marvin's a nervous wreck but he should calm down a bit now he knows that you've arrived.' She thrust a menu into Mikey's hand. 'Here you are, chef, but please don't order the salmon parcels – they've exploded.'

Lyn snorted with laughter and stroked Mikey's arm. 'Don't worry, Jessica, I won't let him.' Jessica beamed with relief and waved a waitress over. 'What will you have to drink?'

'I'd like a cocktail, please, one of those pink ones and . . .' She looked enquiringly at Mikey, who was still seriously examining the menu. 'I guess chef would like a beer.' The waitress clattered away on delicate silver shoes. Lyn sighed.

'What?'

'Oh, I was just thinking that I'd never be able to wear shoes like that again.'

'You don't wear shoes like that anyway.'

'That isn't the point. I'm condemned to trainers and support socks – it's not a good look.' She slipped her good foot out of her trainer and ran her toes thoughtfully up his calf. The results were spectacular. Mikey gave a yelp of shock and jolted in his seat. 'Christ! What are you doing?' he hissed at her.

'Sorry. Greg used to like it so I thought you would as well.'

'Well, just warn me next time, OK.'

She sniggered. 'OK . . . this is your three-second warning.' She ran her foot further up his leg, just as the waitress arrived with their drinks.

'Are you ready to order, chef?'

Mikey coughed.

'Not quite,' smiled Lyn. 'Can we have a few more minutes?' She inched her foot higher.

'Stop it.'

'I can't reach any further anyway,' she admitted. 'Ah well. Do you like it?'

'Not in my restaurant, no.'

'But that's supposed to be what makes it thrilling.' She grinned. 'I've got a whole repertoire of potentially exciting moves that Greg enjoyed.'

'He was obviously totally warped. Now behave yourself. We're here to do Marvin's entry level assessment, not muck about.'

'I love it when you're stern with me.'

He gave her a reluctant grin. 'No, you don't – you don't like anyone telling you what to do. Listen, if I have the chicken and sauté potatoes, will you have the steak au poivre? We have to try both mains and both desserts but we can share the goat's cheese tart to begin with since the salmon parcels are off.'

132

'What is this?' Mikey was waving a freezer carton.

'What do you think?'

'How the hell do I know? It hasn't got a label on it!'

'Mikey, it's obviously ice cream.'

'What sort?'

'Orange.'

'You've made orange ice cream?'

'Yes, it's delicious. They didn't have strawberries so I used my initiative.'

'You should have made a sorbet – citrus fruit doesn't go well with cream.'

'I promise you, it's great. And stop waving it about – you'll drop it.'

'How are you planning to serve it?'

'In a bowl, with a spoon.'

'No way – it'll need a drizzle of something and frosted peel curls to look anything like right.' He was prising up the edge of the carton. 'Actually it might look OK if you used a melon scoop – a sort of miniature dessert.' He dug a teaspoon into the mixture.

'Huh. Not bad – a bit heavy on the sugar but you're right, it is pretty good. It looks horrible though. It's a very strange colour.'

'Have you finished? What are you doing in the freezer anyway, it's my night.'

'I thought we'd have steak – we've got to eat it at some point and you need to learn how to cook it properly.'

133

It was warm and Mikey was too heavy, so Lyn had squirmed out of his arms and was clinging to the edge of the bed as he restlessly and remorselessly wriggled towards her in his sleep. 'Ooof!' he grunted. She squinted across at him – Spike had landed on his stomach and he was stirring, eyes blinking, hands reaching for her. 'Babe?' he muttered.

'Over here,' she hissed back. Honestly, where did he think she was going to be? She watched as Spike stalked impressively up Mikey's chest, sniffed thoroughly at his nose, then circled before settling down. Mikey stroked him and sniffed back. 'You smell good too, fella.'

She groaned. 'You like the smell of damp cat?'

'Sure. He's been out . . . he smells fresh.'

'Do you want me to go and stand out in the garden as well?'

'Hmmm . . . I think I'll have to check you out first. What are you doing right over there?'

'I'm too hot.'

'Oh, just stick a foot out, that'll cool you down. Now then, let's see.' He dislodged the cat, rolled over, took her hand, turned it palm up and began to sniff her wrist.

'Yeah, nice.' He carried on snuffling up her arm until he reached the inside of her elbow, where he paused, then nipped at her flesh.

She jumped. 'Don't bite me, for heaven's sake.'

'Just a little taste, sweetheart. Well, I'm not sure . . . I'll just have to check a bit further.'

A warmly languorous flicker of something ran under her

skin. 'OK, I give in.' She lay still waiting for his next move. Then she heard snoring. She glanced across at him and he'd dozed off, just like that. She was still too hot. She stuck her foot out from under the duvet and sighed.

134

The knock on the door startled her. Lucas was standing there looking at her gravely.

'You shouldn't be here.'

He looked up and down the empty street and raised his eyebrows. 'Because people will talk?'

'No, Lucas, because Mitch is at the restaurant.'

'That's why I'm here. It seemed like an ideal opportunity. We need to talk.'

'We don't.' She tried to stand her ground although she could feel a sweat breaking out under her headscarf.

'OK, I need to talk and you need to listen.'

'No, Lucas, leave it.'

'We have unfinished business.'

'We don't.'

'Come on, let me in.' Very deliberately he placed both hands on her shoulders and stepped up close.

'No.'

'Yes.' He pushed her back into the hall, shouldering the door closed behind him. His hands ran down her arms to the elbow and he pinned her against the wall for a moment before taking a deep breath and pulling her into an embrace. 'God, that feels good. Look at me, why don't you?'

'You're scaring me, Lucas.'

'You know you've broken my heart, don't you?'

'No, actually I don't.' She swallowed. 'I don't know what you're talking about.'

His grip tightened. 'Why was it always him? Why didn't you choose me?'

'You know I couldn't choose anyone, Lucas, you know how it works.'

Suddenly his grip slackened and he sighed. 'OK, let's have some coffee or a beer or something.' He headed for the kitchen. Lyn hesitated. She could make a run for it but she didn't want to leave him in the house. She could call Mikey but her mobile was in the kitchen. She dithered, took a step towards the door, a step towards the stairs. She couldn't leave him in the kitchen – it was full of potential weapons. She hovered in the kitchen door, watching as Lucas helped himself to a beer from the alco store. 'What do you want?' he said over his shoulder.

'White wine, I guess.' Her knees quivered and she sat down quickly.

'You didn't answer my question – why didn't you choose me?'

'I couldn't choose anyone, Lucas.' Her voice was shaking.

'But you liked me better.'

'No, I didn't.' Her voice was now a yelp.

'You did – all those times we shared jokes in front of all the other morons in the class, you must have known how I felt.' He took a huge gulp of beer, wiped his mouth, leant across the table. 'It was like we were telepathic – we understood each other.'

'It wasn't like that . . . we just shared a sense of humour maybe.'

'So why didn't you love me?'

He sounded so bitterly anguished that she looked into his eyes. They were filled with tears.

'Oh God, Lucas, don't be so upset. Mikey says you've got loads of girlfriends. This is just silly.'

'Silly?' He half rose from his chair and she shrank back. 'I know you. I know what you like. I know what you want. You want somebody with intellectual ability, somebody who appreciates you. Is it because I've got girlfriends then? Fine! I'll get rid of them. I'll show you.'

Keep him talking, she thought, he'll get fed up with it in the end.

'Lucas, you're making too much of this. What's got you so wound up?'

'You won't see me.'

'I haven't been seeing anyone. Most of my hair is missing, I've still got a limp and my fingernails haven't grown back.'

'Do you think I care about that?'

'No, but I do.'

'It isn't your looks – they're nothing special. It's your personality. And you're brave.' He shook his head and put his face in his hands. 'Brave and lively and just everything I ever wanted. Why did you have to marry him?'

'I had no choice. But Lucas, you have to understand that I don't want to be with anyone else.' He didn't respond. 'How about some coffee?'

'Sure.'

She got up and moved towards the coffee breaker and in one swift lunge he had her pinned against the wall again – by her throat this time.

'If I can't have you . . .'

'Nobody can? Not very cool, really, is it, Lucas?'

He didn't release her but he managed a wry smile. 'So, what do you suggest?'

She felt so ashamed, she thought she might shrivel up right there on the floor. She felt so scared she thought she might die of fright. 'What do you want?'

'Everything . . . but for the moment, I guess this will do.' One hand began to fumble with her shirt buttons. She tried to slow her breathing. Ran a hand down his back. Picked up the frying pan with the other and brought it down on his head. He sagged a bit but not enough, so she hit him again and this time he thudded to his knees. 'Stay down, you bastard, or I might have to kill you.'

To her relief he stayed down and coughed. 'Think yourself lucky I couldn't reach the knife rack. Now go away.'

'But I love you,' he mumbled.

'I don't care.'

'You will. I'll make you care.'

'Lucas, piss off.'

He looked up in outrage. 'That's not very nice, is it!'

'It's not supposed to be.'

When Mikey got home she was watering the garden with Spike bounding about at her feet.

'Don't let him get my courgettes, they're coming on really well.'

'I don't think he will – he's not a vegetarian cat.'

'I'm not expecting him to grill them or sauté them but he might decide to dig them up or wee on them.'

'Oh, heaven forbid.'

'You sound a bit ratty, what's up?'

'Luke came over.'

'Did he? I never got round to ringing him.' He dug out his mobile.

'Mikey, he tried to kiss me.'

'He did? What did you do?'

'Hit him with the frying pan – twice.'

'Twice?'

'Well, I thought he wasn't going to stay down.'

'Still, it sounds a bit extreme. Couldn't you just have reasoned with him?'

'Oh, I knew you'd be on his side. Listen, he pinned me against the wall. He had his hands around my throat. What was I supposed to do? Huh?' Her voice was shaking. She turned her back. 'He frightened me, Mikey – he terrified me, if you must know. He said he was in love with me and I'd broken his heart

403

and it was just horrible.' She hurled the watering can across the flowerbed. Spike raced to the end of the garden and hauled his fat body up a tree.

Mikey went back into the house and she sat down on the lawn, dry-eyed, her fists clenched with frustration and misery. It's a disaster, she thought, every time I think I'm getting it right something else goes wrong.

'Here.' She looked up. Mikey was back with a brandy. Despite herself she grinned.

'Not toast then?'

'Sometimes brandy is better.' He took a healthy slug himself then passed her the glass. She took a huge gulp. 'Careful – who taught you to drink it like that?'

'Dylan.'

'Oh, of course.'

He took her hand and held it against his chest. 'Feel that?'

'Yes.'

'It's yours . . . that means I'm faithful to you. That doesn't just mean I don't have other girlfriends, it means that I take your side – not Luke's or anybody's, just yours.'

She sniffed and drank some more brandy. 'I suppose that's what you mean by a romantic declaration?'

He looked undeniably smug. 'Sure, woman, I have the soul of a poet.'

'It was horrible, Mikey.'

'I know, darling. I'll make sure he leaves you alone in future.'

'How?'

'Don't know yet – I'll think of something, don't you worry.'

135

Eyes narrowed against the drizzle, Judith watched as Luke made his way back down the street. He didn't look quite as sleek and jaunty as usual and was shaking his head. She wondered what the undercover centre security guard keeping watch on the front door had been instructed to do – just note comings and goings she supposed, and call in if he spotted her. He'd be lucky . . . she could pass within inches of him and he wouldn't notice her. She wondered what to do next.

After casually walking out of her training camp, she'd hitched a lift back to the city easily enough but knew that she'd have to keep moving. At first she'd thought she could hide out at Lyn's but then she remembered that Lyn had betrayed her and would hardly ask her in for coffee and sit idly by while she killed her cat and her husband. She liked to be in control and she liked to know what was going to happen. It was all getting a bit complicated. Huddled in her anorak, she tried to formulate plan B. Damn, she needed a coffee.

She found one at a vendor's a couple of streets away and immediately her normal confidence reasserted itself. Nothing had to happen this minute – she just needed to set things up in advance. She remembered the bookshop opposite the restaurant – she could hide out there and check on Mikey. That would do nicely.

Dylan sat back as the head of security briefed him. He'd been interrupted at his planning meeting by Larissa, who was practically gabbling with excitement. He'd made his apologies. He was frowning now as he tried to put together the overall picture. Larissa was jabbing her finger at the screen, which was playing a gritty film of Judith sauntering out of a northern training camp, fully armed, laughing chummily with the guard on the gate.

'What?' he demanded.

'She's very clever,' said Larissa. 'Look, she's wearing an all access badge.' The head of security nodded. 'Apparently she just talked her way into the ward station, lifted a set of key cards and helped herself to what she needed.'

Dylan sighed. 'Fatalities?'

'Three: ward manager, security officer and an assessor. Once she was off the ward she was home free.'

'Larissa, we need some witness statements. I'll leave that with you.' Larissa bustled from the room. 'So – she was seen watching the house this afternoon?'

'Yes – it was called in at once but as she didn't try to force entry she wasn't picked up.'

'And where is she now?'

'We don't know – she seems to have ditched her mobile.'

'Ah, well, keep on it. The scanners will pick her up in the end. Oh, and this time perhaps we should give her less opportunity to escape.'

'She was doing very well, Dylan, she ticked all the boxes.'

'Perhaps they were the wrong boxes.'

136

'What were you thinking of?'

'What has she told you?'

'What do you think?'

'I don't know – that's why I'm asking.'

'Lucas, don't try to be smart with me ... she was all over the place. Were you drunk?'

Luke groaned and shook his head. 'No – I was optimistic.' He was looking pale and uncomfortable, his mouth a thin line.

It was in between service and the restaurant was deserted. Mikey poured them some more coffee in silence.

'It was OK with Kylie. I thought you'd be cool with it.'

'That was when we were sixteen, and that was about who was taking her to the disco or whatever. Not sharing my wife. You know I'd never allow that. She isn't some plaything. I respect her too much for that and you should too – you've been a guest in our house.'

'OK, my friend, I stand corrected.'

'Lucas, if she hadn't already hit you then I would. In fact, I still might. I mean, what was all that stuff about having your heart broken?'

'Oh hell, she did tell you everything, huh?'

'Most of it. I think she left out some of the grisly details because she was too embarrassed.'

'Well, it's true.'

'You what?'

'It's true, I really want her. But I'll be good. I won't come round any more, OK. No more surprise encounters when she's out shopping. No more trailing about like a bloody stray dog. Anyway, I'm getting a bike.'

'A bike? You're taking up cycling?'

'No, you goof, a motor bike – a great big silver racer.'

'Great – as long as it keeps your mind off my wife.'

'OK, my man. So, want to meet up at the weekend?' His tone was miraculously restored to its usual drawl.

Mikey stared and sighed. 'No, Lucas, I'm not meeting up with you again. We're finished.'

137

I had to approach this tactfully. I wasn't looking forward to it but I'd promised Mum, so that was that. It was Lyn's night to choose what to put on the entertainment screen and we'd already sat through what felt like hours of boring Shakespeare. She was enjoying herself though, muttering away about interpretation and clarity of vision and I was waiting for a good moment to start. It looked as if some poor old guy was about to be tortured.

'How can you watch that? It's disgusting.'

'No worse than your horror movies.'

'Yes it is, it's revolting.'

'That's interesting.' She swivelled round to look at me. 'Is it because it's his eyes, or because you weren't expecting it or because he's old and helpless and not some nubile young thing?'

At least I'd got her attention. 'Don't know really. What do you normally do for Halloween?' She blinked and stared at me. 'I was just wondering?'

'Oh, were you?'

'Yeah. I mean, we don't make a big thing of it but we normally do something and I just thought that . . .'

Her eyes narrowed in speculation. 'If you are genuinely asking about Halloween then no, I don't usually do anything. If you are asking about my birthday, then the answer is still no – birthdays aren't celebrated after eight years old in the dump.'

'But with Greg?'

'I don't think Greg knew when my birthday was.'

I felt a familiar rush of irritation. I mean, Greg must have known when her birthday was – he'd selected her for God's sake – but he was just too mean to do anything nice for her.

'Did you know when his was?'

'Oh, of course, we used to invite people out for drinks.'

I felt even more annoyed. 'OK – what would you like to do for your birthday?'

She thought for a moment then her brow cleared. 'I'd like to have the family round to watch the Russian version of Hamlet. It's very old and black-and-white with subtitles but I'm sure the centre could locate a copy.' She smiled sweetly up at me. 'I know everyone would just love it.' Then she sniggered and punched my arm. 'Gotcha! As if! I have no idea, chef, but I expect you do, so why don't you just surprise me.'

I ruffled her hair – she'd just had it trimmed and the new bits were starting to blend in with the rest of it, although she was still wearing a scarf when she went out. 'Look, I know what Mum and Krystal want to do but I want to know if there's anything special you'd like.'

'I can't think of anything. I'm not good at this sort of thing, sorry.' Her shoulders slumped a bit and her face fell. 'Sweetheart, come here, you've got time to think about it – it's no big deal.'

We both looked at the screen for a bit – it looked like the good guys were finally getting it together. Then another old man tottered on, carrying a dead body. 'Darling, I can't stand much more of this – it's too depressing.'

'It's a tragedy – it's supposed to be cathartic.'

'Oh, that's all right then.'

'Mikey?'

'Hmm?'

'What are you doing?'

'Just getting a bit more comfortable.'

'But it's nearly finished.'

'That's good because I'm about to distract you. Nothing to worry about, just a little light canoodling. I've got an early start tomorrow.'

138

A dense ground mist was whirling up from the river as Lyn made her way along the footpath. She was completely alone. It was early morning and she had her mobile, plus permission from Mikey to go for a walk. She'd never been out this way on her own, so she felt safe from interruption. Huge drops splashed off the trees above her head and occasionally ran down her neck. Strange gurgles and hoots rose from the river, muted by the mist. When she drew breath she could taste the dampness. She paused and looked up at the sky. The mist shimmered and shifted above her as the sun started to break through.

Skidding a little on the damp grass, she turned and looked back. There was nothing behind her. With a contented sigh she stepped off the path and sat on the trunk of a fallen tree to watch the mist parting from the water. She was trying to get things into some sort of perspective. Judith was far away. Lucas was out of the picture, presumably enjoying his new bike. Dylan had gone quiet. She had finished Marvin's entry level training and was just waiting for the results to come through. The recipe game and accompanying cookbook were both proofed. She and Mikey had started family licence training.

It was all good.

She shifted as dampness seeped through her jeans. The sun was almost fully out now but the morning was still cool. She tried to make out the coots and moorhens on the river but still couldn't tell them apart. She imagined bringing a toddler with her and teaching him things. She thought he'd be a tough little boy, so she'd have to learn to swim if they were going anywhere near the water. How would she manage with a toddler and a baby? In three months' time she might be pregnant. The thought made her shiver in equal horror and excitement.

She supposed she'd have to learn how to knit.

She supposed she'd have to turn the spare room into a nursery.

The feeling of excitement definitely had the edge.

The river was a dancing silver ribbon now and she turned back towards home feeling much better. Climbing the stile back into the lane she noticed a security guard standing at the far end but as she approached, he melted round the corner and by the time she was at the front of the house, he'd gone. She wondered for a moment if she was still designated special interest but then she heard Spike mewing crossly from the other side of the door and hurried to unlock the cat flap for him.

139

Marvin was waiting by the bar when I arrived at the restaurant. He shot forward waving an envelope at me. 'Chef, look.' I didn't need to . . . the expression on his face said it all. Still, I took my time sliding out the letter and turning it in my hands before frowning over the notification.

'Dear Mr Spencer,' I read, 'Re your recent submission of manual CWK1689 (entry level qualification vocational studies – kitchen) we can confirm that you have been awarded . . .'

'Read the bottom bit, chef.'

'As the recipient of the highest point score in the current examination series you will receive a pay scale increment with immediate effect and an exemption from one element only of your Level 1 course.'

He was so pink and excited that I couldn't help grinning. 'Hey, Marvin, good job.'

'Can I start now?'

'What, this minute?'

'Yes.'

'We won't have a porter.' He nodded in resignation. Oh, what the hell. 'OK – off you go.'

He took one step then looked back with obvious pride. 'Chef, where do you want me today?'

I was already digging out my mobile. 'Ask the sous chef – she'll put you on the line somewhere.'

140

On her birthday, Lyn woke fizzing with excitement. Lie still, she told herself firmly, this is ridiculous, probably nothing out of the ordinary will happen. 'But he did ask,' she muttered. It was dark outside but just starting to lighten and she could make out streamers of cloud hurtling across the sky. Beside her, Mikey slept on – a solid, warm, comforting shape. She propped herself up on one elbow and contemplated him.

He needed a haircut, she thought; he'd got curls coming through and they were certainly cute but she preferred it shorter. His skin was like silk and smelled faintly of shower soap. My, oh my, she thought, you are one handsome man, Mr Jones, and no mistake. She bent closer and took a deep breath then snuggled up. Her eyes started to close and she relaxed against him when suddenly she shot upright.

'Jesus . . .' she muttered, 'I'm nuzzling and nestling and loads of other daft things. I'll be wearing his shirts next.'

Mikey stirred, squinted. 'You're awake early, darling. Happy birthday – you're welcome to all my shirts apart from the pale grey one.'

'You remembered.'

'Looks like it . . . what are you twitching about? Come here, birthday girl.'

'I'm hardly a girl – I'm thirty-two.'

'Going on twelve. Come here – do what you're told for once.' She huffed and flumped back down on the pillows. He swung over her. 'What was that about nuzzling and nesting?'

'Nestling, not nesting.'

'Oh, well, it sounded good to me.'

'I bet – I thought you were asleep.'

'With you rabbiting away in my ear? No chance.' He rolled back on to his side of the bed. 'I'm all yours – nuzzle away to your heart's content.'

'I'd rather have a coffee.'

'You sure?'

'Yes.' She glared at him, watching through slitted eyes as he disappeared into the bathroom. Moments later he reappeared shaking his head – water running over his shoulders. She turned on her face and squeezed her eyes shut until she heard him going downstairs. OK, she told herself, just relax and enjoy getting your coffee made for you. After all, it isn't as if you wanted sex anyway.

She opened her eyes when she heard him place her coffee on the table. 'Thank you.'

'Does madam require anything else?' She could hear the laughter in his voice and turned over heaving with resentment. It was all very well for him to make fun of her but she wasn't in the mood. The light was growing outside and he was silhouetted against the window. She couldn't make out the expression on his face but he was standing very still and watchful, as though waiting for her to make the next move. He's waiting for me to ask, she realised.

141

The thing with Lyn is that she doesn't feel comfortable asking. I knew that she wanted sex from the way her feet were beating a miniature tattoo at the bottom of the bed and the way she'd cuddled up to me when she thought I was asleep. But then she got all antsy, so I thought I'd let her stew for a minute or two while I got her coffee. Of course when I got back I couldn't resist teasing her a bit.

Then she looked at me and I couldn't move. Her hair was in a mess, her eyes were enormous and her lower lip was pouting just a fraction. Then she closed her eyes and started to speak. I didn't know what she was going to say . . . I couldn't make her do it and I didn't want her to feel humiliated or foolish. Instead I took a couple of steps towards the bed, gathered her to me and started to kiss her. She made a faint squawking noise, then stopped and somehow got hold of my hair and pulled me closer.

I figured I'd made the right decision for once.

142

Afterwards they curled up and slept for a while. This time Mikey woke first and slid out of bed, pulling the duvet up around Lyn's shoulders and dropping a kiss on her hair. Showered and dressed he put juice, coffee and toast on a tray and went back upstairs. Lyn was sitting up talking to Spike. 'Where's that handsome Daddy of yours, then?' she was saying, holding Spike's face and staring intently into his eyes. 'Is he making Mummy some breakfast? Shall we go and find out?'

'And I thought you were an intelligent woman.'

'Well, Spike's an intelligent cat, you know that.'

'Move your feet.' He put the tray on the bed, then grabbed the juice and the coffee just as she shifted again. 'If you spill this lot, that's it.'

'You are a very bossy man.'

'Secret of my success. Now, nibble your toast, drink your juice and let me tell you what I thought we'd do today.' Her eyes widened and she swallowed. He paused. 'Right – stop looking like that or I'll have to ravage you right now and then all the timings will be out.'

'I thought you'd just ravaged me anyway.'

'Nope. That was consideration personified – this would be strictly on my terms.' Her eyes widened even more. 'Stop it. Behave yourself. OK – you've probably noticed that I've taken the day off. In my back pocket are tickets for the Botanical Centre, where we are booked for lunch and a bulb selection event.' He took her hand. 'Tim has hired a boat for the morning and we are going on the river.'

417

She choked. 'No, Mikey, I can't swim.'

'On the river, not in the river. I promise you'll like it. We'll have to wrap up warm and take a hot drink. It's a great trip.'

'Oh, God,' she moaned, despairingly.

'Tim has to have the boat back by midday, so we'll walk back.'

'What if it rains?'

'It won't. Then we'll get dressed up and go out to dinner. At the restaurant. The family are coming as well. How does that sound?'

She sighed. 'It sounds lovely, apart from the river.'

'That was Tim's idea – I didn't want to disappoint him.'

'No – but the poor lad always sees me in a state of mortal terror, he'll think I'm a complete wet weekend.'

'He told me, you know.'

'What?'

'About that night – he felt really guilty.'

She yanked her hand away. 'Mikey, I told you nothing happened.'

He nodded. 'I know, and I believe you.'

'Then what can he have told you?'

'It wasn't what he did, which was nothing more than Jack or Dad or Krystal or any of us, it was what he felt.'

Her face fell. 'I don't understand it.'

Mikey looked at her. 'No, darling, I suppose you don't. Anyway, it's time you got ready to go out.' He glanced at his watch. 'You've got fifteen minutes. Remember, lots of layers. Have we got a hot flask?'

She shot out of bed towards the door. 'I don't know, I'll look.'

'No, I'll look – you get in the shower.'

143

The day was brightening up but there was a chilly wind, so I marched her down the road at a bit of a gallop. She looked very cute. She was in jeans and a sweatshirt with a waterproof jacket swinging open. The cute bit was a woolly hat and scarf that Krystal had donated to her. It had swinging fluffy bits over her ears that made her look like a teenager. Her hands were thrust into an old pair of gloves that I'd found in my stuff. Her cheeks were pink and she was starting to pant.

'Mikey,' she puffed, 'slow down. I know I'm terrified but you don't have to tug me along quite so fast. I haven't got enough breath left to run away now.'

I took another look at my watch. 'I told Tim we'd be there by ten o'clock.'

'He'll wait, surely.'

'Yes, but I don't like being late.'

We were nearing the river now. It sounded surprisingly busy for a working day. I slowed the pace a little to reorganise my arm firmly across her shoulders and steered her across the footbridge. She stumbled and I glanced down to see that her eyes were shut tight. 'Lyn, don't close your eyes – you need to see where you're going.'

I looked up and down the moorings and spotted Tim chatting to a couple who were just pulling out. A shriek made me jump. Krystal clattered on to the towpath and rushed towards us screaming, 'Happy Birthday, isn't this great!' at the top of her lungs. People turned and smiled as she grabbed my wife and jigged up and down with her, perilously close to the water.

'Calm down,' I said, 'I don't want anyone falling in before we've even got into the boat.'

'It's lovely,' prattled my irritating sister. 'It isn't very big so it feels a bit wobbly until you sit down but it's got cushions and little cupboards and enormous life jacket things. Oh – and there are distress flares.'

'Distress flares,' murmured Lyn, 'how useful on a river trip. Tim, good morning.'

Tim beamed and held out his hand. Lyn hesitated and he looked puzzled. I smacked her hard on the bottom and she shot forward.

'Steady there,' said Tim, pulling her aboard. 'Guess you're not really used to boats, huh?'

Krystal clambered in behind her, all legs and squeals. I groaned as I bent down to untie the mooring rope, stepped into the boat and sat down next to Lyn. She shot me a reproachful look and shifted on her cushion. 'Sorry,' I mouthed at her. She turned her head away, looked across the water then turned back and buried her face in my chest.

'Are you all right?' said Krystal.

'Fine, thanks,' mumbled Lyn. I stroked her back under the waterproof.

'She's just overcome with excitement,' I explained, 'and gratitude.' Lyn jabbed me hard in the ribs. Tim had already manoeuvred the boat out into the river and was happily guiding her away from the other craft that bobbed about around us.

'What did you bring?' demanded Krystal. 'We've got all sorts – hot chocolate and gingerbread and bananas. I'm starving.'

Lyn looked round at her. 'I think we've got coffee. We've only just had breakfast.'

'So?'

I snorted. 'We're only going up to the Botanical Centre, little sister, not on a sea voyage.'

Krystal tossed her head. 'Fresh air makes you hungry. Lyn, what do you want?'

'I'll settle for coffee.'

I dug out the thermos. The coffee steamed in the cold air. We had to share the mug and huddled together over it, taking alternate mouthfuls and spluttering because it was too hot. Lyn was visibly relaxing now that she realised we weren't all going to perish at sea. I ran a finger down her cheek and mouthed, 'All right?' She nodded, and mouthed, 'I love you, chef.' I suddenly noticed that the sound of Krystal slurping hot chocolate had stopped. She was gazing at us with rapt attention and a soppy grin.

'Shouldn't you be in school?' I queried, wondering why it hadn't struck me before.

'No, we've got a study day. You two are so romantic, it's like a fairy story.' Beside me a frightening rigidity shot through my wife.

'Tim,' I called, 'do you want a drink? Let's swap over and I'll show Lyn how to steer.'

'I want to steer,' said Krystal.

'And I don't,' said Lyn.

'And I'm in charge so it's up to me.' I said firmly.

'But Lyn's the eldest by miles,' said Krystal. Lyn immediately started to snigger. 'What?' said Krystal, 'what have I said that's funny?'

'Tim, why did you bring her?'

'I dunno, I couldn't shake her off.'

Krystal flounced and the boat rocked but Lyn didn't scream although she bit her lip. We shuffled about until she was standing at the helm with me tucked in close behind her covering her hands on the wheel. 'Surely we don't have to do anything apart from point it forwards?' she queried.

'More or less, but we're going up a backwater in a minute so then there'll be a bit more action.'

'Oh, have you done this a lot then?'

'When we were younger.'

I felt very comfortable with my arms round her . . . she'd

relaxed again and although some of her questions made Tim snort with derision she seemed interested and happy. Behind us Krystal and Tim were bickering and flicking water at each other. The sun shone fitfully. It was turning into a great day.

144

The wind was dashing her hair across her face and her eyes and nose were running. 'Full steam ahead,' said Mikey, into her ear. She twisted to glance up at him and he grinned. 'You look frozen.' He touched her face and pulled her scarf tighter. 'Here, blow your nose and look where you're going.' The boat began to jump about as it started to cut across the current and she stiffened in horror. 'It's OK – we're just getting into position to go down here.' Sharp little waves were slapping at the bow. 'Hey, calm down,' whispered Mikey, 'it's too broad in the beam to capsize.'

'I have no idea what you mean,' she muttered.

'I mean that we're not going to roll over with the death of all hands.'

'How can you? When I was just starting to like it.'

His arms were very solid, she thought, so even if she did fall in he would probably save her without too much difficulty. She could feel her confidence growing. I would risk anything with this man, rock climbing, fell walking, canoeing. 'Will you teach me to swim?'

'Yes, darling.'

The boat rocked madly as Krystal wobbled towards them. 'It's my turn now. Lyn, you look frozen – get out of the way both of you and let me have a go.'

Mikey took Lyn's arm, gave a tug and amazingly she was sitting down in the stern while Tim moved to the front to keep an eye on Krystal. Mikey stretched his legs out beside her.

'Where are all the other boats?'

423

'We're in a backwater now – not many other boats but lots of wildlife to look out for. We'll drift up here for a bit then turn round and go back to the Botanical Centre. Here, you'd better have some more coffee, you look . . .'

'I know, frozen. It's just that I'm not a sporty type.'

'Actually I was going to say edible – all pink and white and very, very cute.'

'That's ridiculous, I'm too old to be cute.'

'Darling, you are not. Now drink your coffee and shut up . . . Look . . . squirrel.'

She peered about but couldn't see it. 'In the trees, you plank!'

'I knew that.'

'That's why you were looking at the river then. Come here . . . look, moorhens.'

'Oh, now they are sweet.'

'Hmm . . . didn't you do nature study at the dump?'

'I don't think so . . . I can't remember it anyway, so I guess not.'

Somehow he'd arranged things so that she was leaning against him with his arms round her, yet she could see everything floating by. It was extraordinarily comfortable.

'You know, I feel really comfortable,' she said.

'Well, don't sound so surprised.'

'No, really, it's strange. I thought I'd be too frightened to appreciate anything but I feel really safe.'

Mikey looked down at her and smiled . . . he was confident that they were back to normal. Tim came back down the boat: 'Time to turn back.'

'OK, skipper.'

Together they turned the boat and Krystal went to sit with Lyn. 'Are you looking forward to tonight?'

'Yes, of course. What are you going to wear, Krystal? Have you thought?'

'Not really, something fairly flash. I've only eaten at Michael's restaurant once before and it was really grand.'

The boat was getting up speed and Lyn could see the Botanical Centre green house glinting in the distance. She stared in alarm at the tiny landing stage. 'How are we going to get off?' Mikey grinned and slung his backpack out first, then casually stepped on to the slippery wooden planks. Lyn flapped as the boat rocked up and down and the gap widened, then gave a muted shriek as a launch passed and the boat swung into the river in its tumbling wake. Tim caught her arm in a steadying grip, turned back towards the little jetty and nodded. In one abrupt move Mikey took her hands, wrapped them round his neck and swung her out of the boat. She clung to him. Krystal glared. 'The gap was only about six inches,' she huffed. 'Honestly!'

'Thanks, Tim, see you later. Try not to drown little sister on the way back.'

Tim laughed and waved and the boat shot off.

Lyn was still clutching Mikey's jacket. He brushed the hair from her face and tipping up her chin, lowered his lips to hers. He tasted salt and pulled back slightly to study her face.

'You're crying.'

'No, I'm not – it's just my eyes watering.'

He ran his thumbs under her eyes. 'You look like a mermaid. A very sweet pink-nosed one.'

She sniffed hugely. 'You didn't think I'd let you fall in, did you?'

'No, I knew you wouldn't but I felt . . .'

'You felt as if I would?'

'No – I felt as if you'd left me behind.' It was a muffled wail. Rain started to fall. 'I thought you said it wouldn't rain.'

'I lied.'

145

'What should I wear?'

'Sweetheart, you've eaten out more than I have ... just dig something nice out of your wardrobe.'

'What are you going to wear?'

'I'm going to amaze you.'

'God ... what does that mean?'

Mikey was stretched across the bed playing mouse-under-the-duvet with Spike. 'It means that I will amaze you.' He glanced up. 'No, don't wear that black thing, it's boring.'

'Greg liked it – he said it was elegant.'

'Give it here.' He dangled it in front of Spike who looked completely disinterested. 'See, Spike hates it.'

'Oh, well, if Spike doesn't like it ... but I haven't got anything else dressy.'

'Just look, woman, what about that blue thing?'

'I haven't got a blue thing.' She turned back to the wardrobe and rattled the hangers, stopped, looked again. 'Mikey?' Her voice was little more than a whisper. 'How did this get here?'

'This' was a deep blue silky top with a floating panel skirt.

He grinned irritatingly. 'Is it the right size?'

'You know it is. But how did you ...?'

'I smuggled it in while you were feeding Spike.'

Lyn fingered the skirt and looked at the bodice.

'It's got one of those wrap things as well,' he added trying to sound casual, 'and I thought it would go with your sandals OK.'

She slid the hanger carefully over the wardrobe door and

stepped back. 'Yes – they'll be fine with it. But why did you get it?'

'Darling, it's your birthday present from me.'

'But the bulbs were my present, weren't they?'

'Well, this is a surprise present that you can't plant in the garden.'

Her eyes filled up. 'I wasn't expecting anything else.' She looked at him thoughtfully.

'That's what makes it a surprise, darling.'

146

Spike leapt out of the way as she launched herself at me. 'Whoa, careful!' I yelped as she landed on top of me.

'You have to be the kindest man alive. Sorry, but there's about to be a bit of serious snogging going on.' She kissed me very thoroughly and hugged me even tighter. 'Thank you, thank you. You are a marvellous husband and I just adore you. I might even start sorting your socks.'

For a minute or two I lay back and enjoyed myself but then I figured I'd better confess. 'Lyn, darling, I had help.'

'Well, obviously. My guess is Jessica, right? It's too formal for Krystal and too floaty for Claire.'

'You don't mind?'

'No, of course not. I could have ended up with a bin liner otherwise.' She smiled into my eyes. 'That isn't the point.'

She slid her hand under my T-shirt and I grabbed it. 'Hold it right there, we've got to get ready to go out.' She nodded, gave me one last, lingering kiss and, trailing her fingers across my lips, started to get up, pulling off her sweatshirt as she went. Then she paused, looked over her shoulder and gave me a glinting blast from her lovely eyes. 'Sure?'

'Sure.'

'I could help with your T-shirt.'

I cleared my throat, started to get up, fumbled at my top.

'Oh, come here, what's the matter with you?' She was laughing, her eyes shining. My top hit the floor in record time and she grabbed for the button on my jeans.

'Christ, woman, you are a witch.' Her smile widened and I tried once more. 'Lyn, I really don't want to be late.'

She pushed me down. 'We can spare a minute or two.'

'What?'

She grinned. 'You look really offended.'

'I should think so. No, don't do that. Just lie still for a moment, I'll show you.'

'You are a very bossy man, Mr Jones, but if that's what you want, take your time.'

147

'Where did you get that shirt?' It was charcoal with a thin matt line. It looked very elegant. Lyn studied it thoroughly. 'How does it look on?'

'I have no idea – you won't let me get dressed, woman.'

'OK, let's see. Oh Lord, don't tell me you chose this on your own.'

'I told you I'd amaze you.'

'But it fits . . . properly. You look astounding.'

'Thank you, madam, we aim to please.'

'Somebody must have helped you.'

'Only the guy in the shop. I just wanted something that would go with my tie.'

'Hmm. Jessica will go crazy.'

'I hope not, we've got a full house tonight. Oh, and we won't be able to buy any new clothes for about three years.'

148

'Hi, Lyn. Happy birthday, you look lovely.' Jessica ushered them towards their table. 'I don't know what you've done to chef,' she muttered, 'but he looks great. Don't let him in the kitchen looking that hot, the girls will rip him to shreds.' She took a closer look. 'Doesn't he just make your heart turn over?'

Lyn smiled. 'Sometimes, like tonight, I definitely agree with you,' she murmured back. 'And Jessica, thanks for helping him with the dress – I've never had anything like it.'

'Get on with it, you two, stop standing about gossiping,' roared Mikey. 'Jessica, drinks!' Jessica simply shrugged, whipped out her pad and began to describe the cocktail selection.

Claire said, 'Michael Jones, how dare you. You apologise to this young lady right this minute.'

Jack smirked and said, 'Nice one, mate, very smooth.' Ray shook his head grimly. Mikey looked sheepish and sat down.

Lyn put her hands on his shoulders. 'It's all right, Claire, he's just being a perfectionist as usual. He used to make me jump but he doesn't mean anything by it.' Mikey's hand clasped hers and squeezed and she dropped a kiss on his head. There was a stunned silence, then Krystal burst out. 'I told you, it's the most romantic thing I've ever seen.'

Claire nodded. 'Right, what do you recommend, Lyn? What are those ones with the mint leaves in?'

Lyn slid round the table and sat down. 'That's a mojito – very refreshing but quite alcoholic. I think I'll have a soft drink to start but I usually have a strawberry daiquiri.'

'Well, I'll live dangerously for once. How was the river this morning?' Her voice had the slightly odd formality of someone dining in an expensive restaurant, and Lyn's heart sank.

'It was fine – I was absolutely terrified to begin with but Tim and Michael know their stuff and Krystal distracted me. And the bulbs at the Botanical Centre were a revelation. Michael was bored to death, though – next time it'll have to be a cabbage selection event. I don't think I've ever spent so long out of doors.'

'It's given you some colour, though. You look very well and that dress really suits you.'

'Yes.' She fingered the skirt thoughtfully. 'It's not my usual sort of thing but it's lovely to dress up sometimes. Claire, I feel such an idiot. I didn't know that Mikey would get me a special present.'

'What do you mean, love?'

'Greg, my last husband, didn't even say "Happy Birthday", and we never exchanged gifts at all. Does Ray give you special presents on your birthday?'

'He'd be in trouble if he didn't. But that must have been a nice surprise for you?'

'Oh, yes. I was so overwhelmed I practically ripped the clothes off him.' A sudden silence fell round the table. Lyn looked down at her lap and squirmed.

Claire patted her arm. 'Don't worry, Lyn, nobody heard . . . much.' She looked up to find them all gazing at her. Mikey raised his eyebrows.

'Way to go,' muttered Jack. 'I cannot wait to select someone.'

Krystal's mouth was an 'O' of astonishment. 'Does that mean you initiated sex?' she gasped.

'Right, up you get, back in a moment.' Mikey pulled Lyn out of her seat and hustled her into the darkened garden at the rear of the restaurant.

'I'm so sorry.'

'Don't sit down, the seats are all wet. Here, do you want to blow your nose?' Soft lamps glowed on the wall and glimmered in the puddles.

'It's cold.'

'Sure. This'll only take a moment.' His voice was quivering and as she looked up apprehensively, he started to laugh. 'I've never seen anything like it. Do you remember our first night when you thought I was going to take you upstairs and start banging away? This was much funnier than that. I thought Tim was going to faint. And Dad looked as if you'd grown two heads. And Krystal . . . you are going to be her role model for ever. Sorry, my darling, I'll be OK in a second.'

He heaved a steadying breath, put his arms round her and stroked her hair. Then another thought struck him. 'Oh Lord, Mum will try to give you a talking to. I'll tell her not to, otherwise you'll get all stressy again.'

'Will you? I mean, I'll have to apologise.'

'Sure, but a general "Oops, sorry" should do it. Come on, cheer up, it isn't the end of the world. OK to go back now?'

Their reappearance at the table was greeted with a burst of casual conversation. Tim slid a drink into her hand and Claire shook her head at her. Lyn took a gulp and said, 'I'm so sorry, everyone, my tongue just ran away with me.' Mikey snorted helplessly.

Ray stood up. 'Claire, let's go and dance.' With immense dignity they moved across to the dance floor.

Krystal leant across to Lyn. 'Can I come round tomorrow and you can tell me what you did?' she begged.

'No, you cannot,' said Mikey. He looked fondly at Lyn. She was sipping her drink and still looked downcast as her eyes followed Ray and Claire's progress round the dance floor. 'It's fine, sweetheart, they're just doing the outraged parent thing – it proves they think of you as another daughter.'

'Yeah,' added Krystal, 'he's right. They always get huffy with me if I say the wrong thing. Now, do you want your present from me? Say yes.'

'Yes,' said Lyn.

149

Her eyes were shining in anticipation. It struck me that although she was great at getting presents for other people she hadn't had too many herself ... well, of course, I knew that. She fumbled with the wrapping and Krystal immediately grabbed it back. 'I'll do it for you, isn't it exciting!' I reached out to get it back but it was Jack who snatched it first.

'Krystal,' said Tim, 'come on now, you've had your birthday.' She pouted. Jack passed the present back to Lyn with a grin. She was looking a bit bothered as she pulled at the tape but suddenly everything worked and there was a very cute wooden necklace made of tiny shoes. 'Oh, Krystal, it's lovely, wherever did you find it?'

'When we went to the market that time – I'm good at secrets.'

'You are indeed.'

Jack punched her arm. 'And modest as well. OK Lyn, this is from me.' Automatically her gaze swivelled to my face. Jack went to say something but I cut in. 'Come on, darling, let's see what it is.' I put one arm round her and whispered, 'It's all right, it's family.' She leant against me and together we fumbled it open. 'What do you think?'

'I think it's lovely, what is it?'

'It's a game, look,' explained Jack. 'You have to line up the circles and the triangles in the right colour combinations and you've got an owl.' Lyn stared. Stretched out her hand. 'No, wait, let me re-set it, there you go, you try.' He passed back a tangle of wood and metal and looked at her expectantly.

'Later,' said Tim. 'Let her open mine next.'

434

It was a book: sonnets by Elizabeth Barrett Browning. Lyn gasped. 'Oh, Tim, how thoughtful . . . you are clever.'

Jack looked a bit huffy. 'I'm supposed to be the clever one.'

Lyn beamed round the table. 'Thank you so much . . . I've never had a birthday like it.'

Jessica came over and touched my arm. 'Are you ready for starters, chef?' I nodded.

'Are they OK back there?'

She smiled at me. I'd never noticed but she had a very sweet smile that transformed her face. 'You are not allowed in the kitchen tonight, that's all I've got to say.'

Lyn turned in her seat. 'Jessica, look . . . I've got more presents.'

I saw Jessica blink but she didn't give anything away. 'Hey, that's so cute – must be from Krystal, right?' Krystal smirked proudly. Jessica smiled. 'I'll just get them to bring your starters out – are you all right for drinks?'

Krystal waved madly at Mum and Dad and they came over. 'Your dance floor is too small,' said Dad, 'it'll be crowded later.'

'Oh,' said Mum, 'you've done presents already.'

'That was Krystal,' said Jack. I looked at Lyn – her face was taking on the paralysed rabbit expression. Mum was delving in her bag. 'Here you are, love, it's from Ray and me . . . it's waiting for you at home.' She shoved an envelope into Lyn's hands. My darling wife opened it and her eyes filled with tears. Mum looked at me uncertainly. 'We know you like books, love, but you don't seem to have anywhere to put them.'

There was a bit of a silence then she pulled herself together, got up and gave Mum a hug. 'I love it,' she snuffled. 'It's one of the things I've always wanted – you are so kind to me.'

'It's only a boring old bookcase,' said Krystal.

'Hush,' said Dad, 'behave yourself for once.' I noticed that his voice was a bit gruff and I felt like bursting into tears myself. I looked at my place setting instead and noticed that my goats' cheese tart with rocket salad had arrived – minus the rocket salad. 'Who sent this out?' I began.

Lyn, miraculously dry-eyed was back at my side. 'It certainly looks wonderful,' she said loudly, and kicked me very hard.

150

Outside the restaurant Luke leaned against the wall, watching. Lyn looked very lovely and quite different. Someone had dressed her up in a dark blue floppy number that wafted about when she moved. He was hoping that she'd get up to dance soon so he could have a closer look. She and Mitch had already left the table once but he hadn't been able to see what they were up to. He wouldn't have changed anything about her but Mitch was old fashioned in lots of ways and probably liked her dressed as the little woman.

He thought about how she'd felt in his arms that afternoon. As if she was made for him. He thought about how she'd bashed him over the head and grinned. Boy, that had hurt but it had been worth it to feel her trembling in his arms. Next time he'd make sure that she couldn't fight back. She was getting up again but not with Mitch. Tim was leading her on to the dance floor and he could see the dress clearly. It was shimmery and drifted and swirled as she moved. He began to see the point of it and wondered how it would feel, sliding beneath his hand.

She looked happy, he thought. Very like the woman he remembered from college – sparky and confident. He thought that he'd like her to live in his apartment. Her house was OK but a bit boring and he didn't want a garden. His apartment had a lot more gadgets and plenty of room ... since he'd been upgraded at work he'd been able to run a very classy serviced establishment, and he had a cleaner and a man who kept the freezer full of decent food.

His parents weren't an issue as they lived miles away, so Lyn wouldn't have to worry about being nice to them. He squinted through the window again . . . she was dancing with Jack now. There'd be none of that once she was with him; the rules were there for a reason, after all. He wondered if she'd give in to him straight away once they were married or if she'd try to fend him off. He quite liked the idea of her struggling against him. He wanted to see her submissive and adoring but he wasn't anticipating an immediate capitulation. He found that he was looking forward to forcing her surrender.

She was back at the table now. As she sat down she murmured something to Mitch and stroked his cheek lightly. He slung a possessive arm across her shoulders and she grinned at him before turning to his father.

Luke scowled. She was definitely too free with her smiles and her chatty conversation. He took a pace forward, then noticed that Mitch was staring in his direction out of the restaurant window. He didn't think he could see him but he moved off anyway.

151

A bitter wind gusted fitfully across the plaza as Lyn headed for the bookshop. She'd decided to get Ray a waterways map for his birthday that she'd seen in the window a couple of weeks previously – it showed the old canal system in the surrounding area and was covered in bright illustrations of ducks and swans and other creatures that she couldn't name. While she wasn't sure of its accuracy, she loved the rich colours and thought it would make an interesting talking point as the family argued about its reliability.

The warm late autumn had abruptly turned to unseasonably cold and Mikey's mittens were doing nothing to keep her hands warm. In theory she shouldn't call at the restaurant but she thought she might drop in for coffee to warm up before she went back. A sudden flurry of sleet smacked her in the face as she turned the corner and she gasped. A hooded figure crossed in front of her and she swerved away automatically with a reflex shudder of fear.

'Lyn?'

She glanced behind her and wilted with a combination of resentment and relief. Dylan came up at a jog. 'I saw you cross the plaza and thought I'd see how you were.'

'Cold, Dylan.'

'Of course – blasted weather.' He took her arm in a familiar way and carried on down the street with her. 'Goodness, you're perishing. Here.' He tugged off his scarf and wrapped it round her neck then put an arm across her shoulders. 'Where are you heading?'

'The bookshop. Dylan, what do you think you're doing? You can't manhandle me like this.'

He smiled down at her and steered her towards the shop doorway. 'Here we are. I just felt that I should apologise for the way I spoke to you the last time we met. I only have your interests at heart and I meant what I said about not wandering around on your own at night. But I realise I could have been less abrupt with you so I'm sorry.'

He looked round the shop and beamed again. 'I haven't been in here for quite a while – what are you after?'

Lyn decided to play along – after all, it wouldn't be very intelligent to get on the wrong side of Dylan who obviously had fingers in many pies. 'I'm looking for a present for Mikey's father. I thought one of those maps would be interesting.'

Dylan went over to the wall and peered closely at it. 'Not an original.'

'No, Dylan, but then I wouldn't be able to afford an original.'

The purchase completed they hesitated on the doorstep. 'Were you going to the restaurant?'

'I thought I might call in, just for a coffee, to warm up.'

He rubbed his hands. 'Excellent idea.'

Taking her arm he crossed the road with exaggerated care and held open the restaurant door for her. Struggling with embarrassment Lyn passed him. It was still early. 'If you'll just wait here, Dylan, I'll find someone to get you a coffee. Have a seat.' Her legs quaking she went through into the kitchen.

Mikey looked up from the counter where he was demonstrating that evening's ravioli starter. 'Hi. I thought you weren't coming in today.' The general chatter in the kitchen was stilled for a moment, then rose again in a buzz of conjecture.

'Can I have a quick word?'

'Sure.'

In his office Lyn leant against the door and gulped.

'What is it?'

'Dylan's here.'

'Oh, OK, is someone looking after him?'

'Not yet – I said I'd find someone.'

'Right, hang on.' He went back to the kitchen. 'Who's on front of house? We've got a customer – no charge. Right, Toby, get on with it. Oh, and tell him Lyn and I'll be out in a minute to join him.'

He banged back into the office. 'And he's here because?' Lyn shook her head. Mikey instantly put his arms round her. 'Did you just bump into him?'

'Sort of – I didn't even know he was there until he caught up with me. Then he came to the bookshop with me and I couldn't shake him off.'

'Perhaps he just wants a coffee then and a bit of a nose around. We do get the odd tourist. Come on, we'd better go and see what he's up to.' He lifted her chin. 'Smile, darling, I'll be with you.'

'I don't know why I'm such a coward,' she groaned, 'but he makes me so nervous . . . he never used to but he does now.'

Dylan was happily drinking coffee and admiring the restaurant. 'Mitch, what a splendid job you've done here. Only to be expected, of course.' Mikey pulled out a chair for Lyn. 'Coffee, darling?'

'Yes please.'

'And Dylan, anything to go with that?'

'I wouldn't say no to a small tincture – it's a bitter day.' Mikey went over to the bar and Dylan beamed again. 'Do you think I'll be allowed a look in the kitchen, later on?'

'I'm sure you will, Dylan, but it probably won't be as interesting as you think.'

'Rubbish,' said Mikey, handing her a coffee, 'it's great and you know it. You're very welcome to look round, Dylan.'

There was a short silence while Lyn tried to think of something safe to talk about and then she realised that Mikey and Dylan were chatting pleasantly enough about the maps in the bookshop and if they should invest in some for the restaurant walls. She started to relax and try to rationalise what had just happened. For some reason Dylan didn't think that the rules of contact applied to him and, after all, it wasn't as if he'd been anything other than polite.

She looked up. 'Joining us?' Mikey had shoved his chair back and was gesturing towards the kitchen. She nodded and escorted by both men, headed for the kitchen. She felt as if she was under arrest and a sudden urge to make a run for it made her snort loudly just as they went through the door. Mikey began his patter immediately and she hoped that no one had noticed. She drifted along behind them pointing out the odd thing that she thought might be of interest but mainly nodding and smiling.

Dylan was expansive in his praise of everything and delighted to sample anything that was on offer. Finally Owen wrapped up some pastries for him and Mikey ushered him back into the restaurant. Customers were starting to drift in for lunch service. 'Ah, time to go,' murmured Dylan. 'I'll just see your lovely wife home, Mitch, we can't be too careful in this cold weather.'

Lyn rolled her eyes in horror but Mikey simply smiled. 'Thanks, Dylan. See you later, sweetheart.'

Outside it was even more dismal. The sleet had stopped but the pavements were slick and there was a nasty, dense ground mist that muffled footsteps and blurred sound. She sneezed and Dylan tutted fussily. He stopped and carefully wrapped her up in his scarf once more. 'That waterproof is a rag,' he observed. 'No wonder you've got a cold.'

'I haven't got a cold, Dylan, it's just a damp day.' She flinched as a figure brushed past them and Dylan once more put a solid arm round her. 'Come on then, let's get you back.'

At the house he refused another coffee and set off back up the street without waiting.

She started to pull off his scarf and then realised. 'Dylan,' she called, 'Dylan, your scarf.' He turned and called back, waved and carried on. She frowned. She thought he'd said, 'Keep it.' She sighed, shut the door and hung the scarf carefully on the coat rack she'd varnished only last week.

152

When I got home she was already asleep, curled up on her side, her bright hair fanned across the pillow. Spike was a fluffy, solid bundle under her arm. He glared at me accusingly. 'OK, fella, you're going to have to move in a minute.' When I came out of the shower he was still on the bed but had moved down to her feet . . . maybe she was right and he was an intelligent little guy.

I eased myself under the covers and put an arm round her, holding her close. I didn't want to wake her and for once I didn't want sex but I wanted to talk.

'Sorry I'm late back, baby. It was a good night and I'm back on days again next week so I can help out with the garden if you want. I just wanted you to know that I really do love you and if you want to start children now I'm definitely up for it.' I paused a moment while I pictured family days at the park, more pets around, Lyn knitting . . . well, perhaps that was a fantasy too far. 'But I want you to know it's up to you and whatever you decide is all right with me. And I really want you to know that you have always been my girl and I truly love you.'

That would do for now. I closed my eyes and felt the day washing away from me. Just as I drifted off I felt her arm snaking across my chest as she shifted closer in sleep. I thought I heard her say, 'I love you too, darling.' But she never called me that so I couldn't be sure.

153

It was dark and misty when Mikey left the restaurant. The street lighting had dimmed to a faint glow and the pavement was slick and shiny. 'Chef, wait!' He turned. The sous chef was waving a foil wrapped package at him. 'You forgot your doggy bag.'

He turned back with a grin. 'Thanks, Owen, that's tomorrow's romantic dinner.'

'Sure, mustn't disappoint the lovely wife.'

He was still grinning as he stepped into the road.

'Mikey.' He froze for an instant, then turned. Judith was just yards away. As he watched, she pulled out her weapon and took aim. He felt exasperated rather than scared. 'Judith, what . . . ?'

There was a yell from the restaurant. 'Chef! Behind you! Look out!' Confused, he spun back round into a chaos of light bearing down on him, a shriek of brakes, a roaring engine.

He was dead before he hit the ground.

154

The sous chef was shaking uncontrollably, great spasms of fear and grief that made his chair knock against the wall of the interview room. The security man glared. 'You want us to believe that you were six feet away from the incident and you don't know what happened? The street camera shows you shouting a warning so you must have seen something.'

'I closed my eyes.'

'Very responsible. The thing is, Owen, we need to know what you heard – the camera has recorded what happened but the microphone was out of action, so it doesn't matter if you closed your eyes or not really. Just tell us what you heard.'

'It's all confused.'

'OK. Let me tell you what we know so far, OK? The chef leaves the restaurant and you call him back.'

'Yes – he'd forgotten something.'

'What? Come on, kid, he's dead. It doesn't matter if he was stealing the silver or emptying the till.'

'It wasn't anything like that. He'd just cooked an anniversary dinner for his wife, then he left it in the fridge.'

'OK – so then what?'

'He said thanks and he left.'

'And?'

'There was this security guard with a gun . . . then a motorbike was driving at him and that's when I shouted – and closed my eyes.'

'Did the security guard say anything?'

'Only his name.'

446

Upstairs Dylan was observing via the on-desk screen link. The head of security was with him. Their eyes met. 'From the film it looks as if he was shot before the bike hit him.'

'Yes, but why would she shoot him?'

'Why would anyone run him down?' Dylan shook his head. 'That's immaterial at this juncture. I can't think how your people lost track of her.'

'I'll get my team on to it retrospectively but that won't alter the facts. Where have you got her?'

'In one of the interview rooms, but she's not talking.'

'Well, nothing unusual in that. She must know what's going to happen.' He tapped the screen and considered a moment. 'I'm sorry about this, John, I know you hoped that the re-conditioning would work but . . .'

The head of security interrupted him briskly. 'No, no, Dylan, not after what happened up north – and no exceptions just because she's female either.'

'Fine.' Dylan keyed in his access code, called up Judith's records and made one entry, then snapped off the screen.

'I still don't quite follow this unhealthy interest thing.'

'Quite simple – she had a childhood shared history with Mrs Jones in a dump facility. Your girl just didn't grow up.'

'Those dumps have a lot to answer for. It's hardly the first time and I guess it won't be the last.' Dylan glanced up at him for an instant. 'Present company excepted, of course.'

'What about the guy on the flash bike?'

'Skidded when he braked, apparently. Nothing to suggest he was actually aiming for Mr Jones.'

'So he's in the clear?'

'Yeah. Actually, he wants to see you when we've finished. I sent him down to reception.'

'And the wife – my office?'

'Yes. I don't envy you, that's for sure.'

'Normally I'd agree with you but on this occasion I have no

fears. Mrs Jones will have a whole new set of things to distract her from her grief.'

The head of security gave a faint smirk. 'As long as you know what you're taking on.'

'Oh, have no fears, John, I know exactly what I'm doing.'

Down in reception, Luke was waiting, leaning against the wall. He straightened up when he saw Dylan approaching. 'Dylan, right? Can you get me in to see Lyn?'

Dylan shook his head. 'No, definitely not. She needs complete quiet.'

'OK, I guess. Can you give her a message then?' Without waiting for an answer he hurried on. 'Tell her that she doesn't need to worry. I'll keep an eye on the Bulletin and as soon as she's listed I'll get the forms in . . . It won't be like the last time, I'll take it slowly with her.' His eyes met Dylan's. 'She'll need someone she knows.'

Dylan nodded. 'No doubt. By the way, Luke, what were you doing at the restaurant?'

Luke shrugged. 'Thought I'd swing by and pick Mitch up. It was a bit of a mucky night. The next thing I know this crazy bitch is waving a gun at him in the middle of the road. I nearly skidded right into him but I only clipped him with the wing mirror.' He paused, frowned. 'Couldn't believe it when I got off the bike.'

Glancing up at the security screens Dylan caught a glimpse of Judith being escorted down the back stairs. Luke was still talking. 'It was always a bit of a competition really, when we were kids. But it wasn't really until Mitch selected her that I realised what I felt about her. Then it was too late . . . but not this time.'

Dylan considered the arrogance and complacency of the younger, more stylish man. 'Ahh,' he said and turned towards the stairs. Then he turned back. 'A word to the wise.' Luke looked up. 'Mrs Jones will not be released for general selection on this occasion. Her next selection has already been approved and I would hate to see you waste any more time on her.'

He paused on the first landing to check with the body scan team. 'I'm about to see the widow. I need an update.'

'Well, I'd be inclined to say he was a very unlucky young man,' said the team leader.

'He was?'

'Definitely – I've got the preliminary scan right here. The bullet went through his shoulder, the motorbike just spun him round. He died of a heart attack. I've redirected the scanner to look for toxins but it looks like a congenital weakness – could have happened at any time.'

'OK, send me the confirmation via closedown security link for the moment. I don't think we need to share this with everybody as it will only cause more distress. But I'll sleep on it.'

Disconnected, he stared across the atrium out of the window. It was still dark . . . the middle of the night. The situation struck him as darkly humorous – shot, run over, heart failure . . . how doomed could one person be? He took a few minutes to compose himself before continuing up the stairs.

155

In the interview room Owen was trying to regain some control. He could hear a female weeping in the cubicle next door and his heart sank. 'That ... that isn't chef's wife, is it? I won't have to see her, will I?'

'No and no.' The guard sighed. 'It's the other witness – another one of you lot.'

'Jessica,' said Owen. 'Of course.'

'You've remembered something then?'

'Yeah. She was finishing up inside when it happened and she ... Christ! Is she hurt?'

'Listen, kid, just tell me what you remember.' Owen shrank back in his chair.

The door opened and a calm voice said, 'That'll do. Owen, isn't it? Yes – you can go.'

'But sir, I haven't finished the interrogation ...'

'No need – we have what's necessary.' Dylan looked more closely at Owen and his expression softened. 'Owen, collect your colleague from next door and help her to get home, if you would. She's very shaken.' He glanced at the guard as Owen rubbed at his eyes and shuffled out. 'Just remember you're dealing with civilians, and innocent civilians at that.'

'Sir, the girl was very fast on her feet for a civilian.' He indicated the on-desk screen where the vital few moments were playing on a loop. Judith raised her weapon, took aim and fired. The bike skidded. The sous chef covered his face. Jessica hurled herself out of the restaurant door and knocked Judith flat on her back, grabbed her hair and began to bang her head on the pavement. It was the sous chef who tottered over to the body on the ground and started to cry.

156

She leant against the wall with tears running down her face. When the door hissed open and Dylan walked in, she didn't move.

'I guess you'll want to tag me again.'

'No, that won't be necessary. Please sit down.'

She sat opposite him and bowed her head so she wouldn't have to look at him. She knew she looked like a submissive woman but for once she didn't care.

'You are aware of what's happened, aren't you, Lyn?'

She nodded. 'You knew she was here, didn't you.' It wasn't a question.

'We'd received a report that she'd absconded from her base but we didn't realise she was in the city or we'd have increased surveillance.'

She nodded again. 'I suppose you have to say that. It can't be true though ... you knew she was here.'

He didn't comment and after a moment she covered her face. Dylan tapped a key and the door opened again. 'Coffee,' he instructed. When the coffee arrived he pushed one in front of her and said, 'Drink that while it's hot.' She shook her head. 'Don't argue with me, Lyn.' To his relief she picked up the mug and began to drink.

'Good. Well, as Shakespeare put it so appositely, the centre has "devised a sudden day of joy" for you. You've been put on the priority selection register and you've been selected.'

She nodded.

'Don't you want to know who it is?'

452

'No. Yes. It's Lucas, isn't it?'

'No – it's me.'

She looked up, her gaze sliding over his face but not meeting his eyes. He stood, walked around the table and stopped behind her, his hands on her shoulders.

'You're very tense, Lyn. Come on now, drink your coffee.' He began to mould and massage her shoulders while he continued to talk. 'Now, we need to cover some of the details. I have a first floor apartment – very pleasant but with no garden – but I expect you'll want to keep Spike, so I'll be moving into your current address. I know that you redecorated the last time so, unless it's very tasteless – and I can't imagine that it will be, having seen what you've done downstairs – we'll probably just change some of the pictures around. I'll expect you to reduce your workload, certainly to begin with, so you can concentrate on getting the domestic details right but we won't suffer financially – I earn a substantial salary.'

She gave a loud, outraged sniff and began to stand up but he held her down quite easily. 'You've planned it all without talking to me, let alone allowing me any grieftime whatsoever.'

'I'm talking to you now.'

'But why me? There must be loads of women you could have selected. It can't be right – you're my counsellor.'

'Ah . . . something I suppose I should have mentioned earlier. You need to know that although I'm a counsellor, among other things, I'm actually head of Centre.'

'Oh God.' Her voice was a despairing mutter. 'Naturally . . . what else could you be? No wonder you knew what I was doing all the time.'

'I won't be your counsellor any more because that would be unprofessional to say the least. Dear lady, I've got to know you and I think you can make me happy.' He gave her shoulders one last encouraging squeeze. 'After all, you have an excellent track record in making husbands happy.'

'But they're both dead.'

'Maybe, but you didn't kill them.'

A spark of something kicked in and she glanced fleetingly up at him. 'You haven't tried my cooking yet. I once cooked a boot.'

He laughed. 'Lyn, I'll risk it. Believe me – we are going to be very happy.' He leant over and tapped the on-desk screen.

Once again the door opened and an assistant appeared clutching a form. 'Ah good, the paperwork . . . just sign here . . . there we go. Congratulations Mr Elliot, Mrs Elliot.' The door hissed shut leaving them alone.

Unable to stop herself she put her face in her hands again and sobbed. Dylan walked over to the window and looked out. It was dark and the plaza was sparkling with frost.

'Dylan, can I ask you something?' Her voice was low and hesitant.

He turned back from the window and nodded. 'Of course, but if you are seeking my permission to contact Mr Jones' relatives then the answer is naturally no, and no circumstances will change that.'

'It isn't that. I understand that.' She looked up at him with appealing eyes and he felt a surprising thrill of satisfaction that he was in charge. 'I was wondering how old you are. I have no idea.'

He laughed. 'The perfect age for you, dear lady, I'm just thirty nine – comfortably within tolerance and able to look forward to a long and happy association.'

'And have you been married before?'

'No, my work at the centre and my other interests have failed to allow for . . .' He paused. 'To be truthful you are the only woman who has sufficiently engaged my interest.' She looked amazed. He moved closer and pulled her to her feet. 'You needn't be afraid. I've no interest in beating you or bullying you.'

She stared at the floor trying to control the feeling of panic that was building in her. He gently took her chin in his hand

and tilted her face upwards. His other hand was positioned firmly in the small of her back. She was quite unable to move but couldn't repress a judder of fear.

'Keep still, Mrs Elliot, and let's start as we mean to go on.' When he released her he considered her carefully. She was still dry-eyed and her face was completely blank.